Also by Mark Hollingsworth

The Press and Political Dissent – A Question of Censorship

Blacklist – The Inside Story of Political Vetting (with Richard Norton-Taylor)

The Economic League – The Silent McCarthyism (with Charles Tremayne)

MPs for Hire – The Secret World of Political Lobbying

A Bit on the Side – Politicians, Who Pays Them? (with Paul Halloran)

Thatcher's Fortunes – The Life and Times of Mark Thatcher (with Paul Halloran)

The Ultimate Spin Doctor – The Life and Fast Times of Tim Bell

Defending the Realm – Inside MI5 and the War on Terrorism (with Nick Fielding)

Saudi Babylon – Torture, Corruption and Cover-Up Inside the House of Saud

Londongrad – From Russia with Cash, The Inside Story of the Oligarchs (with Stewart Lansley)

Against the Odds – President Goodluck Jonathan and the Threat of Boko Haram

AGENTS of INFLUENCE

HOW THE KGB SUBVERTED WESTERN DEMOCRACIES

MARK HOLLINGSWORTH

ONEWORLD

A Oneworld Book

First published by Oneworld Publications in 2023

Copyright © Mark Hollingsworth 2023

ISBN 978-0-86154-216-1
eISBN 978-0-86154-533-9

Plate section credits: Putin © Pictorial Press Ltd/Alamy, Valentyn Nalyvaichenko
© Private Collection, Hans Peter Smolka © Centropa, Victor Louis © Evening
News/ANL/Shutterstock, Robert Maxwell © Bettmann/Getty, Vassily Sitnikov
© Valentin Mzareulov, 2009, Oleg Lyalin © Harry Myers/Shutterstock, Anthony
Courtney © John Franks/Stringer/Getty, Zina Volkova © Private Collection, Helen
O'Brien © Private Collection, Charles Elwell © Private Collection, Zbigniew
Brzezinski with President Carter © White House/ZUMA Wire/Shutterstock,
Brzezinski leaflet from Zbigniew Brzezinski Papers, Carter Administration,
Box 48, Folder 9, Manuscript Division, Library of Congress, Washington DC,
20540, Senator Henry Jackson © University of Washington Libraries, Special
Collections, Henry Wallace (public domain), Hubert Humphrey licensed
under CCBY20 from Kheel Center, Seacox Heath © The Times, Brompton Oratory
© Mark Hollingsworth

Typeset by Geethik Technologies
Printed and bound in Great Britain by Clays Ltd, Elcograf S.p.A.

Oneworld Publications
10 Bloomsbury Street
London WC1B 3SR
England

MIX
Paper from
responsible sources
FSC® C018072

For Lisa

'No', said the priest, 'you don't need to accept everything as true, you only have to accept it as necessary.' 'Depressing view', said K. 'The lie made into the rule of the world.'

The Trial, Franz Kafka

Nothing is more dangerous to a state than a political police force and an intelligence service which goes off the deep end at the slightest sign of crisis.

Sir Basil Thomson, Director of Intelligence,
Home Office, 1919–21

When you chop wood, the splinters fly.

Czech proverb

Contents

1

THE COVERT ART OF WAR

What baseness would you not commit
To stamp out baseness?
If you could change the world
What would you be too good for?
Sink in the mire
Embrace the butcher but
Change the world
It needs it

The Measures Taken by Bertolt Brecht

IT IS MIDNIGHT ON 17 MARCH 1999, and the stern-faced newscaster on the Russian state TV channel, RTR, suddenly makes a dramatic announcement. The next item – entitled 'Three in a Bed' – is not appropriate for viewers under the age of eighteen. The grainy black-and-white video depicts a middle-aged man frolicking on a bed with two naked, dark-haired younger women in a lavishly decorated flat in Moscow's Polyanka Street. The man in the flickering video, although difficult to identify, appears to be Yuri Skuratov, Russia's powerful prosecutor general.

The late-night broadcast was the culmination of an epic power struggle between Skuratov and the Kremlin. Six months earlier the prosecutor general had opened an investigation into allegations of serious wrongdoing by the daughter of President Yeltsin and two of his deputy prime ministers. In late 1998 Skuratov filed a lawsuit against the Yeltsin administration, alleging that one of its most senior officials had been paid an estimated $60 million in bribes to obtain lucrative construction contracts, including for renovations in the Kremlin.

As the evidence of corruption mounted, the Federal Security Service (FSB), Russia's most powerful intelligence agency, intervened and in January 1999 handed the video to the president's chief of staff, Nikolay Bordyuzha, a former KGB officer. A few days later Skuratov was summoned to the Kremlin and the chief of staff played him the murky footage, implied that it could become public and asked him to resign. Even though he strongly suspected the video was a fake, the prosecutor agreed to step down.[1]

But then Skuratov changed his mind, returned to work and decided to fight back, especially as it was unclear whether the naked man really was him. He knew that his resignation needed to be ratified by the Upper Chamber of Parliament. These were the days when the Russian parliament was an independent body and not simply an adjunct to the Kremlin. They asked the prosecutor to testify about corruption in Yeltsin's inner circle.

The night before Skuratov's appearance before the Russian parliament, the infamous video was again broadcast on RTR. The prosecutor refused to resign and the Russian parliament's upper chamber supported him. And so RTR decided to show the tape yet again, this time on the programme hosted by the notorious and popular media hit man Sergei Dorenko, who announced that Skuratov's behaviour would make it harder for Russian parents to bring up their children patriotically. 'After all, this was the prosecutor general, not Mick Jagger who can run around the beach with a naked behind', shouted Dorenko.[2]

The involvement of intelligence agents in the smear operation was revealed when a photograph was published of a high-ranking FSB officer delivering the video to the RTR offices in Moscow. Soon afterwards, on 7 April 1999, that mysterious FSB officer held a dramatic and unusual live press conference: 'The initial evaluation of the video tape indicates that it is genuine', said the spy, with no expression in his voice or face. 'The man who looked like Skuratov was indeed Skuratov. He must retire and there must be a more robust inquiry into this affair.' That senior FSB officer was Vladimir Putin.

Putin then announced that Skuratov was under criminal investigation by his own office. The next day Yeltsin signed a decree suspending the prosecutor until the probe was complete. Skuratov's telephone lines were cut, his office sealed, his bodyguards replaced and he was banned from entering his former workplace and any government building.[3]

The power struggle between Putin – backed by the Kremlin – and Skuratov continued for several months until the prosecutor reluctantly resigned. The involvement of the two young prostitutes unquestionably ended Skuratov's career – but no one knew who paid them. One of the girls said that she and a colleague charged $500 per sex session and they had earned $50,000 over the previous eighteen months from entertaining the prosecutor.

Putin's use of this crude *Kompromat* video resulted in his rise to power. As a result of Skuratov's demise, Putin's main presidential rival – Yevgeny Primakov – was severely damaged, because he had been the prosecutor's political patron. Primakov had been often and openly referred to by Yeltsin as his successor and now he was compromised by his association with the man in the sex video. Putin had protected Yeltsin, who paid him back handsomely by backing his presidential bid. And when he entered the Kremlin, Putin repaid his gratitude by granting all members of Yeltsin's family immunity from criminal prosecution.[4] But if it were not for the honey trap and the video, Putin may have never become president of Russia.

The smearing of Skuratov was a classic FSB tactic, inherited from its predecessor, the KGB. The video had been made nearly a year before being shown to the prosecutor and months before he launched the corruption investigation. It was stored away to be used at an opportune moment as blackmail, by threatening public disclosure. Moreover, it emerged that the prostitutes had been hired by a third party. And so the FSB *Kompromat* operation was akin to a trawler, gathering anything and everything in its path, just in case the netted fish produce something incriminating against a potential target.[5] This cannot be dismissed as a one-off incident, for it encapsulated the most important secret weapon in the intelligence war against the West for the past hundred years and can be summed up by one Russian word – '*zapachkat*'. It means 'to besmirch' or 'make someone dirty' and it has been a crucial component of advancing Russia's interests and foreign policy right up until the war in Ukraine in 2022.

For Putin, then director of the FSB, *zapachkat* and covert operations to destabilise the West have been a key component of his foreign policy. After all, he had been a KGB officer between 1975 and 1991, and was acutely aware of the power of the security services. 'What amazed me most of all was how one man's effort could achieve what whole armies could not', Putin said later. 'One spy could decide the fate of thousands of people.'[6] He may as well have been quoting Sun Tzu (often cited by former KGB officers as an inspiration), who wrote in *The Art of War*: 'The skilful leader subdues the enemy's troops without any fighting. He overthrows their kingdom without lengthy operations in the field.'[7]

Putin had joined the KGB after reading espionage novels about its heroic exploits against the Nazis during the Second World War and watching films like *The Sword and the Shield*, a title drawn from the secret service emblem. The inconspicuous Putin was perfect spy material. His first posting was in St Petersburg, where for nine years, according to former KGB officer Oleg Kalugin, he 'harassed dissidents and ordinary citizens and hunted futilely for spies'.[8] In 1985 Putin was transferred to Dresden, East Germany, where he served in the First Chief Directorate (foreign intelligence). Using a cover as a translator, he recruited informants, procured intelligence and sent reports to Moscow. Much of his work involved mundane paperwork, but he did oversee Soviet illegal spies working without diplomatic cover.[9] An insight into Putin's pedantic, ascetic personality emerged when he visited East German breweries. 'I would order a three-litre keg', he recalled. 'You pour the beer into the keg, you add a spigot and you drink straight from the barrel. So I had 3.8 liters of beer every week. And my job was only two steps from my house, so I didn't work off the extra calories.' But he is remembered as a tough and relentless negotiator. The goal, Putin said, was to uncover information about the 'main opponent' (NATO).[10] 'What I was doing, which was my speciality, was political intelligence', he said. 'I was engaged and researched in international politics and I never regretted working with the external intelligence department of the Soviet Union.'[11]

Oleg Kalugin and former Stasi chief Markus Wolf are disparaging about Putin's intelligence career and argue that his espionage activities were limited to assessing unimportant reports from informants about foreign visitors. His work may have been dull but his KGB career influenced his mindset towards the West and the use of intelligence. 'A few years ago we succumbed to the illusion that we don't have enemies and we have paid dearly for that', he later told the FSB.[12] But there is an intriguing sub-plot to his career in the secret world. Catherine Belton, author of the authoritative *Putin's People*, argues that Putin has deliberately downplayed his role as a cover for more sinister operations. She documents how the Russian president was involved in coordinating the support for the left-wing terrorist Red Army Faction, whose members frequently hid in East Germany.[13]

As a KGB lieutenant colonel, Putin was expected to spend 25% of his time conceiving and implementing what the KGB called 'active measures' – political warfare as a tool of foreign policy. This involved covert operations to influence and destabilise NATO, especially the USA and the UK, by the use of disinformation,

forgery, paying agents of influence, honey trapping, secret place-
ment of media stories and setting up front organisations.

The collapse of the Soviet Union and the fall of the Berlin Wall
in 1989 devastated Putin. His final days in Dresden left a lasting
impression on the young spy. On 5 December 1989, a crowd of
demonstrators surrounded the local KGB headquarters and Putin
confronted them. 'Don't try to force yourself into this property', he
told them. 'My comrades are armed and authorised to use their
weapons in an emergency.' The group withdrew but an agitated
Putin telephoned the headquarters of a Red Army tank division to
ask for protection. The answer was a life-changing shock: 'We cannot
do anything without orders from Moscow and Moscow is silent.'[14]

Confounded, Putin spent his final days of the Cold War
destroying documents. 'I personally burned a huge amount of
material', he recalled. 'We burnt so much stuff that the furnace
burst. We burned items night and day. All the most valuable items
were hauled away to Moscow.' Crowds demonstrated outside the
KGB outpost. 'Those crowds were a serious threat', Putin added.
'We had documents in the building. And nobody lifted a finger
to protect us... I got the feeling then that the country no longer
existed.'[15] The phrase 'Moscow is silent' haunted Putin for decades
afterwards. Political elites could be supplanted. Regimes could be
overthrown. The security of the state could be dismantled.

On entering the Kremlin in late 1999 as acting president,
following Yeltsin's resignation, Putin systematically restored the
KGB to control all levers of political and financial power. A few
days after becoming acting president, Putin visited KGB headquarters and addressed 300 intelligence officers. 'A group of FSB
operatives, dispatched under cover to work in the government of
the Russian Federation is successfully fulfilling its task', he joked.
'Instruction number one of the attaining of full power [by the
KGB] has been completed.'[16] But the reality was deadly serious. He
swiftly installed former KGB veterans into all areas of Russian life.
Known as the 'siloviki' (power guys), they controlled the key
government ministries, law enforcement agencies and state owned

companies. A research report in 2006 found that 78% of the Russian elite had ties to the security services.[17] These people represented a psychologically homogenous group, ultra-loyal to roots traced back to the Soviet political police. Putin had created a neo-KGB state and he articulated this reality six months after becoming president, when he was asked questions about a former KGB officer. 'There is no such thing as a former KGB man', he replied.

The use of active measures by Russian spies has also been revived as an insidious weapon of foreign policy, notably in Ukraine in 2014 and 2022. Putin does not regard war and politics as separate spheres. He rejects the West's notion that the world fluctuates between conflict and peace. Instead, he adheres to the view of General von Clausewitz (incidentally much read by KGB officers) that war is simply a continuation of politics by other means – sometimes military like the invasion of Ukraine but usually clandestine intelligence operations against adversaries. But active measures are more pervasive than mere propaganda. For the KGB and the FSB, political warfare involves covert funding of politicians, disinformation and recruiting agents.

The aim is to exert influence by any means possible in order to curry favour, negotiate diplomatic and military outcomes and manipulate public opinion. And then there are the dirty tricks – forged documents, doctored photographs, blurry videos of illicit liaisons with prostitutes hired by the secret state, planted drugs, assassination, smears using black propaganda techniques via covert front groups and blackmail.

But *Kompromat* contains an extra dimension: it is not always used and is instead dangled in front of an official, who then faces perennial uncertainty about his or her status – frightened that such information could be used to destroy their career, even if it is false. 'If everyone sees potential land mines everywhere, it dramatically increases the price for anybody stepping out of line', said the Russian academic Alena Ledeneva. 'It is the fear that generates the vulnerability and the willingness to work for a hostile state like Russia and how far they will go.'[18]

Such malign tactics are not relics of the Cold War but alive and flourishing in Putin's Russia. They are enabled and expanded by technology and adapted for a globalised world. Their modern incarnations are much more terrifying, with far greater range, speed and impact via the internet, and so they are able to influence popular and elite opinion on a frightening scale.[19] As the intelligence expert and author Edward Lucas noted: 'Russia's spymasters are now using not only old tools against us, but also new ones of which their Soviet-era predecessors could only have dreamed.'[20]

Today the KGB no longer exists but its legacy operationally lives on in the FSB and the GRU, Russia's military intelligence agency and successor to the KGB. The only real difference is the technology that enhances the methodology. The ghost of the KGB's past not only lingers but haunts – state-sponsored assassination of dissidents (Alexander Litvinenko), persecution of dissidents (Alexei Navalny), disinformation (social media), honey trapping (Anna Chapman), secret illegal surveillance (hacking of emails) and subverting democracy (2016 US presidential election). Russia may no longer be a Communist regime, but it remains an authoritarian superpower governed by a former KGB spy who is surrounded by former KGB officers determined to restore the Soviet Union and cash in on its oil and gas resources.

Western intelligence agencies also implemented some of these measures. During the Cold War the CIA was actively engaged in regime change and orchestrating coups, notably Iran in 1953, Guatemala in 1954, Cuba in 1961 and Chile in 1973. America's spies also secretly owned and funded news outlets around the world and recruited journalists as agents of influence. And Radio Free Europe, a CIA-funded station, often deployed disinformation in Eastern Europe. But America's worst excesses in political warfare were eventually curtailed by the checks and balances imposed by its legal and political system. The Soviet agencies were untroubled by such unwanted and troublesome interventions. 'The problem is that you can't do to them [Russia] what they do to you', remarked Estonia's president, Toomas Hendrik Ilves, after his country was cyber-attacked by Russia in 2007. 'You can't disrupt their elections, particularly since they are already decided.'[21]

This lack of accountability – especially in Putin's Russia – has enabled the KGB and the FSB to implement such covert active measures and influence operations without any fear of repercussions. On an official level, the FSB – like its predecessor the KGB – is a state within a state, immune from any accountability, and so can run amok. Now it has become the state. In their seminal book on the Russian secret state, *The New Nobility*, Andrei Soldatov and Irina Borogan liken the FSB to the Mukhabarat religious police in Saudi Arabia – impenetrable, ruthless and brutal: 'The intelligence bureaucracy considers itself above criticism, impervious to the demands of democracy.'[22] And in this system *zapachkat* in Russia and abroad is crucial and encouraged. It is the weapon by which power and influence is exerted.

Throughout the Cold War the KGB was used as a ruthless instrument of that power rather than a mere intelligence-gathering agency. The covert operations selected in this book unveil the hidden hands of Russia's dealings with the West: the use of espionage for manipulating opinion, for influence and ultimately for military and political power, which clearly resonates well into the twenty-first century.

Political Warfare

Political warfare – the use of covert operations to influence and subvert events in foreign countries – has been an instrument of foreign policy for centuries. In *The Art of War*, Sun Tzu, writing in the fifth century BC, stressed the importance of undermining the enemy's will through the use of secret agents who can 'create cleavages between the sovereign and his ministers' and 'leak information which is actually false'.[23] And the ancient Indian treatise *Artha-shastra* provides detailed advice on how to destroy the morale of political enemies by spreading false rumours and engaging in political intrigue.[24]

In Russia, the ruthless use of a secret police force was integral
to the political culture of dictatorship. 'From the very first ghastly
dawn of her existence as a State, she [Russia] had to breathe the
atmosphere of despotism; she found nothing but the arbitrary will
of an obscure autocrat at the beginning and end of her organisation', wrote Joseph Conrad in his essay 'Autocracy and War'.
'Autocracy has moulded her institutions and with the poison of
slavery drugged the national temperament into the apathy of a
hopeless fatalism.'[25]

The roots of the KGB can be traced back to the tsar's secret
police force of the sixteenth century, confided Dick White, former
head of both MI5 and MI6, to fellow intelligence officers during
the Cold War.[26] Known as the *Oprichniki* ('the thing apart'), it was
set up by Ivan the Terrible, the first tsar of Russia, as an instrument
to enforce autocratic rule in certain wealthy areas and detect
subversion. As in Stalin's Russia, most of the treason that it swept
away existed only in the mind of the *Oprichniki* and its ruler. Its
victims included whole cities. Ivan himself oscillated between
periods of sadism and prayer and repentance, and after a seven-
year reign of terror the *Oprichniki* was disbanded.[27]

The next political police force was Peter the Great's Preobraz-
hensky Prikaz, at the end of the seventeenth century. Those who
perished in its torture chambers ranged from nobles who had tried
to evade state service to drunks who had dared to make jokes
about the tsar. Peter the Great is remembered as the pioneering
moderniser of the Russian state but he used his spy agency as a
weapon of fearsome cruelty. Yet today he is revered, not least by
Putin who installed a towering bronze of the visionary tsar, which
looms over his ceremonial desk in the cabinet room. 'He will live',
declared the Russian president, 'as long as his cause is alive.'[28] And
during the Ukraine war, Putin has likened himself to Peter the
Great, equating Russia's invasion with the tsar's expansionist wars.

After the Napoleonic wars, a new agency was formed in 1826.
Known as 'The Third Section', it sought to distance itself from its
predecessors and grandly referred to itself as 'the moral physician'

of the nation. Instead, the Third Section was tasked with monitoring and crushing political dissent and operated in tandem with
thousands of police officers and innumerable paid informers. Its
surveillance reports on Russia's citizens were then distributed to
the tsarist regime. 'Public opinion', declared the Third Section's
Count Alexander von Benckendorff, 'is for the government what
a topographical map is for an army command in time of war.'[29]

Throughout the nineteenth century, political activity was crim-
inalised and in 1845 Tsar Nicholas issued a law which laid down
draconian penalties for all 'persons guilty...who aroused disrespect
for Sovereign Authority'. Dissidents were deported in marching
convoys to a bitterly cold exile in Siberia, based on Third Section
investigations. Many were raped, trafficked and flogged, or died
from malnutrition. But after the fatal stabbing of the Third Section's
chief in 1878, a new state security apparatus named the Okhrana
was instituted to eradicate political activity. Opponents of the tsar
were executed and Okhrana officers were empowered to imprison
and exile suspects on their own authority. The Okhrana was a law
unto itself. An elite within an elite. 'Every country has its own
constitution', a prominent Russian remarked to the German
diplomat George Munster at the time. 'Ours is absolutism, moder-
ated by assassination.'[30]

By 1908 Lenin had developed new underground networks, which
sought to overthrow tsarist absolutism by organising workers into
a mass movement that was too populous for Okhrana repression.
But the tsar's secret agents continued to penetrate the revolutionaries, report on their plans and remit secret material. Their foreign
agency – based in Paris – kept the Bolshevik insurrectionists under
trans-European surveillance, notably by bribing concierges in
hotels. To counter the Okhrana's highly paid informants, the insurgents held clandestine meetings and were adept at writing secret
letters which were sewn into the lining of clothes, but only on
linen because it did not rustle loudly if a courier was searched.[31]

The overthrow of the tsarist autocracy in 1917 was achieved
by peasant discontent and brutality. 'How can you make a revo-

lution without firing squads?', asked Lenin at the time. 'Do you really believe that we can be victorious without the very cruellest revolutionary terror?'[32] Soon he instituted 'People's Courts', which were mob trials in which barely literate judges ruled on cases based on 'revolutionary justice'. But the Bolshevik seizure of power also relied on propaganda, political influence techniques and covert operations. 'We must be ready to employ trickery, deceit, law-breaking and withholding and concealing the truth', declared Lenin. 'There are no morals in politics. There is only expedience.'[33]

The Bolsheviks' first intelligence agency was formed on 20 December 1917, with the ostensible mission of defending the revolution against its enemies. Known as the Cheka, it deployed agents provocateurs to identify political opponents. But its methods went beyond intelligence-gathering. In reality it was a terrorist organisation committed to the extermination of all Communist opponents.

The Cheka received authority from Lenin to execute or sentence suspects at will. He sent telegrams to officers commanding them to employ 'mass terror' against 'bourgeois vermin'.[34] And so they liquidated, tortured and exiled what they called counter-revolutionaries and conspirators, who were inevitably accused of being foreign agents. As the Cheka founder Felix Dzerzhinsky declared in 1918: 'We stand for organised terror... The Cheka is not a court... The Cheka is obliged to defend the Revolution and conquer the enemy even if its sword does by chance sometimes fall upon the heads of the innocent.'[35] And as the historian Richard Davenport-Hines wrote: 'The Chekists of the 1920s believed themselves superior to bourgeois scruples about guilt and innocence or truth and lies.'[36]

The Cheka also set up the Secret Political Department for surveillance of the population and a foreign unit to gather intelligence on political enemies and discredit anti-Communist émigrés, using undercover agents, notably in Paris and Vienna. 'There is no sphere of our life where the Cheka does not have its eagle eye', said a Chekist leader in November 1918.[37] The atrocities perpetrated by the new secret police included mass executions. But the Cheka was lauded by the Soviet leadership. 'Every Bolshevist should make himself a Chekist', said Lenin. 'The Cheka is indispensable.'[38] In effect, every Communist was given a mandate to spy, falsify documents and kill.

For Russian spies, the Cheka symbolised a badge of honour, not shame. Its emblems of a shield to defend the revolution and a sword to smite its foes were later used as the insignia of its ultimate successor agency, the KGB. And until the disbandment of the KGB in 1991 many of its officers, including Putin, boasted of their Chekist heritage. Indeed, Putin often celebrated the twentieth of December as 'the day of the Cheka' after he became president. 'The history of the security services is rich in outstanding deeds and legendary names', he declared. 'In Russia, we respect every generation of those who have protected our country from external and internal threats. We bow before the heroism and resilience of our veterans.'[39]

In 1923 the Cheka was reconstituted as the OGPU and visitors to Moscow were struck by a red star and a huge placard outside the opera house, urging citizens 'to strengthen the sword of the dictatorship of the proletariat – the OGPU'. Its mission was to 'upset the counter-revolutionary plans and activities of the opposition' by determining how much the enemy knew about the Soviet Union, creating and passing to them false information and documents and disseminating such intelligence in the press of various countries.[40]

The Soviet Union believed that Western intelligence agencies were involved in a deep-laid labyrinthine plot to overthrow the new regime. Stalin was convinced that their chief instigator was 'the English bourgeoisie and its fighting staff, the Conservative Party'.[41] And so in 1920 Soviet agents were dispatched to London to set up a front organisation, the All-Russian Co-operative Society (ARCOS), based at 49 Moorgate in the heart of the City. It was ostensibly the official Soviet trade mission. But MI5 soon discovered that ARCOS operated as a secret vehicle for Soviet propaganda, espionage and subversion against Britain.

In March 1927, a classified British Signal Training manual from the Aldershot military base had been copied at ARCOS head office – a clear act of espionage against the armed forces. MI5 consulted Prime Minister Stanley Baldwin, who swiftly authorised action. And so, on 12 May 1927, several hundred police and Special Branch officers raided the ARCOS office at 'Soviet House'. It was an inept operation: the ham-fisted policemen brandished guns and ordered employees to empty pockets and handbags, while ARCOS employees frantically burned secret documents in the basement. Nobody was in charge and a lack of Russian speakers prevented the police from translating the documents in order to uncover incriminating evidence. But they did remove several truckloads of filing cabinets and safes.

The raid proved that the Soviet trade delegates were in fact spies. It was the first indication that an espionage network had been set up in London and an early warning shot of the Cold War. The foreign secretary, Austen Chamberlain, informed the Soviet chargé d'affaires at the embassy that Britain was breaking off diplomatic relations because of Moscow's 'anti-British espionage and propaganda'. He quoted from an intercepted telegram to Moscow 'in which you request material to enable you to support a political campaign against His Majesty's government'.[42]

A consequence of the ARCOS raid was that Soviet intelligence switched from using legal residents based at their British embassy to greater use of illegal agents who were not connected officially to the diplomatic delegation. The illegals were dedicated Communists who had been recruited by the NKVD, the latest incarnation of the Soviet spy agency, because they were intelligent, committed, sophisticated and ruthless. They were also prepared to operate underground and integrate themselves into London society and the political establishment.

The most notable Soviet 'illegal' agent was Alexander Orlov, who obtained a US passport in the name of William Goldin and operated as a member of 'trade delegations' throughout Europe in the early 1930s. In London, Orlov's cover was managing the

American Refrigerator Company Ltd, set up with funds from the NKVD (£110 in operational expenses). Based at Imperial House, 84 Regent Street, the firm was housed on the floor above the London branch of Hollywood's Central Casting Bureau and the Duckerfield School of Dancing. On the surface Orlov sold fridges, and lived a cosmopolitan lifestyle in his house at 41 Beaufort Gardens, Knightsbridge. He travelled back and forth doing courier work and even placed advertisements for the company in the *Daily Telegraph*. But in reality he ran Soviet spies in Britain and actively recruited new agents. His wife Maria was also an NKVD officer, while operating on a false Austrian passport.

Orlov adopted foreign accents, kept regular office hours and distributed business cards (Regent 2574 was his phone number) to avert suspicion. But one evening in September 1935 his cover was blown when he bumped into his former English professor from Vienna, who knew him by his real name. By then he was one of the few Russian agents who knew about the recruitment of Kim Philby, Guy Burgess and Anthony Blunt. On 10 October Orlov was ordered back to Moscow and the next day he resigned from the refrigerator company and transferred all his shares to one Herbert Kearon. Curiously, the firm did not close down until 1941. But the Orlov spy ring in London had demonstrated an ominous sign of future operations.

The Cold War

By the end of the Second World War, Stalin was not only resentful and suspicious but felt threatened by what he saw as the American and British growing sphere of influence. The perennially paranoid Stalin believed that this alliance could, if unchecked, infringe his country's sovereignty and deny it access to the resources it required to rebuild the Soviet economy and fulfil its destiny as a great power in the postwar world.[43]

This fear governed Soviet foreign policy and its intelligence agencies were used as the weapons to counter this threat. Sitting in his office in the British embassy in Moscow, Sir Frank Roberts, the Russia minister and an adviser to Winston Churchill during the Yalta conference, surveyed postwar Soviet intentions. 'The Kremlin is now pursuing a Russian national policy which does not differ except in degree from that pursued in the past by Ivan the Terrible, Peter the Great or Catherine the Great', Sir Frank argued in September 1946.[44]

The new Soviet–West tension was best articulated by George Orwell when describing the impact of the nuclear bomb in October 1945. Indeed, he was the first person to use the term 'Cold War':

Looking at the world as a whole, the drift for many decades has not been towards anarchy but towards the reimposition of slavery. We may be heading not for general breakdown but for an epoch as horribly stable as the slave empires of antiquity... Few people have yet considered its ideological implications – the kind of world view, beliefs and the social structure that would probably prevail in a state which was at once unconquerable and in a permanent state of a 'cold war' with its neighbours.[45]

In the early postwar period Soviet attitudes were further hardened by US initiatives to stabilise Western Europe, such as the Truman Doctrine in 1947 and the Marshall Plan in 1948. The Soviets saw both of these as dangers to their realm of influence and as a Western propaganda coup. Their response was to set up the Communist Information Bureau later that year, an avowed declaration of ideological warfare against the USA and the UK. It was the first salvo of what the Soviets called 'active measures' – disinformation and the circulation of Soviet propaganda in Western languages. The UK responded by setting up the equally secretive Information Research Department, a unit inside the Foreign Office with close ties to MI6, whose purpose was counter-disinformation. The information war had begun.

The Soviets intensified and expanded covert operations abroad as part of the Cold War and on 13 March 1954 the KGB was born.

This new agency absorbed the traditional functions of the political police, harassing dissidents and counter-revolutionaries and guarding the borders. Families lived in fear of informants, independent thought was banned and the state was all-powerful. As Stalin told the British ambassador to Moscow, Sir Maurice Peterson: 'There are no private individuals in this country.'[46]

The all-powerful KGB was also responsible for all secret missions abroad (apart from the GRU, which collected military intelligence). The new political police force became a law unto itself in clandestine operations – euphemistically referred to as 'pro-active measures' – against 'The Main Adversary' (USA and UK). But they were inextricably tied and subservient to the Communist Party and the Politburo. 'The [Communist] Party was the boss. The KGB was the servant, particularly in foreign affairs', the former KGB officer Oleg Gordievsky told his MI6 debriefers after he defected to the UK.[47] This was confirmed by Vladimir Putin no less. 'If for some reason a person left the Communist Party, they were immediately fired from the KGB', he said.[48]

During the Cold War, covert operations were the chief weapon of Soviet foreign policy and yet the high-spirited President Khrushchev had the temerity to deny that his country spied at all. 'Espionage is needed by those who prepare for attack, for aggression', he wrote in a letter to the Japanese Communist Party in 1962. 'The Soviet Union is deeply dedicated to the cause of peace and does not intend to attack anyone. Therefore it has no intention of engaging in espionage.'[49] Even the most earnest KGB officer must have struggled to keep a straight face when he heard that statement, for the Soviet Union has practised the art of espionage more aggressively and actively than any other nation in the past one hundred years, on an unimaginable scale. This fearlessness was articulated in 1957 when Sir Patrick Reilly, then British ambassador to Moscow and a former adviser to the MI6 chief, Stewart Menzies, asked Vasily Kuznetsov, the Soviet minister: 'I don't understand. What are you afraid of?'

He replied: 'Afraid? We are afraid of nothing.'[50]

In contrast to the West's morally ambivalent relationship to its intelligence agencies, KGB officers have always been regarded and portrayed as heroic figures in Russia, working selflessly for the Motherland against the foreign enemies. 'Like most of my peers I devoured the works of Arkady Gaidar who produced a series of what might best be described as Communist Hardy Boys books', recalled Oleg Kalugin. 'They were superpatriotic tales filled with young characters constantly doing courageous and noble deeds for the good of the Motherland. It was Gaidar's books that first planted the seed in my mind of becoming a KGB officer. One work, *The Military Secret*, featured a boy who died protecting secret information from the enemies of Communism. Another, *The Fate of the Drummer*, recounted how a boy discovered a gang of spies and was shot by them.'[51]

The television screens also touched the emotional chord of patriotism. In the early 1970s Russian viewers watched the exploits of their best-known fictional spy, Max Otto von Stierlitz (to give him his German cover name). His wartime mission was to penetrate the Nazi high command. But unlike James Bond, Stierlitz shunned guns, girls and gadgets. Instead his secret weapon was his mind and his rat-like cunning, motivated by implacable patriotism. The hero of another movie, *The Starling and the Lyre*, countered a Western plot to create discord between the Soviet Union and her allies and delivered long speeches about the US military–industrial complex while enjoying a touching romance with a female spy.

These books and films were compelling and the best recruitment agency for the KGB. They so captivated a tough teenager in the backstreets of 1970s Leningrad that he walked from the cinema to the city's KGB headquarters at the Bolshoi Dom and volunteered his services. But the sixteen-year-old Putin was told that the organisation did not accept walk-ins: you should study law and wait to be approached. 'When I accepted the proposition from the [KGB] Directorate's personnel department, I didn't think about the [Stalin-era] purges', Putin said. 'My notion of the KGB came from romantic spy stories. I was a pure and successful product of Soviet patriotic education.'[52] Five years later the future president was a KGB spy.

During the Cold War the KGB enjoyed a mystique and prestige that still lingers over its successor agencies. The Order of Lenin was bestowed on scores of intelligence officers who were well-paid and with privileges only dreamed of by ordinary Soviets. 'Such privileges inevitably give KGB people a sense of their own exclusivity and importance as well as their superiority over the rest of the population', recalled former KGB officer Ilya Dzhirkvelov in his book *Secret Servant*. 'This has the effect of cutting them off psychologically and physically from the Soviet people and turns them into an elite.'[53]

The KGB's status also provided a crucial advantage: living and operating above and outside the law, especially if they worked for the elite foreign espionage division, the First Chief Directorate. In other intelligence agencies, this may have sparked a crisis of faith or conscience. In *The Spy Who Came In from the Cold* the spy boss, Control, agonised about the relative morality of methods used by the KGB, CIA and MI6:

> We do disagreeable things so that ordinary people here and elsewhere can sleep safely in their beds at night. Is that too romantic? Of course, we occasionally do very wicked things.... I would say that since the war our methods – ours and those of the opposition – have become much the same. I mean, you can't be less ruthless than the opposition simply because your government's policy is benevolent, can you now?

Le Carré had hoped that his novel would prompt readers to ask: 'For how long can we defend ourselves by methods of this kind and still remain the kind of society that is worth defending?'[54]

Such liberal anguish has never troubled Communist spymasters. Markus Wolf, the ruthlessly effective head of the East German agency Stasi, who worked closely with the KGB, argued that the repressive and intrusive behaviour of his organisation was justified by the purity of its ideological aspirations. If anything, he reflected in his memoirs, his agents could have been more brutal. 'Our sins and our mistakes were those of every other intelligence agency. If we had shortcomings, and we certainly did, they were those of too much professionalism, untempered by the raw edge of ordinary life.'[55]

The notion that the KGB and the Stasi could have been more vicious would no doubt shock and anger their victims. But behind this dubious self-justification lies a deeper and more shadowy secret history of deception, fear, manipulation, surveillance, sexual blackmail, political subterfuge and subversion, which starts in the unlikely setting of an atmospheric cafe amid the rubble-strewn streets of Vienna.

2

AGENTS OF INFLUENCE

The end aim of spying in all its varieties is knowledge of the enemy. And this knowledge can only be derived, in the first instance, from the converted spy. Hence it is essential that the converted spy be treated with the most liberality.

Sun Tzu, *The Art of War*

CAFÉ MOZART'S INTERIORS, WITH ITS DANGLING chandeliers and resplendent furnishings, call to mind Vienna's Old World charm. But it became the focal point in a very modern Cold War. Here, Russian, American and British spies met their informants and agents for hushed conversations over thick black coffee or elaborate cocktails. Fear, intrigue and suspicion lurked in every street. Austria was the easternmost area of Western influence and its capital lay in its far corner, making it a cross-roads between the Soviet Union and the West. And so Vienna was the front line for those escaping the Communist Eastern bloc and a conduit for intelligence agents aiming to penetrate it. For the KGB, CIA and MI6, the narrow, dimly-lit, cobbled streets of Austria's capital city were the stage for espionage surpassing any thriller novel.[1]

It was here at Café Mozart one evening in February 1948 that Graham Greene, the mercurial thriller writer and former MI6 officer, could be seen locked in conversation with the bulky, buccaneering correspondent for *The Times*, Hans-Peter Smolka. Over the next several hours, and later over drinks in the Red Bar at the nearby Sacher Hotel, Smolka was Greene's tour guide for the seedier subterranean subculture of rubble-strewn Vienna. The novelist was in town to research his screenplay for *The Third Man*, the iconic atmospheric film noir masterpiece.

The idea to capture postwar Vienna on celluloid – especially its moral ambiguities, which contrasted so sharply with the entrenched certainties of the war – came from the Hungarian-born film producer Alexander Korda, a former MI6 asset. His company, London Film Productions, had been secretly funded by the British Secret Service in the 1930s and provided useful cover for travel to places that spies would otherwise find hard to access. Korda discovered that he had royalties accrued before the war locked up in Austria. It was the perfect opportunity to make a movie about the city of secrets, which was still occupied by the four powers.

Over drinks at Claridges, Korda hired Smolka, the Austrian-born journalist who knew the Vienna underworld intimately, and commissioned Greene to write the script.[2] A month later Greene and Smolka met at Café Mozart and then drank until the early hours of the morning in seedy clubs like the Oriental and Maxim's, whose floor shows harked back to pre-war Berlin. Smolka took the author into the Soviet sector of the city, where they spent seven hours together discussing plot lines and locations. The story revolved around Holly Martins, a hack thriller writer, who visits an old friend, Harry Lime, in Vienna only to find him dead. A mysterious third man had been observed at the scene of the crime and so Martins tries to track him down. He then discovers that the third man was in fact Lime himself, who had faked his own death in an attempt to escape prosecution for selling black market bogus penicillin, which was killing children.[3]

None other than Smolka provided this plot line, and the journalist also introduced Greene to the city's rat-infested sewers controlled by the Russians – the setting of the climactic scene of the film. He asked for no credit but Greene felt obliged and so when Major Calloway, the upright English army officer played by Trevor Howard, barks an order to his driver to 'Take us to Smolka's!' It was a coded form of thanks to the Austrian reporter. True to Greene's fascination with sin, guilt and lost innocence, 'Smolka's' was a subterranean bar in the backstreets of Vienna.[4]

Smolka's influence on *The Third Man* was such that Harry Lime – the movie's charismatic, morally squalid central character, played memorably by Orson Welles – was partly based on the shadowy foreign correspondent. But what nobody knew at the time was that Smolka was in fact an NKVD agent of influence and had been secretly working for the Soviet Union since late 1939, after being recruited by the notorious double agent Kim Philby. Codenamed ABO, his role was to covertly influence and manipulate public opinion and policy in the West. And Smolka performed a successful mission when he persuaded the film's director, Carol Reed, to remove a scene from the shooting script in which Russians kidnapped a woman. The NKVD agent argued that the incident was simplistic and smacked of superficial anti-Soviet propaganda. And so Greene duly inserted an inside joke in which an army intelligence officer offers a shot of vodka to an American visitor. The vodka was Russian and the brand name was Smolka.[5]

The mysterious Smolka could have been a character straight from the pages of one of Greene's Cold War thrillers, notably *The Human Factor*. He was born in 1912 in Vienna, the son of the owner of a ski binding business. Descended from bohemian Jewish rabbis, Smolka grew up in relative comfort despite the hyperinflation of the 1920s. As a teenager he embraced the new Marxist creed as the shadow of Fascism threatened Austria and by 1931 he was the editor of his own political magazine, *The New Youth*. A dedicated Communist, he refused to take over the family business because he 'did not want to become a capitalist'.

At the age of seventeen, he caused his first security scare when he was detained for fifteen hours as a suspected spy and expelled from France after taking photographs of military installations in Marseilles. A month later, in September 1930, the precocious young journalist arrived at Dover with a press pass from the Austrian newspaper *Der Tag*, to report on a conference about the future of India. He was now under the radar of Special Branch, who watched him as he moved into the Manhattan Hotel in Upper Bedford Place, Bloomsbury. MI5 suspected 'Communist tendencies' but had no evidence that he was engaged in espionage.[6]

By May 1933, the enterprising Smolka was the London correspondent of the influential *Neue Freie Presse*, an Austrian Catholic Monarchist newspaper. He was intelligent and wrote fluently but colleagues found him arrogant, with a gauche manner, a brittle temperament and a deep booming voice. Despite his youth, he wore a bow tie and cultivated the air of a condescending intellectual. 'Smolka is a Jew, rather a bore but decent', a Foreign Office official told Colonel Harker of MI5.

In the spring of 1934, Smolka met an upper-class charismatic young English Marxist who would change his life. His name was Kim Philby. Philby was in love with an Austrian Jewish revolutionary firebrand called Litzi Friedmann, a postgraduate student who was a close friend of Smolka's. During a visit to Vienna, civil war broke out after the neo-fascist Chancellor Engelbert Dolfuss suspended the constitution and outlawed strikes. For the next two weeks Smolka, Friedmann and their new English comrade worked tirelessly – at significant risk to their lives – smuggling political activists out of Vienna, many through the sewers. As Peter Foges, Smolka's godson and a former BBC foreign correspondent and producer, reflected later: 'Sharing risk forges bonds.'[7]

On returning to London, Smolka and Philby remained close. 'We used to run into each other at receptions and cocktail parties and we had many friends in common', recalled Philby, who was by now an NKVD agent. 'He often came to me with news items, sometimes in the form of ordinary routine gossip... He brought me very valuable information.'[8] They later shared a flat at Downing Court in Bloomsbury.

Their relationship was formalised on 3 November 1934, when the young Marxists set up London-Continental News Ltd, which supplied specialised news items on events in Central Europe to the Exchange Telegraph Company. Such anonymous sounding press agencies were often used as a vehicle for pro-Soviet propaganda. Based in a tiny but discreet office in Printing House Square near *The Times* newsroom, Smolka owned 98% of the shares and Philby held a 2% stake.

Philby later tried to downplay the importance of the news agency and told MI5 that it 'never actually functioned'.[9] In fact, the accounts reveal that the company traded for three years, Smolka was paid director's fees and it even made small annual profits.

The Austrian Marxist hoped that London-Continental News Ltd would exploit his journalistic work and even asked for Foreign Office blessing. But it was not a success and so he focused on promoting the Communist cause. He delivered a lecture to the Royal Geographical Society which stated that the Soviet Union was 'wholly occupied with itself at present and will be so for a long time to come' and Stalin had 'no designs' on Western Europe. In the summer of 1936 he travelled to the Soviet Arctic regions and on his return wrote vivid articles for *The Times*, which were expanded into a book, *Forty Thousand Against the Arctic; Russia's Polar Empire*. It was a beguiling work of propaganda which extolled the virtues of Stalin's plans to extract coal, oil and nickel from the Arctic regions, and eulogised the virtues of the factories, aerodromes and Five Year Plans. The book reflected Smolka's Soviet sympathies, with phrases like 'give credit where it is due'. 'Russia today', he told his readers, 'is like a house under construction. They cannot hide the dirt, disorder and atmosphere of improvisation which astounds us in all building plots.'[10]

But Smolka's true colours emerged in his portrayal of the horrific brutality of the Gulag during the Great Terror, as an idealistic experiment in social reform: 'What I found new was the great and

sincere belief of the young [NKVD] administrators that they were
really pioneers of the soul in the wilderness of these ruffians [the
prisoners]: He depicted the Gulag as a humane labour penal camp
for murderers, thieves, peasants and Trotskyite counter-revolutionaries, rather than a prison. 'They are the victims of history',
he wrote. 'Pitiable perhaps as individuals. But we had to sacrifice
them to save the country.'[11]

By November 1938, Smolka was gradually infiltrating the British
Establishment. He changed his name to Harry Peter Smollett,
moved into a house on Fitzjohn's Avenue, Hampstead, and joined
the Shanghai Club, an informal dining club in Soho composed of
young left-wing journalists, notably George Orwell, David Astor
and John Strachey. He became a British citizen under the sponsorship of Sir Harry Brittain, founder of the Empire Press Union.
And he ingratiated himself with Lord Astor, who later offered him
the deputy editorship of the *Observer*, which he declined.

There is some dispute about when Smollett first became a Soviet
spy. Some historians argue that he was recruited by the NKVD's
super-agent and former Catholic priest Teodor Maly, before he
arrived in Britain and used his journalism as a cover. But Philby,
by now a senior MI6 officer, claimed the credit and in late 1939
briefed Smollett on the tradecraft. One day he whispered to his
Austrian fellow Marxist: 'Listen, Hans, if in your present job you
come across some information that in your opinion could help
me in my work for England...' Philby then paused, winked at him
and added: 'Then come over to me and offer me two cigarettes
out of a pack, one for me and one for you, and hold them in the
shape of the letter "V". I'll take one, you'll keep the other and that
will be a signal that you want to tell me something important.'
Smollett agreed and provided intelligence which Philby later said
'was very good material.'[12]

Using the cover of working for the Exchange Telegraph Company,
the prominent press agency, Smollett cultivated Rex Leeper, head
of the Political Intelligence Department in the Foreign Office. He
asked for introductions to British diplomats in central Europe and

Leeper agreed, writing that Smollett 'is well known to this department and has achieved a considerable reputation as a writer in
international affairs'.[13] It was perfect timing for the NKVD agent.
A fluent German speaker, Smollett was put in charge of the Foreign
News Department of the Ministry of Information (MoI), distributing propaganda to Switzerland, Belgium and the Netherlands.
And he insisted that all reports by British press attachés be vetted
by him first.

The Second World War was now underway and leaks of classified
information from the MoI resulted in MI5 investigations. Smollett,
a self-proclaimed Soviet sympathiser, was a suspect and rejected
when he applied to join Military Intelligence. He did not help
himself by his abrupt, abrasive manner. Former colleagues regarded
him as an uncouth bull of a man with a decidedly shady air.[14] But
as a senior adviser in the Press Department of the MoI, he had
power and influence. And so the security services became concerned
about his access to secret material. A military intelligence officer
complained to MI5's director-general Sir Vernon Kell: 'I may be
chasing rather a tired hare...but Smollett's employment in his present
position seems to me nothing short of a scandal.' But Roger Hollis,
then an MI5 counter-subversion officer, concluded that Smollett
was 'too closely concerned with his own prosperity to commit
himself to any side until he is sure that he is on the winning side'.[15]

However, Dick White, then an MI5 counter-intelligence officer
and later its director-general, attributed the suspicion of Smollett
to his temperamental failings and anti-Semitism. White was also
conditioned by the public mood of the time, which regarded
Communism as a relatively benign disease. During his time in
Whitehall the MI5 officer met Smollett on several occasions and
found no cause for alarm. During their encounters the Soviet spy
told White that Stalin had no intention of dominating or occupying
postwar Eastern Europe. And so MI5 did not raise any objections
to Smollett's continued employment.[16] It was a cleverly planted
piece of disinformation that proved hugely helpful to the Kremlin
as a way of diminishing the Communist threat to postwar stability.

Despite MI5's scrutiny and scepticism, Smollett attracted the attention of Brendan Bracken, former proprietor of the *Financial Times* and the *Economist*, former Tory MP and one of Churchill's most influential advisers. The dynamic self-made Bracken was much favoured by Churchill, who often preferred rogues to conventional people and so appointed him minister of information in his War Cabinet.

In the summer of 1941, Hitler invaded the Soviet Union and the Nazi Panzer tanks soon punched hundreds of miles through Red Army lines. Suddenly the Communists and 'Uncle Joe' were on the same side. Bracken set up a new Soviet section of the MoI to promote the image of Britain's new unlikely ally and turned to the brash Smollett to be its director. The NKVD now had a mole at the heart of the government. Smollett's power was such that the Soviets had a secret veto on all official British information regarding the USSR. An early MoI meeting decided that 'no statement about Russia or action to present Russia in England should be taken without Mr Smollett approving it from the angle of its suitability in the eyes of the Russian Embassy'.[17] 'His influence and tentacles were extensive', wrote the historian Richard Davenport-Hines. 'He was not merely a Soviet informer but a master at misdirection by hints, distractions, suppressions and diversions. He hid his part in the toadying of official information and propaganda and hence in inducing unofficial civilian obsequiousness towards Stalinism.'[18]

Despite Churchill's interest in the MoI countering 'the tendency of the British public to forget the dangers of Communism in their enthusiasm over the resistance of Russia', Smollett cleverly redefined its role. The priorities were to 'combat anti-Soviet feelings in Britain' and also, cunningly, 'curb exuberant pro-Soviet propaganda that might seriously embarrass the government'. This would be done by keeping Russian-accented and openly partisan apologists at bay and hiring British commentators instead. Smollett planned to win the hearts and minds of England by stealing the thunder of the radical left propaganda machine through outdoing it in pro-Russian publicity and controlling the message with native

British voices. He blurred the line between the brutal Communist state and the brave Russians. In response the Soviet ambassador Ivan Maisky assured Bracken that 'every effort will be made to assist Mr Smollett to maintain close contact with the Embassy'.[19]

Smollett's strategy involved praising the Red Army in a way that identified the Russian people with the Soviet regime. This culminated one evening in February 1943, at the Albert Hall, with a lavish party to celebrate the twenty-fifth anniversary of the Red Army, which included songs of praise by a massed choir, readings by John Gielgud and Laurence Olivier and speeches by Soviet embassy officials. Leading politicians from all parties attended and official posters paid tribute to Russian civilians as well as soldiers. In one month alone, Smollett organised the screening of the film *USSR at War* to factory audiences of over a million and 207 public meetings about the Soviet Union.

The cinema played a key role in the propaganda war. By 1942 the MoI had produced twenty Soviet short films, which were shown around Britain with the aid of seventy mobile projectors. Known as 'The Celluloid Circus', an estimated three million people viewed such documentaries as *Salute to the Soviets* and *Soviet Women*. Its success resulted in Smollett approaching Ivor Montagu, an aristocratic film-maker, for more pro-Soviet material. Montagu was in fact an agent for the GRU. It is not known if they were aware of their mutual interest in spying for the Soviets but Smollett described the son of the 2nd Baron Swaythling as 'a film affairs advisor of the USSR' between 1941 and 1945.

When he was younger, Montagu's father gave him pocket money of £500 per year on the condition that he did not set foot in the Soviet Union. In 1925, aged 21, he broke that promise when he visited Moscow to ask for authorisation to exhibit Soviet films in London.[20] As founder of the Progressive Film Institute, Montagu handled the purchases of films from the Soviet Union on behalf of a British film company called Kino Films Ltd. Based at 84 Gray's Inn Road, London, Montagu oversaw their film production and in the late 1930s they released documentaries like *If War Should*

Come and *Soviet Parliament*, which portrayed the Soviet Union as a democratic ally of Europe. Another film, *Lenin in October*, depicted the events of the October Revolution in 1917. Their pro-Communist proclivities attracted the attention of MI5, who corresponded with the British Board of Censors about their films.[21] But for Smollett, Montagu was a valuable accomplice in portraying the Soviet Union in the best possible light.[22]

MI5's keen interest in Montagu took place between 1926 and 1950. In 1929 he joined the Communist Party and was active in the Cambridge Film Society where he was accused of 'parlour Bolshevism' by an MI5 officer. A thick MI5 file focuses on Soviet film propaganda and his screening of a silent movie about revolutionary factory workers entitled *Mother*. In 1931 an MI5 memo noted that Montagu visited Hollywood and worked with the Atlas film company, the main distributor for Soviet movies.

In the mid-1930s Montagu, a capable Russian linguist, composed the English dialogue superimposed on several Soviet films, notably *The Thirteen*. Special Branch and MI5 constantly monitored his trips abroad and international money orders he received. During the war he worked as a journalist for the *Daily Worker* after being refused enlistment in the armed forces and the RAF and even the Home Guard.

After Hitler's invasion of the Soviet Union Montagu was involved in Communist propaganda, the dubbing of Soviet films into English and a protest against the BBC's refusal to broadcast 'The Internationale'. 'The Soviets are not only fighting the Nazi Germany but also the forces of reaction everywhere', he told the Russia Today Society. An MI5 memo stated: 'Montagu's only loyalty is to the Communist cause... inadvisable that he should be allowed into any position of trust or responsibility.'[23]

The BBC was another target for Smollett, who delivered talks and propaganda bulletins and vetted scripts about the Soviet Union as a senior MoI official. He used the opportunity to inform the BBC that a 'major change of direction has taken place under Stalin', whose policy 'continues to be maintaining friendly diplomatic relations with other governments. The ideologues and doctrinaire international revolutionaries have increasingly been replaced by people of the managerial and technocrat type.'[24] It just so happened that his producer was the infamous Communist double agent Guy Burgess. The NKVD now had a powerful voice inside the BBC.

Smollett wielded huge influence in the information war, notably when he persuaded the MoI to avoid using 'both White Russians and Red Englishmen' to speak on Soviet affairs. This apparently even-handed policy suited the NKVD perfectly, given that White Russians were enemies of the people and counter-revolutionaries. But the NKVD also preferred to have the Soviet case put by apparently impartial British speakers rather than by hard-line Communists.[25]

For the unreconstructed Marxist, Stalin was virtually sacrosanct. In 1944 Smollett discreetly persuaded Jonathan Cape not to publish George Orwell's novel *Animal Farm* because 'it would be unhelpful to the Anglo-Soviet cause' and 'not in the national interest'. No doubt he was also unhappy that Soviet spies were depicted as 'savage dogs' in the satirical novel. Orwell was told that in the current political climate *Animal Farm* was offensive because the central characters were unpleasant pigs. As a result, publication was delayed and Orwell was enraged when he discovered Smollett's covert role at literary censorship. The revered author would extract his revenge in May 1949 when he sent a list of crypto-Communists to the Foreign Office. Next to Smollett's name, Orwell wrote: 'said to be mere careerist, but gives the strong impression of being some kind of Russian agent. Very slimy person.' He concluded: 'If (the list) had been done earlier, it would have stopped people like Smollett working their way into important propaganda jobs where they were probably able to do us a lot of harm.'[26]

Despite his official role at the MoI, MI5 was still concerned about Smollett as a security risk and sought to impress on him 'the importance of exercising the utmost discretion in his use of information'.[27] In September 1942, an MI5 officer named Richard Brooman-White spoke to Philby about the Austrian-born Communist. While admitting that he knew Smollett 'quite well',

Philby was disparaging about his character and falsely claimed that he was 'mildly left-wing' and 'had no knowledge of the Communist Party link-up' in order to put MI5 off the scent. 'Commercially he [Smollett] is a pusher but nevertheless rather a timid character with a feeling of inferiority due in part to his repulsive appearance', said Philby. 'He is a physical coward and was petrified when the air-raids began... He is extremely clever but harmless and would be too scared to do anything sinister.'[28]

Meanwhile, the director of the MoI's Soviet section was covertly meeting his NKVD controller Anatoly Gorsky, the grimly efficient and humourless spy based at the Soviet embassy in London. But then Gorsky believed Smollett was a double agent and part of an elaborate plot by MI6 to hoodwink the NKVD, and so terminated the relationship. A measure of Smollett's importance was that Philby disagreed and secretly continued to use the MoI director, who was tasked to report and deliver information to Burgess, a fellow NKVD agent and colleague at the BBC.

The Austrian Marxist peddled his familiar line that the Soviets were not interested in territorial expansion and recommended a passive foreign policy. 'The ruling class of Russia must therefore be free of fear from foreign intervention', he wrote. 'In order to free the Russians from this fear and allow them to become democratic, we must show them that we intend to leave them alone and trust them.' It was exactly what Moscow wanted to hear.

Among the secret documents that Smollett leaked to Burgess were typed versions of remarks by William Ridsdale, head of the Foreign Office's News Department, in May 1942: 'The talks with Vyacheslav Molotov [Soviet foreign minister] are one long sweat', said Ridsdale of the negotiations. 'These bastards are absolute shits to deal with. The trouble is that they know they are shits...and don't seem to care a damn what we think of them... You make a little concession to them and being an English gentleman you instinctively expect that the other fellow will make some decent countermove or at least acknowledge that you have been trying to be decent to them but they go straight on to their next demand.'[29]

As Moscow was sceptical of Smollett, Burgess passed off these confidential documents to his NKVD controller in London as his own work. 'Guy [Burgess] established contacts with Smollett and got a number of tips from him, and he managed to get very valuable information', Philby said.[30] The ploy constituted a major breach of intelligence protocol and when Gorsky, head of the NKVD station in London, discovered the deception he was furious and even considered ending the relationship with Philby. Despite suspicions that he was an MI6 plant, Moscow resumed the agent relationship with Smollett, although they forbade the acceptance of any information from him unless it had been specifically authorised by the NKVD station in London. 'Our task is to understand what disinformation our rivals are planting on us', ordered the NKVD.[31]

After the Second World War Smollett left the MoI with his reputation intact and was even awarded an OBE by King George VI. In 1947 he returned to Vienna as the foreign correspondent of *The Times*. His posting only lasted two years because a diagnosis of multiple sclerosis deprived him of the use of his legs and he became dependent on using a wheelchair. But he inherited the ownership of his father's prosperous sports equipment business and in recognition of his espionage work the Soviets granted him preferential treatment, despite the factory being based in the Russian zone of control in the city.

As Smollett lived in the Soviet sector of Vienna and was an enthusiastic member of the Communist Party, MI6 closely monitored his activities. In February 1952, his summaries of conversations between Foreign Office officials, MoI reports and a letter to former foreign secretary Anthony Eden were discovered in Burgess's flat and so suspicions that Smollett had been a Soviet spy were renewed. These documents were identified as emanating from Smollett's typewriter, due to its faulty 'm' key. Later that year MI6 officers based at the British embassy in Vienna believed that he might 'come over' (defect) because he seemed 'too intelligent to swallow the Communist line'. But an MI6 officer then reported that 'turning' Smollett was a lost cause. 'Our hopes seem to have been dashed', he concluded.

In fact, Smollett was a bold and irredeemable believer in Marxist doctrine and never lost his faith. He was ideologically motivated and hence it was relatively easy for the NKVD to recruit him. MI5 counter-intelligence officers remained keen to interview Philby's former business partner as part of their investigation into the Communist cell in Britain. At the time, some Soviet agents, notably Anthony Blunt and John Cairncross, were undetected and evidence was circumstantial.

For several years Smollett avoided MI5's clutches, as he was living in the Soviet sector of Vienna, but eventually, on 19 September 1961, he arrived in London for a reunion dinner. He checked into room 387 of the Savoy hotel, paying ten pounds per night for an extended stay. As soon as his presence was noted, MI5 tapped his telephone in his hotel room, based on a Home Office warrant. He was then placed under surveillance while he drove around London in a rented Austin Cambridge car with his wife and on 2 October he was interrogated at the War Office by Arthur Martin, the renowned counter-intelligence officer.

By now MI5's previous view that Smollett was too rapacious, idle and cowardly to be a fervent Communist had been discarded. Based on the documents found in Burgess's flat, Smollett was now regarded as an active Soviet agent inside the heart of government, almost at the level of the infamous 'Cambridge Five'. But the former Soviet agent was a wily operator. He arrived at the MI5 interview in a wheelchair with a rucksack tied to the back, chain-smoked and exploited his disability to gain sympathy. Whenever he was asked a challenging question and needed time to think, he fumbled with lighting a new cigarette and occasionally distracted the MI5 officer by asking him to hold the lighter while he pondered his answer.[32]

MI5 struggled to extract any incriminating confessions from the former NKVD agent, who was adept at sophistry, half-truths and convenient memory lapses. 'Smollett is a forceful personality with a quick, shrewd mind who said nothing which was demonstrably false', stated Arthur Martin in his report for MI5. But the former Soviet spy falsely claimed that Philby had shunned him after 1935 because he was 'anti-Jewish'. Smollett accurately described Burgess as 'a colourful and attractive nut and very vain' but claimed that his secret MoI notes and diaries were given to his fellow Soviet agent because Burgess was 'attached to MI5'. And he categorised himself as a 'fellow traveller' who never joined the Communist Party during his time at the MoI. Instead he portrayed himself as an admirer of President Tito, the independent Communist ruler of Yugoslavia, rather than as a Soviet sympathiser.

Two days later, on 4 October 1961, Smollett checked out of the Savoy hotel and returned to Vienna. He had presented himself to MI5 as an enfeebled man with an incurable disease. Again this was being economical with the truth. He continued to live for many years in a comfortable villa in Vienna, running the family business and dabbling in journalism as the editor of the magazine *Austria Today*. It was not until November 1980, at the age of sixty-eight, that Smollett died – almost twenty years after the MI5 interrogation.

Despite suspicions, it took another two decades before Smollett was fully unmasked as a spy and his secret life was revealed. In 1999 NKVD documents smuggled out of Russia by former KGB archivist and officer Vasily Mitrokhin demonstrated that the Austrian foreign correspondent and former MoI Soviet director was in fact a Soviet agent, recruited by Philby and assigned the codename ABO. This was confirmed by Oleg Gordievsky, who had helped to run Soviet active measures in London. While working on the classified official history of the First Chief Directorate (the international section), Gordievsky concluded that Smollett was an important agent of influence for the Soviet Union. And he considered the NKVD's 'active measures coup' of having Smollett direct pro-Soviet propaganda and influence Anglo-Soviet liaisons during the Second World War to have been a remarkable achievement.[33]

Historians now believe that Smollett's influence at the MoI was far more insidious and important than was realised at the time.

In *Stalin's Holy War*, Steven Merritt Miner argues that he did not single-handedly hijack the BBC and transform it into a propaganda mouthpiece for the Soviet Union. Instead he played a Machiavellian game of disguising his own views and objecting to reports which were excessively sycophantic and subservient to the Soviets. By tempering his Marxist sympathies, he preserved his cover as a spy. Miner wrote that:

> His chief asset was the ineffable spirit of the wartime alliance which fostered admiration of the Soviet people's martial achievements and suppressed critical thinking about the Stalinist system – or at least stifled its public expression. In this extraordinary milieu, Smollett was able to hide in plain view – even managing to appear rather moderate compared to some of his colleagues at the Ministry of Information.
>
> Orders might have come from the prime minister to cease overly indulgent propaganda about the USSR but Smollett always managed to appear enforcing these instructions while in fact flouting them whenever possible. By no means did Smollett ignite the wartime popular enthusiasm for the USSR but he stoked them constantly and whenever his superiors' attention was diverted, he surreptitiously squirted gasoline on the coals.[34]

When I spoke to Smolka's son, Dr Timothy Smolka, in Vienna he was reluctant to discuss the allegations against his father but he did tell me: 'My father was not a spy. The whole thing about him being a [Soviet] spy was invented by George Orwell after the publication of his book *Animal Farm* was delayed.' I asked Dr Smolka if his father objected to *Animal Farm* and he replied: 'This was not my father's idea. He was working in the Soviet department of the Ministry of Information and was told to tell Orwell to delay the publication of the book until the end of the Second World War.'

*

The clandestine activities of Peter Smollett were a curtain-raiser for the most sinister and occasionally most dangerous KGB intrigue of the Cold War – the deployment of agents of influence. In the covert operations to destabilise, disrupt and weaken the West, these undercover spies played a crucial role in what KGB officers called 'decomposition work'. Through this prism the Soviet Union endeavoured to develop its own disguised voices by smuggling Soviet views into foreign governments, parliaments, media organisations, corporations, trade unions and cultural and academic circles. The agents' role was to penetrate such citadels of power by holding senior positions, while their true loyalty was always to Moscow. While agents of influence occasionally transmitted intelligence to the KGB, their overriding mission was to manipulate and alter policy in the interests of the Soviet Union. It was a top priority for the KGB.

The term 'agent of influence', a literal translation of the Russian term '*agent vlyiyania*', is both elastic and multifaceted. Many such agents are not official spies in the conventional sense – that is, hired to complete a mission assigned by a KGB case officer. Some are not even aware that the Soviet diplomat they are meeting is in fact an intelligence officer. Only a few become registered agents. Instead the relationship is informal and covers a broad spectrum of social and professional relationships – from casual lunch partners to close personal friendships. Usually they are journalists, politicians, civil servants, bankers, lobbyists and, in more recent years, IT and social media specialists. Their mission is simple – to secretly exert influence, spread disinformation and destabilise the enemies of Russia.

Agents of influence have a perfect cover – their professional positions – and so evidence of their allegiance to the KGB is more difficult to detect. Indeed, their relationship with Moscow is so loose that they are not even agents but classified as informants and assets. 'Many persons whose actions may benefit the Soviet Union cannot be classified as agents of any kind', stated a secret Foreign Office report in 1964. 'It follows that successful agents of influence can be most dangerous and if they are in a position to influence policy then they may be even more dangerous than a spy who is selling military secrets.'[35]

During the Cold War the value of this type of agent was based on how they could be used politically to benefit the Soviet Union. In the United States the KGB targeted the growing array of congressional staffers in Washington DC. An expense account was authorised to cover a lunch at the Hay Adams hotel or cocktails in a Georgetown bar. In New York each KGB officer ostensibly moved in his own official circle determined by his cover job: the UN diplomat, member of the Soviet mission to the UN, the trade representative and TASS correspondent. But their real job was to make friends, influence people and cultivate agents.

This tactic can be risky. In 1959 the KGB launched a painstaking operation to install an agent inside the heart of New York City politics. Based at the United Nations, KGB officer Yuri Mishukov cultivated a New York law student called Richard Flink by commissioning him to write relatively unimportant research reports. After Flink became a lawyer, the undercover KGB officer continued to pay him for innocuous research and kept signed receipts which would provide leverage for blackmail if required. Then in 1962 Mishukov offered to finance Flink's campaign as a Republican candidate for the New York State Assembly. In return, he asked the ambitious young lawyer to insert statements into his speeches which would benefit the Soviet Union foreign policy agenda. But what the KGB officer did not know was that Flink had been suspicious from the outset and had reported the approach to the FBI. As soon as the offer to bankroll his campaign was made, the FBI terminated the KGB operation by exposing it. If Flink had not been a patriotic and honest lawyer, he might have embarked on a political career secretly financed, abetted and manipulated by the KGB.[36]

The motives and methodology of Westerners being recruited were carefully assessed. Between the mid-1970s and mid-1980s, Kim Philby ran an annual seminar for young KGB officers responsible for operations in Britain, Ireland, Scandinavia, Australia and

New Zealand. The famous double agent adopted the roles of a foreign politician, civil servant, intelligence officer, businessman and journalist, and told his students to try and recruit him. At the end of each course Philby wrote individual reports on each student and some of their careers prospered by such preparation. And in 1976 the KGB systematised agent recruitment for all targets, which required information on a wide variety of personal traits, ranging from personal discipline to sexual perversion.[37]

The easiest agents to recruit were those with an ideological allegiance to the Soviet Union and Communism. One variant of this formula, introduced in the late 1980s, was to exploit sympathy for glasnost and President Gorbachev's attempt to lead the USSR into a new era of openness and freedom. For senior aides to foreign presidents, being an informal KGB informant provided political benefits because this connection could be useful as a confidential diplomatic back-channel. But this was risky, as exposure of the relationship could be misinterpreted as espionage rather than backdoor diplomacy.

Agents were invariably persuaded to accept cash in order to strengthen the KGB's hold over them. If the agent declined the payment, then he or she was told that it was merely to cover their expenses. For such a momentous life-changing decision, it was remarkable how the human factor played such a crucial role. Flattery and attention were successful and so was the exploitation of an individual who wanted to exact revenge against his or her boss or management. For some people, it was the excitement of secret late-night meetings in underground car parks or hotel rooms, which spiced up their mundane existence. And then there were the dirty tricks and the fear – blackmail by honey trapping or threats to expose personal embarrassing secrets and peccadillos. But blackmail did not always work.

'Money is a very persuasive tool', recalled former KGB officer Stanislav Levchenko. 'But I did not find blackmail to be a useful technique. Of course, it has been used by the KGB but personally I did not like blackmail because I felt it could drive the agent into the hands of the target nation's counter-intelligence branch.'[38]

Journalists were prime targets because of their power to publish quickly and reach large numbers of people. The KGB focused on recruiting two types of reporters. Firstly, a specialist in a useful subject area who possessed both sensitive information and connections with important individuals. Secondly, a columnist with a wide and large following of readers and an influential audience. The KGB recruited reporters all over the world. In Japan the powerful *New Times* newspaper was completely compromised and infiltrated by the KGB. In the mid-1970s the *New Times* had twelve foreign correspondents of which ten were KGB agents, according to Levchenko, who recruited most of them personally. Even the other two were involved with the International Department of the KGB. 'During my time, the two so-called "clean" correspondents were assigned to the United States and West Germany', he remembered.[39]

In France there were more KGB agents of influence than in any other NATO country during the Cold War, usually at least fifty in government alone. The French intelligence agencies were thoroughly penetrated by Soviet spies, who recruited several state officials. One agent – codenamed 'German' – was so important and useful to the Soviet cause that he was awarded the 'Order of the Red Star' – a rare honour. Even today, a list of the names of valuable KGB agents and their codenames compiled in 1954 is deemed too sensitive to be published in France. But the name of one KGB agent can be published because he was convicted and jailed for his activities as a Soviet agent of influence. He was the journalist Pierre-Charles Pathé.

An unapologetic advocate of the Soviet Union, Pathé, son of the millionaire film magnate who had founded Pathé newsreels, attracted the attention of the KGB in 1959 when he published a naively pro-Soviet essay. 'The cruelties of Stalinism were only childhood illnesses', he wrote. 'The victory of the Soviet Union is that of a correct vision of the march of history. The USSR, this laboratory of new ideas for the most advanced development of society, will overtake the gigantism of the United States.'

After a meeting with the Soviet ambassador in Paris, Pathé was recruited under the codename Pecherin and the KGB funded a new news agency called CISEP. Between 1961 and 1967 the KGB paid Pathé 6,000 French francs a month to publish a weekly newsletter, which was sold by subscription but sent free to opinion-formers in government, business and foreign embassies. The Soviets did not give completed articles to Pathé for publication. Instead, he was provided with general instructions and briefing notes on which to base his columns. The newsletter's purpose, according to leaked KGB documents, was to damage US–French relations, promote a Franco–Soviet rapprochement and distance France from NATO.[40]

Pathé's advocacy was to some extent effective, especially during the presidency of Charles de Gaulle, who attached little importance to ideological differences and liked to use the Soviet Union as a counterweight to American influence in Western Europe. He made a triumphal state visit to Moscow in 1966, which reinforced his conviction that the Soviet Union remained a traditional great power and was evolving from ideology to technocracy. 'If one leaves aside their propaganda statements, they are conducting a peaceful foreign policy', pronounced de Gaulle.[41]

The KGB was delighted and closed down the news agency CISEP. But Pathé continued to work as a Soviet agent of influence, writing regular articles in national newspapers under the pseudonym of 'Charles Morand'. Between 1967 and 1979 he was paid a total of 218,400 French francs plus 68,423 francs for expenses and bonuses. In 1969 Pathé was one of the organisers of the Gaullist dominated Mouvement pour l'indépendance de l'Europe, which the KGB regarded as a potentially valuable means of destabilising NATO.[42]

By 1974 the KGB was so confident of its influence on French politics that it attempted to sway the outcome of that year's presidential election. Soviet spies believed that the Socialist candidate, François Mitterrand, had a real chance of victory and so launched a major dirty tricks operation against his Conservative opponent, Giscard d'Estaing. A well-connected journalist – codenamed

BROK – was recruited as a paid agent of influence and supplied with a fabricated copy of secret campaign advice supposedly given to d'Estaing by the Americans, on ways to defeat Mitterrand. But the publication of the fake document did not prevent d'Estaing from being elected president.

Frustrated by Giscard d'Estaing's pro-American stance, the KGB rehired Pierre-Charles Pathé and launched the newsletter *Synthesis* (codenamed CACTUS). In essence it was a Gaullist publication designed to destabilise NATO by portraying France as a subservient sycophant of the USA. Between 1976 and 1979 the KGB invested 252,000 francs to secretly bankroll this newsletter, which was sent to 70% of French parliamentarians and influential journalists. 'France was portrayed as the victim of an "underhand" American economic war in which the US balance of payments deficit allowed Washington to act as a parasite on the wealth of other states', wrote the distinguished intelligence historian Christopher Andrew in *The Mitrokhin Archive*. 'Giscard d'Estaing was portrayed as an "Atlanticist" who was failing to protect French interests against American exploitation. The United States was a sinister "police democracy" which employed systematic violence against its black minority and all others who stood in its way, and the assassination of President Kennedy was "an essential aspect of American democracy".'[43]

This message was faithfully published and disseminated by Pathé. But his secret life was unmasked in 1979 when his KGB controller, Igor Sakharovsky, in Paris was placed under surveillance by the French security service, the DST. Eventually Sakharovsky inadvertently led his DST watchers to one of his clandestine meetings with Pathé. On 5 July 1979, the leader of a DST surveillance team was heard over the radio-intercept frequency. 'The actors are in place', he shouted. 'Let's start the show!' Soon afterwards Pathé was arrested in the act of receiving cash and documents from the KGB officer. In May 1980, the French 'journalist' became the only Soviet agent of influence ever convicted in a Western court. Pathé was sentenced to five years in jail but was released the following year. During his trial he admitted to having received small sums of money for articles written on Moscow's behalf. But his KGB file revealed that in reality, by the time of his arrest, he had received a total of nearly one million French francs in fees and expenses.[44]

*

The KGB loved agent-of-influence operations because they were elaborate and so difficult for their CIA and MI6 counter-intelligence officers to unravel. Moscow utilised such operatives as one element of a carefully orchestrated strategy called 'kombinatsia'. This refers to the skill of relating, linking and combining various agents of influence in a complex web deliberately designed to confuse the enemy.

The informal status of such an agent was especially useful because it provided ambiguity and deniability. Unlike full-time KGB intelligence officers, there was no paper trail. The relationship was casual, assignments occasional and intermediaries were used to distance the agency and the agent. Disinformation could be leaked via the agent and unsuspecting sources could be spied on to obtain compromising intelligence. And none of these operations could be directly traced back to the KGB.

The most celebrated KGB agent of influence was Vitali Yevgenyevich Lui, better known as Victor Louis. As the Moscow correspondent of the London Daily News and the Sunday Express, freelancer for the Washington Post and prolific author, the diligent, charming Louis developed a remarkable network and relished his image as an international man of mystery. But, according to his KGB controller until 1982, Major General Vyacheslav Kevorkov, and multiple Soviet defectors, the Kremlin's favourite journalist was also one of the most effective agents during the Cold War.[45]

Born in 1928 in Moscow, Louis's mother died a week after his birth but he enjoyed a relatively affluent upbringing. As a teenager, he worked as a messenger and police informer at the New Zealand and Brazilian embassies in the capital. He also dabbled in black marketeering and clearly made enemies, as he was accused of being a foreign spy and thrown into a concentration camp in Kazakhstan while only eighteen. During his nine-year internment, Louis was an eccentric if engaging prisoner. One fellow inmate recalls him arriving at the camp in Kazakhstan wearing a pith helmet and an outfit resembling a British tropical dress uniform. Louis was also a gifted linguist and sought out interned intellectuals who confided in him.[46]

On his release in 1956, aged twenty-eight, Louis qualified as a lawyer but returned to the black market. Carrying his wares in a large suitcase, he quite openly – and recklessly – sold ikons and exchanged foreign currency, acts for which most Soviet citizens would have been shot. He also circulated among diplomats as a dealer in black market goods and a fixer eager to ingratiate himself. It was at this time that he attracted the attention of the Moscow district of the KGB, according to former KGB officer Major Yuri Nosenko. While never employed as a full-time officer, Louis involved himself in intelligence operations. He tried to recruit as an agent an American the KGB were already trying to ensnare. 'Gribanov [the KGB officer in charge] ordered the Moscow district to get him [Louis] away from our operation', recalled Nosenko. 'But you must understand that the local KGB got only the crumbs of operations and to them Victor [Louis] was a big thing. He could work against foreigners very well and they thought that through him they could get into important operations.'[47]

And so Victor Louis the intelligence agent was born. As he was fluent in English, he soon secured a job at the CBS News bureau in Moscow and tipped off his boss Daniel Schorr about the imminent Soviet invasion of Hungary in 1956. Based on that scoop, the London Daily News provided him with official press credentials. He was the archetypal foreign correspondent – a plausible manner, some literary ability and a lateral thinker. He was also charismatic: just under six feet tall, he wore spectacles and had a pale, pink face that smiled often and many people liked him. He was always curious, often generous with information and stories and possessed a sharp intellect. And he appeared to know everyone.

But at the time few knew that Louis had a secret relationship with the Soviet state. To make him more attractive and accessible to foreigners in Moscow, the KGB fed him inside information and soon he was breaking stories that the Western foreign correspondents could not access. Former KGB officers and Foreign Office diplomats say that Louis crossed the line from being a sympathetic reporter to becoming an agent of influence and disinformation. He was involved in an operation to discredit, disrupt and defame Stalin's daughter, Svetlana Alliluyeva, in 1967 when she published her memoir *Twenty Letters to a Friend* and some intimate family photographs. The next year Louis published an article about the Soviet dissident and esteemed novelist Alexander Solzhenitsyn in the *Washington Post*, purportedly based on an 'interview'. The Nobel Prize-winning author was portrayed as a whining, self-pitying attention seeker and martyr – far from his established reputation as courageous and principled. Louis even suggested that Solzhenitsyn regarded the Nazi wartime occupation of Russia favourably. Readers were perplexed by the article. This was not surprising because Solzhenitsyn was adamant that the interview never took place.[48]

Perhaps the most dangerous disinformation operation occurred in September 1969, at a time when Sino-Soviet relations were at a low ebb and a delicate stage. Soon after the Soviet prime minister Alexei Kosygin returned from Peking after unsatisfactory talks, Louis sent a dispatch to the *London Evening News* which indicated that the Soviet Union was considering a pre-emptive nuclear strike against China. Simultaneously, KGB officers stationed at Soviet embassies in Europe and the USA were briefing influential Americans that the Russians were seriously considering such a surprise attack. It was a classic KGB underhand tactic: by not officially threatening the Chinese and exposing themselves to the charge of reckless warmongering, the Russians could pressure the Chinese into re-entering negotiations in the Sino-Soviet dispute.

By 1975 Louis's activities were creating tension in US–Soviet relations. In April, Henry Kissinger, then secretary of state, summoned the Soviet ambassador Anatoly Dobrynin, a former aircraft engineer and member of a new professional generation of Soviet diplomats who had been entrusted with state secrets, to discuss 'a highly confidential and delicate question'. While he had no objection to the ambassador holding private meetings with opposition figures in Washington DC, Kissinger said that it was 'a different matter' when Moscow dispatched secret, unofficial emissaries to spread 'political disinformation' among the opposition and create tension in US–Soviet relations.

The Soviet ambassador was not surprised to hear that Kissinger named Louis as an example of an unofficial agent of influence. In his memoirs, Dobrynin describes Louis as being 'directly used by Soviet intelligence' and 'a dubious character': 'When Louis visited Washington he did not contact our embassy and I never saw him in the United States or at home. In their own search for political information in the West, Louis and people like him presented themselves as more knowledgeable than Soviet diplomats about the inner secrets of the Kremlin and more suitable for finding "compromises" in our relations.'[49]

While there is no evidence that Louis was a KGB officer, multiple sources say that he was used to leak stories to foreign correspondents and spread speculation that the Kremlin did not want to be attributed to them directly. Sometimes sensitive information was leaked to Louis even before the event took place – just to test the water. Vyacheslav Kevorkov later described how he would meet Louis at safe houses – never at the KGB HQ at Lubyanka – and give him his assignments, usually from Yuri Andropov, then head of the Soviet intelligence agency.[50]

Buried in the UK National Archives is a Foreign Office profile of Louis entitled 'Agent of Disinformation'. It is an unflattering portrait. Known as 'Red Pimpernel' and 'Louis the Leak', the report stated: 'Louis has become so notorious that the Soviet authorities make little effort to disguise his role as a Russian intelligence agent.... His task is to sow confusion, plant lies, peddle fraudulent or stolen manuscripts and smear the reputations of dissenting Soviet intellectuals such as Alexander Solzhenitsyn.'[51]

Former British diplomats describe the power and presence of Louis on the Moscow landscape. 'What his actual [KGB] description was I have no idea, but of his role as an agent there could be little doubt', recalled Sir Curtis Keeble, former British ambassador to Moscow between 1978 and 1982. Louis's hotline to the KGB was illustrated by Sir Brian Barder, former first secretary at the UK embassy. In 1971 the diplomat was concerned that he would be expelled from the Soviet Union as part of counter-expulsions after KGB officers had been evicted from London.

'I asked him [Louis] the day after the expulsions whether I should start packing', said Sir Brian. 'He telephoned me the next day and said "No, you will be staying".'[52]

Unlike his fellow foreign correspondents, Louis lived an unusually luxurious lifestyle. He travelled the world in a style alien to any Soviet citizen, flashing his credit cards and staying in expensive hotels. Together with his English wife Jennifer, he entertained royally at his opulent dacha in Bakova, west of Moscow. The three-storey mansion contained five bedrooms with an indoor swimming pool, a tennis court, a Porsche, a Bentley, a Mercedes and a reception room full of ikons, sculptures, framed letters from foreign dignitaries and paintings. There the hospitable and gracious Louis would entertain British diplomats and luminaries of the media aristocracy, amid tables laden with salmon, imported cheese, caviar and tsarist memorabilia. For his British guests a TV showing a video of *Match of the Day* would be in the background. The house acted almost like a Soviet press centre, complete with the latest fax and telex machines, at a time when it was difficult just to send a telegram from Moscow.

As Louis and his servants served Pimms and brandy and handed out Cuban cigars after dinner, in the garden or by the pool, guests asked each other: 'How on earth can he afford all this?' He had bought the dacha in 1965 but also owned a spacious apartment on Leninsky Prospect in Moscow, where he retained a chauffeur. It was a lifestyle which only the privileged Communist Party elite enjoyed and most of the Russian population could only dream of.

'He is testimony to the fact that Soviet bureaucracy is flexible and a talented Russian can juggle the system to his own advantage', said the journalist Stanley Karnow.[53]

The sources of Louis's wealth were diverse. But he had made a Faustian pact with the KGB. 'Louis had a licence to operate', a former MI6 officer stationed in Moscow during the Cold War told me. 'He did the KGB's bidding and was very much a member of their inner sanctum and met Andropov privately on several occasions. As long as he delivered their message, he was left alone.'

And so Louis became an information entrepreneur. He sold stories to multiple newspapers, translated *My Fair Lady* into Russian and collected royalties and was paid vast sums for videos by American TV companies. He was also fortunate that his English wife Jennifer, who had been a tutor to the children of a diplomat at the British embassy, was a hardworking, articulate journalist. Together they wrote detailed guide books for motorists and tourists, and compiled the only English language telephone directory and street map of Moscow.

It was all very rewarding but it was his work as an agent of influence that enabled him to keep and expand his wealth, according to Vyacheslav Kevorkov. The KGB allowed Louis to keep all his money from international media outlets in foreign currency, which would have been a crime and unthinkable for regular Soviet citizens. This enabled him to buy his luxury items from abroad and import them from Western countries.[54]

One lucrative source of wealth was his business relationship with Robert Maxwell, the buccaneering publisher. Maxwell had long been interested in obtaining the rights to translate and publish Soviet scientific journals and books in the West, alongside his British publications. It was a slow negotiation in the mid-1960s but the British media tycoon had an ace up his sleeve: he had been a KGB agent of influence since 1947. After patiently waiting and playing chess and drinking vodka, Maxwell was told by Yuri Gradov, the lawyer for the Soviet copyright agency, that the KGB had approved his venture. 'I was ordered to conclude a deal at any price', recalled Gradov. Indeed, the price paid by the avaricious publisher to sell the books was remarkably low and he was then introduced to his new sales representative in Moscow, one Victor Louis.[55]

It was a financially interdependent relationship. In the early 1970s Maxwell's business empire had crashed after accountants discovered that the accounts of his publishing company, Pergamon Press, were fraudulent. In 1974, after regaining ownership of his company, Maxwell returned to Moscow. This is what happened next, according to the definitive biography of Maxwell by Tom Bower:

> Ambitious to rebuild Pergamon, he agreed with the KGB and with General Secretary Leonid Brezhnev to publish biographies of Soviet and other Communist leaders in the West. He would be paid by the KGB for undertaking to publish 50,000 copies of the books, though understandably the KGB's subsidy would never feature in Pergamon's accounts. Maxwell in fact deceived the KGB about the number of copies that he actually printed but he did satisfy the dictator's vanity.[56]

Four years later Maxwell met President Brezhnev for a private conversation at the Kremlin and the businessman was accorded what appeared to be 'a state visit' to his birthplace, a border zone normally forbidden to foreigners. During the visit the Soviet president inscribed on the title page of one of these books in his quivering hand, 'To my dear friend Robert Maxwell'. But this was then incorrectly translated from Russian into Cyrillic and so the publisher asked the ageing Brezhnev to sign again.

Throughout the late 1970s and early 1980s, the Soviet Union bought vast numbers of Pergamon's academic and scientific books from Maxwell at inflated prices and Louis was his representative in Moscow. The books were dry, bland and highly technical but it was a method used by the KGB to pay Maxwell, who was also a Labour MP until 1970. Like Louis, Maxwell was a willing agent of influence. In 1968 he delivered a speech in the House of Commons which urged the West to give a restrained response to the Soviet invasion of Czechoslovakia. But what ministers were not aware of was that two months earlier Maxwell had been secretly briefed by Yuri Andropov, the KGB chairman.[57]

By the late 1980s Maxwell was the owner of the Mirror Group of newspapers and for a brief period the *New York Daily News*. And so the KGB regarded him as a useful agent who could influence the West. The beleaguered press baron was summoned to Moscow and met Vladimir Kryuchkov, the KGB chief, on several occasions. 'He was a friend of the USSR', Kryuchkov said. 'He was sincere and wished us well.' According to his biographer Tom Bower:

> Kryuchkov reminded Maxwell that to repay the debt he owed the country, he should explain Russia's policies to other statesmen. In the KGB's newly sanitised parlance, Maxwell was an 'unusual foreign relation' who could be relied upon to share information to which he enjoyed privileged access. 'We would try and exploit him and vice-versa. It would be mutually profitable', attested Leonid Shebashin, then the suspicious chief of the KGB's foreign intelligence branch.

One joint venture that the KGB boss Kryuchkov was intrigued by in the late 1980s was the establishment of a new English newspaper, to be edited and printed in London but secretly controlled by the Russian intelligence services![58]

The importance of Maxwell in the covert propaganda war was illustrated by documents leaked just days after the media tycoon died in 1991 in the Atlantic Ocean, found not far from his yacht. A civil servant in the International Department smuggled out files which revealed that $200 million had been transferred to Communist-linked parties abroad in order to fund the KGB's political and influence operations. One of these schemes was what the Soviets called 'friendly firms'. These were crony companies at the heart of a vast system of black market operations that

kept the Soviet Union afloat. A priority corporation listed was
Pergamon Press, owned by Maxwell, and its Moscow agent was
Victor Louis.[59]

A year later, on 18 July 1992, Victor Louis died prematurely of
a heart attack in London, just a few months after the demise of
the Soviet Union. He was just sixty-four. His wife Jennifer, who
had worked so hard to advance her husband's career, was devastated
and remained in the UK. When asked about Louis's dealings with
the KGB, she replied:

> I will tell you this. Whatever business Victor has with the Soviet
> government is his alone. I know nothing about it, and I don't
> want to know. That's one part of his life which is separate from
> mine and the boys. It is Victor's exclusively. Early in our
> marriage we decided on that sort of arrangement because it is
> best for the family. If anything should happen and officials
> should suddenly question me, say about 'your husband's last
> mission', then I honestly wouldn't know what they were talking
> about.[60]

When I asked his son, Nicholas Louis, about his father's relationship with the KGB, he smiled enigmatically and shrugged off the
allegations as speculation and gossip. 'The family is very philosophical about these claims', he said. 'I never spoke to my father
about his work and so I know nothing about it. We always found
it frustrating when people came to dinner and asked whether he
was a spy. We just didn't know.'

When Victor Louis was alive, his fellow correspondents would
often tease him because he always maintained that he was a regular
journalist. 'Come on, Victor, stop it. Tell us the truth', Michael
Binyon, *The Times* correspondent in Moscow, would jibe. 'We know
regular people don't live like you do.' But Louis would always strongly
deny that he was a KGB agent. 'It was a game', Binyon said. 'We
knew and he knew that we knew, but no one ever admitted
anything.'[61]

To some extent, Louis enjoyed and even encouraged the notoriety, mystery and celebrity status. When a friend asked him about
the KGB, he joked: 'I am a double agent. I am loyal to both sides.'

For the UK and US governments and some Soviet diplomats,
the activities of Victor Louis were deadly serious. They regarded
him as a menace, a disruptor and an agent of disinformation. One
former Foreign Office mandarin told me that Louis often sowed
confusion and planted half-truths in the international press, which
created diplomatic discord and tension at a time when detente was
on the agenda. 'It was almost as if he was a semi-official exponent
of a parallel foreign policy on behalf of the KGB', he added.

'He [Louis] was just a part of that whole sub-world of the Soviet
Union', recalled Sir Curtis Keeble, former British ambassador to
Moscow between 1978 and 1982. 'It was a kind of under-water
jungle which you might observe through a glass-bottomed boat
but into which you dived at your peril and an old chart might
bear a sign – "Here be strange sea monsters" – and they were liable
to come up from the depths to swallow the unwary.'[62]

Both Victor Louis and Hans-Peter Smolka operated in an underworld of intrigue and influence for the benefit of the KGB. They
had different motives: Louis wanted to be the ultimate insider and
Smolka was the committed Communist. But both masqueraded
behind their public roles – Louis as a journalist and Smolka as a
government propagandist – to secretly promote the Soviet foreign
policy agenda and destabilise the West.

3

FAKE NEWS

For the great enemy of truth is very often not the lie – deliberate, contrived and dishonest – but the myth – persistent, persuasive and unrealistic. Too often we hold fast to the cliches of our forebears. We subject all facts to a prefabricated set of interpretations. We enjoy the comfort of opinion without the discomfort of thought. Mythology distracts us everywhere – in government as in business, in politics as in economics, in foreign affairs as in domestic affairs

President J. F. Kennedy, Commencement address,
Yale University, 11 June 1962

Words are like tiny doses of arsenic, swallowed unnoticed and then after a while the toxin sets in.

Victor Klemperer, *The Language of the Third Reich*

THE FAVOURITE AUTHOR OF MANY KGB officers during the Cold War was not Leo Tolstoy, Fyodor Dostoevsky, Alexander Pushkin or Maxim Gorky. Instead it was the Chinese military strategist, general and philosopher Sun Tzu, born around six hundred years before Jesus Christ. Best known for his treatise *The Art of War*, Sun Tzu argued that the most effective way to win a war was not on the battlefield but through influence operations, disinformation, propaganda and psychological tactics. 'All warfare is deception', he wrote. 'Hence, when able to attack, we must seem unable. When using our forces, we must seem inactive. When we are near, we must make the enemy believe we are far away. When far away, we must make him believe we are near.'[1]

One of Sun Tzu's most devoted admirers was a KGB officer called Yuri Bezmenov. Between 1965 and 1970 he worked ostensibly for Novosti Press Agency but in reality he operated as a Russian intelligence officer based in the classified department of 'Political Publications'. For the sake of secrecy this group was not based in the Novosti HQ on Pushkin Square but in a discreet office on Kutuzov Avenue. Bezmenov placed disinformation and fake stories in the press in foreign countries in order 'to change the perception of reality of every American', as he recalled later.[2] He was so effective that when the KGB set up a new secret unit in India called ~~'Research and Counter Propaganda' he was made its deputy chief~~ of operations. He later defected to Canada.

The Cold War was fought through the hearts and minds of the combatants and Bezmenov's task was to distort reality to such an extent that despite the abundance of information, no one could reach sensible conclusions in order to defend themselves and their country. For the committed KGB officer, Sun Tzu was his operational guide and mentor.

'The highest art of warfare is not to fight at all but to subvert anything of value in your enemy's country', recalled Bezmenov. 'These include moral and cultural traditions, religion and respect for leaders and authority. And so anything that puts white against black, old against young, the rich against poor works. As long as it disturbs their society and cuts the moral fibre of their nation, that's good. And when everything in this country is subverted, disorientated, confused, demoralised and destabilised, then the crisis will come.'[3]

For the KGB the use of disinformation – now known as 'fake news' – was a primary weapon in their armoury during the Cold

War. Its purpose was to create a climate of chaos, fear and pervasive uncertainty in which nobody could be trusted. In his
perceptive book *The War of Nerves*, Martin Sixsmith, former BBC
correspondent in Moscow in the late 1980s and early 1990s, argues:

> The aim of Soviet disinformation in the Cold War was to under-
> mine the confidence of people in the West in the open nature of
> their 'free' society and in the probity of the men who ran it.
> Moscow sought out the potential weak points in a nation's psyche,
> applying pressure, hoping to speed its degradation. Tacitly,
> Washington acknowledged the importance of such methods.
> 'There are no rules in such a game', concluded the Doolittle report
> of 1954. 'Hitherto acceptable norms of human conduct do not
> apply.'
> The impact of fake news on the human mind is profound. The
> mind creates mental maps and finds it hard to redraw them once
> they are settled. Accepting the unreliability of a 'fact' on which
> others have subsequently been built throws the mind into intol-
> erable doubt. Perversely, the more unlikely an assimilated 'fact'
> might seem, the harder it is to dislodge.[4]

The word 'disinformation' was first used in Russia in 1949 and
defined as 'the dissemination of false and provocative information',
according to the *Soviet Political Dictionary*. A more incisive defi-
nition was contained in a leaked KGB training manual: 'Strategic
disinformation assists in the execution of State tasks and is directed
at misleading the enemy concerning the basic questions of State
policy, the military-economic status and the scientific-technical
achievement of the Soviet Union.'[5] It was one component of a wider
strategy called 'active measures' – a uniquely Soviet intelligence
term translated from '*aktivnyye meropriyatia*'.

For KGB officers, the deployment of disinformation was a top
priority against the USA, the UK and NATO. 'Only about 25 per
cent of our time, money and manpower was spent on espionage
as such', Bezmenov said. 'The other 75 per cent was a slow process

focusing on what we called ideological subversion or active measures.'[6] This was confirmed by Ladislav Bittman, former deputy head of Czech intelligence, who worked closely with the KGB. He said that all KGB officers were required to spend most of their time conjuring up ideas for 'deliberately distorted information', which was secretly 'leaked through a variety of channels in order to deceive and manipulate'.[7] By the mid-1980s the KGB's annual budget for active measures was a staggering $3.63 billion, and it employed a total of 15,000 people – inside and outside the Soviet Union – who were deployed officially and unofficially. It was a small army of which Sun Tzu would have been proud.

The sponsorship of grand strategic deception and subterfuge is, of course, nothing new nor restricted to the KGB. The Greek philosopher Plato argued in the fifth century BC that a ruler was entitled to deceive the population in the interests of their own safety and the security of the state. Disinformation is even more powerful if those in authority believe in it. In the Soviet Union its roots can be traced back to Lenin. In a memo written to Foreign Affairs Commissar Tchitcherin in 1921 he said: 'To tell the truth is a petty bourgeois habit whereas for us to lie is justified by our objectives.'

Based on Lenin's diktat, 'a special bureau for disinformation' was created in the state political directorate on 11 January 1923. It was mandated by the Russian Communist Party 'to break up the counter-revolutionary plans and schemes of the enemy'. At the time the group focused on internal not external opponents of the regime. But during the Second World War this bureau collected foreign and military intelligence about the Red Army which was used to hoodwink the enemy. After the war when the Russians were threatening Greece, Iran and Berlin, the NKVD – the predecessor of the KGB – leaked data grossly exaggerating the strength of the Red Army. This was designed to intimidate the West. Instead, ironically, they provided an incentive for Western rearmament and the formation of NATO.[8]

In 1947 a new disinformation unit called K1 was set up 'to unmask the anti-Soviet activity of foreign circles, influence the public opinion of other countries and compromise anti-Soviet officials and public figures of foreign governments'. Its aim was to create 'a carefully constructed false message leaked to an opponent's communication system in order to deceive the decision-making elite or the public', according to Ladislav Bittman. To succeed, wrote Bittman, 'every disinformation message must at least partially correspond to reality or generally accepted views because without a considerable degree of plausible, verifiable information, it is difficult to gain the victim's confidence.'[9]

The KGB took advantage of the maxim that there is rarely an unvarnished, undeniable truth. As Oscar Wilde once quipped: 'The truth is rarely pure and never simple.' For many people, there is no incontrovertible reality. When the left-wing Labour firebrand Aneurin Bevan first met his future wife Jennie Lee at a party in London, he opened with 'I'll tell you my truth, if you tell me yours'.

But the KGB cynically distorted reality to a new low level of falsehood. 'The great Russian lie was born as an essential instrument of self-preservation – to tell the truth was likely as not to be fatal in the most literal sense', argues Sir Rodric Braithwaite, the British ambassador to Moscow between 1988 and 1992 and former chairman of the Joint Intelligence Committee. 'But it goes much beyond that. All those who have dealt with the Russians over the centuries have commented on their indifference to the truth.... Russians have a word for it, "*vranyo*".'[10]

The KGB believed that the production and dissemination of black propaganda and disinformation would significantly alter the balance of power between the Soviet bloc and NATO. 'Our main objective was to note and dissect all the enemy's weaknesses and sensitive or vulnerable spots and to analyse his failures and mistakes in order to exploit them', recalled Bittman, who defected to the West in 1968. 'The formula of special operations might remind one of a doctor who, in treating the patient entrusted to his care, prolongs his illness and speeds him to an early grave instead of curing him.'[11]

The KGB's disinformation desk was overseen by General Ivan Agayants, a tall, aloof, cultivated Armenian with a pencil-thin moustache and receding hairline. Ascetic and solemn, Agayants combined puritanism with a penchant for professional ruthlessness. He was a senior experienced intelligence officer who had long been the central figure in Soviet clandestine manipulation and deception abroad, mainly in the Middle East. His career began in 1930 at the knee of Artur Artuzov, the mastermind of cunning deception operations like the infamous 'Trust'. This was a fake organisation set up by Russian spies, which pretended that a huge underground group of anti-Communists was eager to receive outside help. Nothing of the kind existed. The Trust was an invention to ensnare anti-Bolsheviks, who were then captured and executed. Using similar subterfuge methods, Agayants became the KGB's first resident in Paris after its liberation in 1944. Under the code name 'Ivan Avalov', Agayants exploited President de Gaulle's interest in postwar Soviet cooperation by recruiting highly placed French civil servants and intelligence officers. For decades they undermined Western efforts to cope with Soviet subversion and espionage, as the French administration was heavily penetrated by the KGB.

In 1954 Agayants deployed his Soviet-friendly agents to influence the French parliamentary vote on the proposed European Defence Community treaty. Exploiting old fears of German militarism, the Soviet spymaster arranged for secret payments to be given to French MPs and Communist organisations to mount noisy street demonstrations. He then planted fake stories about supporters of the treaty and the French parliament duly rejected French ratification of the plan. Most of these agents of influence were never uncovered and to this day their names remain classified.

Inspired by Agayant's success, the KGB chairman at the time, Alexander Shelepin, realised that such clandestine operations could enhance Soviet foreign policy and coordinate covert global political action. In 1959 a proposal for a unit to distribute disinformation through trusted channels as a way of 'exposing and compromising' anti-Soviet policies was agreed and Department D was born. The cunning Agayants was ideally suited for the job. He gathered forty officers at a secluded KGB office on Gogolevsky Boulevard and another twenty at the residency in East Berlin. And it was not long before Agayants was given a top-level assignment. During a visit to Washington DC in September 1959, President Khrushchev privately tried to undermine confidence in US intelligence agencies during talks with President Eisenhower at the White House. According to a CIA report that was later declassified, his briefing notes were prepared by Agayant's disinformation unit.[12]

Department D's top priority was to discredit and destroy American prestige and institutions in order to create distrust and rifts between the USA and its NATO allies. Practically every evil and misdeed in the world was attributed to the Americans: the CIA was accused of assassinating President Kennedy and attempting to murder Pope John Paul II and when the esteemed UN secretary-general Dag Hammarskjöld died in a plane crash, the KGB fuelled rumours that American spies had orchestrated the accident.

Such fake news was part of an organised, authorised operation which routinely invented stories to discredit Westerners who were anti-Soviet (three per day was not unusual). It was a tsunami of falsehood. Smearing anti-Communist electoral candidates was a favourite, according to the former deputy head of the KGB's disinformation department, Sergei Kondrashev. 'Almost every day, somewhere Service D officers forged letters "exposing" their rumoured misdeeds or illicit associations', he recalled.[13]

This was confirmed by another KGB defector, Peter Deriabin, who said in 1954: 'The Russian Intelligence Service's purpose is not only to acquire information but to manufacture information, destroy sources of foreign information, terrorise, assassinate and proselytise as occasion demands. In short, Soviet intelligence sets out to subvert the political and social life of a foreign country.'[14]

By the early 1960s the KGB's disinformation unit was deemed so vital that its staff was increased to over a hundred officers and its status raised to 'Service' and redesignated as 'A'. The depth of its operations was illustrated by a booklet attacking Allen Dulles, CIA director between 1952 and 1961 and a bête noire of the KGB, which was published and distributed in London in January 1961 and later reprinted. Entitled *A Study of a Master Spy*, the ostensible authors were the left-wing maverick Labour MP Bob Edwards and a British journalist called 'Kenneth Dunne'. In fact, 'Dunne' was a fake name and the real author was a senior KGB disinformation officer called Colonel Vassily Sitnikov, chief of the American desk and deputy head of the station in Vienna. He was also stationed in Berlin, where he led a covert operation to smear the prominent conservative German politician Franz Josef Strauss before returning to Moscow. Sitnikov had researched the manuscript of the Dulles booklet, translated the documents, written the draft and sent it to Edwards, who polished up the final version. The pamphlet was then published and distributed by Housmans, a radical bookshop near King's Cross station.

The role of Edwards was significant in that he acted as an agent of influence inside and outside Parliament and was occasionally paid, according to former KGB officer and defector Oleg Gordievsky, who read his file. The eighty-page KGB pamphlet on the former CIA director was extremely detailed and poorly, if cunningly, written. It pretended to be a serious study and was not personal. 'We haven't the slightest desire to damage the reputation of this honourable man', stated the introduction, but then it proceeded to launch a character assassination. The principal allegation was that Dulles had cultivated pro-Nazi business interests just before the Second World War and so was compromised and illicitly sympathetic to their cause. 'Hemmed in on all sides by the black slime of Nazi interests, he could not help put a foot in the mire', stated the booklet. 'Mr Dulles had planted a tree that bore German Nazi fruit.' The authors concluded that the CIA director and the USA were planning a war against the Soviet Union which, just like the

Nazis, they would lose. When the hidden hand of the KGB was later revealed, Dulles was philosophical. 'Sitnikov has a whole dossier on me', he commented. 'I've read some things there about myself that even I didn't know.'[15]

The booklet was, in fact, part of a wider covert operation against Dulles and the CIA, according to a top-secret KGB document compiled on 7 June 1960, and distributed widely. This report by KGB boss Alexander Shelepin urged its officers to 'carry out measures targeted at further discrediting CIA activity and compromising its leader Allen Dulles'. KGB operatives were ordered to activate the following covert measures:

> Mail anonymous letters to Dulles' political and personal enemies using the names of CIA officers criticising his activity and authoritarian leadership.
>
> Prepare a dossier of articles from the foreign press which had criticised Dulles personally and send it – using the name of a Democratic Party member – to the US Senate Committee on Foreign Relations which is already investigating CIA activities.
>
> Send to some members of Congress, the Senate Committee and the FBI specially prepared memos from three US State Department officials with attached private letters received [allegedly] from dead American diplomats. These 'documents' would demonstrate CIA involvement in domestic decision-making, the persecution of foreign diplomats who took an objective stand and that the CIA sends deliberately false data to the State Department.
>
> Study the possibility to disseminate through appropriate channels a document by Allen Dulles which would make it clear that he was exploiting the resources as leader of the CIA and fabricating compromising materials on his private and political adversaries.
>
> Prepare and publish articles in the bourgeois press to demonstrate that Dulles got big bribes from the Lockheed corporation for allocating contracts to produce reconnaissance planes.

Present a list of American intelligence officers and agents who
have refused to work for Dulles on political, moral and other
grounds.

Dulles' successor at the CIA, John McCone, was also targeted. In
June 1963, a pamphlet entitled *Spy No. 1* was issued by the State
Publishing House for Political Literature in Moscow. This booklet
was more honest about its origins but riddled with disinformation:
'John McCone is the director of the CIA. Behind the exterior of
a respectable gentleman is hidden the seasoned spy, the organiser
of dirty political intrigues and criminal conspiracies.'

The following year *Pravda* published another attack on
McCone. Under the headline 'The Spy with the Slide Rule', it
claimed: 'Under the leadership of McCone, the CIA was transformed from just an invisible government to a government of US
oil monopolies, mainly Standard Oil and the Rockefeller Group.'[16]

The dissemination of such fake news and conspiracy theories
focused principally on the under-developed, unaligned and newly
independent nations. As the former BBC Moscow correspondent
Martin Sixsmith argues:

Weak, disenfranchised individuals, or indeed nations, appear to
be more likely to turn to conspiracy theories. It is comforting to
be able to ascribe the troubles in their lives and the lack of control
they have over their fate to a single outside factor that is not their
responsibility and cannot be overcome by their own effort,
relieving the individual of the usually unavailing effort of reme-
dying them.[17]

And so Soviet black propaganda targeted Asia, Latin America and
Africa, caught between the Cold War demands of East and West,
where pressure to conform fuelled suspicion of the USA, especially
the sinister CIA. One KGB document highlighted 'the assisting in
stepping up the activity of anti-imperialist forces in Asia, Africa
and Latin America and deepening the contradictions between

these countries and the developed capitalist states'.[18] But this was merely Marxist jargon for fabrication and disinformation, according to Oleg Kalugin, who was based in Washington:

> One of our dirty tricks involved a nasty letter-writing campaign against African diplomats at the United Nations – an idea cooked up by KGB headquarters in Moscow. Our KGB staff, using new typewriters and wearing gloves so as not to leave fingerprints, typed up hundreds of anonymous hate letters and sent them to dozens of African missions. The letters, purportedly from white supremacists as well as average Americans, were filled with virulent racist diatribes. The African diplomats publicised some of the letters as examples of the racism still rampant in America and members of the American and foreign press corps quoted from them. I and other KGB officers working as 'correspondents' in the USA reported extensively on this rabidly anti-black letter-writing campaign. I lost no sleep over such dirty tricks, figuring they were just another weapon in the Cold War.[19]

The KGB planted articles in relatively obscure, often left-wing, publications in Third World countries to sow distrust and create disruption and disturbance. This tactic had the bonus that a story could be laundered and recycled from a little-known magazine and eventually appear in the mainstream press. 'When the disinformation department wanted to carry out a big campaign in one country, it used to surface the disinformation message in another country in order to protect the people involved', Ladislav Bittman explained. 'An anti-American black propaganda campaign in Indonesia in 1965 started with an article published in a Ceylonese newspaper. Only after that first publication was it transplanted in the Indonesian press.'[20]

Oleg Kalugin said that he would always first try and place a story in a Third World country like India or Thailand – where journalists could be manipulated – or Japan – where reporters could be bribed. 'That gave the story acceptability when nobody was searching about its origin', recalled the former Russian spy.[21]

A Machiavellian manoeuvre was to exploit the willingness of non-Communist countries to exchange intelligence with one another, combined with their reluctance to disclose their sources. The following scenario is reminiscent of a Len Deighton novel or 'a wilderness of mirrors', as former CIA counter-intelligence director James Jesus Angleton once said. 'It is easy for the KGB to plant information through a source in one country relating to the security of another country which is not in a position to make its own assessment of the source', stated a secret Foreign Office report.

> The information planted may be true or false. In either case, if it is sufficiently sensitive, then embarrassment or loss of confidence between the two countries may be caused. In a military context, intelligence may be planted in one country containing deception material intended for a second country with which the first country is in intelligence liaison. The original recipient may not be in a position to spot the deception and will pass the material in good faith to the second country which will be inclined to accept it because it carries the seal of approval of the original recipient.[22]

Disinformation did not need to persuade people to believe that a conspiracy theory was true – merely to consider it. If there was enough fact to make it plausible, even if it was outlandish, this might be enough to convince them that it was possible. Hence a feverish atmosphere could be created whereby the population were willing to believe the worst excesses of their government. Like a virus, lies spread often untraced, circulating further and faster and gaining traction every time they are repeated. KGB disinformation operations were egregious and reckless, precisely because the Russian authorities did not care whether they were detected or not. 'The KGB would strike lots of matches, then light them up and hope that the whole field would catch fire and blow up', David Major, the former director of FBI counter-intelligence told me.

Such vulnerability was shamelessly capitalised on by the KGB. The main adversary – '*Glaval Vrag*' in Russian – was the USA. But the disinformation outlets were initially and relatively marginal – *The Nationalist* in Tanzania, *The Patriot* in India and *The Ghana Evening News*. In June 1965, 'The US Master Spy' – a revival of the description of Dulles – was the headline in the Greek newspaper *Avghi* about the CIA officer William Raborn. And the circulation of anonymous pamphlets was a favourite tactic – *CIA Over Asia* (Kanpur, 1964), *America's Undeclared War* (Bombay, 1963) and *American Intelligence – This is Your Enemy* (Cairo, 1964). The KGB were especially active in Ghana. On 15 May 1965, the front page headline of *The Spark* newspaper splashed 'The Secret War of the CIA – The Killer at Your Door' and claimed: 'This murderous game, which goes by the innocent-sounding name of "intelligence", has its world nerve centre in America's CIA.' The article illustrated its theme with eight photographs of spy equipment. Four of these pictures had earlier appeared in *West Berlin – The Facts* – a KGB-inspired, anti-CIA tract that was published in Moscow three years earlier. Later in 1983 the newspaper published a story head-lined 'CIA Assembling Mercenaries to Attack Ghana'. It was based on a forged document which the country's President Rawlings accepted at face value and it was several months before he agreed that it was KGB disinformation.

The sensitive issue of racial tension and anti-Semitism was also on the secret agenda. 'Our active measures campaign knew no bounds and did not discriminate on the basis of race, creed or colour: we went after everybody', Kalugin explained.

Attempting to show that America was inhospitable, we wrote anti-Semitic letters to American Jewish leaders. My fellow KGB officers paid American agents to paint swastikas on synagogues in New York and Washington. Our New York station even hired people to desecrate Jewish cemeteries. I, of course, beamed back reports of these misdeeds to my listeners in Moscow who no doubt thanked the Lord or Comrade Lenin that they had been

born in a socialist paradise and not in a hotbed of racial tension
like the United States of America.[23]

The problem with psychological warfare and disinformation is that
they have an unfortunate tendency to take on a life of their own.
The KGB was a state within a state and accountable only to the
Communist Party. There was constant political pressure to produce
'evidence' of Western evil for propaganda purposes. The truth took
second place. It was vital to demonise the enemy. There were no
limits and operatives were encouraged to implement increasingly
daring and outlandish plots. In the early 1980s even battle-hard-
ened, cynical intelligence veterans were uneasy when the KGB
manufactured neo-Nazi propaganda in imitation of crude Western
style language and posted the leaflets to the disaffected youth in
West Germany. This was done at a time when there were some
neo-Nazi activities in Berlin. But the KGB-written leaflets were
accepted as authentic and caused outrage in the West, creating
needless fear and placing people's lives in danger – all for the sake
of trying to embarrass West Germany politically.[24]

By 1985 the number of KGB and Communist bloc spies had
reached an unprecedented level. There were some 4,000 Soviet
intelligence officials stationed in the USA, of which 1,300 were
trained operatives and 700 were undercover, while the FBI only had
350 specialist intelligence officers to counter that threat. And
spreading disinformation was the priority. Hundreds of millions of
dollars of KGB cash poured into covert political operations. Some
of the funds went to National Liberation front organisations, as well
as subsidies to foreign Communist Parties and anti-NATO campaigns.
But most of it was given to media outlets staffed by intelligence
officers – TASS, Novosti, *Pravda*, *Izvestia*, foreign newspapers like
New Times and radio stations. In the mainstream press, *Paese Sera*
in Italy, *Blitz* in Delhi and *Die Furche* in Vienna were the most
cooperative, according to former KGB officer Kondrashev.[25]

Journalists were very important to the KGB, according to defectors. 'The press is our chief psychological weapon', President

Khrushchev said in 1964. As many as 75% of the TASS bureau
correspondents were in reality intelligence officers. In one six-man
TASS bureau in West Germany three were KGB, two were military
intelligence and only one, the bureau chief, was a professional
full-time journalist. Senior KGB officers also regarded reporters
from the West and developing countries as agents of influence, or
'useful idiots', as they were known. They could be exploited for
their love of sensationalism and opposition to the government.
'Our programme for counter-propaganda work is aimed at influencing public opinion in Western countries to our advantage and
at compromising specific politicians and statesmen', confided
Agayants to a fellow officer.[26]

One method of disinformation was for an undercover KGB
officer to ingratiate himself with a new, naive Western journalist
or diplomat under the guise of being a friend. The spy cultivates
the wide-eyed new resident in Moscow, provides favours and introductions and through a series of calculated indiscretions becomes
a 'confidential source'. The Russian 'friend' is then in a perfect
position to spread disinformation through this channel. 'Journalists
were particularly vulnerable to this ploy', a former MI6 officer told
me. 'They could not resist a scoop or being on the inside track,
especially when the news was so controlled by the state and it was
hard to find new sources and know what was really happening.'

Some newspapers were supported by Soviet funds to manipulate
public opinion in the West, while appearing to be independent or
privately-owned. 'We did not exclude the possibility of using a
journalist to set up an independent newspaper or magazine to
disseminate disinformation', recalled Ilya Dzhirkvelov.[27] This
happened in Japan in 1975, when a leading member of the Socialist
Party was given one million yen to set up a Soviet-friendly newspaper. For the KGB, it was a perfect vehicle for laundering
disinformation. 'If they did not have press freedom, we would have
to invent it for them', quipped one former KGB disinformation chief.

At the height of the Cold War, the renewal of the nuclear arms
race was high up on the KGB target list of active measures. In 1983

alone the Soviet Union spent $200 million on what it called 'special campaigns' against NATO plans to deploy intermediate range nuclear weapons in Western Europe in response to their own SS-20 missiles. Earlier that year Konstantin Chernenko, just before he became president, publicly highlighted the importance of the strategy: 'Comrades, our entire system of ideological work should operate as a well arranged orchestra in which every instrument has a distinctive voice and leads its theme, while harmony is achieved by skilful conducting.'

As negotiations faltered and both sides promoted the instalment of nuclear missiles, the stakes were very high. But according to one former career Russian intelligence officer, the notion of a nuclear winter was one of the KGB's most successful disinformation operations. This allegation was made by Sergei Tretyakov, a former colonel in the SVR, the successor organisation to the KGB after the Cold War. Between 1995 and 2000, Tretyakov was the deputy at Russia's second-largest intelligence outpost in New York, where he was responsible for all covert operations in the city and at the UN. He defected in 2000 and handed over five thousand cables to the CIA. His story was later told by Pete Earley in the book entitled *Comrade J*, in which he made the extraordinary claim that the KGB had deliberately exaggerated the prospect of a nuclear war of mutual destruction to scare the West into reducing their nuclear arsenal.[28]

Key vehicles for KGB propaganda were international front groups that on the surface appeared to be independent, harmless and benign but in reality were a conduit for promoting the Kremlin message. The use of fronts can be traced back to Lenin, who referred to them as 'transmission belts'. Most of these organisations, like the World Peace Council, the World Federation of Trade Unions and the World Federation of Democratic Youth, were set up in the 1950s with affiliates in Western Europe. Their role was to influence politicians and the media and manipulate non-Communists who were unaware of their hidden pro-Soviet agenda. The World Peace Council (WPC) was the most prominent and active and adept at attracting members from a broad political spectrum. With affiliates in 130 countries, the WPC's head office was in Helsinki, after being expelled from Vienna in 1951 for espionage and subversive activities.

Publicly, the WPC claimed that its national peace committees were its major donors but their contributions were minimal compared to the covert funding from the Soviet Union and Communist Parties in Eastern Europe. 'The Soviet Union financed this movement', said Vladimir Yakunin, who served in the KGB's foreign intelligence division based in New York City between 1985 and 1995.[29] By 1980 the WPC's annual budget was $31.5 million – 50% of the total funds that Moscow provided to its thirteen major international fronts. It also acted as a clearing house for channelling payments to European peace groups. But its primary purpose was to reinforce, and at times, generate opposition to the deployment of intermediate nuclear and enhanced radiation weapons by NATO.

The hallmark of the WPC's approach was its flexibility. 'The Politburo can turn its propaganda on and off like a tap', said former MI6 officer Norman Reddaway, who investigated KGB-sponsored front groups.[30] The KGB realised that any heavy and overt Soviet involvement in the WPC caused legitimate peace groups like CND to distance themselves from the more transparently Soviet-controlled fronts. And so in 1983 the Kremlin dropped its demand that peace groups provide unequivocal support for the hard-line Soviet policy. Instead they were encouraged to forge alliances with broad political coalitions, even if they criticised the Moscow line.

A favourite propaganda vehicle was the private peace conference, which was funded and organised by unaffiliated individuals who on the surface had no ties to governments or intelligence agencies. But the reality is some of them were pro-Soviet fronts. In 1984 businessmen and former government officials participated in a conference in West Germany organised by a West European busi-nessman who derived a substantial amount of his income from trade with the Soviet Union. And the participants included a retired

KGB general, the local KGB chief of station and a KGB officer working undercover.[31]

The Art of Forgery

Deep inside the KGB's headquarters at 2 Bolshaya Lubyanka was a secret sub-group (*sektor*) known as the 'documentation' section of Service A. Its purpose was to forge documents. Like a scientific laboratory, its officers skilfully imitated signatures, logos and passport entries and wrote false life histories (or 'legends') of KGB 'illegals' – operatives sent to work abroad using Western identities. Overseen by chief forger Pavel Gromoshkin, his artisans were engaged in producing often crude letters, US state department cables, UK Cabinet papers, internal memoranda, telegrams and even military manuals on an industrial scale throughout the Cold War.

A favourite ploy was to acquire blank stationery from the US Congress and the FBI and extract the letter-head and signature from genuine letters. Based on this paperwork, the KGB's creative artists would then get to work. The standard technique was for the KGB to create the fake document and then photograph it – usually on microfilm. Copies were then inserted into envelopes purchased in the area and mailed anonymously to the targeted recipients – journalists, politicians, diplomats, campaigners. If the forgery imitated an official document, the mailing list was likely to be small. In order to conceal and protect the clandestine relationship with the KGB agent of influence, that source also received a copy of the forged document. The names of the recipients were not always carefully chosen because KGB operatives believed that some journalists were naive or lazy enough to publish without checking. If the target countries abroad were near, then the fake letters and documents were delivered to them by special courier and dropped into public mailboxes.

Fake newspaper articles were disseminated and channelled via agents of influence. The first draft was drawn up in KGB headquarters in Moscow, usually describing how the CIA was organising a coup, infringing on sovereignty and abusing human rights. 'The articles were received from Moscow on microfilm and then reproduced as enlarged photocopies at the Embassy', recalled former KGB information officer Alexander Kaznacheev, based in Burma.

> It was my job to translate them into English. It was then arranged through local agents for the article to be placed in one of the Burma newspapers, usually pro-Communist orientated. The newspaper would then translate the article into Burmese, make slight changes in style and sign it 'Our Special Correspondent in Singapore', for instance. Upon publication of the article, the illegitimate creation of Soviet intelligence received an appearance of legitimacy and becomes a sort of document.
>
> But the work was not yet finished. I then took the published article and checked it against the original Russian text. I noted all the changes and variations made by the newspaper and wrote down in Russian the final version which was then immediately sent back to Moscow through TASS channels. The last stage of this grandiose forgery was under the special care of the Soviet Information Bureau, TASS, Radio Moscow and diplomats abroad. It was their duty to see that the material was republished and distributed in all countries of that region as if they were genuine documents which had appeared in the Burmese press.[32]

The KGB fake news production line was prolific and unrelenting. Almost every week carefully constructed forgeries marked top secret were inserted into envelopes, placed inside diplomatic pouches and dispatched to KGB residences in foreign embassies.

'I kept special white gloves inside a drawer of my desk to open the envelopes so that the forgeries, when mailed out, did not contain any fingerprints of KGB officers. I was careful to avoid leaving any traces on the documents', Stanislav Levchenko said, who was stationed in Japan between 1975 and 1979.[33]

The distribution of the 'articles' was carefully planned by the KGB. Their favourite type of newspaper was small, independent, low circulation, muckraking, non-Communist but anti-American and unlikely to verify or check out the information. When the publication published a planted story they never identified their source except to credit 'our correspondent abroad', who was, of course, ultimately the KGB. These newspapers were easily manipulated by an agent of influence and the story was scattered widely enough throughout the world to enable the KGB to launch a fabrication on any continent chosen for the purpose of disinformation. An estimated twenty publications were Soviet-controlled during the Cold War. Some of these 'Charley McCarthys', as they were known in the intelligence trade, were closed down for slander but some of them remained just enough inside the law to permit years of continuing manipulation in support of KGB psychological warfare.

The use of obscure newspapers in Third World countries had the bonus of disguising the original source. A bewildering network was created whereby the documents and the original draft of the story would be reprinted so many times and in so many locations that the reader would have no idea about its true origins. 'Getting it replayed is often the role of the KGB', said Herbert Romerstein, former director of the US information agency, who investigated Soviet disinformation.

When a forgery appears in a newspaper in India and a few days later appears in a newspaper in Mexico, we know that the Mexican editor is not reading the Indian press and picking up the forgery from there. He is often picking it up because it is being orchestrated by the KGB. It is often the KGB officer that takes the forgery that has appeared in one ostensibly non-Communist publication and hands it to another ostensibly non-Communist paper to replay. We find the same forgery or the same disinformation showing up in various parts of the world and sometimes the CIA is able to advise us of a specific Soviet hand and that a particular KGB officer was involved.[34]

The recycling of fake documents was global. One morning in September 1976, diplomats in the Philippine embassy in Bangkok, Thailand, woke up to read an extraordinary document on their bulletin board. On the surface, it was a US Army field manual marked 'Top Secret' with a reference number 'FM 30-31 B' and it stated that the US was creating terrorist groups in friendly countries which would then force their governments to comply with US foreign policy priorities. This 'manual' would normally be laughed off as a blatant hoax. But it soon developed a life of its own. In 1978 it reappeared in two Spanish language publications and the following year the KGB conjured up a Portuguese version of the forgery and covertly circulated it among military officers in Lisbon. Like a message in a bottle, the document resurfaced in at least twenty countries as diverse as Turkey and Malta.

Then there was a bizarre sequel. In 1981 a scandal broke in Rome concerning the political influence of a controversial Masonic lodge called P-2, which was regarded as a shadow government. The KGB took advantage of the scandal by claiming that the US Army manual had been found in the P-2 files. It was a smart move because P-2 was anti-Communist and anti-Soviet and so the hidden hand of the KGB was far less likely to be detected. The purpose, of course, was an attempt to authenticate and rehabilitate the old fake which had been exposed and link it to the notoriety of P-2, which was corrupting Italian politicians. Two years later, at least two Soviet books repeated the same false story.[35]

The factory of deception was not always crude. On many occasions the KGB did not have to create completely fictitious documents. Sometimes they altered or recreated a genuine Western document and then inserted false phrases or a name in order to exacerbate a political rivalry or sow tension and unrest abroad, especially in NATO. The forgeries were designed to supply the 'factual evidence' required to prove the disinformation that Moscow had already unleashed via other active measures operations, notably through front groups and black propaganda.

Throughout the Cold War at least one hundred forgeries of American government documents were circulated. In 1961 Richard Helms, the former CIA director and a highly experienced covert action intelligence officer, testified to the Senate Judiciary Committee his agency had identified thirty-two documents that had been fabricated by the KGB. He added that seventeen of them were designed to look as if they were written by US government officials and 'showed' US interference in the affairs of what were described as 'free world' countries. But he also pointed out the long history of the Russian art of forgery. 'More than sixty years ago the tsarist intelligence service concocted and peddled a confection called the *Protocols of the Elders of Zion*', he told the Senate.

The *Protocols*, the most notorious anti-Semitic tract of modern times, was fabricated in about 1900 and published three years later when the St Petersburg newspaper *Znamya* serialised extracts from the document. In 1921 *The Times* conclusively exposed the text as a forgery but as late as 1958 this proven fraud was still being circulated by Soviet psychological warfare agencies specialising in anti-Semitism.[36]

By the mid-1950s NATO countries, especially West Germany, were flooded with forgeries. A recurring theme was to 'reveal' the encroaching imperialist ambitions of the USA in the Third World. In February 1957, a letter from Nelson Rockefeller, then a special assistant on foreign affairs at the White House, to President Eisenhower was published in the East German Communist newspaper *Neues Deutschland*. The lengthy letter purported to be a facsimile of a letter in the 'original' English and spelt out a secret plan for American manipulation of military and economic aid in the developing world in order to secure world hegemony:

To put the policy in a nutshell, our policy must be global i.e. include political, psychological, economic, military and special methods integrated into one whole. The task is to hitch all our horses in a single team... Providing all of the recommendations are carried out, the result would be not only to strengthen the international position of the US as a whole but also considerably facilitate the fulfilment of any military tasks that may confront the US in the future.

The letter was a KGB forgery but the targeting of Rockefeller was no accident. Three years earlier he had been appointed special assistant to the president concerning the use of psychological warfare in foreign policy. His brief was to advise on the use of programmes to counter Soviet disinformation and sat on US national security council committees. The former US vice president advocated that foreign economic aid was indispensable to national security and so the KGB used this plan, even though it was opposed by the CIA, as a way to portray US foreign policy as imperialistic. The fake fax was not even signed but was widely distributed by other Communist publications around the world on the basis that at least some recipients would believe its contents.

Three weeks later, on 10 March 1957, *Neues Deutschland* published another KGB fantasy communication to the president. This time it was a memorandum by John Foster Dulles, then secretary of state, which reinforced Rockefeller's 'proposal' of interfering in and influencing other countries. Dulles, brother of the CIA director, adapted the jingoistic Rockefeller theme to the Middle East. In his 'memo' he informed the president that the true goal of US foreign policy was to scuttle national independence movements and replace European colonialism with American domination and the enforcement of its values and culture.

'The main problem', wrote Dulles, 'was the overcoming of Arab nationalism and the filling up of the vacuum. I propose to accomplish the overcoming of Arab nationalism by the formation in this region of aggressive military bases and sending in American military units designated for "special purposes".'

In effect, the US was secretly plotting to rule the world. But it appears the KGB realised that on this occasion such a primitive forgery was too crude and so the newspaper only published 'summaries' of the memo and added its own editorial content: 'It is clear that the memorandum met with the agreement of the National Security Council and served as a basis for the so-called Eisenhower Doctrine.'[37]

A sequel appeared across the Atlantic three years later when a document purporting to be a photostat of a draft Annex to a UK Cabinet paper on British and US trade union policy was suddenly being circulated. It apparently provided proof that the UK and the US privately still harboured imperialist designs on Africa at a time when the independence movements were at their peak. The 'evidence' was their opposition to the formation of the All-African Trade Union Federation and their covert support of a rival trade union organisation. The 'internal policy paper' also asserted that the UK and the US were squabbling over the spoils of Africa and were in dispute – a recurring theme in KGB disinformation.

This carefully crafted hoax first surfaced at the All-African People's Conference in Tunis in January 1960, where Russian 'observers' were seen distributing copies to delegates. News of the 'incendiary' Cabinet paper spread faster than a forest fire. The African press published detailed extracts and for the next decade it was quoted widely as an example of Western imperialist duplicity. In December 1960, the full content was printed in a booklet entitled 'The Great Conspiracy against Africa', with a foreword by a prominent Nigerian trade unionist. And in 1969 the forgery appeared in a radical American magazine called *Ramparts*, which referred to the Cabinet Paper Annex as genuine. It was such a successful fake news operation that for a long time the KGB did not feel it necessary for the Communist news media to highlight the document.

There were no boundaries to this counterfeit mentality so prevalent inside the KGB – not even the frightening apocalyptic prospect of nuclear war, which was the pervading shadow during the Cold War. Despite the high stakes, the KGB had no hesitation or qualms in raising the tension by claiming that the US military was riddled with unstable lunatics. In November 1957, the Soviet president, Khrushchev, set the agenda in an interview with US reporters:

> When planes with hydrogen bombs take off, that means that many people will be in the air piloting them. There is always the possibility of a mental blackout when the pilot may take the slightest signal as a signal for action and fly to the target. Does this not go to show that a war may start as a result of a sheer misunderstanding, a derangement in the normal psychic state of a person? Even if only one plane with one atomic or one hydrogen bomb were in the air, it would not be the government but the pilot who could decide the question of war.

Such fearmongering was intensified by the KGB. Sergei Kondrashev vividly recalled his campaign to portray the officers of the US Strategic Air Command as reckless, psychotic and insane, who were preparing to blow up the world. On 7 May 1958, five months after that interview, his colleagues fabricated a letter from Frank Berry, assistant secretary of defense (health and medical) to the defense secretary, Neil McElroy, which stated that 67.3% of all American flight crews are psycho-neurotics whose symptoms were phobias, unaccountable animosity and varying degrees of irrational behaviour. It added that after undertaking flights with atomic and H-bombs, crew members and flight personnel indulged in excessive drinking, drug consumption, sexual excess and perversions and the ultimate capitalist sin – card playing! Just for good measure, the KGB forger concluded that 'moral depression is a typical condition of all US crew members'. Kondrashev recalls that as part of his clandestine campaign, *Dr Strangelove*, the darkly satirical movie about fear of a nuclear war starring Peter Sellers and directed by Stanley Kubrick, inadvertently helped this operation.[38]

The most brazen active measure against the CIA was the publication of the book *Who's Who in the CIA*. This was devised and authorised by the KGB but implemented by the Czech and East

German security services, who were in reality surrogates for the Kremlin.

'The East German, Czech, Polish, Hungarian and Bulgarian services are directed mainly by the KGB.... Russian advisors influence the planning of each operation and assess the results', said Ladislav Bittman. 'No important decision is made without them.'[39]

Who's Who in the CIA was published in 1968 in East Germany and written by Julius Mader, author of several books on the CIA. In fact, Mader was an East German intelligence agent and *Who's Who's* sole purpose was to expose serving CIA officers.

'I am very familiar with the book because I am very sorry to admit that I am one of the co-authors', Bittman testified before the US Congress. 'About half of the names listed are real CIA operatives. The other half are just American diplomats or various officials and it was prepared with the expectation that many Americans operating abroad would be hurt because their names were exposed as CIA officers.'[40]

Despite the risk to the lives of those listed in *Who's Who in the CIA*, it was published in English and widely distributed. Any objective analysis of the book would discover that many were not CIA officials at all. But their names were now in the public domain and so their lives were in immediate danger. The inevitable happened two years later when Dan Mitrione, an official at the US Agency for International Development who had been falsely listed as a CIA operative, was kidnapped by the Cuban-sponsored Tupamaros terrorists in Uruguay. On 9 August 1970, he was brutally murdered. Three weeks later the Cuban Communist Party newspaper, *Granma*, justified the murder by reproducing the page from *Who's Who in the CIA* that identified the victim as a CIA officer and it later published the transcript of his interrogation.[41] So powerful was the impact of the book that CIA whistle-blower Philip Agee frequently referred to it as source material in his 'Covert Action' bulletin and so did a mainstream US nightly news broadcast on ABC.

By 1976 Soviet forgeries had become more sophisticated and less crude. Journalists and politicians were more adept at identifying a hoax, especially as many of the documents were not signed. And so some fake documents were deliberately not designed for public dissemination and circulated privately. Their purpose was to influence opinion-makers and power-brokers discreetly, as some may accept the document at face value whereas a journalist is more likely to check its authenticity.

However, the volume of forgeries arriving anonymously in the post remained of Stakhanovite proportions and there is not enough space in this book to include all of them (see Appendix). But the focus did change. The new forgeries were directed at NATO. A stream of bogus letters to and from the NATO secretary-general and US defence officials suggested that the US was devising secret plans to secure more support for the use of nuclear weapons in Western Europe. The KGB even had the audacity to falsify the signature of President Reagan on a letter to King Juan Carlos of Spain, in an attempt to prevent or disrupt that country's entry to NATO. In terms likely to offend Spanish sensitivities, Reagan urged the king to join NATO and crack down on groups like 'Opus Dei pacifists' and 'left-wing opposition'. The document contained the correct White House stationery and typescript and was circulated to journalists and diplomats, but swiftly dismissed as bogus. Clearly, the Soviet strategy was long-term. It was like multiple drops of water falling on a stone. After a few minutes, hours or even days, nothing happens. But after five years the stone is eroded and there is a hole. Mission accomplished.

The use of fabrication to galvanise the UK peace movement against NATO was a priority. And so the KGB devised a plan to interfere with the anti-war protests in London. In June 1980, just after the announcement of new cruise missiles, several MPs and newspaper editors received a 125-page booklet in the post. The package was posted anonymously from Paddington and Croydon, was marked 'top secret' and appeared to contain leaked documents. Among the recipients were nine Labour MPs who forwarded a copy to Francis Pym, then the defence secretary, who in turn passed the booklet to the US embassy and the CIA. The targeted MPs had in the recent past all had dealings with the World Peace Council, the KGB front group. A politically wide range of newspapers also received the apparently secret US files – from the conservative *Sunday Telegraph* to the socialist *Tribune* and the *New Statesman*.[42]

The 'leak' was entitled 'Top Secret Documents on US Forces Headquarters in Europe'. The cover showed the logo of the US department of defense in green and beneath it a headline: 'Holocaust Again for Europe'. The book's second page – usually reserved for publisher and copyright information – was completely blank. The third page contained only one line – 'Information Books No.1'. The preface was signed with a curious 'publisher's' note: 'This booklet is published as a public service and as part of the growing campaign against nuclear war and for freedom of information. We hope to extend this service in the future.'

The 'we' referred to the KGB officers in Service A, as the political scientist Thomas Rid pointed out in his book *Active Measures*. The timing of the leak had been made 'horrifically simple', according to the preface of the 'leaked' pamphlet. Presidents and prime ministers of the NATO bloc had forced disclosure by increasing expenditure on nuclear missiles and stationing 'new terror weapons' in Europe. The arguments in favour of NATO modernisation were phoney, the (KGB) authors argued in the booklet. There was no looming Warsaw Pact military superiority in Europe and in fact the US had already planned the destruction of Europe. 'There is no Soviet threat, but there is a very real American threat.' The pamphlet then outlined the old familiar argument that the American military–industrial complex, especially 'electronics interests', stood to make vast profits from researching and producing new cruise missiles.[43]

What followed was a most extraordinary self-reflection, according to Professor Rid. 'That view probably looks very much like Soviet propaganda', the KGB wrote in skilfully colloquial English, 'and pretty cheap propaganda to boot.' It was a cunning move. The anonymous authors then addressed the anticipated counter-arguments: 'Our collection of Top Secret paperwork dates from the early 1960s and last got a major airing in the West European press a decade ago... Newspaper legend has it that an American serviceman photographed the top-secret documents in a NATO vault near Paris and subsequently passed the documents to the Russians. True or false, the legend has never been seriously challenged in the west and neither has the authenticity of the documents.'[44]

Known as the 'Holocaust Papers', the so-called confidential war plans were authentic documents which were altered and falsified to create tension in NATO. They first surfaced in a Norwegian magazine in 1967 and were then revived and placed in a 1980 context. The papers alleged that the USA planned to sacrifice Western Europe by nuclear bombing strikes during a potential World War Three and could be summed up, wrote the KGB, as 'better dead than red'.

'It was a masterful display of disinformation tradecraft, at least at first glance', concluded Rid. 'To further bolster the credibility of the leaked documents and its own analysis, the preface quoted a catalogue of authoritative Western voices – the NATO secretary-general, the respected International Institute of Strategic Studies, *Le Monde* and West German newspapers.'[45]

The leaking of the 'top secret' documents was indicative of a more sophisticated and subtle KGB fake news operation. But it retained the old tactic of believing that even when the US government issued prompt denials of the authenticity of the forged document, the denial will never entirely offset the damage done by the initial release. This was the case in the mid-1980s, when the Kremlin implemented a covert operation to persuade peace organisations to focus only on the US Strategic Defense Initiative (SDI) programme while ignoring the SS-20 missiles already deployed in Eastern Europe. In 1986 a West German journalist obtained a copy of what purported to be a confidential speech back in 1983 by the US defence secretary, Caspar Weinberger, who claimed that the SDI was an offensive rather than a defensive system. He added that the SDI would be used to control NATO allies and enable the US to have a major technological advantage over its allies. Weinberger concluded by saying that the Soviet Union did not have its own SDI programme. If true, the document was a big story and so the West German journalist asked the US government to confirm that the speech was genuine. Within a few hours, the US department of defense was able to establish that the document was a complete fabrication.

By the end of the Cold War in 1989, the use of disinformation and forgery in the dark arts of black propaganda had played a major role in demonising the enemy. The KGB's covert use of fake news in the information war was an integral part of its strategy of destabilising the West and arguably hid the real military and technological substance of the conflict. 'Active measures were the heart and soul of the KGB', Oleg Kalugin once told former head of FBI counter-intelligence David Major.

But the demonisation of the CIA was always a priority and even after his death in 1969 Allen Dulles, CIA director between 1952 and 1961, was a prime target. Stories of his sinister and devilish schemes appeared regularly in Soviet newspapers and in the hugely popular 1973 spy drama *Seventeen Moments of Spring*. In the early 1990s, shortly after the fall of the Soviet Union, a lengthy document called 'The Dulles Plan', purportedly compiled and devised by Dulles in the mid-1940s, was quietly distributed. On the surface it was a self-incriminating litany of clandestine dirty tricks deployed by the USA to destroy the Soviet Union, providing copious details of a black propaganda campaign which was implemented as soon as the Second World War ended:

> We shall throw everything we have – all the gold, all the material might and resources into making the Soviet people into fools and idiots. It is possible to change the human brain, the consciousness of people. After sowing chaos in Russia, we shall imperceptibly replace their values by stealth with false ones... Thus we shall find

like-minded people, our own helpers and allies in Russia. Episode by episode, the tragedy will be played out, grandiose in scale, of the death of the most intractable people on Earth, of the definitive, irreversible dying out of its self-consciousness.

The Dulles Plan portrayed the West as decadent, corrupt and obsessively materialistic, and intent on destroying traditional Russian values. The document attributes to Dulles all the sleazy stereotypical characteristics of an American spymaster plotting their destruction:

> Literature, theatres, cinema – everything will depict and glorify the basest human emotions... We shall support and raise so-called artists who will instil and drum into Soviet consciousness the cult of sex, violence, sadism, treachery – in a word, immorality... Honesty and decency will be mocked. Insolence, lies and deception, drunkenness and drug addiction, an animal fear of one another and shamelessness... Nationalism, enmity and hatred towards the Russian people – all of this we shall cultivate deftly and imperceptibly, all this will blossom wildly. We shall debase and destroy the foundation of spiritual morality.... We shall corrupt, deprave and violate them.[46]

The Dulles Plan was a dream for anyone who suspected that the CIA was Satan and the Soviet Union's mortal enemy. The only problem was that it was a fake and riddled with inconsistencies and falsehoods. Entire sections of the text were lifted directly from a novel by the Soviet author Anatoly Ivanov and adapted from Dostoevsky's novel *Demons*, whose anti-hero character Pyotr Verkhovensky says in a passage that reads like a KGB disinformation manual: 'We will make use of drunkenness, slander, spying. We'll make use of incredible corruption... But one or two generations of vice are essential now – monstrous, abject vice by which a man is transformed into a loathsome, cruel, egoistic reptile. That's what we need.'[47]

The contemporary importance of this forgery was noticed by Martin Sixsmith:

The fake 'Dulles Plan' continues to enjoy widespread credence in Russia, with Oscar-nominated film-maker Nikita Mikhalkov declaring that Putin was the only man capable of preventing the [Dulles] Plan's implementation. It has been cited in support of post-Soviet conspiracy theories naming Mikhail Gorbachev and Eduard Shevardnadze [foreign minister in the late 1980s] as covert agents of the West, dispatched to bring the Soviet Union to its knees. Condemnations of its seizure of Crimea are explained as further evidence of an orchestrated foreign disinformation campaign designed to undermine and marginalise Russia.[48]

*

Disinformation is not new and has been implemented and exploited by authoritarian and democratic regimes for centuries. 'Fake news has been with us for thousands of years. Just think of the Bible', remarked Yuval Harari.[49] The British used deception operations extensively against the Nazis throughout the Second World War. 'All intelligence services carry out active measures', said Vladimir Yakunin. 'Of course, whenever there are conflicts each side tries to find an advantage. The Germans do this. The French do this. The Russians do this.'[50]

The CIA was certainly active in fake news, influencing elections, orchestrating coups and covertly funding and running front groups and publications during the Cold War. In East Germany the agency indulged in 'the art of forging' via its front groups in Berlin. But the CIA, according to Professor Rid, 'retreated from the disinformation battlefield almost completely' later in the Cold War.[51] When it did later wage information war, it was of a different character, notably distributing translated copies of *1984* into Ukraine.

And so when it comes to deception and the faking of documents the KGB was in a class by itself, with unmatched scale and sophistication. 'If the Soviets were as enterprising in the areas of industry and agriculture as they are in disinformation, then they would have overtaken us by all parameters', said Admiral Stansfield Turner, the CIA director during President Carter's administration.[52] Unlike the USA with its myriad of congressional investigations, oversight and legal accountability, Russian spies were given a licence to disrupt, discredit and destroy with impunity. And it was all done without the firing of a gun.

4

SEDUCTION AND SURVEILLANCE

There are many brave men we ask to lay down their lives for their
country. But for brave women we simply ask them to lie down.

Former KGB general Oleg Kalugin (1959–90)

I hope you are not a spy.

President John F. Kennedy to Enud Sztanko, Hungarian foreign
language instructor, October 1962.

AT THE HEIGHT OF THE COLD War the British embassy on the
embankment of Saint Sophia in Moscow was the ornate,
imposing embodiment of political and diplomatic prestige and
status. Built in the 1890s by a Russian sugar merchant and made
available in 1929 on a twenty-year lease, the entrance featured a
heavily panelled Scottish baronial hallway and red carpeted orna-
mental staircase. The ground floor was converted into offices. But
the first floor was dominated by a vast white and gold ballroom
with a fine parquet floor, used for flamboyant parties and exotic
balls reminiscent of a scene from *Anna Karenina*.

Across the river and facing the mansion was the harsh
red-brick Kremlin wall, punctuated by watchtowers, which ran

for half a mile along the opposite bank. Behind this wall a steeply wooded slope was crowned by the palaces and cathedrals which, for so many troubled centuries, had symbolised the power and legacy – barbaric and heroic – of Russia. Here were the five golden domes and cathedrals of the fifteenth century and towering over them the 250-foot-high bell tower of Ivan the Great. Here too were the edifices of the raw brutal power of the tsars and the Soviets: the Armoury and the great Kremlin Palace. 'It is as if St. Paul's, the Tower of London, the Palace of Westminster, Buckingham Palace and half a dozen Wren masterpieces had been assembled in one majestic group, looking down on the Thames', recalled Sir Curtis Keeble, former British ambassador to Moscow.[1]

No embassy had such a clear vision – not just visually – of the very heart of the Soviet empire. From some vantage points in the Kremlin, an irritated Joseph Stalin looked sternly across at the green-roofed, lovingly restored British embassy with the Union Jack fluttering above it. The capitalist enemy was in his sights. One of the final acts of his rule on Christmas Eve in 1952 was to order Britain to find another residence. Three months later Stalin died of a stroke and the British refused the offer of newer and larger sites, even though the lease had expired in 1949.

For the KGB, the embassy was a prime target for undermining, destabilising and disrupting British interests. There were no limits – bugging, arson, burglary, honey trapping, spiking of drinks, blackmail, planting of drugs, relentless surveillance by car and on foot, telephone harassment and entrapment. The aim was to obtain 'Kompromat' – compromising information, recordings and photographs that could be used as leverage to persuade an intelligence officer or diplomat to spy for the KGB or reveal secrets. The incriminating material would be deployed at once or filed away for when the target became more powerful and influential. Kompromat was a tool for political influence-peddling, to improve the outcome of negotiations and sway public opinion. The Soviet Union had become the blackmail state.

On arriving at the British embassy in Moscow all staff were given a security briefing by the resident MI6 officer. It was introduced with a reading from a visitor's account of his Russian experience. He had been subject to eavesdropping and provocative visits to his hotel room and his luggage had been thoroughly searched. This was standard practice by the KGB. But the diplomats were then surprised to hear that this account had been written in the nineteenth century and described the activities of the tsar's secret police against dissidents.

The past was not another country. The only difference was the technology. Accordingly, the staff were told to be careful about what they said during conversations as every apartment was bugged. Dennis Amy, who was in charge of internal security at the British embassy in Moscow between 1961 and 1964, removed two hundred concealed microphones and eight were from his flat alone.[2] This unnerved some diplomats, who were frightened to say anything, while others enjoyed making outrageous remarks to light fittings which were assumed to conceal bugging devices. In fact, the KGB did not expect sensitive state secrets to be divulged through a microphone in the wall and suspected such 'provocations'. Their real motive for the eavesdropping was for intelligence about the individuals' lives. They were listening for any personal weaknesses, vices, marital unhappiness, homosexual inclinations, financial problems, vulnerabilities and misgivings about their government.[3]

When the Cold War began in the late 1940s, the security of the embassy was difficult to maintain. It was flanked on three sides by buildings controlled by the Soviet authorities and the Soviet staff, notably the drivers, were all KGB informants. The surveillance was intense. At that time a typical listening device consisted of a microphone attached to wires which passed through the building to a hidden radio receiver or a listening post outside the embassy grounds. Microphones wired to a location under the embassy were also inserted into the walls of the rooms where diplomats worked and a thick cable had been inserted into a closed tunnel under the building. But the embassy usually had some form of security and so it was difficult for the KGB to secretly install such a device while the building was in use.

The best opportunity came when an embassy moved to a new premises because the KGB would wire up the building before the diplomats arrived. This is primarily why the British declined to move in 1953. But there were other options: if an office or apartment block adjoined the embassy, the KGB eavesdroppers gained access to it and inserted microphones into the wall or ceiling or floor. Another method was to turn the telephones in the embassy into bugs. The receiver would be modified so that it transmitted sound down the telephone even when it was on the hook, effectively making it a bug. This process was known in the CIA as 'hot miking' (the CIA and MI6, of, course, indulged in the same tactics).[4]

In the 1950s and 1960s rapid advances in electronics transformed eavesdropping devices and made them much easier to plant and conceal, according to David Easter, a lecturer at the Department of War Studies at King's College London, who made a detailed study of Soviet surveillance of diplomatic premises during the Cold War:

> The development of the transistor enabled intelligence agencies to miniaturise radio transmitters and reduce their power consumption. As batteries also shrank in size, it became possible to build smaller, battery powered bugs that contained their own transmitters. These new bugs did not need wires to transmit the signal or carry power and could be quickly installed, either through breaking into buildings or by KGB agents within the Embassy staff.[5]

At the British embassy in Moscow, it was relatively simple for the KGB to plant these new small listening devices because Western missions employed Soviet citizens as ancillary staff. The Soviet foreign ministry provided the embassy with interpreters, clerks, telephonists, cooks and drivers. Most were informants and some were actual undercover KGB officers. While they were denied access to the more sensitive areas of the premises like the ambassador's study and the cipher room where messages were encrypted and sent as telegrams, these spies had ample opportunities to place and maintain bugs.

Even though the British diplomats knew the staff were KGB assets, they maintained a friendly relationship.

'They [the staff] were all paid to report to the KGB on our activities but this did not prevent them from being real people with that larger-than-life quality of all Russians – loving twice as warmly, hating twice as bitterly, drinking twice as deeply, weeping with twice the grief and laughing with twice the joy of the English', recalled former British ambassador Sir Curtis Keeble. 'I remember coming back to the Embassy once after a leave. As we walked up the staircase, the staff gathered at the top, welcoming us with hugs and kisses. "Good God", someone remarked, "It's the *Cherry Orchard* played in reverse".'[6]

Once the eavesdropping system was in place and operating, valuable political intelligence could be obtained from unguarded comments by indiscreet diplomats as they spoke on the phone and dictated telegrams and dispatches back to London. But officials were judicious in their remarks and safe rooms were set up so that meetings and cables could be dictated to a secretary without risk of eavesdropping.

'These rooms consisted typically of a transparent soundproof box large enough to accommodate a meeting of eight people', added Sir Christopher Mallaby, a senior diplomat based in Moscow during the mid-1960s and mid-1970s. 'Between this box and the actual walls, floor and ceiling of the room was a space filled with noise. This "cocktail party noise" came from tapes of conversations among many raucous people, recorded and then re-recorded several times on the same tape to produce appalling cacophony. This ensured that any microphones in the outer walls of the room would record nothing but ear-splitting babble.'[7]

Despite these precautions, the bugging of the embassy was endemic. In the mid-1950s a microphone was found in the study of the British ambassador, Sir William Hayter. Wiring was also discovered and it was suspected that the Soviet ancillary staff had removed other listening devices before they could be detected. Microphones were being found all over the building, even in the cipher room. There was also what Sir Patrick Reilly, the ambassador in 1957 and a former MI6 adviser, described as 'a most fantastic system of wires', some of which went down a shaft and out underground through the embassy garden to the building next door.[8]

The penetration of the embassy was so deep that the cipher room could no longer be used and MI5 investigated the impact of the KGB surveillance. In 1960 an official told Prime Minister Harold Macmillan that classified and top secret information had been intermittently compromised between late 1943 and early 1954, and to a lesser extent until 1958. Later that year Macmillan remarked philosophically to President Khrushchev that 'In every Embassy in the world there were listening devices in the walls, on the ink stands, on the telephones.'[9] Even though the installation of secure rooms reduced the damage inside the British embassy in Moscow, the clandestine eavesdropping remained a key factor in breaking the diplomatic ciphers for the rest of the Cold War.

Despite the technological advances in surveillance, the KGB were keen exponents of psychological warfare. 'They used to ring you up again and again and again and there would be nobody there when you answered the phone, and so you would leave the phone off the hook to jam their line but then they would put a blaster on it', recalled Dennis Amy. 'This was hard on the young girls who lived in single flats in Moscow. They would call each other and say "it's time to wake up" and the Russians would tape record that person saying it and then play it back to themselves on the telephone... The Russians were stupidly spiteful. If ever I went out to work and Helen [his wife] was in bed and the curtains were drawn, they would always ring up. Living there was like a Le Carré novel. We were always being followed.'[10]

In Moscow extreme measures were tolerated in the search for compromising intelligence. In October 1964, the KGB actually set fire to the British embassy in an attempt to penetrate the inner sanctum, seize documents and discover the secrets of MI6 surveillance equipment. One evening, while the ambassador, Humphrey Trevelyan, attended a performance of the English Opera Group, the upper storey of the east wing of the embassy – directly facing the Kremlin – was set alight. By the time diplomats arrived at the blazing inferno, the place was surrounded by a posse of surprisingly prompt Soviet firemen, who were battling with embassy staff to secure access to the building. 'It was pretty obvious that some of these people were not firemen at all', said Sir Rodric Braithwaite, first secretary at the embassy, who was present. 'They wanted to get into that section of the embassy to see what was going on, so they set it on fire.'[11]

The diplomats suspected that some of the firemen were KGB officers but they allowed them access to the building on the basis the area on fire did not contain sensitive documents. 'The papers were safe', recalled Sir Bryan Cartledge, a senior diplomat who witnessed the blaze. 'They [the KGB] were much more interested in the communications equipment – that sort of thing.'[12] The decision to allow the 'firemen' inside the embassy was made by Thomas Brimelow, the renowned Kremlinologist and the most senior diplomat on duty. His view was that there was no point in getting into an intelligence firefight because the Soviets played by different rules. And so his motto when dealing with the KGB was 'never get into a pissing match with a skunk'. That was a risky decision and could have backfired but the KGB did not discover anything during the fire.

*

If the Cold War was a 'Great Game', then the KGB took it very seriously, especially the priceless intelligence obtained by eavesdropping on the main enemy – the Americans. Even when the

Soviet Union was an ally of the USA during the Second World War, it bugged their diplomatic mission in Moscow. In 1944 a navy electrician discovered no fewer than 120 microphones in the US embassy. In conditions of intense secrecy, the Soviets were devising ingenious new devices. To bug the private residence of the American ambassador, Averell Harriman, at Spaso House in Moscow, a passive cavity resonator was concealed within a carved relief of the Great Seal of the United States. On 4 July 1945, Independence Day, Soviet Young Pioneers presented the Great Seal plaque to Ambassador Harriman, who proudly hung it in his study in his house. He was blissfully unaware that by directing microwaves at the wall plaque Soviet spies activated the cavity resonator and listened to his conversations in the room. The bug was not discovered until September 1952.[13]

When the Americans moved out of their wartime embassy on Mokhovaya Ulitsa to a new building on Chaikovskovo Ulitsa in 1953, it created new opportunities for the Soviet eavesdroppers. Before the diplomats moved in, the Soviet workers altered and renovated the building. And so the American security officers were on site to ensure that the construction workers did not illicitly install any microphones on the top floors of the new embassy, which housed the the most sensitive offices. But control of the site was remarkably lax. According to the historian David Easter:

> The Soviets were allowed to cover the building with canvas to block the view of the construction and there were no American guards on watch during the night. After the new embassy opened, two State Department security technicians swept it and did not detect concealed microphones, but they warned that bugging remained 'a serious possibility' because 'exceedingly clever and effective installations of such equipment could have been made during the construction of the building'.[14]

The technicians' fears were justified. But it took another decade before the bugs were discovered, when two KGB defectors disclosed the hidden electronic surveillance. The embassy discovered over forty devices hidden in bamboo tubes built into the walls behind the radiators, in order to shield them from metal detectors. A US state department damage assessment concluded that the bugging system had enabled the Soviets to read many, probably all, of the Moscow embassy's communications and also diplomatic telegrams between Washington DC and its embassies in Eastern Europe. Many of these telegrams had been passed to President Khrushchev. This was illustrated in July 1963 when Khrushchev inadvertently and with characteristic indiscretion and bluster made it clear to the US ambassador, Foy Kohler, that the KGB had tapped his coded cables.

'He [Khrushchev] wanted to confront the US Ambassador with the fact we knew that they had personally opposed the delivery of steel tubing from West Germany [to the Soviet Union] for natural gas pipelines', said former ambassador Anatoly Dobrynin. 'Thus alerted, American intelligence presumably acted and our information from the US Embassy in Moscow was much reduced.'[15]

By the late 1970s, some diplomats believed that the intensity of the surveillance operation was having an impact on their health.

'The KGB use of microwave equipment caused anxiety in the American Embassy and to a lesser extent in my own about the damaging health implications', recalled Sir Curtis Keeble, British ambassador between 1978 and 1982.

Tests were done and it seemed that there was no radiation danger. But this is an area where it is very hard to be certain either about the nature of the attack or the long-term physiological consequences and the constant uncertainty added to the other strains of life in Moscow. After a couple of years I developed an irritating facial tic and consulted a doctor in London. He said that there was no sign of disease and I must be suffering from stress. I replied, genuinely, that I did not feel under any strain but he must have been right because it disappeared when we left Moscow.[16]

Despite such assurances, even senior Soviet diplomats believed that radiation arising from electronic surveillance may have caused serious disease. In November 1975, Anatoly Dobrynin was told by Henry Kissinger, then US secretary of state, that the US ambassador in Moscow, Walter Stoessel, was suspected of having developed leukaemia, possibly as a result of extended electromagnetic exposure in the embassy in Moscow. American security specialists believed that it could have been caused by jamming and decoding the embassy's messages. Kissinger added that if the ambassador's illness became public, it would cause a major scandal. He asked the Soviet government to stop the electronic interception which caused the radiation.

Dobrynin was instructed by Moscow to deny that the US embassy was being deliberately subjected to radiation. But the mystery was never fully resolved. 'Many years later I learned the real reason for the radiation', the former Soviet ambassador said. 'The KGB was trying to jam electronic espionage by the American secret service which used the US Embassy as a base to intercept important official telephone and radio conversations which were mostly unscrambled. Both secret services therefore tried to cancel out each other's efforts.'[17]

The CIA was not satisfied and so President Ford demanded that the Soviets stop such electronic surveillance. President Brezhnev replied that the electromagnetic field around the US embassy was of industrial origin and carried no health risk. But the US was not convinced and so a specialist team from Johns Hopkins University studied the medical histories of nearly five thousand US officials who had been stationed in Moscow between 1954 and 1976. They found no influence of the electromagnetic field on their health. The Soviets were also suspicious. Their embassy in Washington DC was bugged by US intelligence agents in the mid-1970s and they believed this had caused serious illness.

'I myself repeatedly suffered from throat and respiratory ailments', recalled Dobrynin. 'Our doctors suspected them to be the result of many years of work in an enclosed electronic space

– my embassy office more than any other had insufficient ventilation because it was enclosed in double walls with a magnetic
field permanently between them. Of course, all these medical
assurances were fine, but who can really say with certainty that in
the long run the health of diplomats in embassies of both countries
[the US and the Soviet Union] was not compromised for the sake
of the Cold War?'[18]

Like the British, the Americans resorted to holding conversations in the bathroom with the water running or had music playing
from a radio or record player to prevent eavesdropping, especially
when they were dictating sensitive telegrams. Many offices were
fitted with loudspeakers which were connected to a record player
constantly playing records. This enabled diplomats to have music
readily available whenever they needed to conduct classified
discussions at short notice. The paranoia was not without its comic
moments. In late 1976, Henry Kissinger was in Moscow for a final
meeting with his Soviet counterpart, Andrei Gromyko. They met
in a private mansion with a ceiling dominated by paintings of
nymphs and semi-naked ladies.

'I suppose we can talk safely here', said Kissinger, as a joke. The
long-serving Soviet foreign minister looked up at the ceiling
intently and replied: 'No, I think it is in her left nipple.'[19]

The fear of eavesdropping was so widespread and pervasive that
two American ambassadors to Moscow – Charles Bohlen and
Llewellyn Thompson – wrote their most secret messages back to
Washington in longhand rather than dictate them. Letters classified
as 'top secret' were not dictated. Thompson even exchanged notes
with an aide rather than have a conversation if the topic was
sensitive.[20]

A more twentieth-century alternative to this archaic option was
to install secure rooms in the US embassy. Known as 'bubbles',
these special rooms consisted of large, soundproof, transparent
plastic and aluminium boxes set up on stilts or suspended from
the ceiling of empty offices. The technicians believed that secure
rooms were bug proof. In the 1980s one American security officer

said the 'bubbles' were '100 percent secure... There are certain physical laws that even the Soviets cannot violate.'[21] But the most secure method of preventing sensitive secrets being discovered was refreshingly old-fashioned: do not speak a classified word outside the 'bubble' which you do not want the KGB to hear.

Honey Trap

The KGB was not naive enough to think that Western diplomats would reveal sensitive state secrets over the telephone. The purpose was to exploit weakness and vulnerability – financial, marital, ideological and, above all, sexual. As one former American diplomat based in Moscow observed: 'Very few people would talk to their wives about sensitive political or military information. The value of the listening devices is to get somebody.'[22]

But sex and seduction were not the only tradecraft to obtain *Kompromat*. During the Cold War the conditions for entrapment were ideal in Moscow. A Western ambassador is recruited because he has a collector's passion for Russian ikons. A Soviet 'friend' volunteers to find some for him and he is hooked after taking the bait, because exporting ikons is illegal. A diplomatic clerk is inveigled into exchanging hard currency for roubles on the black market. And an American woman succumbs to the KGB because she is threatened with official refusal to issue her with an exit visa.[23]

The art of blackmail took many insidious forms. One was the doctoring of drinks.

'The Soviet authorities tried to compromise a Western diplomat quite often', Sir Christopher Mallaby, who served in Moscow in the mid-1960s and mid-1970s, explained. 'When travelling in the provinces two members of the embassy might be given a drink which was fixed. They might pass out and things might happen while they were unconscious which the KGB might exploit for the purposes of blackmail.'[24]

This was corroborated by the former British ambassador, Sir Curtis Keeble: 'I know of at least two cases in which there was good reason to suppose that drinks had been doctored with an emetic [mixed solution that causes vomiting] in order to provide evidence of "hooliganism" with a photographer who was conveniently present... The knowledge that compromise was a standard technique induced a suspicion of normal friendly approaches and itself played a part in KGB policy.'[25]

But sex was the most powerful motive for transforming an apparently patriotic, conscientious public servant into a duplicitous traitor. Listening in on their private conversations, the KGB selected candidates for the honey trap: the lovesick, lonely secretary who has access to documents, the frustrated homosexual, the diplomat trapped in a miserable marriage and the intelligence officer angry at being underpaid. All were vulnerable and easy prey to young, beautiful women known as 'Swallows' and charismatic, confident muscular men known as 'Ravens'.

The KGB regarded sexual entrapment as the most effective tactic to recruit new agents, exploit foreigners and obtain secrets. Actresses from the theatre and the cinema, singers, dancers and teachers were sent off to a 'Sexpionage' training school in Kazan, south-east of Moscow on the banks of the Volga, according to former CIA agent Jason Matthews, author of *Red Sparrow*, a thinly-disguised fictional account of a ballerina trained by Russian spies to seduce.

In East Germany the HVA, in reality a subsidiary of the KGB, trained the Romeo spies like professional pilots. To learn their trade, they were sent to Belzig, a secret training camp outside Berlin. The syllabus was focused on Marxism, political reliability, loyalty, espionage and, most important, psychological manipulation.

'Our screening process was extremely rigorous', recalled Markus Wolf, the legendary charismatic former head of the Stasi during the Cold War. 'For every hundred candidates our staff found through the Communist Party, the universities or the youth organisations, only ten would be interviewed, after we had studied their backgrounds and records. Of that number, only one might end up working for us.'[26]

The Romeos were told to seduce the secretaries at NATO working for presidents of Western countries, and in defence and foreign ministries. It was the early 1950s and the postwar shortage of men was keenly felt among single, lonely, middle-aged secretaries yearning for a partner. They often worked long hours for demanding bosses and it was almost impossible to meet eligible attractive men. Many were desperate. They were easy prey and the HVA and KGB agents ruthlessly exploited their vulnerability. One secretary who worked for West German president Konrad Adenauer passed on secrets for fourteen years to her Romeo spy. And a secretary at the US embassy in Bonn handed over 1,500 classified documents over twenty-two years to her lover. Both women had absolutely no idea that their boyfriends were East German intelligence officers until they were arrested, convicted and jailed for espionage. Despite being later exposed, the Romeo spies claimed they were 'just doing their job' and were not charged.

The typical Romeo spy was about thirty years old. They were well-educated, confident, reliable, serious but with a sense of humour, impeccable manners and attentive. But they were not necessarily handsome or even experienced Don Juans, much less Adonises. 'More important to these women was the inner values of these men who made them think, yes I could share my life with him', said former Stasi officer and Romeo spy Gerhard Bayer. 'He was the kind of man who when he walks into a room, you think he's important. He is tall. He appears to be something special and important… Good espionage work always rests on a firm grasp of psychology. I studied psychology and human behaviour very closely, including Freudian theories.'[27]

For the secretary to fall in love with them, the Romeo spies needed to be potential marriage material.

In the Soviet Union the manipulation was not always so sophisticated. Some honey trap approaches were crude and abrupt: an apparently low-grade prostitute solicits a well-dressed foreigner on Gorky Street in Moscow or an inebriated diplomat is approached late at night in a bar or a disco. Occasionally young, impoverished girls were used, despite having little knowledge of politics or surveillance. But that did not matter. They served as the bait. 'They did not know the difference between transistors and resistors', one former CIA officer told me.

But as a rule the KGB preferred to work with professional educated men and women because they were more articulate and so more credible to foreigners. An ideal operative was a young woman with a good degree working in a junior job, which would provide access to the diplomats. In return the women would be rewarded with cash payments, clothes, promotion in their career, a more spacious and pleasant apartment and a measure of liberty and fun not usually available in the Soviet Union.

In one crude ploy, the KGB placed an advertisement in the *Moscow Times* which stated 'Wealthy American businessman looking for a wife and relationship' and then listed the name and telephone number of a CIA officer based in Moscow. Later that night the intelligence officer received sixteen calls from women who wanted to meet him. 'Are you really rich?' asked one. It was hoped that the CIA officer would succumb and meet one of the women but he declined their kind offers.

Then there were the fake brothels. Before one summit of foreign ministers of the allied powers in Berlin, a specialist KGB consultant told his East German colleagues: 'Of course, you'll be needing a "malina" for the duration.' The HVA spies were mystified. 'Malina' is the Russian word for raspberry but it emerged that the word was code for a bordello, to which KGB and Stasi agents would lure Western officials for some late-night recreation, away from the conference. At breakneck speed, a little house in Berlin was converted into a combined brothel and entrapment centre, with bugging devices and a camera with an infra-red flash hidden in the bedroom light fitting. In those days such devices were very primitive, so the photographer had to squeeze into the bedroom's tiny linen cupboard and stay there until the KGB 'swallow' had entertained her Western prey.[28]

However, it was the lobbies, bars and restaurants of hotels that were the epicentre of operation seduction. Most of the bellboys, drivers, cooks and maids at the Intourist hotel and travel company were on the KGB payroll and they coordinated with the female agents deployed to entrap a foreign politician or diplomat. It was a tightly controlled operation and the KGB-sponsored escorts often chased away freelance sex workers who had not been officially approved.

A hotel room or private apartment was rented and carefully furnished and constructed in preparation for the trap to be set. Known as a 'swallow's nest', it consisted of two adjoining single flats. In one, the girl entertained the foreigner while in the other KGB technicians recorded on film and tape their sexual frolics via holes in the wall, using microphones and special cameras. Within minutes of the Westerner succumbing to the charms of the KGB operative, agents would burst in and attempt to blackmail the victim by threatening to send the photographs to his wife back home. An irate 'husband' would then suddenly arrive, berate the man and demand retribution. According to Oleg Kalugin:

> Occasionally the KGB agent/husband would smack around the foreigner just to scare him. On other times he would merely scream and threaten the unfortunate visitor with death or castration.
>
> But in all cases the KGB agent/husband would phone the police who would arrive in a matter of minutes and go through an elaborate, staged ritual. The policemen, who were actually KGB officers, would say things like 'We're sorry to have to do this but you are a foreigner and we'll have to open an investigation.' By the end of this charade the businessman would usually be a blistering wreck. Then, a few hours later, another of our officers, posing as the good guy, would talk to the man and suggest that the matter could be hushed up if he would do a few things for us when he returned home. The victims often agreed to work for us.[29]

Restaurants in Moscow were also a location for sexual blackmail. In the summer of 1966, a young American engineer engaged in top-secret research in the Soviet Union for a US Air Force contractor was having dinner. Suddenly a waiter ushered him to a table occupied by a pretty blonde with a friendly smile. The next evening they dined together at a cafe in a park. Afterwards she led him down a narrow path to a bench near an amphitheatre. She accepted his embraces and warmly returned them until suddenly she started screaming in Russian.

Flashbulbs popped like a series of fireworks and at least ten men sprang from the surrounding bushes. The bewildered American was arrested for attempted rape. 'If you confess your obvious guilt, your sentence will be from three to eight years', said a KGB officer. 'However, if you insist on denying the obvious, you will be imprisoned from six to sixteen years.'

'Let me talk to someone from the US embassy', replied the terrified engineer.

'You will be allowed to contact the embassy after you are tried and sentenced', said the KGB officer. 'Of course, if you are willing to co-operate with the Soviet government...'

The American felt that he had no choice but to cooperate. He was being held in secret and facing an indeterminate term of imprisonment in an alien land. For the next three days the young engineer was interrogated by the KGB and then flown to Moscow, where he was locked in a hotel suite for another six days while specialists extracted technical details of his secret work. They also extorted from him a promise to become a spy. But when he returned to the USA, his conscience compelled him to confess to his employer, the US Air Force contractor. He lost his security clearance and his job. The blackmail state had succeeded.[30]

KGB officers often played a long game and waited weeks or months before presenting the photographs or recordings. In some incidents, the KGB stored away the evidence for use at a much later date, perhaps when the victim's circumstances had changed, notably after he was married or applied for a visa. If the visa was issued, the KGB had leverage and decided whether to neutralise, influence, recruit or merely watch him or her. There were many cases where people were compromised and left to think that their troubles were over, only to find themselves many years later subject to a threatening approach. In some cases the film footage was filed away to be used at the most politically opportune moment. When the unhappy wife of the former Canadian prime minister, Pierre Trudeau, indulged in an affair in the early 1980s, the KGB placed her under surveillance and filmed her sex sessions. The tapes were retained for future use, just in case Trudeau became too critical of the Soviet Union.

If blackmail negotiations were prolonged, there were more elaborate schemes to coerce the unwary and gullible, according to the respected intelligence historian Nigel West:

> The techniques became so sophisticated that sometimes the victims were the last to realise the true nature of their predicament. They believed the 'kindly Uncle' role adopted by some of the more skilled practitioners, who pretended to be an intermediary, using their supposed influence or negotiating talents to keep the vengeful authorities from exacting the necessary consequences of some supposed infraction of the criminal code. In such circumstances, the wretched victims often went to considerable lengths to protect the very architects of their misfortune.[31]

*

At the height of the Cold War the hazards of diplomats working in Moscow became so serious that in 1969 the British government published an explicit warning to avoid such KGB provocations and entrapments. MI5 even circulated a private – but not secret – booklet called 'Their Trade is Treachery', which outlined the perils of casual late-night encounters with attractive women in hotel bars. The FBI was more blunt: 'The

Soviets never hesitate to employ blackmail, especially against Americans visiting Russia. Sex offers a particularly fertile field – especially perverted sexuality. Suddenly the American is confronted with unpleasant and embarrassing photographs, either legitimate or forged.'[32]

Despite all the warnings, many a middle-aged, overweight and balding politician or diplomat lacked the self-awareness that the attractive younger woman was not interested in his wit, charm and intelligence as they sipped cocktails. The capacity for male self-delusion was ruthlessly exploited by the KGB. One FBI official used to advise US congressmen that they should take a cold, hard, objective look at themselves in the mirror after shaving, before they went to Moscow, and rate their own looks. 'If you are a solid 7 out of 10 that's fine, but if when you travel everyone who comes up to you is a 10 out of 10, you should be concerned', he said.[33]

US and UK agents, of course, also used sex as a weapon in the intelligence war. Sexual entrapment was a constant theme in the James Bond thrillers by Ian Fleming, a former wartime naval intelligence officer. In his first novel, *Casino Royale*, 007 is betrayed by a subordinate who has been blackmailed by the KGB. And in his short story, 'The Portrait of a Lady', an MI6 clerk is compromised in 'some unattractive sexual business' and forced into becoming a Soviet spy. In *From Russia with Love*, Bond and a Soviet defector have an affair and are secretly filmed in his hotel bedroom by a hidden camera – a classic technique.[34] The CIA was not shy in hiring honey trappers to obtain inside information.

'The use of sex is a common practice among intelligence services all over the world', said former assistant FBI director William Sullivan in testimony in 1975. 'This is a tough dirty business. We have used that technique against the Soviets. They have used it against us.'[35]

Inside MI6 there was a debate about whether British agents should use such tactics to persuade Russians to defect or spy. 'I don't believe in blackmail for both moral and practical reasons', said Gerry Warner, deputy chief of MI6 between 1988 and 1991.

An agent who is working because he is being blackmailed and is being coerced into it, then he or she is never going to be reliable. He has every good reason to betray you if he thinks he can get away with it... An agent who is being blackmailed has no reason to tell you the truth and may make things up. He has no loyalty to either himself or to you and so it is not a practical business and quite clearly it is not a moral business. If we had descended to the kinds of practices that the KGB routinely practised, there was no point in doing the job.[36]

MI5 – responsible for monitoring Soviet spies in London – was not so shy. Their officers often tried to ensnare KGB officers by introducing them at a party to high-class call-girls who were on their payroll and then later photographing them in the throes of passion. The prostitutes in Shepherd's Market, Mayfair, just around the corner from MI5's head office on Curzon Street, were also briefed and paid to look out for Russian clients.

But there is little doubt that the KGB was far more ruthless and willing to use sexual espionage and exhibited far fewer scruples in exploiting human vulnerabilities, according to Oleg Kalugin. 'There are many brave men we ask to lay down their lives for their country. But for brave women we simply ask them to lie down', he said.[37]

Even male opera singers were auditioned and recruited to perform for the secret state. The KGB's most effective raven was a strikingly handsome singer called Konstantin Lapshin, who performed at the Moscow Operetta. In the late 1940s and 1950s his secret life involved seducing female officials and diplomats at the American embassy. His *coup de grâce* was Annabelle Bucar, who worked for the US ambassador, General Walter Bedell-Smith. She was so smitten that she accepted the singer's proposal for a secret marriage and then defected. In 1952 Bucar was persuaded by the KGB to write a book, *The Truth about American Diplomats*, which was highly critical of American foreign policy and revealed secrets about the US embassy. According to Bedell-Smith, who recounted the episode in his memoirs *My Three Years in Moscow*, the charismatic Lapshin 'courted almost every unattached young foreign woman in Moscow'.[38]

The sexual dark arts were also used to steal documents as well as for blackmail. In his authoritative book *KGB*, John Barron, who was given detailed information and introductions by MI6 and the CIA, recounts how the Swedish embassy in Moscow was burgled using a 'swallow':

> It commenced with the seduction of an embassy watchman by a female agent who engaged him in regular evening trysts when he was supposed to be on duty. To neutralise a huge and ferocious watchdog, the KGB sent an officer to the embassy grounds two nights a week to feed him choice cuts of meat. The KGB scheduled the raid on a night when most of the embassy staff had been invited to a party.
>
> Surveillance teams and telephone monitors tracked the movements of all Swedes in Moscow starting that afternoon. Squads parked at street intersections surrounded the embassy under orders to ram any Swedish car that approached. While the female agent diverted the watchman and an officer plied the dog with meat, a dozen KGB men unlocked the embassy door and headed for the safes. The locksmiths, photographers and specialists in opening sealed documents emerged in an hour, their work done and undetected. The dog caused the only slight difficulty. The officer feeding him kept calling for more meat, complaining "This dog is eating by the kilo".[39]

By the mid-1950s the KGB swallows swarmed down on the British embassy, hovering and looking for prey. One target was Sir Anthony Meyer, a 38-year-old commercial counsellor and later a prominent Conservative MP. Suave, sophisticated and ambitious,

Meyer was frustrated in Moscow because he could not speak the language and was confined to the diplomatic ghetto. One evening the KGB tried to take advantage of his predicament when an attractive female agent lured him into a taxi by saying she had 'an urgent message' for him. He was immediately suspicious, especially when a 'police officer' suddenly arrived and asked to see his papers. The diplomat reported the approach to the ambassador, who put Meyer and his family on the next plane home, where he returned to the Foreign Office.

But occasionally diplomats succumbed to the temptation. Even the ambassador was vulnerable. When the 57-year-old Sir Geoffrey Harrison arrived at the British embassy, he was already the archetypal Establishment man. Educated at Winchester College and King's College, Cambridge University, he joined the Foreign Office in 1932 and became ambassador in Brazil and Iran before arriving in Moscow in 1965. Tall, patrician and impatient, Sir Geoffrey enjoyed being driven around Moscow in a Rolls-Royce – standard for a diplomat of his status but a dubious asset during the winter. (Ironically, the Soviet president at that time, Leonid Brezhnev, also owned a Rolls, although it was not seen on the Moscow streets.) One day he was incensed when his Rolls' brakes failed and he was informed that he would have to use an ordinary Humber for his meetings in the city. 'Oh, can't you get the Rolls to the front door', he wailed at his private secretary.[40]

Consequently Sir Geoffrey was not the most popular ambassador and did not endear himself to the press when he told his staff that he regarded the Moscow correspondents as 'security risks'. The irony was that the KGB regarded him as someone who could be compromised or even recruited. In early August 1968, at the height of the crisis in Czechoslovakia, the KGB dispatched a stunningly attractive young woman called Galya Ivanova to work for the ambassador as his chambermaid. Blonde and buxom, Galya was already a favourite among the diplomats. Four years earlier George Brown, the foreign secretary, stayed at the embassy and was captivated by her. After a hard day of negotiating and several gin and tonics, he was incorrigible. As soon as Galya entered the Blue Room with coffee and brandy and wearing a tight little black dress, the drunken and arrogant foreign secretary leaped to his feet, kissed her and gave her a hug. 'That's a lot better. I've always wanted to do that to a Russian lass', he declared to the startled guests.[41]

Fellow diplomats then noticed that Galya conspicuously flaunted her charms at the ambassador's dinner table, leaning over the guests in her low-cut uniform. Red light warnings flashed around her. But Sir Geoffrey was oblivious to the danger. During a visit to Leningrad, Galya 'unexpectedly' met him and suggested a romantic tryst at her brother's apartment, which just happened to be nearby, and the diplomat succumbed. For the next few weeks they had brief evening encounters in his first floor flat at the embassy. Galya lived outside the embassy compound and so the ambassador believed the affair would remain secret. 'It was quite separate and I had no reason to suppose that anyone knew about it', he said later.[42]

The KGB, of course, knew everything and the obligatory photographs of their lovemaking were taken. He was threatened with exposure unless he leaked secrets and became sympathetic to the Soviet position on repressing the dissidents in Czechoslovakia, who were campaigning for democratic reforms. The game was up and Sir Geoffrey reported the affair to the Foreign Office. He was summoned to London immediately. 'I felt that, however unpleasant the consequences might be, I had to tell the Foreign Office. Otherwise the Russians might try something', he said later.

The prime minister, Harold Wilson, was informed of Sir Geoffrey's enforced departure and was horrified. His abrupt resignation in August 1968, just a few days after Soviet tanks rolled into Prague to suppress the protesters, weakened the West's diplomatic position. But no action was taken against Sir Geoffrey, who retired early on a full pension. The real reason for his resignation was kept secret, and was only disclosed thirteen years later after it was leaked to the *Sunday Times*.

Fellow diplomats were sympathetic to Sir Geoffrey's demise. They pointed out that he had a disabled daughter who could not be taken to Moscow and Lady Harrison spent large amounts of time in the UK visiting her and so left her husband alone in the embassy flat. But Sir Geoffrey was refreshingly self-critical about his fall from grace. 'She (Galya) was a young attractive girl', he later reflected. 'I did not ask whether she was working for the KGB but the assumption was that every Russian working in our embassy was a KGB employee. As a trained diplomat, it was an aberration on my part. It was absolutely crazy but if you are on a long tour abroad then your defences can drop. It's unforgivable but it happens.'[43]

A more successful KGB seduction operation occurred four years later when a thirty-year-old married British diplomat based in Moscow was seduced by his family's Russian maid. Codenamed KAREV – his identity remains secret to this day – the diplomat was captivated by the young woman, whose code name was CH, according to documents later smuggled out by former KGB officer Vasily Mitrokhin. She successfully deployed a time-honoured KGB tactic of pretending to be pregnant and claimed that a security officer at the British embassy had arranged an abortion.

Karev was so relieved and grateful that he then disclosed biographical information on embassy officials in Moscow and the names of MI6 officers working under diplomatic cover. To compromise Karev further, the maid – in reality a KGB swallow – pretended to be pregnant again and asked for his help in arranging another abortion.

This tawdry tale then took a twist when the maid was arrested on KGB instructions for possessing illegal Western currency given to her by Karev. The disraught British diplomat then dug himself into a deeper hole by asking a Soviet official – whom he probably realised was a KGB officer – both to arrange the second fictitious abortion and for the charges against his lover to be dropped.

Under intense pressure, Karev negotiated with the KGB, as his tour of duty was nearly at an end. As he had already disclosed sensitive secrets, the Soviets backed off. This was unusual but probably based on the advice of Kim Philby no less who, on being shown his file, advised against compromising Karev publicly.[44]

*

For gay men and women during the Cold War, sexual blackmail was far more serious if their proclivities were exposed. It was a criminal offence and in 1954 they were officially branded as security risks and barred from public office.

'They [homosexuals] are open to blackmail and this may lay them open to direct pressure by hostile intelligence agents', stated a Foreign Office report at the time. 'The US State Department believe that Soviet and satellite agents collect information about the sexual habits of members of the US Foreign Service for precisely this purpose... The American security authorities are convinced that homosexuals are a security risk.'[45]

In many countries homosexuality was a criminal offence and regarded as a vice and deviant behaviour. Gay men were vulnerable to social disgrace, family disruption and the destruction of their personal and professional reputations. As Russians are notoriously homophobic, the stress of being a gay diplomat in Moscow was even more intense. If he was successfully compromised in a KGB honey trap, he would be confronted by stern militiamen outraged by this 'disgusting' transgression against Soviet law and decency. Indeed, it was an act of blasphemy, they screamed. And if the diplomat refused to cooperate, he would be locked away in a prison until the early hours, surrounded by threatening KGB officers who shouted the humiliating consequences if he did not cooperate.

Gay men would be treated far more brutally than heterosexuals. During one visit to Moscow in 1954, one young well-connected student was entertained in the customary manner by some Russian 'friends'. In fact, it was a set-up. The young man was interested in student group exchanges and the KGB decided that he could be useful as a valuable talent-spotter for recruiting new agents. Over dinner his friends poured vodka down his throat and spiked his other drinks. By the end of the evening the young man could barely stand and was dragged back to his room at Hotel Moskva, where he crashed onto the bed. But when he awoke he found himself the victim of a homosexual assault while a photographer wearing a black hood took pictures of the incident from the end of the bed. After several cups of coffee, he was shown the photographs and told that he could be 'of assistance' to the Soviet Union. Fortunately, the young man was calm and courageous and he walked straight to the British embassy. He told the security officer on duty and the next day he was flown home to London.

The most notorious case was John Vassall, an Admiralty clerk at the British embassy in Moscow. The son of a Church of England clergyman, Vassall was a promiscuous homosexual in the early 1950s who boasted that he had 'come to bed eyes'. But he was also a loner and aloof and, unlike his colleagues, embraced the night-life of Moscow rather than bridge games, theatre and cocktail parties. He chose a clandestine sexual life which made him more vulnerable and so became easy prey to the KGB ravens.

The KGB chose a handsome young Russian interpreter for the operation. He was adept at seeking travel and theatre tickets and the best food from the markets, which ensured that he was invited to embassy parties. Flattered by the interpreter's attention and invitations, Vassall was enchanted by his exciting new life. After three months the trap was set. The clerk joined his new Russian friends for dinner near the Bolshoi Theatre and the agents moved in for the kill. 'We were taken to the first floor where I first thought was a dining room but they invited me into a private dining room', Vassall later confessed:

> We had drinks, a large dinner and I was plied with very strong brandy and after half an hour I remember everybody taking off their jackets and somebody assisted me to take off mine. The lighting was very strong and gradually most of my clothes were removed... I remember two or three people getting on the bed

with me, all in a state of undress. There certain compromising sexual actions took place. I remember someone in the party taking photographs.[46]

Soon after the interpreter vanished and Vassall was confronted by two officials in plain clothes. One official produced photographs from the party which the KGB had manipulated into a gay orgy. 'After about three photographs, I could not stomach any more', recalled the clerk. 'They made one feel ill.' He was then told that he could be jailed for such activity, banned from leaving Russia and the photographs might be sent to senior embassy staff, including the ambassador's wife, who was presumably not the type to approve of such behaviour. However, if he cooperated... Over the next few weeks the KGB turned up the heat and Vassall agreed to leak classified documents.

On his return to London the clerk resumed his duties at the Admiralty and spied for the Soviet Union for the next seven years. But then in 1962 a tip off by a KGB defector resulted in an investigation by the formidable MI5 officer Charles Elwell, who oversaw the bugging of Vassall's flat in Dolphin Square, near Parliament, and surveillance of his journey to work on the Number 24 bus. A search of his flat revealed two cameras and exposed film concealed in a hidden compartment. Vassall was arrested later the same day. Panting with fear, he confessed his guilt and was convicted under the Official Secrets Act and jailed for eighteen years.

A postscript to Vassall's arrest occurred when Sir Roger Hollis, head of MI5, gleefully told Harold Macmillan, then prime minister, that the spy had been captured. 'I've got this fellow Vassall, I've got him!', he said with rare excitement in his voice. But the prime minister was not happy.

'I am not at all pleased', he replied. 'When my gamekeeper shoots a fox, he doesn't go and hang it up outside the Master of Foxhounds' drawing room. He buries it out of sight. But you just can't shoot a spy as you did during the war... Better to discover him, then control him but never catch him... There will be a terrible row in the press, there will be a debate in the House of Commons and the government will probably fall. Why the devil did you catch him?'[47]

Politically well-connected gay journalists were also targeted as the influence of the press during the Cold War was far more pronounced than today. One of the most powerful American columnists was Joseph Alsop, a ferocious critic of the Soviet Union and a close friend of the esteemed diplomat George Kennan. Self-opinionated and highly articulate, Alsop was a feared political pundit at a time when it mattered. He was a grand nephew of President Theodore Roosevelt and the archetypal Washington DC political insider. While he was a New Deal liberal, he displayed an obsessive anti-Communist streak and his columns mattered in the White House. When President Johnson deployed an extra 50,000 troops during the Vietnam war, he remarked: 'There, that should keep Joseph Alsop quiet for a while.'[48]

The Soviets found his relentless criticism infuriating and so decided to silence him. The KGB discovered that Alsop was a closet homosexual and during his one and only visit to Moscow in 1957 the honey trap was set. They told a handsome young blond man with an athlete's build and a pleasant manner to ensnare him. The seduction was successful and the influential columnist's tryst was filmed in a hotel room. Shortly after Alsop finished having sex, two KGB officers stormed into his hotel room and told him that they had photographs of 'the act' and encouraged him to spy for the Soviets. 'You need to help us a little if we are going to help you', said one of the officers.

The formidable Alsop ignored the overture, returned to Washington and promptly informed the FBI and his friend Frank Wisner, the CIA's deputy director of plans. He continued to attack the Soviets in his column. This angered the KGB, who sent the incriminating photographs of his gay liaison to his friends and enemies. One sordid picture was mailed to the humourist Art Buchwald, who had satirised Alsop. He had written a comedy, *Sheep on the Runway*, featuring a pompous bowtie-wearing

Washington columnist, which was a thinly-disguised portrait of Alsop. Buchwald was not an admirer of the columnist but was appalled by the photographs and so the tactic backfired.

One KGB agent even left a note on the windshield of a car in front of Alsop's house in Georgetown, stating 'Joe Alsop is Queer'. The columnist was flustered. He spoke to Richard Helms, then CIA director of operations, and said he planned to end the ordeal by making a public declaration. Helms advised against it and the CIA fixed the problem via a back-channel with Russian intelligence, reserved for washing dirty laundry. The agency threatened retaliation and the KGB blackmail operation against the esteemed commentator stopped immediately. But nearly twenty years later the same incriminating photographs mysteriously resurfaced in the mailboxes of critics of Alsop's hawkish views on the Vietnam war. It was another failure, as his enemies sent the photographs to Alsop so that they could be destroyed.[49]

One of Alsop's fellow journalistic critics of the Soviet Union was also targeted. Edward Crankshaw, educated at the nonconformist public school Bishop's Stortford College, Hertfordshire, was a distinguished foreign correspondent who predicted the Second World War while reporting for *The Times* in Berlin in 1938. During the war he served as a signals intelligence officer and in 1947 became the *Observer's* Moscow correspondent. He was a vociferous critic of the Soviet Union, notably in 1956 during the brutal invasion of Hungary. At that time, the *Observer* was a highly regarded and authoritative newspaper and was taken seriously by the Conservative government, despite its liberal tendencies.

Like Alsop, Crankshaw was a closet homosexual and in 1959 the KGB launched their entrapment operation. The first attempt was to arrest the two Russians living with the foreign correspondent and force them into falsely confessing to being British spies, in order to persuade Crankshaw to change his reporting. Unperturbed and unfazed, he refused. Shocked by this reaction, the KGB then engaged an attractive young man to seduce the journalist. This was successful, as Crankshaw was photographed while indulging in 'sexual frolics', according to KGB documents later smuggled out by Vasily Mitrokhin.[50] But again the correspondent refused to be intimidated and his anti-Communist coverage continued. He later reported that past atrocities committed by the KGB remained 'part of the present':

'Still no voice in the Soviet Union can be heard to say that the collectivisation, the mass arrests, the deportations and killings were appalling crimes – past now but never to be forgotten. And this means in effect that for all the remarkable changes since Stalin, the Khrushchev Government is still condoning those crimes.'

The Kremlin was furious and so when Andropov became KGB chairman in 1967 he sanctioned a new operation against Crankshaw in an attempt to discredit or blackmail him. The sex photographs were sent to the *Observer*'s office in London. But the operation was abandoned after KGB officers in London advised – correctly – that Crankshaw would not succumb to this crude blackmail and that his editor would stand by him.[51]

Other gay foreign correspondents in Moscow did not fare so well. While Crankshaw was in Moscow, the *Daily Telegraph*'s reporter was 28-year-old Jeremy Wolfenden. A former National Service naval intelligence officer and Old Etonian, Wolfenden spoke Russian and arrived in Moscow in 1962 at the height of the Cold War. He was also a closet homosexual, sensitive by temperament, and the KGB ruthlessly exploited his vulnerability. As he was going to bed with his boyfriend – the ministry of foreign trade's barber – a man jumped out of the wardrobe in Wolfenden's room at the Ukraine Hotel and took photographs of the two men.

The blackmail pitch was delivered: pass on intelligence about Westerners in Moscow or face the consequences. At first the young correspondent resisted. But he was worried that the KGB would tell the *Daily Telegraph*, not known for its liberal tolerance of gay sex, and he would be sacked. He was unsure and so reported the incident to the British embassy. The next time he visited London

Wolfenden was summoned to see an MI6 officer, who asked him to 'cooperate with the Russians' but report back to British intelligence whenever he was in London.

The *Telegraph* reporter was now hooked by both the KGB and MI6 and in reality a double agent. The stress started to take its toll. He began drinking heavily and consumed vast amounts of cognac. He felt trapped but decided to work for the KGB periodically. In 1964 Wolfenden wrote a story for the *Daily Telegraph* saying that British companies which had been associated with Greville Wynne – the businessman who spied for MI6 – would be blacklisted by the Soviet ministry of trade. He later told colleagues that he knew the story was untrue but sent it to London because of pressure by the KGB. And to keep up his double life, he told MI6 about a fellow reporter who knew a Soviet diplomat of interest to Britain.[52]

By now Wolfenden was making frantic efforts to break away from both MI6 and the KGB. Despite being gay, he married Martina Browne, an English girl who had been a nanny for the visa officer at the British embassy in Moscow, who was also a contact man for MI6. But when the correspondent was due to return to Moscow his MI6 controller advised him not to take his wife with him. This confused the young man, who was desperate to escape from the spying game. He was then transferred to the Washington DC bureau, but at a British embassy party his MI6 controller greeted him warmly and persuaded him to renew their working relationship.

The pressure of being a double agent was now almost Kafkaesque. His marriage was not going well and his bouts of drunkenness became more frequent. He barely ate. On 28 December 1965, Wolfenden suffered a cerebral haemorrhage after apparently cracking his head against the washbasin in his bathroom. He died soon afterwards. He was thirty-one years old. A few weeks later his wife decided to move to the United States. One of Wolfenden's friends met her for a farewell drink and asked her what she planned to do there.

'I don't know', she replied. 'I can't go back to my old job. I'm getting a bit old for looking through keyholes. Anyway, I've lost all my Russian contacts.' It was clear that she was an MI6 officer who was tasked to keep an eye on her husband.

The official version of Wolfenden's death was not accepted by his friends. They believed that whatever the physical causes of his passing, the intolerable stress of working for both MI6 and the KGB while being secretly gay drove him to such a deep depression that he had lost the will to live. It was a classic case of how the lives of individuals caught up in the intelligence game during the Cold War were expendable.[53]

The KGB were clearly impervious to the consequences of their actions. They did not just target diplomats and journalists. Ordinary tourists were also victims of sexual entrapment and blackmail. 'Being a Vice-Consul, I was in touch with tourists who were in trouble', Dennis Amy remembered.

> The Russians would set people up. Young people may be fair game and they would set up middle-aged ladies in bed with people and take pictures of them which was absolutely inexcusable. It blighted their lives. We had one man, a senior mathematics lecturer at Manchester University who came out to Russia because it is a centre of mathematical excellence. And they [the KGB] drove him mad. They really gave him a hard time.
>
> I got him home and he was admitted to a hospital in Virginia Water, Surrey, because he was upset. But the day he was released, he killed himself. The Russians killed him just as surely as they had shot him by the pressure they put on him. They would go to any lengths to compromise people. They would drug people and many of my colleagues were sent home with their careers destroyed.[54]

Former spymasters found a way of rationalising their sexual entrapment and blackmail operations.

'When I reflect on their [Romeo spies] contribution to our work and some of the consequences, I have to admit that in several cases, the human cost was high in disrupted lives, broken hearts and destroyed careers', acknowledged Markus Wolf, head of the Stasi who worked closely with the KGB throughout the Cold War. 'The ends did not always justify the means we chose to employ. But it does irk me that Westerners adopt such a strident moral tone against me on the subject. As long as there is espionage, there will be Romeos seducing unsuspecting Juliets with access to secrets. After all, I was running an intelligence service, not a lonely hearts club.'[55]

In the summer of 1961, intelligence on France was a priority, especially as Charles de Gaulle was president. And so the KGB made plans to target the French embassy in Moscow. Hidden microphones in the apartment of Colonel Louis Guibaud, the air attaché and a confidant of the French ambassador, revealed that he quarrelled frequently and fiercely with his wife. To the KGB, this was a signal for a honey trap. And so Guibaud was exposed to a succession of women, until one lured him into an affair.

The KGB allowed the 'romance' to flourish for a year until one day Guibaud was confronted by three men in civilian clothes. Polite but blunt, they spread before him an array of photographs documenting his dangerous liaison. Then they delivered the brutal familiar choice: secret collaboration with the KGB or public disgrace. He chose neither option. Depressed, frustrated and shaken, a few weeks later he took a revolver from the desk of his study in the embassy and shot himself. His body was found sprawled on the floor in a pool of blood while his wife knelt over his body, sobbing and caressing his face.[56]

For a few hours the news of Guibaud's suicide created near panic inside the KGB. His tragic death was of no consequence. The Soviets' consuming fear was that the French diplomat might have left a note exposing the entrapment and the blackmail. Once its agents discovered that this was not the case, the KGB relaxed, breathed a sigh of relief and promptly planted fake news in the diplomatic community that Colonel Guibaud had shot himself because of psychotic depression. Within days the KGB resumed entrapment and blackmail operations against the Western embassies in Moscow.

The extent to which Russian intelligence – from the Cheka in 1918 to the FSB in 2022 – ruthlessly deployed honey trappers to extract *Kompromat* and hence recruit agents by sexual blackmail shows just how far they were prepared to go in the war against the West. No one was beyond their sights or untouchable, even members of Parliament.

5

ANATOMY OF A SMEAR

The neatest trick of the devil is to persuade you that he does not exist.

Charles Baudelaire, 1869

ON THE MORNING OF 4 AUGUST 1965, at the height of the Cold War, a mysterious anonymous package arrived at the House of Commons, the office of the *News of the World*, the Conservative Association of East Harrow, a London flat and a Surrey country house. Inside the buff-coloured envelope was a large foolscap-sized sheet of poor quality glossy paper headed: 'I'm not a Profumo but... (a story in photographs)'. Attached were three grainy if graphic photographs of the prominent Conservative MP Anthony Courtney in various states of undress, accompanied by a blonde Russian woman, in his spacious suite at the National Hotel in Moscow. One picture showed the MP naked and seated alone. In the second the young lady was fully dressed and sitting on the bed. And the third showed the woman reclining on the bed half-clothed while Courtney unbuttoned her pleated blue nylon blouse. A rectangular black patch across her eyes was designed to prevent identification. The clear implication was that the MP was sexually intimate with the young woman.

Another document was a typed letter on House of Commons notepaper, written by Courtney, but its contents were almost completely concealed by an enlarged business card belonging to the MP. The anonymous author added: 'Why not try to become an MP to combine business with pleasure and conduct shady business while "defending public interests"', and concluded ominously: 'To be continued...'

The dossier was addressed and posted to Jo Richardson, the Labour candidate who stood against Courtney in the previous year's general election, George Wigg, a minister without portfolio but in reality the prime minister's intelligence adviser, the government chief whip Edward Short, Theo Valentine, chairman of Courtney's Conservative Association, the news editor of the *News of the World*, four other MPs and his wife Elizabeth. At least one copy was delivered by hand to the London apartment of an MP.

The compromising photographs of Courtney were a crude attempt to inflict maximum damage. The next day the dossier was delivered to his stepson David Trefgarne, the Conservative chief whip William Whitelaw and the chairman of Kodak, who had hired the MP for advice on how to do business in the Soviet Union.

Courtney was unaware of the politically explosive package until he received a phone call from his fellow Tory MP John Tilney, whose only connection to Russia was that he had visited Eastern bloc countries. 'Something important has happened', he said. 'Can we have a word?'

Ten minutes later Courtney and Tilney were sitting in the sombre, stone-flagged magnificence of Westminster Hall within the precincts of Parliament.

Tilney was anxious as he passed the infamous envelope to his fellow Conservative. 'Have a look at that', he said. 'Several Members have already received it.' Stunned and shaken, Courtney gazed at the photographs. Tilney was equally distressed and nervous. 'Why did they have to send one of these foul things to ME?', he sighed.[1]

Staring transfixed at the pictures and documents, Courtney did not respond. After enquiring about their distribution he returned to his flat at Roebuck House, Stag Place, Victoria, and made two telephone calls. The first was to his wife. 'Darling, something terribly important has happened which I must tell you about', he said. The second was to the director-general of MI5, Roger Hollis, an old personal friend and colleague from when he served in Naval Intelligence in his previous life. An hour later Hollis arrived but was not very reassuring. He took a copy of the broadsheet and photographs and promised to discover the origin and source of the smear. As he left the flat, the afternoon post arrived. It included a typed envelope addressed to his wife. Inside was yet another copy of the dossier.

That evening Courtney drove down to see his wife, Elizabeth Trefgarne, at their country house in Chobham, Surrey. She had been brought up in a political family and was familiar with dirty tricks. But she was shocked when her husband showed her the dossier. 'It is too soon to say with any certainty', said the MP, 'but I am sure this is Russian work.'

That night Courtney lay awake thinking. Until he knew more about the broadsheet, he reflected, it was impossible to make any plans to counter it. The photographs had been touched up a little and so were they genuine? If this was blackmail, surely he would be approached by the KGB? And was the smear designed to warn other critics of the Soviet Union that if they stepped out of line, they would endure a similar fate?

The targeting of Courtney was no accident. He had been a trenchant critic of the KGB since his election in 1959 and campaigned for a tough crackdown on the Soviet espionage network which was highly active in London at that time. He believed that Foreign Office complacency enabled the KGB to infiltrate and subvert the UK, principally by exploiting the fact that *all* individuals attached to the Soviet embassy, including chauffeurs and secretaries, were accorded full diplomatic immunity from search and arrest. This enabled large numbers of KGB officers to run amok through London while MI5 struggled to counter their clandestine exploits.

*

Despite being fervently anti-Communist and archetypically English, Anthony Tosswill Courtney grew up with Russia dominating his family. His grandfather was a friend of Peter Kropotkin, the Bolshevik agitator and historian, who was living in exile in Bromley, Kent, where Courtney was born on 16 May 1908. His father, Basil, was an engineer who sold parts for guns and machine tools to the Russian army and navy as Basil Courtney and Co. Ltd, before and during the First World War. He was in Petrograd in the summer of 1917, where he met Kropotkin's daughter who told him about the Bolshevik movement. After witnessing the October Revolution, Basil Courtney escaped to the West via Finland but never returned. He was not a Communist but was captivated by the country. He spoke the language fluently and sang Russian and Ukrainian folk songs at home.

As a nine-year-old boy, Anthony was entranced by his father's adventures, although he could not understand why his father was not in uniform. But his imagination was kindled by the presents he brought back from Russia.

'There were beautifully carved wooden toys, bears and wolves which could be made to perform ludicrous antics and illustrated books of fairy tales, illuminated in blue and gold, whose princess far outshone anything we had previously found in the hag-ridden pages of Grimm or the wishy-washy stories of Hans Christian Andersen', recalled Courtney.[2]

Russia sounded romantic and exciting and the teenage Courtney was keen to explore the world. In 1924, he joined the Royal Navy and as a lieutenant on HMS *Cornwall* he met Russian émigrés in the Far East. Visits to Port Arthur stimulated his interest in the

Russo-Japanese war and trips to Shanghai resulted in meeting girls in the White Russian nightclubs and cabarets, notably 'The Tavern'. Most of these women had brothers in the Imperial Guard and provided an incentive to learn Russian. But he really learned the language when he moved to Romania and spent nine months there with his friend Jack Greenway, a British diplomat, who spoke Russian and educated the young naval officer.

By 1934, Courtney's career was flourishing, enhanced by the status of being heavyweight boxing champion of the Royal Navy. He spoke Russian fluently and the Admiralty was so impressed by his linguistic skills that he was asked to translate intelligence reports. The following year, aged twenty-seven, Courtney joined the Naval Intelligence Division, based in the Admiralty, and was one of the few Westerners to visit the Soviet Union at that time for his summer holidays. He hated Communism but loved Russia.[3]

MI6 soon realised Courtney's value. It was rare for a British officer to have so many Russian friends and speak the language so eloquently. And so Courtney submitted reports to MI6, with details ranging from the battleships he saw to how many roubles a waiter earned a month in a Moscow restaurant. He also drafted papers on what operations could be mounted against the Soviets in the Arctic and the Black Sea in the event of war. 'I'm afraid I have rather violent ideas on what we really could do to the USSR if we tried', he wrote in a 1936 report.

During the Second World War Courtney was sent to the Soviet Union as deputy to Admiral George Miles, head of the Naval Mission which the Russians believed was a front for MI6. His yearning for adventure led him to sail the Arctic to Murmansk, through storms violent enough to detonate mines around the boat. And he remained passionately pro-Russian and donated a litre of his own blood to the Red Army to support their defence against the Nazi invasion. This was done without his admiral's knowledge, which impressed the Russians. He also managed to persuade the Admiralty to give the Russians copies of their operational code books. But his wartime years in Moscow were filled with frustration and obstruction.

'We were handicapped by the ingrained Russian secretiveness and suspicion', he said later.[4]

There was one welcome distraction, however. One evening at the Filial Theatre in Moscow, he noticed an attractive, enigmatic ballerina called Lydia Manukhina leaning against one of the pillars in the lobby, smoking a cigarette. Courtney was married at the time to Elizabeth Stokes, then secretary to the defence security officer in Malta, but was enchanted by the ballerina who, he said later, was 'all eyes' and 'could be irresistible'. He regarded her as 'a greyhound among beagles' and after dinner dates escorted her back to her flat on the site of the old church of St Pimen. While Courtney claimed she was just a friend, in fact they became lovers.

'She became Courtney's mistress – a fact which was well known', stated a top-secret MI5 report. 'Manukhina had a flat to herself and Courtney sometimes stayed there quite openly.' It was not long before Soviet intelligence agents placed the couple under surveillance.

Hypersensitive and outspoken, Manukhina was a widow and her late husband had been an official in the ministry of foreign trade and so she had an appreciation of the outside world. She thought the English were stupefyingly naive.

'Anton, you stupid sailor', she once shouted in a burst of temper. 'When will you come to realise that we Russians are just about half-way between you English and the animals?'[5]

As a ballerina in the state ballet, she was a privileged member of the Soviet elite and taught Courtney about her country, its people and culture. This enabled the intelligence officer to 'go native'. During his time off, the broad-shouldered Englishman dressed like a Russian and spoke like a Russian. This made him less conspicuous, so he could indulge in his intelligence-gathering and nocturnal socialising without attracting the attention usually accorded to foreigners in Moscow.

After the war Commander Courtney and his wife Elizabeth
returned to London and moved into a tiny flat on Thackeray Street,
Kensington, not far from the Soviet embassy. She joined MI5 at
the War Office and he became head of the Soviet section of Naval
Intelligence, based in the Admiralty, and was embedded in the
intelligence infrastructure. He was instrumental in developing new
ideas to use fast surface craft and submarines against the Soviets
in the Black Sea. And he held meetings with MI6 officers and their
chief, Sir Stewart Menzies, to discuss the feasibility of obtaining
intelligence from Turkey and the Black Sea and Baltic states by
using such craft. Unfortunately, the man MI6 assigned to this
project was Kim Philby, the notorious Soviet double agent. Philby,
recalled Courtney, 'listened to my proposals with interest, for he
had a wide knowledge of Turkish affairs and his support was
essential if Naval Intelligence was to make any contribution to the
common effort in the Black Sea where our information was deplor-
ably scanty'.

By 1948 Courtney was the chief of intelligence staff in the Allied
Control Commission based in Hamburg and promoted his idea
of using fast surface craft for the reconnaissance of Soviet activities.
He was also instrumental in dropping highly trained armed MI6
agents behind enemy lines in Latvia. But his efforts were sabotaged
by leaks to the Soviets.

'Little did I know that the penetration of the Foreign Office and
Secret Intelligence Service [MI6] by the Russian Intelligence
Service must have not only doomed our efforts from the start, but
had involved me personally in sending many a brave man into the
jaws of a Soviet trap', Courtney said. 'Even worse, boat crews in
the Baltic and Black Sea had also been penetrated by the KGB.'[6]

On retiring from the navy in 1953, the 45-year-old Courtney
was offered a job by the deputy chief of MI6 but the Foreign Office
objected and it never materialised. And so he found himself
without a career or an income. His only useful assets were his
expert knowledge of the Soviet Union, its people and its language.
And so he set up a private company, Anglo-Russian Business

Consultants Ltd, which advised UK firms on exporting their equipment to the Soviet Union. His clients included Kodak, Associated
British Engineering and EMI, who wanted to sell and exchange
their gramophone records.

Courtney was a fixer and an intermediary, not a businessman.
His role, as he later told MI5, was to bridge the gap between 'the
capitalist profit makers and the suspicious socialist centralisers'.
He would try and find common ground between the entrepre-
neurial West and the rigid state bureaucracy of the East. His
wartime service helped, but he also believed, rather ambitiously,
that his 'appreciation of the irrepressible Russian sense of humour'
would reduce the tension during commercial negotiations. He was
also adept at securing visas for Russia, met with the Soviet trade
delegation in London and threw parties for visiting Russians.
Unsurprisingly, the KGB and their satellite agencies believed his
company was a cover and that in reality he was an MI6 agent.

Courtney's security vulnerability was compounded by having
affairs with several East European women. Between 1955 and 1958,
he had an illicit relationship with Hania Zabenska, a secretary at
the Poznań Business Fair in Poland, which he attended as a member
of the British delegation. She was engaged to a son of a Polish
military general and so it was a high risk relationship for the
former naval intelligence officer. For her part, Zabenska told
Courtney that she was trying to set up a small cosmetics business
but was being obstructed by state officialdom. She was frightened
of the authorities and asked for his help. He complied.

The surveillance of the former naval intelligence officer culminated on 21 June 1958, at the Poznań Fair, when he was summoned
to appear at the Bureau of Foreign Registration. In a top floor
room, Courtney sat at a table facing the light, where he was interrogated by a granite-faced, humourless intelligence official in plain
clothes, accompanied by a drink-sodden interpreter. It was not a
sophisticated operation.

For the next hour he was questioned about his activities in
Poland. The officials clearly believed that he was an MI6 agent

masquerading as a businessman. But there was no attempt to blackmail him with their knowledge of his affair with the young secretary. Their priority was to persuade him to admit that he was a spy and not a businessman.

'Your activities are not in the interests of Anglo-Polish trade', the official concluded. Fortunately, Courtney had alerted the British embassy in Warsaw in advance, so that if he did not emerge from the meeting his whereabouts would be known. He left the next day.[7]

*

While business was thriving in the mid-1950s, Commander Courtney had not quite left the secret world. Between 1946 and 1954 he wrote twelve articles about the Soviet Union for the *Spectator*, using the pseudonym 'Richard Chancellor', an English sailor who opened up commercial and diplomatic relations with Russia during the reign of Ivan the Terrible in the fifteenth century. Courtney had become an exponent of the art of Kremlinology. But as he was still an intelligence officer, he could not be seen to be writing articles under his own name. And so he was authorised to indulge in some covert Cold War propaganda. In his first *Spectator* piece, Courtney delicately tried to keep a balance between not upsetting the Soviet Union while remaining hostile to its ideology. 'Stalin took a lengthy and well-earned rest in the pine-scented hills of Sochi', he wrote in November 1946.

Interestingly, Walter Taplin, his editor at the *Spectator* between 1953 and 1954, also wrote for the Information Research Department, the secretive unit inside the Foreign Office which countered Soviet propaganda during the Cold War.

Despite being a Russophile, Courtney was a passionate anti-Communist and believed that the West needed more rather than fewer nuclear weapons. In December 1958 he became the Conservative candidate for Harrow East after the sitting MP Ian Harvey resigned after being caught in a homosexual act with a Coldstream Guards officer in St James's Park.

'An air of horrified prudishness pervaded the atmosphere in the constituency', recalled Courtney.[8]

And so the sober, respectable local Conservatives chose the upright dapper former navy commander, who could not possibly let them down.

Courtney's past as head of the Russian Section of Naval Intelligence was displayed on election leaflets and in March 1959 he won the by-election with a majority of over 2,000. Six months later he increased his majority to 6,000 at the general election. It was now a safe seat – for the moment. He later admitted that his elevation to the House of Commons 'improved my business affairs' and he was in a better position to lobby the Board of Trade on behalf of his clients. 'They [the clients] felt that their dealings with Russia and the Eastern European countries would be given an aura of official government blessing through the fact that I was now an MP', he said later.

The Russians also treated him with more respect, especially as the Conservatives were in power. Typically the Chinese were the most brazen. 'We would like to know your opinion about the British quota system for trading with our country, Commander Courtney, as we know that you are on the inside', the Chinese commercial secretary remarked.[9]

Blissfully unperturbed by the conflict of interests, Courtney's business thrived and he bought a small Regency house in the unspoilt Sussex village of Slinfold, which delighted his wife. As he represented a safe Tory seat, the commander felt comfortable about resuming his commercial activities. And so in June 1959 he visited Moscow to negotiate the sale to Russia of an early version of the digital computer, on behalf of EMI Electronics.

It was during this fateful trip that he first met Zina Grigoryevna Volkova, a 36-year-old quick-witted beauty with fair hair and hazel eyes, who ran a car service for visiting foreigners based at the Hotel Ukraina. She was ostensibly an Intourist guide and official, but in fact she was a KGB agent and operative. Set up in 1929 by Stalin as the Soviet Union's official travel agency, Intourist secretly functioned as a branch of the KGB. As a matter of routine, the names and passport details of all prospective visitors, based on their visa applications, were sent to the KGB for vetting and intelligence-gathering. In effect, they decided who could visit the Soviet Union. Intourist worked closely with the KGB to control every aspect of the visit – where you went, what you saw and whom you met. The KGB even searched visitors' bags and intercepted their letters home.

'It is no exaggeration to say the Intourist organisation works primarily for the KGB and the whole of its activity is under the control of the KGB', said former officer Ilya Dzhirkvelov. 'Among the huge staff of Intourist employees, there are full-time KGB officers and agents working as guides and interpreters for tourist groups.'[10]

The 51-year-old MP was married but was immediately smitten by the vivacious, cultured and intelligent 'tourist guide', who was a graduate of the Marxist-Leninist Institute. Unmarried and an only child, she lived with her mother in one room of a single storey old Russian house, just off Mayakovsky Square. She was impressed by the broad-shouldered, muscular former navy commander and flattered by his attention, but she also saw an opportunity. She met him for dinner on several occasions, when she expressed a fascination for the British aristocracy and a passion for the books of Angela Thirkell, the prolific novelist who gently satirised upper-class folly and middle-class aspirations in the 1930s. These charms sufficed for Courtney to begin an affair.

In June 1961 Courtney, now a widower, returned to Moscow primarily to attend the first British Industrial Exhibition since the 1917 Communist Revolution. It was at this moment that the KGB decided to set the trap. They instructed Volkova to give up part of her annual holiday from her employer, Intourist, to work at the exhibition for a British company. She was ordered to seduce and ensnare. During an evening when she was off duty, she dined with the MP at the National Hotel. Despite their political differences,

Courtney noticed that Volkova was warmer towards him and she became more animated as they drank the rather acid dry champagne. After dinner she asked if she could come up to his suite, a luxury room dominated by a grand piano. He readily agreed. They made love rather unsuccessfully but she stayed there for several hours. The next day she appeared to 'regret' her behaviour.

The hotel tryst may have been awkward but the brief encounter was covertly recorded by hidden cameras installed by the KGB. Under the code name Operation PROBA, the photographs were filed away to be used at the most opportune moment in the future. Courtney later told MI5 that he was not suspicious of Volkova's motives, despite her sudden forwardness coming as a surprise and his awareness that all Intourist employees were under KGB control.

'In the circumstances, one can only assume that his judgement was impaired by his male vanity', concluded the top-secret MI5 report on the affair.[11]

On his return to London, the Conservative MP became an uncompromising critic of the Soviet Union, despite his private commercial interests. In May 1962, he attacked the Foreign Office and MI5 'for a curious lack of reality' after the security debacle involving John Vassall, the gay civil servant who became a Soviet spy after being honey trapped and blackmailed. While acknowledging the Soviet Union was effectively in a state of war with the West, Courtney referred to the 'psychological dominance' which the Russians endeavoured to establish over members of foreign missions in Moscow.

'Individuals who are not prepared to accept this', he said, 'are usually removed or framed or find it necessary to go.'

He told the Commons the harassment of British diplomats in Moscow was designed to secure greater leverage when demanding diplomatic privileges for their embassy staff in London. 'We have seen an utter failure [in security] after a succession of failures in face of a ruthless and efficient enemy', he told the Commons.[12]

During the debate on the infamous Profumo security scandal, Courtney claimed the KGB was able to conduct nefarious and illegal operations under the cover of diplomatic immunity. He argued that all of the staff in the Soviet embassy in London enjoyed immunity even though 60% of them were KGB officers, according to the KGB defector Oleg Penkovsky. Protected by their diplomatic status, they could 'bug and burgle their way across London', to use former MI5 officer Peter Wright's phrase. He said that only the Soviet Union, Hungary, Czechoslovakia and Bulgaria enjoyed such blanket immunity. It was unprecedented.

Publicly, the government was disturbed by the shadow of the KGB.

'I feel it right to warn the House that hostile intrigue and espionage are being relentlessly maintained on a large scale', the prime minister, Harold Macmillan, said on 14 November 1962. But in private he was curiously unconcerned. During a briefing at 10 Downing Street, Macmillan looked uninterested and expressed a patrician disdain for the MP's anxiety about Soviet intelligence penetration of the British Establishment. He clearly regarded the secret world as rather grubby and vulgar and best left alone to the spies.[13]

In June 1964 Courtney turned up the heat and accused the Soviet Union of abusing its diplomatic privileges. He claimed that the twenty Russian chauffeurs employed by the embassy in London were in fact undercover KGB officers.

'Why was the Soviet Embassy allowed to have Russian drivers while British diplomats in Moscow were forced to hire local drivers and staff, all recruited from an agency clearly under control of the Russian intelligence services?', asked the MP.

The loophole provided a 'legal' network for recruiting intelligence agents in the UK.

The relentless criticism attracted hostile attention in the Soviet Union. Unsurprisingly, the ambassador in London refused his invitation to drinks at his country house in Chobham and Anatoly Strelnikov, the resident KGB officer at the embassy, warned the MP that his criticism of the KGB was causing intense irritation back in Moscow. Courtney was now a prime target, and the KGB plotted their revenge. According to former KGB officer Mikhail Lyubimov, there was an attempt to blackmail the MP into becoming an agent, a claim that the MP strongly denied.

In August 1964, Courtney flew to Eastern Europe for a business trip on a private aircraft with a navigator. The Soviet Union refused to allow the plane to enter their air space and so on 24 August 1964 the MP discarded his aircraft and flew by Aeroflot to Moscow, where he stayed at the National Hotel. By this time the MP had remarried. His new wife was Elizabeth Trefgarne, the widow of a peer and former minister. He told her about his affair with Zina Volkova. But he was living dangerously. He had been unfaithful during other business trips in Eastern Europe.

In November 1961, five months after his liaison with Volkova, Courtney had a brief affair with a young Russian woman called Evgenia Korolikhina. During a visit to Leningrad he picked up Evgenia at the theatre and escorted her to dinner at the Astoria Hotel where he was staying. After dinner they slept together but MI5 later concluded that because Courtney made the approach, it was unlikely she was a KGB swallow. MI5 also believed that there was no KGB entrapment motive when the MP indulged in another casual sexual encounter in August 1964 with a Bulgarian woman called Veska Spursova, in her flat in Sofia. The MP later told MI5 that none of his romantic escapades led to the KGB attempting to blackmail him or recruit him as an agent.[14]

It is unlikely that Mrs Courtney was aware of her husband's dalliances. But she was unhappy. The MP was either abroad on business or in London, when he would attend late-night parliamentary sessions. On his own admission he was thoughtless and neglected her. The marriage was in trouble. But when Courtney arrived at the National Hotel in Moscow on 28 August 1964, he was still shocked to receive a letter from his wife saying that she was leaving him. He then made a fateful if characteristically reckless error. In an attempt to change her mind, he picked up the phone and called her on an open line and sent letters to her at their Sussex country retreat. The KGB listened in to his calls and read his letters. It was the vulnerability the KGB was looking for. Operation PROBA could now be implemented.

Meanwhile, just before Christmas in 1964, Courtney resumed his attack on Soviet abuse of diplomatic privileges in London.

'Setting aside the specialised illegal espionage networks operated by the Soviet and associated Intelligence Services, the clandestine activity of the Communists in this country depends for its effectiveness on the immunity and the secure lines of communication with Moscow provided by Embassy "cover"', the MP declared. 'Much of the KGB success in the past has been due to the saturation of our counter-espionage defences by the sheer number of potential KGB agents involved.' He added: 'When will the government stop behaving like hypnotised rabbits in the face of an efficient Soviet espionage organisation?'

The KGB decided that it was time to strike. In January 1965, Sir Alec Douglas-Home, then leader of the Conservative Party, Courtney and his stepson David Trefgarne received anonymous letters about Courtney's private life. They were posted from his constituency in Harrow and concluded: 'We think that you should resign as our MP before there is a further public scandal in the Party.' This was a clear reference to the recent sex security case, when the war minister John Profumo had an affair with a woman who was also sleeping with a KGB officer and then lied about it in Parliament.

As MPs often receive anonymous threats, Courtney informed the chief whip, Willie Whitelaw, who was sympathetic but advised caution and discretion. Scotland Yard investigated the letters but were unable to trace the source or whether they were even authentic.

Courtney was nervous but decided to ignore the letters. He thought that while they remained private and anonymous there was no danger and so he continued his campaign against KGB activity in London. In March 1965, he flew to Moscow on business. Sensing potential danger, he left a letter for his wife with the foreign secretary, to be sent to her if something should go awry. But he resumed his relationship with Zina Volkova in Moscow, although instructing her to refuse to answer his telephone calls. Despite this precaution they went to the opera and saw *Sadko* at the Bolshoi Theatre. He also telephoned his former girlfriend Lydia Manukhina, who had ceased to be his mistress in 1946. But his call struck an uneasy and discordant note. The number he had dialled for twenty-three years produced an irritated response from a strange voice, who denied all knowledge of Lydia or of the flat in which she lived. She had changed her number. Courtney found her new number and called her.

'Lydia, this is Tony.'

There was silence and she hung up. And so he dialled once more. Again her familiar voice responded abruptly: 'I don't know anyone called Tony. I am not Lydia and I don't know any of these people. Stop bothering me.'

Shocked and upset, Courtney walked over to her flat in the Tverskaya area of Moscow. He knocked on the door. '*Kto tam?*' ('Who is there?') was the response.

'Vaska', he said, using a Russian password which they had adopted.

There was a pause. 'I don't know you and I have no idea who you are', she said. A confused MP checked with the neighbours next door, who confirmed that it really was Lydia.

Courtney walked back to the National Hotel with a nervous and tense feeling he had not experienced since he was interrogated by the Polish Secret Police in Poznań police station in 1957. Taken in its Soviet context, the incident was an important warning sign. She might as well have posted a sign outside saying 'Danger – keep right away'.

MI5 had few doubts. 'It was clear that Lydia must have been got at by the KGB and probably told them all she knew about him', stated an MI5 report.[15]

On his return to London Courtney resumed his anti-KGB campaign. On 29 June 1965 he met Prime Minister Harold Wilson privately and outlined his concerns about how the KGB was abusing its diplomatic status in London. He also mentioned the attempted entrapment of the Conservative MP Anthony Meyer, while he was a diplomat in Moscow.

The prime minister responded that the security situation was 'in hand' and refused to reform the 'special arrangements' the Foreign Office had with the four Soviet bloc governments. He added that the normal conduct of diplomacy would be impossible without them. He said Courtney's proposals would be 'impractical and unhelpful', arguing the existing system protected British embassy officials in Communist countries. And he concluded by claiming that British consular officials would be expelled from Soviet bloc states or be more open to blackmail and that MI5 had sufficient personnel to keep suspected KGB officers under surveillance.[16]

Courtney walked away from 10 Downing Street despondent but declined to back down. On 27 July 1965, he tabled a Commons motion which recognised the damage of recent security breaches, conscious of the handicaps imposed on MI5 by the 'extraordinary degree of diplomatic immunity accorded to certain foreign embassies which habitually abuse this privilege for espionage purposes'.

By now the bluff former naval commander believed any potential smear campaign had subsided. He was deluded. A week later, on 4 August 1965, the photographs of the MP and Volkova together in the Moscow hotel room and the anonymous broadsheet were distributed to MPs, journalists and anyone else who could make his life difficult. This was no speculative attempt to blackmail the MP. It was an unambiguous threat: stop criticising the Soviet Union or else.

Stunned and horrified, the beleaguered MP sat down at his desk in his London flat and studied the material, in the hope of finding a clue that proved its suspected Russian origin. He could just about see the genuine letter that had been stolen, with his large business visiting card superimposed on it. If he could find the carbon copy of that letter, that would identify at least the country of origin. After a forensic exercise, Courtney was delighted to discover the duplicate of the letter. It was in English, dated four months earlier, and was addressed to Nina Gromov, the wife of a Russian general, regarding the arrangement of a meeting in Moscow. At the very least someone from the Soviet Union was involved.

Clearly, there were security implications and so Courtney met Roger Hollis, the director-general of MI5 and an old and close friend, at his London flat. Aloof and austere, the MP found the spy rather too cynical for his taste. Courtney had been startled when Hollis visited him in West Germany in the late 1940s and said: 'My experience is that every man, without exception, has his price – but mine is a very high one.'[17] He was also mildly irritated by the fact that Hollis was having a long affair with his secretary at MI5, which reeked of Establishment double standards.[18] But they were friendly enough. The MP's first wife had worked for MI5 throughout the Second World War and on one occasion Hollis stayed with the couple for a week. However, after Courtney became an MP, the MI5 director-general avoided contact, partly because he did not want Whitehall to think he was responsible for the attacks on the Foreign Office.

Privately, Hollis thought that Courtney was trying to rationalise his difficulties on the grounds that he was engaged in a crusade against the KGB. But he was broadly sympathetic to his plight. Soon after the broadsheet was distributed, one important recipient told the MI5 director-general that he thought 'the technique of the anonymous letter was a despicable one'. He added: 'Whatever the truth of the allegation, Courtney should not suffer from this filthy attack.' After that comment, Hollis told the cabinet secretary, Sir Burke Trend: 'This seems to me a good, robust British point of view and I very much hope that we may follow it.'[19]

At first MI5 and Scotland Yard forensic experts believed that the dirty dossier could have been forged. But this was soon discounted and Courtney received a visit from an unassuming MI5 officer who was known as 'Soames'. The MP was pleased to hear that 'Soames' was an expert on the KGB but disappointed to learn that he neither spoke Russian nor knew the meaning of the word 'Oprichniki' (Russia's earliest secret police). But he had a sympathetic manner and listened carefully to Courtney's frank account of the saga, the documents, his relationship with Zina Volkova and his grudging admission that he was the man in the photographs.

Meanwhile, a parallel investigation was being conducted by the mercurial and mysterious Colonel George Wigg. A shadowy character, his role was to alert and safeguard 10 Downing Street against security scandals and risks. As Harold Wilson's official biographer observed:

> Wigg's passion was secrets, the more malodorous the better. He was at his happiest in the twilight world of spies, counter-spies and Chapman Pincher [the legendary *Daily Express* security correspondent] and viewed his fellow MPs with the same ferocious suspicion as he would have lavished on an accredited agent of the KGB.[20]

The Courtney dossier had been delivered to Wigg's London flat and he was also given a copy of the file by MI5. The MP telephoned Wigg and they met at 10 Downing Street alone.

'He was excited and his eyes sparkled as we talked', recalled Courtney.[21]

The prime minister's intelligence trouble-shooter was intrigued, sympathetic and alarmed but did not indicate what action might be taken. Later that day, Wigg sent a confidential memo to Wilson in which he mentioned that there was no attempt to blackmail Courtney. He focused on the phrase 'To be continued....' at the end of the dossier:

'The possibility must be considered that "To be continued" may relate not to Courtney but to some other person... in order to provide a hint to some other person as to what may happen to them'.

Wigg believed at the time – and for the rest of his life – that the KGB was 'cracking the whip' at somebody else to warn them that a similar fate was in store if they ever stepped out of line.

By sending the dossier to MPs, the KGB clearly aimed to destroy Courtney's political career. Now they went after his marriage. The day before he visited 10 Downing Street, an additional copy of the broadsheet and photographs were posted to his wife in Chobham. Two days later the MP arrived at his London flat to find a note from his wife asking him not to come home, and she added: 'By the time you get this, I may be abroad.' At that moment his lawyer rang and told him she was filing for divorce.

It was a mortal blow. Courtney sat on the bed with his head in his hands as he considered his situation. His marriage was already in trouble because of his nomadic lifestyle. He had told his wife about Zina and even introduced her during a trip to Moscow. But his wife did not believe that the affair had ended before their marriage, especially when MI5 told her that her husband had continued the affair on at least two occasions during subsequent business trips to Moscow. The receipt of the extra copy of the dossier was like a dagger in the heart.

Under siege, Courtney moved out of his flat at Roebuck House, Victoria. His friends deserted him. And two anonymous phone calls made him even more neurotic. He compared himself to the character on the run in the spy novel *The Thirty-Nine Steps*. He even dug out an old swordstick from a bag of golf clubs and kept a .38 revolver loaded at his bedside table. One day he contemplated suicide. Another evening he would dream of shooting a KGB agent or any Russian.

The incriminating photographs would inevitably leak when Elizabeth Courtney cited Zina Volkova in her divorce petition on the grounds of his adultery. And so on 6 September 1965 Courtney visited 10 Downing Street and met with the prime minister, Harold Wilson, and George Wigg, who assured him that they would not exploit the affair for party political advantage. He was received with personal sympathy but with no commitment to take retaliatory action. He walked back with Wigg, who was excited and voluble.

'What I want to know is – who are they getting at', he almost shouted. 'They are cracking the whip at someone and I want to know who that someone is. This may be just the tip of the iceberg.'[22]

But Courtney was more concerned about the political consequences. Two days later he visited the Conservative Party leader Edward Heath at his set at the Albany, Piccadilly. The chief whip, William Whitelaw, joined them and counselled his backbencher to be silent. Heath was characteristically cold and the shadow of the Profumo scandal hung over the meeting. In headlining the broadsheet 'I'm not a Profumo but...', the KGB had carefully focused on how to implement maximum political damage.

Despite the risks involved, Courtney decided to proceed with a business trip to Moscow to show the Soviets he was not going to be intimidated. But his hopes were dashed later that afternoon when the MI5 officer 'Soames' visited him at his London flat to brief him on the inquiry. As he was leaning on the piano, he told the MP: 'The last time I saw you I said that there would be no risk to your personal safety if you continue with your intention to visit Moscow. I am afraid that I must withdraw what I said then. It is no longer safe for you to go to Moscow.'[23]

The next morning Courtney was summoned to 10 Downing Street by Wigg, who confirmed MI5's advice: 'Our strong advice to you is not to go to Moscow in the present circumstances.'

In fact, Courtney had already decided to put the journey off. He believed there was a connection between the timing of the smear broadsheet's release and his planned trip to Moscow.

'I believe that had I in fact gone to Moscow, as I had intended, I should have been arrested and used as a hostage in an exchange to enable George Blake [a KGB agent in jail in the UK] to return to the Soviet Union.'

Meanwhile, the KGB dossier had inflicted the intended political damage. The Conservative Party leaders were determined to avoid another Profumo-type scandal, which had brought down their government just the year before. On 6 October 1965, Courtney had lunch with Jack Shrimpton, chairman of Harrow East Conservatives, who told him that constituency officers were turning against him. 'The possibility of your resignation has been discussed', he said.

Even worse, the newspapers now believed the photographs were genuine. On 14 October 1965, Peter Gladstone-Smith, a *Sunday Telegraph* reporter, met Courtney in the Commons.

'There is a rumour going around Fleet Street that your wife is filing for divorce based on information given to her by the Soviets', he told the MP.

Sensing that the game was up, Courtney agreed to help Gladstone-Smith with his enquiries, but only if the *Sunday Telegraph* allowed him to read the first draft of the article before publication.

A deal was done and three days later the *Sunday Telegraph* published a story which discussed the possibility of Courtney's arrest for espionage in Moscow and mentioned the bugging of his hotel room, under the sympathetic headline 'My Fight Against a Soviet Smear'. This was followed by a well-informed and hostile article in *Private Eye*, which revealed the more salacious aspects of the scandal, notably the photographs, using the apt headline 'Under Plain Cover'.

It has long been speculated that *Private Eye* was the recipient of anonymous intelligence leaks, notably from MI5, and former *Eye* journalist Patrick Marnham recalls seeing 'Secret Service Information Packs' arrive at their Soho office.[24] It was the only story that Richard Ingrams, then editor of *Private Eye*, regretted in his entire twenty-three years as editor.

'After Courtney was photographed in bed with a woman in Moscow, the KGB circulated the [Courtney] pictures to various newspapers like the *News of the World*', he recalled. 'The fact this happened was mentioned in *Private Eye*... That was a clear case where we were wrong to do what we did since we were really playing the KGB game.'[25]

When I asked Ingrams in 2021 about the source of the Courtney story, he could not remember who wrote the article and the *Eye* does not keep archives identifying anonymous authors.

Five days later the Soviet Union newspaper *Izvestia*, which claimed to be only 'gently guided' by the Kremlin but in fact was a propaganda sheet, published an equally detailed story about Courtney. It claimed that the MP had the same weak character as Profumo and the photographs were distributed by his political and commercial enemies. The article was dismissive of the honey trap claim: 'If there was a trap, why did the Russian government decline to issue Courtney with a visa?' In fact, he had already received a visa.

By now the MP's world was falling apart. His consultancy business had collapsed, his wife threatened divorce proceedings and his political career was in peril.

'The Russians knew that I had for years accepted the risk that my business might be brought to a standstill overnight should I incur their displeasure – and this had now taken place', Courtney added.[26] It was open season.

Whatever the outcome, the seeds of doubt about the MP had been planted and the KGB operation – codenamed Operation PROBA – was deemed a success. The KGB's aim, of course, was to remove their arch critic as an MP. On 17 November 1965, Courtney was summoned to a meeting of Harrow East Conservatives officers. They listened to Courtney's side of the story attentively and asked questions politely. But they believed he had been irreparably damaged. The chairman, Theo Constantine, who had received the smear sheet, described it as 'political dynamite' and accused him of being a compulsive womaniser.

'It is our opinion that we cannot win an election in Harrow East in the present conditions with you as the candidate', he told him.

Courtney refused to stand down but did not help himself by flying off in his private aircraft for a two-week holiday in Las Palmas in the Canary Islands, while his political enemies in Harrow were conspiring against him. On his return the MP introduced yet another bill in the Commons to curb diplomatic immunity, citing the KGB's abuses of the system. But Harrow East Conservatives were not impressed and one official hinted darkly at 'further revelations' to come at election time. They passed a resolution that forced the MP to seek reselection and other candidates were invited to stand against him.

At a packed meeting on 21 February 1966, at Harrow Grammar School, Courtney's opponents focused on his 'moral character'. But he retained some support. One Young Conservative said he had been a good MP and he did not care if he slept with the entire Bolshoi ballet, as long as he served his constituents. The shadow of the KGB dossier hung over the proceedings and Courtney argued that the real issue was whether a foreign power should dictate to the electors of Harrow East. It was a persuasive argument and Courtney survived with a vote of 454 to 277 in his favour.

It was a pyrrhic victory. The MP had been abandoned by his party, his government and MI5. There was a half-hearted verbal protest by a Foreign Office official at the Soviet embassy in London. But it was too little, too late. The perception of scandal and the divisive rancour had inflicted political wounds. At the general election campaign six weeks later, Courtney's share of the vote collapsed and he lost his seat by just 378 votes after two recounts.

Within two months Courtney's wife Elizabeth launched a second divorce petition (she had withdrawn her original case). This time she accused the former MP of committing adultery in Westminster with a lady called Mrs Barbara Fane and did not cite Zina Volkova. The irony of this saga is that Elizabeth knew about his past relationship with Volkova, met and liked her and even invited the Russian femme fatale to a summer holiday in England. But Volkova never responded to the invitation. Courtney did not contest the adultery allegation and both husband and wife admitted to extra-marital affairs.

The KGB had their scalp. It was a ruthless operation. As the KGB file on PROBA later revealed in the Mitrokhin archive, the motive was not just to remove Courtney as a political enemy and MP but to destroy his business and marriage.

'We did a Profumo on him', a former GRU officer now based in London told me. 'Usually we would have blackmailed him privately but Courtney was an exception because he was so vocal against the Soviet Union and so needed to be removed. It was very effective.'

Courtney remarried, left the political arena and returned to business. Soon after the election he wrote to the prime minister and asked for advice regarding the resumption of his trips to the Soviet Union. MI5 was consulted and wrote to the Home Office permanent secretary Sir Charles Cunningham:

> There is no intelligence available about the intentions of the Soviet Union or any other Communist country towards Commander Courtney, and it is arguable that the Governments concerned would think it unwise to harass him further. On the other hand, it is known that he has been under suspicion of being a British Intelligence agent and, having regard to his previous career in Naval Intelligence, it would not be difficult for them to fabricate a colourful case against him.

MI5 concluded that Courtney should not visit the Soviet Union or Eastern Europe, and advised the Home Office to convey this view orally and not in writing. It was another victory for the KGB.

Unperturbed, Courtney continued to protest about how the KGB abused their diplomatic privileges. And five years later, in September 1971, he was vindicated when 105 Soviet 'diplomats' were expelled from the UK for espionage and for doing precisely what Courtney had been complaining about while he was an MP.

The former naval commander remained a vociferous critic of the KGB until he died in 1988, aged seventy-nine. But he retained a sense of humour and in retirement offered some advice to British businessmen travelling to Moscow during the Cold War.

'Beware Russian women knocking on your hotel door who will be only too anxious to give you a real socialist "good time"', he told his audience. 'I have had some experience and perhaps inevitably I have been accused of seeing "Reds under the Bed". Well, I had one in mine and the repercussions ever since have taught me that it simply isn't worth it.'[27]

*

At the height of the Courtney affair on 19 October 1965, MI5's director-general Roger Hollis and his colleagues met at their head office on Curzon Street, Mayfair, to discuss the implications of the phrase 'To be continued...' at the foot of the infamous broadsheet. Did it mean that other KGB critics would receive similar treatment in the near future? Hollis disagreed.

'If the KGB had compromising information which they wanted to use to bring pressure upon an important agent or potential agent, they would be more likely to do this by a direct threat to that agent', he wrote to the cabinet secretary, Burke Trend, the next day.[28]

The consensus inside the secret state was the KGB had regarded Courtney as an MI6 agent since the early 1950s and had tried to recruit him by using several East European swallows to entrap him. They failed, which is why MI5's report on Courtney concluded: 'He is not a hostile agent.' And so the KGB's Plan B was to distribute the compromising photographs and broadsheet, and hence destroy the MP's career and remove him as someone who could jeopardise their espionage operations based at the Soviet embassy in London. It was a warning to Courtney: 'Shut up or we will reveal more secrets about you.'

The meaning of the phrase 'To be continued...' may never be known. The KGB officer who wrote that line is probably dead, but the message was unmistakable. If you criticise the Soviet Union, we will destroy your political career, marriage and livelihood. As George Wigg told Courtney, the smearing and honey trapping of the KGB's most outspoken critic was a strategic weapon during the Cold War. The operation against the MP was in fact an implicit threat against all critics of the Soviet Union and a warning shot: if you take on the Kremlin, the KGB will bring you down.

6

ALL ABOUT EVE

It appears that this Club is a sort of sub-department of the Foreign Office

Sir Laurence Dunne, Chief Metropolitan Magistrate,
Bow Street Court, 14 September 1954

IT IS 11 P.M. IN A spacious dimly-lit basement nightclub just off Regent Street, sometime in 1958. Decorated extravagantly as the first earthly paradise by being hung with vines and what looked like the foliage of a metallic banana plantation, the Eve Club's lights are blue, red and purple but low key. The stage show takes place on an illuminated glass floor where exotic half-naked women in outlandish headdresses dance to cabaret numbers like 'Fantasy in the Jungle' or slow routines. In the crimson velvet-lined booths, the hostesses smile obligingly and murmur interest in the gentlemen clients' conversation, however slurred and familiar it may be, as they drink Bollinger 66 champagne and smoke Pall Mall cigarettes.

But this is no ordinary private club. In one plush upholstered corner, you can see Earl Jellicoe, a former MI6 officer and later leader of the House of Lords, with a fellow aristocrat. At another table there is a QC in conversation with an MP or an ambassador. And in a more discreet booth you will find KGB, Czech and Romanian intelligence officers talking in hushed tones while being discreetly observed by an MI5 officer pretending to be a businessman with an expense account.

Presiding over this unique den of political, sexual and espionage intrigue is the eagle-eyed, diminutive, vivacious, blonde figure of the joint owner, Helen O'Brien. As she sits at Table One, as it was known, chain smoking a black, gold-tipped Balkan Sobranie cigarette and sipping a glass of Drappier champagne, she is not just checking that her young girls are not being harassed by the middle-aged men. She is scrutinising the faces, comments and behaviour of her members, especially the spies or 'diplomats' as they describe themselves on their application forms. She does not trust many people and has a cutting wit with a sharp tongue.

'Don't insult my intelligence', she would remark, if a member made an unreasonable request.

The KGB officers, posing as bankers, and their fellow spies from Romania, East Germany and Czechoslovakia enjoy the company of the young hostesses, the exotic cocktails and the innovative floor shows. But they also relish the discretion and secrecy. Unlike other clubs, photographers and journalists are banned and new members are carefully vetted. For intelligence-gathering and networking it is the perfect venue for observing and perhaps even compromising leading members of the British Establishment. Three years earlier, Sir Laurence Dunne, the chief metropolitan magistrate of London, presided over a hearing in Bow Street Court to decide whether the Eve Club was serving alcohol after hours. As he read through the list of members, Sir Laurence, who had overseen a court hearing involving the infamous atomic spy Klaus Fuchs, raised his eyebrows several times. He paused and commented, 'This [club] appears to be a sort of sub-department of the Foreign Office' and dismissed the case.

The membership list was of great interest to the KGB. It included nine MPs, twelve ambassadors, thirty diplomats, Earl Jellicoe (later leader of the House of Lords), five QCs, two Romanian diplomats and seventy titled Englishmen, including the Duke of Devonshire, the Duke of Rutland and the Duke of Norfolk. Perhaps the most intriguing member was John Profumo, a Conservative MP and then a Foreign Office minister, who held his stag night at the club in December 1954. He later became the war secretary and was embroiled in a notorious security scandal after having an affair with Christine Keeler, who was sleeping with a KGB officer at the same time.

The magistrate's comment attracted the KGB's attention and the Eve Club became a late-night den of espionage which lasted throughout the Cold War. But what they did not realise was that the charismatic, acerbic Helen O'Brien spoke fluent Russian, Romanian and French and was in fact a registered MI5 agent and informant, who was determined to discover the KGB's deepest secrets and counter their operations.

*

Helen O'Brien was not even her real name. She was born Elena Constaninescu in Romania, on 14 December 1925, into a family of landowners. Her mother was a duchess of German origin who had left Russia before the revolution. Her father was an engineer who also cultivated the family farm. She was educated at a German school where she developed a gift for languages. As a teenager during the Second World War, Elena was a wilful, fearless child. She lived in the rural village of Barcanesti, where she learned riding tricks from Cossack prisoners-of-war when Romania was allied with Germany. On one occasion she travelled to the port of Constanza and found herself on a German ammunition train. In 1943, aged eighteen, she landed in a village with a German officer in a Fieseler Storch aircraft – the first plane seen in the region. But Elena also lived under the shadow of the invading Red Army and a year later she escaped on the king's racehorse from the marauding Russian cavalry, after Romania switched sides.

'They were shooting away but they were on half-starved nags', she recalled.[1]

The Russians then confiscated Elena's horse and that started a lifelong hatred for the Soviet Union. After the war her family's affluent ancestry was unacceptable in the new Communist Romania. Her parents were arrested and investigated but survived. Her father was not jailed because he convinced the authorities that he could invent a device which would extract gas from the Danube. Elena's elegant mother destroyed all evidence of her aristocratic origins, apart from a handkerchief with the family heraldic emblem. But she was still taken to the police station, where a military officer leaned menacingly towards her and shouted: 'Are you a Countess?'

Elena's mother believed she would be given a life sentence, perhaps even shot, and so she decided to depart the world with dignity. 'Young man, if you want me to answer your questions, take your hands out of your pockets, tuck in your tunic and be respectful', she replied.

'Are you a Countess?', the officer yelled again.

'No, no, no, I am a Duchess', she responded.

Furious, the lieutenant rushed into his office, slammed the door and told his subordinate: 'She's crazy. Let her go. She thinks she is a Princess.'[2]

Many families were jailed and died in prison when Romania became a Communist country but Elena's parents survived, despite their land being confiscated. It was an uncertain time for Elena. Romania was still under Soviet occupation when she married a young RAF officer called Kenneth Archer. But the marriage ended abruptly when a drunken batman fired a gun through the door of their room and hit her husband. The bullet ripped his body apart and then the man burst through the door with the gun.

'Are you going to kill me?', she shouted. 'Go on then, kill me.'

The man was ashamed but the Romanian authorities were not sympathetic to her situation. She was told to leave the country or renounce her British citizenship, so she decided to leave. She

Vladimir Putin while he was a KGB officer stationed in East Germany in the 1980s. He was an intelligence officer between 1975 and 1991. 'What amazed me most of all was how one man's effort could achieve what whole armies could not,' he later reflected. 'One spy could decide the fate of thousands of people.'

Former head of the Ukraine intelligence agency, Valentyn Nalyvaichenko, for nearly five years. He oversaw investigations into how the FSB infiltrated and recruited agents in Ukraine well before the 2022 invasion, sometimes using kompromat.

Soviet agent Hans Peter Smolka in a London park in 1937. As head of the Russia section of the Ministry of Information during the Second World War, he was instrumental in promoting Soviet propaganda. His controller in London was Kim Philby.

The ultimate agent of influence Victor Louis. On the surface he was a well-connected Soviet foreign correspondent sending dispatches from Moscow to British and American newspapers. In reality, he was used by the KGB to smear dissidents and critics.

The press baron Robert Maxwell with Soviet premier Leonid Brezhnev in the Kremlin in 1978. The former owner of the *Daily Mirror* and *New York Daily News*, Maxwell was a KGB agent. His company Pergamon was paid by the KGB to publish sycophantic biographies of Soviet and Communist leaders.

KGB spy Oleg Lyalin at a drinks party in London in 1969. By day he was a clothes importer, by night he devised sabotage operations to spread turmoil in the UK. But two years later he defected to the West and his disclosures resulted in 105 KGB spies being expelled from London.

Former KGB officer and disinformation specialist Vassily Sitnikov, chief of the American desk at the height of the Cold War. He was the secret author of *A Study of a Master Spy*, an attack on former CIA director Allen Dulles – published under his KGB pseudonym 'Kenneth Dunne'.

Above: Conservative MP Anthony Courtney on the campaign trail in 1959. A relentless critic of the Soviet Union and its intelligence operations, he faced retaliation from the KGB. They deployed a female agent to honey trap the MP in a Moscow hotel while they took photographs. British politicians and journalists later received the pictures anonymously.

Right: KGB operative Zina Volkova, tasked with seducing Courtney at Moscow's National Hotel in 1961. She was a travel guide working for Intourist, a travel agency in Moscow notorious for being a branch of the KGB during the Cold War.

Helen O'Brien who was recruited by MI5 to spy on East European intelligence officers when they frequented her exclusive Piccadilly nightclub. The KGB never knew that she spoke Russian and reported back to her controllers in a Hampstead safe house the next day.

Former MI5 officer Charles Elwell with his wife Anne at a wedding in London in 1960. Regarded as the most effective counter-intelligence officer during the Cold War who investigated KGB spy rings in the UK, Elwell was Helen O'Brien's controller.

US National Security Adviser Zbigniew Brzezinski with President Carter in the White Office in January 1977. Brzezinski was an articulate and ardent critic of the Soviet Union. In retribution, the KGB fabricated a government document in which he advocated regime change in Poland.

This leaflet falsely claimed that Brzezinski was secretly anti-Semitic and bribed by Arabs. Officially it was written and distributed by the Jewish Defence League in New York City in 1978, but it was made by the KGB.

Senator Henry Jackson with the Soviet dissident Alexander Solzhenitsyn. The Soviets regarded the Senator as their arch-enemy and tried to find compromising information about his personal life. When they found nothing, the KGB forged an FBI memo, alleging that Jackson was a member of a secret gay club.

Henry Wallace, the Democratic US Vice President between 1940 and 1944. A year later, while Commerce Secretary, he met with Soviet intelligence officers and discussed the possibility of his presidential campaign being financed by the Kremlin. In 1948 he stood unsuccessfully as the Progressive Party candidate.

Democratic Vice-President Hubert Humphrey on the campaign trail against Richard Nixon in 1968. The Soviet ambassador Anatoly Dobrynin offered Humphrey secret funding and assistance from Moscow for his presidential campaign. He declined.

The KGB's country house Seacox Heath, a nineteenth-century four-storey castle near Tunbridge Wells which boasts mock-Gothic turrets and terraced lawns. To this day the property is used as a weekend retreat by Russian spies.

Here in the Brompton Oratory in Knightsbridge, KGB agents hid secret documents and film cassettes wrapped in newspapers. These items were placed behind the right hand of the two columns to the left of the altar, their dead letter box of choice.

packed some ikons and jewels that her mother had brought from Russia before the revolution and fled to London.[3]

It was 1947. London was cold and polluted and rationing was still in place. But the 22-year-old Elena had a confident manner, a showgirl's figure and a head for numbers. She found a job as a dancer and cigarette girl at the Paradise Club on Regent Street and then at Murray's Cabaret Club on Beak Street, Soho. A private members' club, Murray's was renowned for the hostesses being scantily clad and for later employing Christine Keeler. Described as a 'visual brothel', it was not the job that Elena had envisaged. But she found the club scene exciting and met and fell in love with the handsome general manager, Jimmy O'Brien.

The couple dreamed of owning their own club. The opportunity came when a large basement at 189 Regent Street, Piccadilly, modelled on the first-class passenger desk of an ocean liner, became available. O'Brien secured a bank loan and the Eve Club opened on a packed Valentine's night in 1953. The staircase led members to the lower ground floor and down a long corridor to the reception area, where they were greeted by a tall, imposing gold statue of a naked young woman. The clients were then escorted by the cigarette girls to select tables or booths with red plush lampshades, where they would be offered Bollinger 66 champagne, vodka or gin and tonic. The hostesses could only drink champagne or fruit juice. As membership was a guinea a year the club was beyond licensing laws and so it was open until 3 a.m.

Elena conceived the club as a 'journey into fantasy' and there was a mysterious as well as a glamorous atmosphere. She was inspired by Aldous Huxley's *Brave New World*, *Doors of Perception* and *Heaven and Hell* and created a mood between a nightmare and a dream. On stage the stunning showgirls wore fig leaves and outrageous headdresses, often with masks on their faces, accompanied by calypso music. The Folies Bergère-quality floor show often resembled musical theatre, notably a performance called 'The Temptresses of History'. There were magicians and a juggler, although he was renowned for how many items he dropped.

But there were also darker avant-garde performances, notably 'Astrological Witchcraft' based on Goethe's ballad. In 1953 it was the most daring show in the West End.

The Eve Club was celebrated for its style but also its discretion and exclusivity. There was no sign outside the entrance. Elena operated a tough staff selection policy, interviewing 100 hopefuls to find one hostess, who needed to be 'just perfect'. Christine Keeler applied and failed the audition.

'She wasn't suitable', recalled Elena. 'She was too young and I felt lacked the *savoir-faire* that was required. I also felt she was an easily-led girl – and I was proved right.'[4]

The convention was that men bought drinks for the girls. But unlike similar clubs, there was no ban on the girls going home with the customers afterwards.

'It was a great aphrodisiac. Of course, there was sex, but not on the premises', Elena added. 'We were not a whorehouse. But if a girl and a client wanted to begin a relationship beyond the club, we knew nothing about it.'[5]

Some eminent Establishment figures frequented the club undercover. One member signed in as 'G. D. Savage', but in reality he was the bishop of Southwell. A gentle, generous man, the bishop spent most nights at Eve's, drank two gin and tonics and bought the girls perfume and cigarettes.

'I must confess, I am a great sinner', he told Elena. 'I like women.'

But he then fell in love with one of the topless dancers, who was appropriately named Amanda Lovejoy, and was later forced to resign as a priest.

The subterranean atmosphere was completed by the office being situated in another basement below the lower ground floor. It was here that Elena sat down and read through *Who's Who* and *Debrett's* to find the names and addresses of potential new members. She wanted respected Establishment figures and chose aristocrats. The Duke of Bedford and Michael Bowes-Lyon, nephew of the Queen Mother, joined and so did lords Samuel, Anson and Ulick Browne and the earls of Dudley and Jellicoe. She was amused to notice that under the heading 'occupation' in the application form, they wrote 'Gentleman'. Like many East Europeans, she loved old-fashioned English society and the landed gentry. 'What is a gentleman without his Prairie Oyster?', she asked a bemused member.

The political classes joined, including Foreign Office ministers, peers and MPs. The banker Evelyn de Rothschild, the press baron Jocelyn Stevens and businessman Greville Wynne, later recruited by MI6, became members. And so did celebrities like Frank Sinatra, Errol Flynn, Judy Garland and the international jet set. The leaked membership list included the Greek shipping magnate Aristotle Onassis, two sultans, nine maharajahs and even the King of Nepal. It was the club to frequent late at night without the unwanted attention of the paparazzi, and Elena was delighted that on the evening after Queen Elizabeth II was crowned in 1953, all the European aristocrats who attended took taxis for cocktails at Eve's.

By 1955 the club was thriving, Elena and her co-owner Jimmy were married, and the charismatic owner had changed her name to Helen O'Brien. But despite its exotic, semi-erotic floor show and aristocratic members, the atmosphere in the club reflected her Central European roots. It was as if the place operated in a frontier city of the Cold War, with its discreet purple-lit sign outside, reminiscent of Vienna nightlife, where Harry Lime would have dropped by for cocktails in a scene from *The Third Man*. If the club had not existed, Graham Greene would have created it.[6]

Helen's only disappointment was that she could not obtain a visa for her parents to move to London. It was this frustration that resulted in her entry into the world of spies and espionage. She bombarded the Romanian government and its embassy in London with letters pleading for a visa and even sent a telegram to President Ceausescu. But it was all to no avail. Then on 14 November 1957, Colonel M. V. Gavrilovich, a military attaché at the Romanian embassy in London, walked into the club and asked to become a member. After checking him out, Gavrilovich was accepted and later returned to have dinner. Helen was fascinated by his presence, although she pretended not to notice him. The colonel and his wife did not touch their dinner of turtle soup and Tournedos Rossini but invited Helen to their table.

'Please sit down and drink something with us', said the Romanian diplomat. 'We have to make friends. You need friends from your own country, right? Do you have relatives in your own country?'

'Yes, my parents', replied Helen.

'Have you been to see them?'

'I can't. I've got work to do here and I have a baby to look after.'

Gavrilovich invited Helen to a reception at the Romanian embassy on Belgrave Square on 30 December 1957. She accepted and wore her mother's jewels and drank Romanian Riesling wine. The attentive colonel promised to send more bottles of wine to the club.

'This will symbolise our new friendship', he said.

'I would like to send my mother a birthday present but the customs duties on some items are so high', remarked Helen.

'Prepare the gift but make sure it is not bigger than a bottle of wine', he replied quickly. 'I will take care of it personally.'

As Helen drove home with her husband in their black-and-white Bedford to their house on Frognal Way, Hampstead, she was happy. She felt that finally the Iron Curtain was opening and she would see her parents.

'Everything will work out the way I wanted', she said.

'Are you sure?', he replied.

'I'll make sure everything goes my way.'

Two days later Helen was at home washing her hair when the phone rang. It was Colonel Gavrilovich.

'Is the package ready?', he asked.

'Yes', she replied.

'Good, please come to my house at 41 Cadogan Square at 4 p.m', he said.

Helen arrived at the Belgravia mansion on time, where they had tea alone. 'It's great, of course, to send a package', she said. 'But it would be more wonderful if I could have my parents here.'

'Hard, very hard', replied the colonel. 'But, as friends, we can try. I know someone who could help you. He might be coming to London soon. Would you like me to introduce him and the three of us can have a chat? You will need to make friends with him as well.'

Helen was delighted and a few days later she was invited by Gavrilovich to dinner at The Trojan Horse, a Greek restaurant. When she arrived, both men were waiting outside and she was introduced to the new 'friend', a short man with a military presence who appeared to be Russian. His name was 'Mr Pierre'. It was a fake name. His real name was Ganciu.

'Let's go', he said impatiently. 'I know a place where we can talk quietly.'

'Who are the two men in raincoats on the street corner?', she asked. Pierre did not respond but seemed anxious. They jumped in the car and Helen noticed that the two men were following them.

'Drive fast', she shouted. Helen persuaded her new 'friends' to drive to the Eve Club, where they could talk in her office in the sub-basement. There they would not be disturbed or over-heard.

On arrival, Pierre launched into a monologue about collaboration and friendship. 'You have been recommended', he said. 'I can help you, especially as by chance I was friendly with your parents.' He then produced a photograph of her parents sitting with him on a park bench. Helen was shocked but pleased. Pierre then ripped off the section of the picture where he appeared. 'I don't think you want to keep that part', he said. 'Let's meet again tomorrow and I will bring six bottles of Romanian wine.'

Helen agreed but she was worried. After showing the two men out through the back door of the club, she discussed their approach late into the night with her husband. They both felt threatened. 'They are like invisible monsters lurking in our shadows', she said. *They must be spies*, she thought. *But what action do I take? Tell someone. But who? Should I tell the secret services? But how do I*

find out who I need to talk to? Helen was anxious and nervous but
decided to wait and see what transpired.

'I will accept gifts and, if necessary, give inconsequential information but I will not disclose information that exposes me to being
blackmailed', she told her husband, 'I'm not going to lose hope but
I will do my best to look naive and vulnerable.'

The next evening at 10.30 p.m. Pierre returned to the club, armed
with the six bottles of wine. He then lit a cigarette and asked her
several questions. How did you get to England? What was your
attitude towards the UK? Do you know other Romanians who
have come to England? And then the leading question that revealed
his secret agenda.

'A friend needs the help of another friend but she must agree
to certain rules', he said. 'The first of these rules is that the friend
should not criticise the Soviet Union or Soviet satellite policies
because that would almost certainly amount to betrayal. If I was
in the presence of someone who made negative statements about
the Soviet Union, I would have to change the subject.'

Pierre repeatedly mentioned collaboration, friendship and
loyalty. 'Oh, by the way, have you had any trouble with the police
or been investigated?', he asked.

'No, I have had no problem', replied Helen.

'Very well', said Pierre, who had just smoked a whole pack of
cigarettes, 'The prospects are good. I think we can help each
other.' It was 3.30 a.m. Pierre had been sitting in Helen's basement
office for five hours. She escorted him quietly through the back
door and he disappeared into Regent Street and the pale light of
dawn.

After the late-night meeting Helen was confused. Her hopes
were mixed with fear. It was clear that Pierre was a Soviet bloc
spy, and it was no secret that Eastern bloc intelligence officers act
on the direct instructions of the KGB. And so she could be in
trouble with the UK authorities for consorting with an enemy
agent. I need advice, she thought. Someone I can trust. Six weeks
went by and her anxiety levels were running high. She needed

proof he was a Romanian spy and so she decided to record her next meeting with Pierre. When he called and said he would be at the club at 11.20 p.m. the next day, she was ready. She gathered all the microphones, cables and wires used by her performers – working or defective – and placed them on the coffee table, and then connected one of the microphones to a cassette recorder underneath.

By now Helen was keen to know about the plan for her parents to move to England.

'My proposal is to bring your mother to Vienna for ten days', said Pierre. 'You want to see your mother, don't you?'

'No, I don't want to see her in those circumstances', she replied.

At that moment there was a squeak from just beyond the door. The sound was from an eccentric musician who was playing a single string violin made from a matchbox! It was excruciating.

'So, you don't want to see her', said Pierre.

'No, I want both of my parents to come and live with me in London', said an irritated Helen. 'My Mum is old and sick and so why take her to Vienna?'

Helen was then unnerved when she heard the violinist rehearse 'The Teddy Bear's Picnic'. She was worried that the sound would suppress the voices on the tape. Worse, the cassette only had a few minutes to go. She would be in trouble if Pierre heard the inevitable click of the recorder. *I have to get him out fast*, she thought.

But then Pierre said: 'You told me your brother was a sailor. We know he was a general in the Italian navy and had an important function.'

'I told you he was a sailor because that's his job', she replied curtly. 'I don't think it is that important.'

At that moment the stage show started and Pierre agreed to enter the club upstairs. Over a smoked salmon dinner, the Romanian spy enthusiastically applauded the violinist with one string. But he frowned sternly when the dancers with naked breasts and with enormous ornaments on their heads performed. Clearly, it was conclusive evidence of the decadence of Western capitalism!

Pierre and Helen then resumed their conversation. 'What I was trying to tell you is that we could jeopardise your brother's situation', he said. 'We might even, if need be...'

'Very well', interrupted Helen, implying that she would help him. Pierre then peppered her with questions about the club's members. What kind of people were they?, he asked. She briefed him in general terms without providing details and he left.[7]

In the ensuing weeks, Helen was increasingly worried about her conversations with Pierre. She felt she had been inadvertently sucked into a web of espionage. Could she be pressurised, or worse, blackmailed? But then in October 1958, she received a brown envelope at her Hampstead house that alleviated her anxieties. When she nervously opened the package, there was another smaller envelope marked 'Strictly Secret'. Inside was a letter from Room 055 in the Ministry of Defence.

'We believe that you have information of possible interest', stated the letter. 'Would you be so kind enough to come to the War Office for a talk?'

Based at the Old War Office building on Whitehall, Room 055 was the secret address used by MI5 to interview and recruit new officers and agents. 'Thank God', sighed Helen when she read the letter. She called the number immediately and within days presented herself at the Ministry of Defence, where she was led to Room 055 and greeted by a secretary who looked more like Miss Marple than Miss Moneypenny. She was then introduced to the formidable MI5 officer Charles Elwell. Sharp-witted and single-minded, with a direct manner and a passion for classical music, Elwell was one of the most effective counter-intelligence officers during the Cold War against the KGB. He later led the MI5 investigations into the Portland spy ring, when two civil servants supplied sensitive Royal Navy and NATO secrets to the KGB.

'Take a seat, please', said Elwell, smiling and wearing a pin-striped suit. 'I would like to ask you a few questions. Of course, you are perfectly free to answer or not. It is up to you to choose.'

'I will answer any question', replied Helen.

'We would like you to explain your friendship with the Romanian Embassy.'

'I am not sure it was friendship.'

'Would you like to clear it up?'

'There was pressure on me. I was being blackmailed. I tried to defend myself as best as I could but I felt lonely and defenceless. I've been waiting a long time for you to come to my aid.'

'Well, now I am here', said Elwell, pleasantly surprised.

Helen was delighted by the MI5 approach. In essence, she was told: 'You can work for us or the Communists.' It was an easy decision. A fervent anti-Communist, she despised the Soviet Union and their satellite states, especially Romania, where the state had seized her family's property. 'You have twenty-four hours to leave your house', her parents were told. She wanted to do everything to prevent the spread of Communism in England. And so the West End nightclub owner became an MI5 agent and informant, but not a paid intelligence officer.

From that moment the Eve Club became a focal point for late-night spying on KGB agents in London. Helen hired a Russian-speaking manager and every time Soviet or Eastern bloc diplomats or businessmen visited the club as members or guests, they would be under surreptitious surveillance. The next day Helen would telephone Elwell or one of her assigned MI5 handlers, and they met at the club or an MI5 safe house, where she disclosed their names, addresses, financial details and habits. The hostesses were trained to chat up the Russian clients, gleaning information, sometimes unwittingly, when the inebriated punters whispered comments as they slipped a five-pound note into their handbags. Some girls even learned a few words of Russian.

For Helen, the only disappointing aspect of being an MI5 agent was that her friendships or relationships with all fellow Romanians in London stopped. 'You never know who you are dealing with', Elwell told her. It was upsetting for Helen to turn her back on her compatriots. But she wanted to help and, besides, it was exciting to be 'on the inside' and meet real-life James Bonds, although their appearance rarely matched that of Sean Connery. Her work for 'the department', as she called it, involved mainly identifying KGB and Soviet bloc intelligence officers.

One afternoon Elwell met Helen at an MI5 safe house in north London and she revealed her conversations with 'Pierre', the Romanian spy. MI5 was desperate for a positive identification for surveillance purposes. After looking through several photo albums, she found Pierre. Elwell was ecstatic. He abandoned his English reserve and his eyes lit up like a Christmas tree. Later, they met in the Queen Mary garden in Hampstead while Helen was playing with her daughter. As they walked through the garden, she quietly gave him the tape of her conversation with Pierre and explained the circumstances of its recording. The seasoned MI5 officer was surprised but happy. 'You are a great spy. Bravo', he laughed, almost shouting.

On her way home Helen's young daughter asked: 'Who was the man in the park?' As he was carrying a large diplomatic bag, this inspired her.

'He was a doctor', she replied.[8]

When surveying the nocturnal habits of spies posing as diplomats in her club, Helen did not distinguish between the KGB and Eastern bloc operatives. Indeed, she regarded spies from Romania, Czechoslovakia, East Germany and Bulgaria as 'dangerous nephews of the KGB'. Her assessment was accurate. The security services behind the Iron Curtain were appendages of Soviet foreign policy. Any covert action in the UK needed to be authorised by the KGB 'advisers'. 'These services are subordinated formally to their governments but they are directed mainly by the KGB', said Ladislav Bittman, who defected in 1968. 'Russian advisors influence the planning of each operation and assess the results. No important decision is made without them.'[9]

The Czech intelligence officers were subservient to the KGB, according to defectors. But they were more operational on the streets of London because MI5 had identified so many KGB officers. And so the Eve Club became a natural magnet for intelligence-gathering. On 30 December 1965, a 43-year-old Czech spy, Josef Piskula, became a member and visited the club several times throughout 1966 and 1967. He was usually accompanied by Josef Frolik, a handsome 37-year-old Czech counter-intelligence officer, and Tom Dunley, a talkative English businessman and club member who also secretly reported to MI5. As soon as Helen met the Czechs, she clocked them as KGB agents and called Charles Elwell. And she was correct.

Codenamed 'Petran', Piskula was a spy working undercover as a commercial attaché based at the Czech embassy and a flat at 6 Upper Belgrave Street. His main task was to handle Ernest Fernyhough, a Labour MP and parliamentary private secretary to the prime minister, Harold Wilson, between 1964 and 1967. Codenamed 'Koza', Fernyhough also reported to the KGB and provided intelligence on the prime minister's private telephone conversations with President Johnson on Vietnam and the devaluation of the pound. The Czechs and the KGB had a spy inside 10 Downing Street. The KGB then suspected that Fernyhough was informing the government about their clandestine meetings and ended their six-year association. But Piskula retained the MP's services and lavished him with gifts, mainly chocolates and free holidays to Czechoslovakia, until he was recalled to Prague in 1967.[10]

The charismatic Frolik continued his visits to the Eve Club, although mainly to seduce women he thought could be connected to the government. In fact, he was so successful that his Czech spymasters gave him a monthly quota of ladies with Whitehall or parliamentary jobs. He was required to sleep with them in order to obtain security secrets during pillow talk. His controller was unforgiving when the Czech spy explained that the daughter of a former prime minister was gay and so seduction would be fruitless. In 1969 Frolik defected and disclosed details of how MPs and trade union leaders were recruited as Soviet agents of influence. Years later, Frolik was asked by the BBC where spies meet when they are in London. 'At the Eve Club', he replied instantly.[11]

By the late 1960s, KGB operations in London were at full throttle. As the Foreign Office had granted diplomatic privileges and immunity to all staff at the Soviet embassy, it was easier for the KGB to function. They had more agents in place than in any other period of the Cold War and MI5 were struggling to cope. For Russian spies, the Eve Club had an intoxicating atmosphere and they felt comfortable because of the ban on photographers and journalists. They flocked to the club most evenings, while Helen scrutinised their every move and reported back to MI5 the next day or to undercover officers who sat with their backs to the walls while they nursed a weak gin and tonic.

As Helen could speak fluent Russian, her antennae were sharply tuned. One evening she noticed a heavy drinking Russian who made abusive comments about the British and used extremely vulgar expressions. Helen suspected that he was a KGB informant, not an officer. *How do I find out his real name?*, she thought. He had signed in but Helen was sure it was a false name. The opportunity came when he invited her for drinks. He got spectacularly drunk and consumed three bottles of Dom Perignon. He then muttered something about titanium, the precious metal used for explosives. This alarmed Helen, but then the orchestra played 'Moscow Nights' and the drunken Russian started singing loudly. *Now is my chance*, she thought. She asked for the bill and prayed that he would sign using his real name. Without any hesitation and while he kept singing he shouted: 'Give it here. I will sign. My signature will be honoured.' Success. Helen had discovered his real name. The combination of the champagne, the music, the girls and the atmosphere made the Russian forget his location and his sense of security. It was classic spycraft.

The identification of KGB officers was often a challenge for Helen. Of course, not every Russian sitting in the Eve Club was a spy. But she learned to read between the lines. MI5 always suspected that many employees of Moscow Narodny Bank Ltd were in fact connected to the KGB, and this was confirmed when some of its directors and officials were expelled from the UK in 1971.

Founded in 1919, the bank promoted and funded East–West trade, but it also facilitated illicit funding of the British Communist Party. And so many Moscow Narodny executives were under scrutiny. In April 1968, German Skobelkin, a director of the Moscow Narodny Bank, was accepted as a member of the Eve Club six days after his thirty-fourth birthday. Polite and sophisticated, he lived in a detached house in Robin Grove, Highgate, in north London suburbia, and when he signed his receipts at the club they were sent to the bank's head office at King William Street in the City.

The following year Skobelkin proposed his colleague Albert Voronin, forty-one, a vice president of Moscow Narodny Bank, and soon they arrived at the club with another banker called Vyacheslav Ryzhkov, a thirty-year-old former army officer who was an expert in foreign exchange, foreign loans and cash operations. Ryzhkov worked for Vneshtorgbank but was a close friend of Skobelkin as they lived next door to each other in Robin Grove. Helen liked these Russian bankers. They behaved impeccably, they were polite and one of them, Albas Khshtoyan, thirty-two, played the piano. But she noticed that Ryzhkov in particular spent vast sums of money at the club. On Valentine's night in 1970, he signed a cheque for £126 (£1,900 in 2022) without even glancing at the bill. Again the Moscow Narodny Bank settled the account.

While Helen passed on their names to MI5, she could not be sure these Russian bankers were intelligence officers, although she recalled that six years later Ryzhkov was named as a KGB agent in a BBC news report, after he was expelled from Singapore.[12]

*

By the early 1970s Helen's covert work for MI5 intensified and she was involved in more delicate and sensitive operations. She was aware that the Security Service was using her club to compromise KGB and Eastern bloc agents.

'I know that The Department [as she used to call MI5] bring people to Eve's as a honey pot to entrap people', she told a friend.

Her husband Jimmy was concerned about the pressure and MI5, in effect, recruiting the club's staff. But only two of the hostesses knew about Helen's secret relationship with MI5, whose officers authorised their role. One evening Helen was told to take a photograph of a suspected East German intelligence agent. But there was a problem. The club banned cameras. And so Pauline, one of the hostesses, agreed to snap a picture through a window using a flash, as soon the East German emerged from the bathroom. Helen's role was to sit on the ventilation basket with her dress high enough to show her legs and distract the suspected spy. The ruse worked perfectly and MI5 got their photograph.

The focus on secrecy resulted in Helen feeling increasingly insecure and frustrated about her role as the years went by. She found it difficult to lie to her two young daughters about her whereabouts during the day and who she was meeting.

'I could feel the uncertainty tormenting me', she recalled in her memoir, which was published in Romania but not in the UK. 'My suspicions and fears were torturing me. Doubts were emerging. Some operations failed, some ended abruptly. But I was doing everything in my power to help because I was so grateful to Britain which had given me the freedom to live and earn my own living unlike the Communist countries where they confiscated everything.'[13]

Despite her reservations, Helen's commitment to British intelligence remained undiminished. In 1972 she bought a first floor flat at an apartment block called Greenhill on Prince Arthur Road, Hampstead, just around the corner from her house on Frognal Way. It was used purely as a safe and secure house for Helen's secret meetings with her MI5 officers – Charles Elwell, Brigadier Mike Lennard and Harry Wharton. She spent her own money on decorating the flat, complete with psychedelic posters on the walls and state-of-the-art furniture. Her expenditure was refunded, however, and it was the only occasion on which she received cash from MI5. But the Security Service did lavish her with expensive gifts – liqueur chocolates, silk scarves from Hermès, bottles of

Armagnac brandy and vintage champagne and lunches at luxury restaurants.

MI6 also utilised Helen's services. The area around the Eve Club was a hive of espionage. MI6 rented a small office directly across the street, while one KGB agent moved into an office nearby at Imperial House on Regent Street and another KGB officer, Oleg Lyalin, set up a fourth floor office in Marcel House. They all watched each other and Helen was in the midst of the great game.

One day she received an urgent phone call from an intelligence officer. An MI6 agent needed to visit the club that night with a Chinese source but could not disclose his real name when he signed in at the desk. 'He needs to give the impression that everyone knows him and so choose the right girls', he said. 'He does not have time to sign up as a member and he will use the name "John Kellogg". Can you arrange that?'

Helen knew what to do. She made up a backdated membership card and a fake address under the false name of 'John Kellogg' and the MI6 agent was all set. He duly arrived at 10 p.m. with his Chinese contact, who was impressed and pleased by such unfamiliar surroundings. For Helen, it was all part of the service.

However, countering, disrupting and investigating KGB activities in Britain was the nightclub owner's priority. In April 1973, a threat by a gangster resulted in Helen playing a secret role in one of Britain's most famous security scandals since the Second World War. One evening Helen received a visit from a thug on behalf of an East End gangster.

'Wouldn't it be terrible if something nasty happened to your club?', snarled the man.

It was a classic shakedown and so Helen called the police and was visited by Detective Sergeant Brian Boyce, a formidably intelligent officer from south London. The two formed an effective alliance against organised crime in Soho. They trusted each other and became lifelong friends. Helen taught Boyce that only gangsters wore jewellery, never gentlemen, and he educated her about drug dealers and users.

Two weeks later Helen called Boyce. 'I've got something for you', she said. 'We need to meet.'

Their rendezvous was the Coffee Cup on Hampstead High Street and MI5's nightclub agent was hardly incognito in a huge Ascot-style hat and smoking ostentatiously.

'What have you got?', he asked.

'A bit of difficulty', she replied. 'As you know, I am in contact with MI5 and my girls provide tips and information about the Russian spies who come to the club. Well, one girl who used to work for me has been to see me and she has a problem.'

The girl in question was Norma Levy, a prostitute who entertained Soviet spies, politicians and the criminal underworld at her flat at 9 Marlborough Court in Maida Vale, London. Helen employed Levy at the Eve Club in 1966 for four days but did not think she was suitable.

'Beautiful body, good showgirl but hard and mercenary', said Helen. 'I had a sixth sense she might bring trouble and she really didn't have the requisite breeding.'[14]

But she was willing to hear what Norma Levy had to say. It transpired that her husband, Colin Levy, did not mind her extra-curricular activities but he was now blackmailing her.

'My husband knows that I have been sleeping with spies and all sorts but one of my clients is the minister for defence', she told Helen. 'He comes to see me regularly and pays me well. The problem is that the Minister leaves me letters and signed open cheques and allows me to fill in the amounts. I am worried that my husband has photocopies of the documents and will force me to help him in one of his drug deals with his business partner, James Humphreys.'

The involvement of Humphreys, an international cocaine smuggler, attracted Boyce's attention. He had been investigating Humphreys and wanted to charge him. And Levy's wife could be the route to that conviction. Helen then arranged for Norma Levy to meet Boyce at West End police station. 'He is the only police officer you can trust', she said.

Levy told Boyce everything and then on 6 April 1973 they met again for coffee at a Jewish restaurant on St John's Wood High Street. She was frightened that if her husband knew she was informing the police about his drugs deals, he would carry out his threat of publishing the documents that would incriminate a senior minister in the government. 'I don't want this to happen', she said.

'Who is the Minister?', asked Boyce.

'I am the girlfriend of the minister for defence', she replied.

'You mean Lord Carrington?'

'Yes.'

Levy said that the minister had been visiting her regularly for several years at her flat, which he had bought for her. He had been paying her about £10,000 per year. Her husband knew about the relationship but she was worried that he had copied some cheques and notes and taken down the registration numbers of the Ministry of Defence cars which delivered the love letters to her flat. He had also noted down the car number plates of other clients, notably the chargé d'affaires at the Soviet embassy, who was in effect the deputy ambassador and possibly KGB. She was worried that her husband would blackmail her by threatening to leak her client list.

Boyce was only interested in Humphreys and his cocaine smuggling but felt duty bound to inform MI5 about the potential security risk posed by a defence minister being blackmailed by the KGB or another agency. And so on 6 April 1973 Boyce met three MI5 officers – Brian Oliver, Harry Wharton and Mike Lennard – at the Tatty Bogle, a wine bar on Kingly Street in Soho. The officers were concerned that the documents held by Colin Levy proved that the defence minister was sleeping with a prostitute who was also servicing Soviet agents. It could be a major security breach.

'Help us', said one of the MI5 officers. 'If you arrest Levy at Heathrow Airport, can you arrange to collect the documents and give them to us?' Boyce agreed.

Three days later, on 9 April, Boyce met Norma Levy at the King's Arms, on Edgware Road. She was distressed and frightened. She had admitted to her husband that she was a police informant and was worried about the consequences. And she also referred to the minister who was her boyfriend as 'Tony', and admitted that she had lied when she named Lord Carrington as the minister in question. By 18 April 1973, Boyce was sure that Norma Levy's secret ministerial lover was in fact Lord (Tony) Lambton. This was confirmed later that day when he met her husband Colin Levy, who disclosed that he had a cheque with no amount of money stipulated but signed 'Viscount Lambton'. That night Boyce called an MI5 officer and named Lambton as the minister under suspicion.

Lord Lambton was an eccentric aristocrat who was frustrated by his ministerial responsibilities in the Conservative government. Later, when asked by MI5 officer Charles Elwell why he slept with prostitutes, he replied: 'My job at the Ministry of Defence was so boring that the only way to relieve the tedium was sex and vigorous gardening.'

The security risk of the KGB or another agency blackmailing the RAF minister has never been established. Most historians believe that Lord Lambton would not have submitted to blackmail. But at the time the risk was very real. MI5 took it seriously enough that they placed Lord Lambton under surveillance to check whether the KGB was aware of the potential for blackmail. What is certain is that if the KGB obtained the letters or cheques or photographs, they would have used them against the minister, just as they did with Commander Courtney eight years earlier. It was eerily reminiscent of the Profumo affair.

Meanwhile, back at the club, Helen was fully aware of the ticking national security time bomb. She was concerned about the security implications and the political consequences. *I need to protect the minister's political reputation from being sullied by the likes of Norma Levy*, she noted in her diary. By chance one of her members, Earl Jellicoe, then leader of the House of Lords, was wrongly named and implicated. In fact, his only 'impropriety' was engaging a Mayfair escort agency. The earl was a regular of Eve's and even took his red ministerial boxes into the club as he drank half bottles of champagne. Helen decided to act. She telephoned an aristocratic friend of Prince Philip and he arranged for her to meet James Prior, then leader of the House of Commons, and Robert Armstrong, principal private secretary to the prime minister, Edward Heath.

At twelve noon on 4 May 1973, Helen met Prior and Armstrong at the Cabinet Office and she explained the security risk and political danger of a senior defence minister who was vulnerable to blackmail. She detailed her involvement and argued that Lord Lambton should resign on 'health grounds' to avoid an embarrassing scandal and denied that Earl Jellicoe was involved in pornography. There was silence from across the table, apart from the prime minister's private secretary informing her that her statement was being tape-recorded.

'Are you an MI5 agent?', he then asked her sternly.

'You don't really expect an answer to that question, do you?', she replied tersely.

She found Armstrong's unsmiling attitude 'patronising and reminiscent of a priest in a confessional'. But the prime minister's private secretary was impressed by the depth of her knowledge. 'She was an honest and intelligent witness', he recalled years later. 'She was a remarkable lady, impeccably reliable and intensely patriotic.'[15]

After the meeting Helen informed MI5 and was convinced that Lambton and Jellicoe would resign. At 4 a.m. every Sunday morning she walked to Leicester Square to buy the newspapers in the hope that the scandal would break. But the story was kept under wraps because MI5 still did not have the cheques or the love letters. Eventually, with Boyce's help, MI5 officers obtained the incriminating evidence and they celebrated at the Eve Club with champagne.

Unfortunately, Boyce had called Norma Levy, whose phone was tapped, and told her: 'Clear your papers.' This was constituted as tipping off someone who was a witness in a potential case involving national security and so he was arrested under the Official Secrets Act and detained in jail. He had been stitched up.

A furious Helen called an MI5 officer and protested. 'Too bad', he replied.

Enraged, she dressed in her most formal outfit and walked up to 10 Downing Street and knocked on the door. 'My name is Helen O'Brien', she told the security officer sternly. 'I have an urgent appointment to see the prime minister's private secretary. Mention my name and he will come down and see me.' Within minutes she was ushered in to see Robert Armstrong. Helen briefed him on Boyce's predicament. 'Something must be done', she said. But it was not until another intelligence officer, Hamilton Macmillan, told the Foreign Office about Boyce's crucial work for MI5 that he was released from jail.

Looking back on Helen's secret involvement in preventing what could have been a defence minister being blackmailed by the KGB, Brian Boyce told me she was indispensable. 'Norma Levy would not have spoken to anyone apart from Helen and MI5 would never have known about Lord Lambton', he reflected. Boyce, who later led the investigation into the Brink's-Mat robbery, held Helen in high regard as an intelligence asset and informant.

'You are cleverer than me', he once told her.

'No, I just speak more languages', she replied.

*

By the late 1970s discos had taken over from old-fashioned night-clubs and Eve's was gradually losing its appeal. The strip clubs of Soho made the Eve Club look tame. Helen introduced raunchier and racier floor shows with topless girls and strippers to keep the clients happy. But the club was in a 1950s time warp, when men dressed in dinner jackets and women wore ball gowns. Its unique appeal of glamour, intrigue, sex, sophistication, daring floorshows and mystery was fading. Helen enjoyed the occasional foray back into espionage. Her father found his way to London and she introduced him to Charles Elwell, the MI5 officer who first recruited her. It turned out that her father was a goldmine of intelligence about Romania and Elwell's pencil broke as he wrote down page after page. 'Deus ex machina', a delighted Elwell concluded about the meeting.

But the Eve Club's final years were not so happy. Taxi drivers were bribed by other clubs to say that Eve's had closed or burned down or moved. The owners increased the rent to an unaffordable amount. The water installation resulted in constant floods. And Eve's health worsened. She took sleeping pills but suffered from nightmares. But the reality is that the world had moved on. By 1990 the Cold War had ended and the Eve Club had become an anachronism. Its film noir shadowy smoke-filled atmosphere, which reminded guests of a combination of *The Third Man* and *Casablanca*, in which Helen O'Brien played the Humphrey Bogart role, was no longer in vogue. On Valentine's night 1992, the Eve Club closed. For a brief period the venue retained its musical roots: in 1994 the Britpop group Menswear played their first gig there and Pulp filmed a video. Today on the ground floor Lululemon sells yoga clothing and sadly the basement is now a large stock-room. 'It's big enough to turn into a nightclub', said a member of staff without a trace of irony.

As for Helen O'Brien, she retired to Valbonne in the south of France with her two daughters and her husband. She spent most of her time and energy negotiating the return of her family's land and property which the Communist regime had confiscated without compensation. Only some land was returned to her and so her final years involved gardening, walking her dogs and relaxing before she died in 2005, aged seventy-nine. It was a far cry from the cosmopolitan late-night world of intrigue and espionage. The only connection to her nightclub past was that visitors would always be served with champagne.

'She was a remarkable person', recalled Clive Entwistle, the crime journalist and TV producer who knew her in the 1980s during the club's final years. 'She was tough with the girls, knew how to manipulate men but she was extremely intelligent and understood people. Above all, she loved the intrigue and probably lived the equivalent of twenty lives of other people in her one life.'

It is unlikely that the KGB knew that Helen O'Brien – AKA Elena Constaninescu – was an active MI5 agent. Their officers frequented her club for most of the Cold War – at least until 1973 – and so if her cover was blown Moscow would have banned their membership. As they walked into the intoxicating, seductive atmosphere of the Eve Club in the heart of Piccadilly, KGB agents no doubt thought they would simply enjoy a discreet drink and an exotic floor show. They were reassured by the absence of reporters and photographers. But there is little doubt that many KGB secrets were spilled late at night or in the early hours of the morning, and some of their operations were curtailed.

7

OPERATION WHITE HOUSE: THE KGB'S SECRET OFFERS TO AMERICAN PRESIDENTIAL CANDIDATES

We are in a position to influence the outcome of the US Presidential elections, you know.

General Dmitry Yakushkin, KGB station chief
in Washington DC, 1975–82[1]

We are opposed by a monolithic and ruthless conspiracy that relies primarily on covert means for expanding its sphere of influence, on infiltration instead of invasion, on subversion instead of elections.

President John F. Kennedy, 1961

O N 5 JANUARY 2017, AT THE height of the controversy surrounding revelations that Russian intelligence agents intervened in, hacked and meddled with the previous year's US presidential election, James Clapper, former director of US National Intelligence, told Congress: 'The Russians have a long history of interfering in elections. Theirs and other people's…. This goes back to the 1960s from the heyday of the Cold War.'

That remark by Clapper, at the time the most senior and long-est-serving official in the US intelligence community, went almost unnoticed. And yet what he called the 'unprecedented' role of Russia's intelligence agencies in 2016 represented the revival of Soviet interference, smear and influence operations against American politicians that predate even the Cold War.

Secret funding and recruitment of congressmen and presidential candidates can be traced back to the Stalinist era of the 1930s, at a time when Soviet foreign intelligence was expanding and the US had almost no counter-intelligence capabilities. Soviet agents, then working for the NKVD, were rampant in Washington DC. One even became the piano tuner for Governor Nelson Rockefeller, later vice president of the United States, and succeeded in bugging the meeting room of the Senate Foreign Relations Committee.

One of the earliest recruits by the NKVD was a Democratic congressman called Samuel Dickstein, who represented New York City. A Lithuanian Jew born in 1885, Dickstein emigrated to the USA with his parents when he was six. His family settled in a Lower East Side apartment block in Manhattan, a neighbourhood that Dickstein would later represent in Congress. After qualifying as a lawyer, he served as a deputy state attorney general and then in 1923, aged thirty-eight, won a Democratic seat in the House of Representatives, where he would serve eleven terms over the next twenty years.[2]

The congressman first came to Moscow's attention in 1937 when he assisted Soviet 'illegals' – secret NKVD agents without an official diplomatic cover – in obtaining false passports and visas. He charged one Austrian and his wife $1,200 for a US visa, a vast amount at that time. 'Others take huge money for these things and become millionaires', he told an undercover NKVD officer, 'and I, Samuel Dickstein, am a poor man.'

In fact, according to the NKVD station chief in New York, the congressman was 'heading a criminal gang that was involved in shady businesses and selling passports'.[3]

But then Dickstein's value as an intelligence asset to his Soviet controllers increased. He became the founder of a congressional committee which investigated – ironically – Communist and Nazi covert activities and black propaganda. Almost overnight, Dickstein became actively involved in domestic intelligence operations. This gave him access to inside political information and so he offered to relay this intelligence on anti-Soviet activities within the USA by Russian émigrés to the NKVD. This almost certainly placed their lives in danger.

The congressman's access to such secret material was via the newly formed House Committee on Un-American Activities. The NKVD tasked Dickstein to steer the committee away from targeting Communists and towards anti-Bolsheviks and Fascists. The congressman agreed but wanted to be paid, his NKVD handler Peter Gutzeit, under diplomatic cover at the Soviet consulate in New York, reported back excitedly to Moscow. Through Dickstein, wrote Gutzeit, 'we can gain information on not only Russian nationalists, Nazis, Ukrainian nationalists and Japanese operatives but also supporters of Leon Trotsky'.[4]

The Soviet Union agreed and by 1938 NKVD operatives were passing $1,250 in cash per month to Dickstein and planned to 'throw him a round sum for his re-election campaign'. In response the New York liberal Democrat delivered pro-Soviet speeches in Congress, including impassioned attacks on the House Committee on Un-American Activities, whose allegations resulted in many innocent individuals losing their jobs and being blacklisted. The bleak irony, of course, was that Dickstein had in effect set up the infamous Un-American Activities Committee.

It was apparent that Dickstein was purely motivated by financial gain and his NKVD codename – 'Crook' – revealed exactly what his Soviet controllers thought of him. 'A very cunning swindler' was how one operative described him. Their relationship became fractious and by February 1940 the NKVD had mostly given up on the congressman, who increasingly demanded larger amounts of cash for his spying but provided little documentation in return.

The congressman claimed that he was ideologically sympathetic to the Soviet Union but he displayed all the hallmarks and instincts of a petty criminal. Dickstein did provide some documents, notably details of the war budget for 1940, but the value of his information was increasingly limited. He also argued with his Soviet handler over his understandable concern over signing receipts for cash received. The NKVD was cautious about retaining his services. As one cable from Moscow noted, he represents 'a danger because this type is not simply a crook but a mercenary of many intelligence services'.[5]

However, the NKVD did attempt to make greater use of Dickstein. In April 1939, a leading official reviewed his activities and even agreed to pay him without receipts. The Soviets asked the congressman to provide 'information about all the important political questions regarding your country and its relations with other countries'. The NKVD also asked Dickstein to penetrate US intelligence agencies to obtain information 'about our enemies'.[6]

Typically, the congressman replied evasively and demanded additional thousands of dollars to pay an FBI source and a lawyer to defend Moscow's interests. This was declined. Instead, the NKVD decided that Dickstein's only possible use was to deliver speeches in Congress under their direction, for which he would be paid $750 on each occasion. During one of his speeches Dickstein went completely off-message and called for more funds for the FBI, which had begun counter-intelligence efforts against Soviet agents in the USA. An infuriated NKVD official sent a cable to Moscow: 'This source cannot be a useful organiser who could gather around him a group of liberal Congressmen to exercise our interest and, alone, he doesn't represent any interest.'

Frustrated by the congressman's dishonesty and avarice, in early 1940 the NKVD terminated the relationship. By then they had paid Dickstein a total of $12,000 – equivalent in 2022 to nearly $254,000. The NKVD had long regarded the congressman as 'a complete racketeer and blackmailer' but he was still a useful agent of influence. Fortunately for Dickstein, his corrupt and treacherous activities as a spy were not discovered until the NKVD archives were made available decades later. He spent his final nine years as a judge in the New York State Supreme Court until his death in 1954. The irony was not lost on his NKVD handlers.

For the Kremlin, the Dickstein experience provided the basis for an expanded strategy that would allow the NKVD to influence American elections, Congress and the White House. Dickstein's NKVD handler – Peter Gutzeit – identified other politicians, notably New Deal Democrats, who could be recruited as agents. He did not advocate the payment of crude bribes to politicians (as was the case with Dickstein), but rather spending big money to influence the US political agenda in order to benefit the Soviet Union. In one report in 1938, the Soviet spy wrote that it was important 'to have several people of ours among Congressmen and even Senators if we decided to penetrate seriously and actively into the politics of this country [the USA]'. He added:

> Very big money will be needed for this purpose... Helping during the elections with money means to define relations with a future Congressman or Senator, possibly for some years. It does not mean that they should be obligatorily recruited by all traditional rules (some could be recruited). But it does mean that we create a group of our people in the legislative bodies, define their political positions and insert them there to actively influence events.[7]

Moscow responded to Gutzeit's proposal with zeal. In fact, the NKVD even suggested that he add the purchase of a newspaper to his list of targets and buy the pens of journalists as agents. Such a publication, stated the NKVD, could be used to influence events in favour of preferred and sympathetic congressional and senatorial candidates and provide a vehicle for a critique on American domestic politics.

Gutzeit replied that it was extremely difficult to calculate the spending, especially the financing of congressmen's election

campaigns. But he discussed an annual budget of $500,000 or
even $1 million – a huge amount of money at that time. The
purchase and ownership of a US newspaper appeared to be less
problematic. 'It does not represent any major difficulty to protect
ourselves from any surprises on the part of the so-called newspapers' owners', wrote Gutzeit. 'Controlling shareholders of these
newspapers can be easily re-registered to a Soviet citizen and kept
in the Soviet Union.'[8]

Unfortunately, there is no reply to Gutzeit's detailed proposal
in the NKVD archives and so it is not known if his grandiose and
insidious scheme was ever implemented. However, it provides an
insight into the type of secret agenda that the Soviet Union intelligence agencies were planning to pursue after the Second World
War.

The next stage was to infiltrate the Oval Office in the White
House. Declassified FBI files reveal that in October 1945 Henry A.
Wallace, the radical left-wing Democrat and former vice president,
held at least one meeting with the NKVD to discuss secret Soviet
funding and support for his presidential campaign.

Born in 1888, in Iowa, Wallace was the son of Henry C. Wallace,
agriculture secretary under President Harding in the 1920s. After
graduating from Iowa State College, Wallace became a farming
expert and campaigned against the Republican policies of high
tariffs. He successfully delivered Iowa, usually a conservative state,
for the Democrats in the 1932 election and President Roosevelt
appointed him agriculture secretary. During the devastating Great
Depression, he played a key role in devising and implementing
New Deal policies which raised and stabilised farm prices and
conserved soil. He believed only radical state intervention could
help the rural poor who lost their farms through no fault of their
own, which was so graphically described in *The Grapes of Wrath*
by John Steinbeck.

Wallace was rewarded by becoming vice president during
Roosevelt's third term between 1941 and 1945. He also became a
goodwill ambassador and assumed emergency powers in national

economic affairs when the USA entered the Second World War. But his intense advocacy of radical causes alienated moderates and so a cohort of senior Democrats around Roosevelt plotted to remove the left-wing firebrand from the ticket for the 1944 presidential elections. They correctly perceived Wallace as being overly sympathetic to Communism and emotionally unstable. After some controversy, they succeeded in convincing both Roosevelt and the Democratic establishment, and chose Harry S. Truman, the senator from Missouri, as their favoured candidate. After three rounds of balloting at the 1944 Democratic National Convention (the first round of which Wallace led) Truman finally obtained the vice-presidential nomination.

A furious Wallace viewed his removal as a betrayal, but accepted the role of commerce secretary. After Truman became president in April 1945, he told Wallace he could remain as commerce secretary. The radical left-winger accepted but became increasingly aggrieved and decided to exploit secret information he had learned in the White House. And so on 24 October 1945, only eight months after he left the White House, Wallace sat down for a secret breakfast meeting he had requested with Anatoly Gorsky, then the Washington DC station chief for the NKGB (People's Commissariat of State Security). Gorsky was stunned but delighted and sent a detailed report back to Moscow several days later. Its contents were so explosive that the document was sent to the foreign minister, Vyacheslav Molotov, who responded curtly: 'It must be sent to Comrade Stalin!'

Wallace began their conversation by discussing the Truman administration's attitude towards the Soviet Union. He reported that the president would like Soviet scientists to visit the United States to witness American successes in nuclear power. But his comments soon became indiscreet and betrayed his motives. 'Truman is a petty politician who reached his current post by accident', he told the enthralled Soviet agents. 'He often has good intentions but too easily falls under the influence of people around him.'[9]

Wallace was still the commerce secretary at the time of this meeting but he did not hesitate to highlight his policy disagreements with the new administration. The Soviet spies were delighted to hear that Wallace wanted America's nuclear arsenal to be controlled by the UN Security Council. He blamed his failure to implement this idea on lobbying by 'big capital – Du Post, General Electric and Union Carbide'.

The cabinet minister explained to Gorsky, the NKVD intelligence officer, there were two main factions 'fighting for Truman's soul'. He disclosed there was a smaller pro-Soviet group (centring on Wallace) and a larger anti-Soviet group, made up of secretary of state James Byrnes and attorney general Tom Clark. Wallace, already eyeing the 1948 Democratic nomination, then suggested to the NKVD station chief that the Soviet Union should help his pro-Soviet faction. 'You [the USSR] could help this smaller group considerably, and we don't doubt... your willingness to do this', he told the spy. He did not elaborate on this proposal and concluded their breakfast meeting by remarking: 'US Congressmen spread lots of anti-Soviet lies here [Washington DC].'[10]

This remarkable conversation, preserved in the Russian archives, both highlights Wallace's indiscretion and his perception of Soviet willingness to influence the American political establishment. While Gorsky's report of the conversation was sent to Moscow with alacrity, the NKVD declined to finance Wallace or his supporters.

Incredibly, if Wallace had succeeded and won the 1948 presidency, he would have turned the US government into an appendage of Soviet intelligence or, at the very least, a government that was sympathetic to the Soviet Union. While this sounds hyperbolic and far-fetched, Wallace later suggested that he would have appointed Laurence Duggan and Harry Dexter White, both long-serving Russian intelligence assets in the US government, as his secretary of state and his treasury secretary. It was a serious possibility and the consequences for the course of the Cold War would have been extraordinary and potentially devastating.[11]

As the Iron Curtain descended upon Europe and President Truman adopted a hard-line policy against the Soviet Union, Wallace became increasingly disillusioned and in 1946 was dismissed from the cabinet. In his 1948 campaign for the presidency, the left-wing progressive advocated closer cooperation with the Soviet Union and arms reduction. He received more than one million votes but his volatile temperament was not conducive to collegiate politics and he resigned from the Progressive Party. At the age of only sixty, he returned to private life and wrote several books before he died in 1965. His secret meeting with Soviet spies remained unknown until the FBI declassified Wallace's file in 1983 and it was published in *The Haunted Wood* by Alexander Vassiliev, a former KGB officer, and Allen Weinstein.[12]

As the Cold War escalated in the 1950s, Premier Khrushchev was anxious to find someone in the US political establishment he could do business with, now that the inevitable collapse of capitalism and the implementation of Communism was not going to happen. He selected Adlai Stevenson, the erudite Democratic presidential nominee in 1952 and 1956 and still the titular head of the party. The Soviet leader considered Stevenson to have 'a tolerant – I'd even say friendly and trustworthy – attitude towards the Soviet Union'. They had met in 1958, when the Democratic grandee toured the Soviet Union with his two sons. Khrushchev advised the boys to marry Russian girls and told Stevenson: 'In 1956 I voted for you in my heart'.[13]

During the 1956 campaign Khrushchev clumsily intervened by instructing his prime minister to issue a public letter praising 'certain public figures' for endorsing a nuclear test ban. It was a thinly-veiled endorsement of Stevenson's bid for the White House and President Eisenhower complained about Soviet meddling in the election. The vice president, Richard Nixon, used the Soviet letter to claim that Stevenson's 'dangerous scheme' would play 'disastrously into the Communist hands'.[14]

For the 1960 presidential campaign – a pivotal and transformative election after eight years of Dwight Eisenhower – the

Kremlin planned to influence the outcome without their finger-prints being discovered. The secret conduit was Mikhail Menshikov, the energetic if eccentric Soviet ambassador to Washington DC.

In late 1959, while Ambassador Menshikov was on home leave in Moscow, Khrushchev ordered him to pay a secret call on Stevenson and ask him: 'Which way can we be of assistance?' Soon after the New Year, the Soviet ambassador telephoned Stevenson at his Chicago law firm office. Menshikov told him that he had gifts and messages from Premier Khrushchev.

'I would like to deliver them to you in person in Chicago', he said.

Stevenson was puzzled but curious and agreed to meet, but only at the ambassador's residence.

Two weeks later, on 16 January 1960, Stevenson arrived at the heavily guarded Soviet embassy, then based at the old George Pullman mansion on 16th Street in Washington. The veteran Democrat regarded the Russian diplomat as a competent and outgoing, if unconventional, figure. He told friends how, at a Georgetown garden party, the Russian envoy unwittingly insisted on delivering his own toast to the ladies present: 'Up your bottoms!' And the ambassador later turned up at the White House with a terrified small white fluffy dog called Pushinka as a present. Pushinka was checked for eavesdropping devices and then became a pampered and valued member of the White House family and staff.

Over copious amounts of caviar, wine and fruit in the family dining room, Menshikov thanked Stevenson for helping arrange a visit to the USA by Khrushchev the previous year. Diplomatic pleasantries were exchanged and then the ambassador came to the point. He carefully withdrew from his pocket a folded sheaf of notes written in ink and, clearly under strict instructions, launched into an extraordinary monologue. He told Stevenson in a serious low voice that the message he was about to deliver came directly from the Soviet president himself:

When you met in Moscow in 1958, Premier Khrushchev said to you that he had voted for you in his heart in 1956. He says now that he will vote for you in his heart again in 1960. We have made a beginning with President Eisenhower and Khrushchev's visit to America toward better relations, but it is only a beginning. We are concerned with the future, and that America has the right President.

All countries are concerned with the American election. It is impossible for us not to be concerned about our future and the Presidency, which is so important. In Russia, we know well Mr. Stevenson and his views regarding disarmament, nuclear testing, and peaceful coexistence. When we compare all the possible [presidential] candidates in the United States, we feel that Mr. Stevenson is best for mutual understanding and progress toward peace.... We believe that Mr. Stevenson is more of a realist than others and is likely to understand Soviet anxieties and purposes.

Because we know the ideas of Mr. Stevenson, we in our hearts all favour him. We don't know how we can help to make relations better and help those to succeed in political life who wish for better relations. Could the Soviet press assist Mr. Stevenson's personal success? How should the press praise him and if so, for what? Or should it criticise him, in the hopes that would get him support at home? Are there other ways that we could be of assistance to those forces in the United States which favour friendly relations? We Russians are open to suggestions. Stevenson will know best what would help him.

The ambassador said that the Russians saw Stevenson's 'rival' – Vice President Richard Nixon, the likely Republican nominee – as being hostile to their interests. The distaste and distrust of Nixon was expressed cautiously but clearly. The diplomat concluded by asking the Democrat grandee to keep his comments 'in confidence'.[15]

Despite repeated declarations that the ambassador's presentation was not a desire to interfere, in fact it was a politically primitive attempt to covertly influence the 1960 presidential election.

Stevenson was shocked and appalled. He told the ambassador bluntly and politely that he did not expect to be a candidate in 1960 and the offer of assistance was 'highly improper, indiscreet, and dangerous to all concerned. I have grave misgivings about the propriety or wisdom of any interference, direct or indirect, in the American election.' He concluded by reminding his visitor that the last time an ambassador expressed a preference for a presidential candidate – the British ambassador back in 1888 – the US president, Grover Cleveland, promptly expelled him from the country.[16]

The next morning Stevenson wrote to a friend: 'As I think about it, I get more and more indignant about being "propositioned" in that way, and at the same time, more and more perplexed by the confidence they have in me. I shall do one thing only now: politely and decisively reject the proposal – and pray that it will never leak, lest I lose that potentially valuable confidence.'

Stevenson was true to his word. Six days after the meeting, he told Menshikov in a diplomatic manner that even if he were a candidate in 1960 he would not accept the assistance offered by the Russians.

'The confidence expressed in me during our conversation and Premier Khrushchev's interest in my views were flattering', he wrote. 'I am sure you and Premier Khrushchev will understand my feelings about the proprieties we discussed and I trust that my reaction will not be misconstrued as discourteous or ungrateful.'[17]

Despite his desire that the Soviet approach would remain secret, Stevenson remained concerned. He told his colleagues privately that the Russians were showing a keen and active interest in the presidential election and displaying 'appalling ignorance' of the dangers in commenting on it.

'Menshikov has been talking openly about his opinions of the candidates and the Soviet preference for who should win', he confided. 'We cannot tolerate foreign interference in our elections.'[18]

Notwithstanding Stevenson's objections, the Soviets were unperturbed about interfering. After Richard Nixon and John

Kennedy were nominated, Premier Khrushchev told colleagues in Moscow: 'We have to make a choice in our own minds. We can still influence this American election.'

For Khrushchev, the ruthless Republican candidate was his nemesis. He described Nixon as 'a puppet of the American Cold War Establishment', an 'unprincipled careerist' and an ally of that 'devil of darkness McCarthy'. While Nixon was no longer a hard-line anti-Communist Cold Warrior, the Soviet Union remained hostile.

But Kennedy was an unknown factor. 'He was a young man, very promising, very rich', said Khrushchev. 'He was distinguished by his intelligence, his education and his political skill.'

While the charismatic Democrat had been critical of the Soviet Union in his Senate oratory, he now favoured a nuclear test ban. And so the Soviets chose Kennedy.[19]

When the 1960 election campaign started, Khrushchev remained hostile towards Nixon, but there was also personal animosity. In Moscow, the pair had attended the opening of an exhibition devoted to the United States, and launched into a public argument about the merits of capitalism versus Communism while standing inside a model kitchen. 'You don't know anything about communism – except fear of it,' Khrushchev told Nixon.

And so the Soviet premier desperately hoped that Kennedy would win and took an active interest in him. The KGB station chief in Washington, Alexander Feklisov, recalls that 'the rezidentura [KGB station] had been instructed to inform the Center in Moscow periodically about the development of the electoral campaign and to propose diplomatic or propaganda initiatives, or any other measures, to encourage and facilitate Kennedy's victory'. A KGB agent even tried to contact Robert Kennedy but was met with a polite rebuff.[20] The Soviet premier deliberately delayed the release of captured American soldiers and spies in the Soviet Union until after the campaign. Any release before the election would strengthen the hand of the incumbent, Vice President Nixon.

Khrushchev also intervened to help Kennedy when a U-2 surveillance plane operated by the CIA was shot down by the Soviet air force while flying near Yekaterinburg. The US initially said the plane had been studying weather patterns for NASA and had simply strayed off course. But information recovered from the plane's wreckage quickly proved it was a spy plane. The pilot, Gary Powers, was taken prisoner and put on trial for espionage, eventually being sentenced to a decade in a Soviet prison. Powers' fate became a point of tension in the Cold War.

The Soviet premier sensed an opportunity. If he stalled the negotiations and delayed the release of Powers, then he could prevent the Republican White House, especially the despised Nixon, from claiming the credit and reaping the political benefit from any release. And so when the United States asked for Powers to be released, Khrushchev refused. 'Now is not the time to do it,' he told a colleague.

Noting that the 1960 election was too close to call, Khrushchev believed that if Powers or the other Americans were set free before the poll, it could give Nixon a boost. Kennedy won the election by a majority of only 118,550 votes, a tiny margin. The slightest movement either way would have been decisive. The Soviet premier believed he had made a decisive intervention.[21]

Powers was eventually released in 1962, in exchange for a KGB officer who was serving a prison sentence in the United States for espionage (later portrayed in the film *Bridge of Spies*). The American pilot spent the rest of his life tainted by accusations that he had been too weak-willed in the face of Soviet interrogation, although the CIA's own report found he had acted honourably.

It is likely the Soviet decision not to release the hostages influenced the election result and Khrushchev is adamant that President Kennedy acknowledged his assistance. According to his account, Kennedy laughed when the Soviet premier brought up his role a year later when they met in Vienna.

'You know, Mr President, we voted for you during the elections.'

'You're right', replied Kennedy jovially. 'I admit you played a role in the election and cast your vote for me, but I am sure whatever position the Soviet Union took in the media, I don't think it affected the election in any way.'

The former Soviet ambassador, Oleg Troyanovsky, suggested Kennedy was very doubtful – or did not want to admit – that the Kremlin had been helpful.

By now it was apparent that the Soviet Union would try and influence each presidential election. In 1964 the KGB made a crude overture to President Lyndon Johnson, which was swiftly and abruptly declined. In retaliation, Moscow authorised a smear campaign against LBJ. Colonel Boris Ivanov, head of the KGB station in New York, was ordered to investigate and circulate the unfounded conspiracy theory that the president was responsible for the assassination of JFK the previous year.[22] The KGB also sent fake news to African newspapers that President Johnson had secretly planned policies to keep black people in a subordinate status and bribed Martin Luther King to tame the radical elements of the civil rights movement.[23]

Despite its reservations about Lyndon Johnson, the Kremlin preferred his candidature to the right-wing Republican Barry Goldwater. A hard-line Cold Warrior, Goldwater was a relentless critic and arch enemy of the Soviet Union. 'Let's lob a nuclear bomb into the men's room at the Kremlin', he once declared. In the run-up to the 1964 election, the KGB regarded Goldwater as a dangerous rival to Johnson. A smear and disinformation operation was launched against the Republican candidate in conjunction with Hungarian and Czech agents. According to Ladislav Bittman, the strategy was to portray Goldwater as a racist, a Ku Klux Klan sympathiser and a member of the extreme neo-Nazi John Birch Society:

> It was a leaflet of several pages attacking Mr Goldwater as a racist. Some facts in this leaflet about Mr Goldwater were picked up from American books and newspapers and they were mixed

up with sensational ingredients attacking Mr Goldwater as a racist... They were distributed anonymously. I think that these letters were sent to the United States in diplomatic bags and then mailed by members of the Czech intelligence station in the United States.[24]

Czech and KGB officers combed through telephone directories and reference books like *Who's Who* for the addresses of prominent voters and opinion-formers.

'I would say several thousands of these anti-Goldwater pamphlets were printed in English and French and then mailed and distributed throughout the Third World, pointing the United States as the enemy of non-white nations', Bittman later testified before Congress.[25]

The false claim that the Republican presidential candidate was a member of the neo-Nazi John Birch Society was promoted by the American Communist Party in alliance with the KGB. In 1963 – the year before election year – a booklet suddenly appeared which claimed that Goldwater was conspiring with the society to organise a coup or violent insurrection to take over the United States the following year. Entitled 'Birch Putsch Plans for 1964', the booklet contained no address for the publisher, Domino Publications. The author was 'John Smith, as told to Stanhope T. McReady' – not a very imaginative pseudonym.

There was nothing to tie this publication to the Kremlin or the Communists until April 1963, when an advertisement for this booklet appeared in the pro-Communist *National Guardian* and listed the address of Domino Publications as Suite 900, 22 West Madison Street in Chicago. This was in fact the address of Translate World Publishers, which was registered as an agent of the Soviet Union under the Foreign Agents Registration Act. And the company's two owners were active pro-Soviet Communists.[26]

It was clear evidence of collusion between the KGB and its US surrogates to discredit a presidential candidate. The impact of this operation was limited and in November 1964 Lyndon Johnson beat

Goldwater in a landslide. But it was a rare insight into how the KGB meddled in US presidential elections.

Four years later the prospect of their nemesis Richard Nixon becoming president galvanised the Kremlin into more decisive and riskier covert action. This time they devised an operation to secretly finance the campaign of his Democratic rival, Hubert Humphrey. The offer was made by Anatoly Dobrynin.

In March 1961 Dobrynin became Soviet ambassador to Washington and established a diplomatic rapport with the new president, John F. Kennedy. Despite the public Cold War rhetoric, Premier Khrushchev wanted a closer, constructive relationship with the young charismatic Democrat. A confidential channel was set up in strict secrecy, which operated outside the normal diplomatic exchanges, between the US state department and the Soviet foreign ministry. It was handled by the president's brother, Robert Kennedy, and Colonel Georgi Bolshakov, a military intelligence officer, via coded messages.

'Whenever you need to convey something to me in a confidential way, he [Dobrynin] will be able to transmit this to me personally', the Soviet premier told the president.[27]

By 1968 the Kremlin's animosity to Nixon was undiminished and Dobrynin had established trusting and discreet relationships with American politicians. From their private conversations Dobrynin believed that the Democratic candidate, Hubert Humphrey, would provide more stable relations with the Soviet Union if he became president, and the Kremlin agreed. But Moscow was concerned that the hated Nixon, who had built his career on opposing Communism and the Soviet Union, would win the election.

The Kremlin and Premier Brezhnev took an unprecedented and momentous decision: they authorised their ambassador in Washington to offer a bribe to the Democratic presidential candidate soon after his nomination. Dobrynin was horrified and, according to his memoir *In Confidence*, did his utmost to persuade his Kremlin bosses not to proceed.

'It was a dangerous venture which if discovered certainly would have backfired and ensured Humphrey's defeat', he recalled.

But it was to no avail. Nixon was regarded as 'profoundly anti-Soviet'. Brezhnev approved the operation and instructed Dobrynin to approach the Democratic candidate. 'This is the decision. You carry it out', the foreign minister, Andrei Gromyko, told a shell-shocked ambassador.[28]

In the late summer of 1968, Dobrynin had breakfast at Hubert Humphrey's house and, against his better judgement, made what he described as an 'extraordinary' proposal. After discussing the election campaign, the Soviet diplomat asked about Humphrey's finances. 'We would like to offer you any conceivable help for your forthcoming election campaign, including financial aid', he told the Democratic candidate, who was vice president at the time. Humphrey was stunned and politely declined the offer. It would have been illegal to accept foreign money and his candidacy would have been destroyed if word leaked out that Moscow was secretly backing his campaign in any way.

'He knew at once what was going on', Dobrynin said, who served under five Kremlin leaders and six US presidents. 'He told me it was more than enough for him to have Moscow's good wishes which he highly appreciated. The matter was thus settled to our mutual relief, never to be discussed again.'[29]

During the 1968 election campaign, the Kremlin changed their view of Nixon. The KGB believed that Nixon's fervent anti-Communist stance could work to their advantage: such a president would have the power to improve US–Soviet relations, because nobody would ever dare accuse Nixon of being soft on Communism. This new approach had been reinforced before the election campaign, when a KGB officer called Boris Sedov established a back-channel relationship with Henry Kissinger, then an influential foreign affairs adviser to Nixon. They met frequently.

'Officially, he [Sedov] was in Washington as a reporter for the Novosti Press Agency', said Oleg Kalugin, the KGB station chief in Washington at the time. 'In fact, he was one of my underlings in the KGB's political intelligence line… We encouraged Sedov to cultivate his relationship with Kissinger but we never had any illusions about trying to recruit Kissinger. He was simply a source of political intelligence.'[30]

After Nixon became president in 1968, the KGB–Kissinger back-channel continued. Brezhnev sent a confidential note to Nixon through Sedov, which expressed the hope that relations between the superpowers would improve. For the next six years Kissinger, then US national security advisor, and his top aide Richard Allen met KGB officers regularly to exchange information, ask questions and float ideas. Until Watergate resulted in his resignation in 1974, Nixon was rehabilitated in the eyes of the KGB as someone who genuinely believed in detente. Many Soviet intelligence officers liked Nixon. They respected his pragmatism, aggression and intelligence and were bemused by his downfall. The president's criminal attempts to cover up and conceal the use of dirty tricks against his opponents were, as Ambassador Dobrynin later noted, 'a fairly natural thing to do. Who cared if it was a breach of the constitution?'[31]

'We never understood Watergate', a former Russian military intelligence officer told me. 'What did Nixon do wrong?'

*

The 1976 presidential election was one of the most important in American history. The country had just experienced the trauma of Watergate, and so the candidates campaigned on restoring trust and integrity in government and reviving human rights in foreign policy. The KGB was not impressed by President Ford, regarding him with mild contempt.

'It sometimes happens that a man will occupy a high state position and yet will be written of and spoken of only in passing', wrote Foreign Minister Andrei Gromyko. 'Gerald Ford, president for barely two years, belongs in this category.'[32]

Despite being dismissive of Ford's ability and frustrated by his cautious approach to foreign policy, Moscow remained anxious for him to win the election. As the premier intelligence historian Christopher Andrew wrote:

> The Kremlin's innate conservatism made it prefer a known light-weight like Ford to the unpredictable Democrat candidate Jimmy Carter. Under Ford, it was believed, the 'back channel' between Dobrynin and Kissinger could continue. As the election approached, both the Soviet Embassy and the KGB Residency in Washington received increasingly urgent appeals (from Moscow) for advance notification of the winner.[33]

But in the early days of the 1976 campaign, the Kremlin was confronted by one of its most articulate and hostile critics, the liberal Democrat Senator Henry 'Scoop' Jackson. The KGB Centre in Moscow regarded Jackson as a relentless foe who needed to be discredited and marginalised. They considered the senator as an enemy of detente and head of the 'Jewish lobby', who were campaigning for unrestricted emigration by Soviet Jews to Israel, supporting dissidents and advocating increased arms expenditure. Politically, he was the key figure in holding together a credible anti-Soviet coalition. The secretary of state, Henry Kissinger, considered Jackson as 'the indispensable link between the liberals, preoccupied with human rights [in the Soviet Union], and the conservatives who became anxious about any negotiations with the Soviets'.[34]

The senator epitomised the perennial struggle of US foreign policy to reconcile ideals with the nation's self-interest. His aggressive approach to the Soviet Union, which focused on supporting human rights, put him at odds with classical realists such as George Kennan, who preferred a more pragmatic stance. The Kremlin, argued Jackson, was an implacable adversary and it was naive to think that stability could be achieved by 'managing' the Cold War.

For the senator, the Soviet Union was an evil empire bent on the destruction of the West.

'The basic aim of the Kremlin remains unchanged – a Moscow dominated world', he told the Senate in 1956. 'Let us pay the devil his due. The overlords of the Communist men are not stupid men. They are skilful practitioners of the art of conquest. They have read their Machiavelli, their Clausewitz, just as they have read their *Mein Kampf*. The Soviets have profited from the mistakes of aggressors in ages past. Unlike Hitler, they might wait for years, or even decades to achieve their ends.'[35]

Jackson rallied those who disliked detente and repression around a new cause. Economic relations with the Soviet Union, he insisted, could only improve if Moscow allowed Russian Jews to emigrate if they wished. The Kremlin refused and then in 1972 the senator introduced an amendment to the Trade Reform Bill, which prevented the Soviet Union from receiving favourable trade credits until it had lifted restrictions on emigration. The Kremlin was furious. Ambassador Dobrynin reported to Moscow that Jackson 'kept escalating his demands' in order to win the backing of the Jewish lobby in his bid to win the Democratic nomination at the 1976 election.[36]

It was time for the KGB to intervene. Its New York resident, Boris Solomatin, informed the KGB Centre in Moscow that Jackson appeared to be in a strong position for the presidential primaries:

> Jackson's strong point is the fact that, during his 35 years in Congress, he has never been involved in any sort of political or personal scandal. In the post-Watergate period, the personal integrity of a presidential candidate has had exceptionally great significance. It is necessary to find some stains on the Senator's biography and use them to carry out an active measure which will compromise him. We must discuss with the American friends [the US Communist Party] the most effective ways and means of opposing Jackson's plans to become President of the USA.[37]

According to KGB documents smuggled out by former officer Vasily Mitrokhin, the senator's relative reticence 'probably points to the existence of compromising information which could be used to discredit him'.[38]

The KGB operation was launched in early 1974 and was extraordinarily extensive. Despite the fact that Jackson's parents had left Norway as long ago as 1885, KGB agents in Oslo were ordered to investigate his Norwegian relatives. Declassified FBI documents show that they believed that the KGB colluded with Communist Party activists in Seattle, Washington State (Jackson's constituency) 'to do research' on the senator. This coincided with a public attack by a Soviet UN delegate, who accused Jackson off being 'a foe of detente'.

The FBI later 'confirmed his [Jackson's] suspicion that there was a concerted effort by the Soviets and the US Communist Party to monitor his activities'. The senator then told the FBI he 'would like to bring these Soviet actions to public attention, but wanted to make sure that he did not compromise any sensitive information'. The operation was not made public.[39]

Meanwhile, KGB officers in Washington DC were desperately trying to find *Kompromat* on the senator. The most promising – and only – lead was his sexuality. Jackson had married at the age of forty-nine and his KGB file records that his colleagues were 'amazed', as they considered him a 'confirmed bachelor'. But the KGB agents could not find any evidence he was gay apart from the fact that the senator once shared an apartment with a male childhood friend – hardly incriminating.

The boring truth was that Senator Jackson had married late in life and was not homosexual. But the KGB was unperturbed. They simply fabricated a document to 'expose' him as gay. Codenamed POROK (meaning 'vice' in Russian), the KGB forged an FBI memo, dated 20 June 1940, in which the FBI director, J. Edgar Hoover, reported to the US department of justice that Jackson was homosexual. Photocopies of the forgery were then sent to the *Chicago Tribune*, the *Los Angeles Times*, the *Topeka Capital* in Kansas and

Jimmy Carter's campaign headquarters. At the time it was still controversial to be gay in conservative politics and so the clear intention was to destroy his chances of becoming the candidate.

The KGB portrayed the senator as a sexual hypocrite. In fact, Jackson was homophobic and heterosexual. During the primary campaign he told a gay rights activist that he did not want his vote, and once said 'homosexuality leads to the destruction of the family'. The KGB attached press reports of these statements to the bogus FBI memo and other fake documents purporting to show that Jackson was a member of a gay sex club. These were sent to newspapers, Senator Edward Kennedy (a potential rival for the Democratic nomination), the columnist Jack Anderson and *Playboy* and *Penthouse* magazines.[40]

On 1 May 1976, barely a month after the fake FBI memo was circulated by the KGB, Jackson dropped out of the campaign after losing the critical Pennsylvania primary to Carter by 12%. His former colleagues recall the smear operation but do not believe it had any discernible effect. Richard Perle, the senator's chief foreign policy adviser who was also falsely named in the document as being a member of a gay sex club, told me: 'I don't think it had any real political impact at all.' Journalists ignored the fake documents when they landed on their desks. But the episode revealed just how far the KGB was prepared to go in order to demonise and discredit their critics.

Interestingly, the KGB forgery may have been inspired by a similar smear during Jackson's attempt to be the candidate in 1972. During the primaries, Donald Segretti, the infamous Republican exponent of dirty tricks, fabricated a letter on the stationery of Edmund Muskie, a rival for the Democratic nomination. The detailed document accused Jackson of 'being involved' with a seventeen-year-old schoolgirl and being 'arrested twice in Washington DC as a homosexual'. The letter was distributed widely. Segretti, who was later jailed for his role in Watergate, later admitted that he wrote the letter 'off the top of his head' after 'two or three glasses of wine at the local pub', not expecting anyone to believe it.[41] But its contents were uncannily similar to the KGB forgery four years later.

Despite the fact that Jackson failed to secure the Democratic nomination in 1976, Operation POROK continued. This was because of the senator's opposition to the ratification of Soviet–American arms limitation agreements. In private conversations with the Soviet ambassador, Dobrynin, Jackson said that he was not the Cold War hawk or warmonger that had been portrayed.[42] When he advocated a strong military arsenal it was not to start a war with the Soviet Union but to deter the Kremlin from starting one.

In 1977 agents attempted to incite the gay press into attacking the senator as a closet homosexual who hypocritically criticised homosexuality in public for his own political advantage. In May a KGB officer in New York forged another FBI document which 'reported' that Jackson had been an active homosexual while working as a state prosecutor in the 1940s and sent it to *Gay Times*. Handwritten on the fake memo was the heading 'Our Gay in the US Senate'.[43] Jackson did not stand for the presidency again and died in 1983.

As soon as Jimmy Carter was the Democratic candidate, the Kremlin was even more scornful of his candidature than that of President Ford. Known as 'The Dreamer', Carter's focus on human rights, especially the Soviet dissidents, infuriated the KGB. And so they recruited an agent inside the Democrat's campaign headquarters. This KGB spy, who has never been identified, was a Democratic Party activist recruited during a visit to Russia. He was regarded as a key operative because of his influential contacts inside the Democratic Party, notably Governor Jerry Brown of California and senators Alan Cranston, Eugene McCarthy and Edward Kennedy. On one occasion the agent spent three hours discussing the campaign with Carter, Governor Brown and Senator Cranston in Carter's room at the Pacific Hotel. According to the Mitrokhin archive, his dispatches to Moscow showed direct access to the US presidential candidate and inside information on his

foreign policy plans. The agent's reports were regarded as so important that Yuri Andropov, then head of the KGB, forwarded them
to the Politburo under his signature.[44]

Even before Carter moved into the White House, the KGB were
focusing what *Kompromat* could be obtained on influential administration officials. They concentrated on Zbigniew Brzezinski, the
highly intelligent, Polish-born US national security advisor and a
hard-line Cold Warrior. At first the KGB thought he could be
recruited as an agent but that plan was soon abandoned. Then on
3 January 1977, two weeks before the presidential inauguration,
Andropov approved an operation to collect 'compromising information' on Brzezinski as a means of putting pressure on him and
influencing his decision-making.

Brzezinski was targeted because of his visceral anti-Sovietism.
When Carter spoke on foreign affairs, complained Ambassador
Dobrynin, 'we tended to hear echoes of the anti-Sovietism of
Brzezinski'.[45] The US national security advisor's strident rhetoric
and advice differed from that of Cyrus Vance, the secretary of
state, who was more conciliatory between the superpowers. And
so the KGB aimed to diminish Brzezinski's influence and, if
possible, engineer his dismissal by active measure to discredit
him.[46]

Just like the muckraking operation against Senator Jackson, KGB
agents throughout the USA were told to find any negative information against the US national security advisor. Was Brzezinski
concealing his Jewish origins? Was he having an adulterous relationship with the Hollywood actress Candice Bergen? And was
there any compromising material about his relations with his staff
or the Polish émigré community?[47]

By early 1978, the KGB was struggling to find anything.
Consequently, they resorted to fabricating documents. The idea
was to create artificial tension with Poland, the home country of
Brzezinski (his father was a Polish diplomat before the Second
World War). Dated 17 March 1978, Brzezinski purportedly sent a
secret memorandum to President Carter on US national security

council notepaper, in which he outlined a more aggressive policy towards Poland and the Soviet Union. The document – 'copied' to the CIA director – suggested 'an offensive strategy' and added: 'The policy of detente designed to strengthen it [postwar division of Europe] constitutes no more than a temporary phase... The time is ripe for a more forward policy aimed at influencing the inevitable process of change in the Communist world... We have reached the conclusion that Poland is currently the weakest link in the chain of Soviet domination.'

In essence, Brzezinski was advocating regime change in Poland.

'Trade between the US and Poland should be further developed in order to foster indefinitely Poland's dependence on the West in finance, industry and food supplies', stated the memo. 'It is also necessary to increase anti-Soviet and anti-Russian feelings... In such a climate, created by politics, diplomacy, trade and the mass media, covert activities are aimed at contributing to the destabilisation of Poland.' It concluded 'Very truly yours'.

While drawing on Brzezinski's anti-Communist rhetoric, in fact the memo to the White House was a KGB fake and later leaked to the Spanish press. The US national security advisor never signed his letters 'Very truly yours' and never sent this memo. I found the document buried in congressional archives with a handwritten note: 'Phoney KGB document'.

By the summer of 1978, the KGB campaign against the national security advisor was in full swing. The FBI discovered that the KGB was colluding with Communist Party activists in New York City to denigrate and castigate Brzezinski.

'The order from Moscow was to depict him [Brzezinski] as a warmonger, a zealot and a mad dog', said a US department of justice official.[48]

An FBI file on the operation was handed to the White House.

Disinformation was a primary weapon. The Soviet newspaper *Pravda* raised the stakes in July 1978, when it claimed Brzezinski said that he would 'without too much hesitation' recommend to the president to push the nuclear button in case of 'necessity'. This comment was based on an interview nine months earlier when the national security advisor actually said that he would recommend retaliation only if a nuclear attack was being launched against the USA. 'We don't want to use them and we're not going to use them first in an attack', were his actual words.[49]

When in doubt, the KGB resorted to a smear that Brzezinski was secretly anti-Semitic, on the basis this would damage his standing in the White House and reduce his influence. In early August 1978, the KGB drafted a bogus report by an Israeli Zionist organisation which alleged that the national security advisor had been a CIA officer and was 'a secret anti-Semite'. The document concluded there was compromising information on his personal life which would seriously discredit him. In fact, the KGB had nothing on the parsimonious, intellectual former Harvard professor. But on 20 August, this bizarre 'intelligence report' was inserted through the window of a car parked by an American diplomat in Jerusalem.[50]

A week later two anonymous graphic leaflets about Brzezinski were distributed throughout New York City. On the surface, the leaflets were written and circulated by the US Jewish Defence League. One contained a photograph of the national security advisor and underneath stated in large bold headlines: 'Brzezinski is anti-Semite, has been bought out by Arabs and trades in Jews.' It then concluded: 'There is no place for the Polish-born anti-Semite Brzezinski in this country.'

The second leaflet also contained the emblem of the Jewish Defence League. Headlined 'To All Jewish and Zionist Organisations', it posed several questions, notably 'Can the Anti-Semite Brzezinski be non-partisan in mapping out US foreign policy?'. It then provided the answer: 'No'. Underneath, the leaflet stated: 'We urge you not to accept the anti-Semite Brzezinski as a representative of the American people who are true friends of democrats the world over, including Israel'; and: 'We urge you to write to Americans and President Carter in order to reveal the real face of the anti-Semite Brzezinski.'

New York Jews were shocked to receive this leaflet and copies were sent to the White House. On 31 August 1978, an official in the US national security council asked Rabbi Israel Miller, head of the Jewish Defence League in New York City, if these documents were authentic. Within hours a horrified Miller disavowed them as fraudulent. In fact, they were a crude KGB forgery. Buried in the Congress archives, a note attached to the file on this episode puts it baldly: 'Another phoney KGB document'.

The covert war against the national security advisor did not succeed in its ultimate aim, but that was not always the KGB's intention with fake news, letters and memos. The secret agenda was to spread false smears like a virus to discredit Brzezinski, regardless of whether it was effective. 'We just wanted to scare him, to be honest', a Soviet former military intelligence officer told me.

During the 1980 presidential campaign the Kremlin so distrusted Carter that it could not bring itself to support him even against the rabidly right-wing Republican Ronald Reagan. The Carter administration had been unexpectedly confrontational, especially on human rights violations, and dominated by the KGB's bête noire, Brzezinski. And so the Soviet Union remained neutral, partly because they did not believe that Reagan would reject detente and return to the paranoia and tensions of the Cold War. 'Fed up with Carter and uneasy about Reagan, it decided to stay on the fence', wrote Ambassador Dobrynin.[51]

Soon after Reagan was elected president in November 1980, the KGB was shocked by his apocalyptic confrontational outbursts. At his first press conference, Reagan accused the Kremlin of being willing 'to commit any crime, to lie and cheat' in order to promote a world Communist revolution. Later in his presidency, he set the tone by declaring that the Soviet Union was 'the focus of evil in the modern world' and an 'evil empire'. The Kremlin accused Reagan of reviving the 'worst rhetoric of the Cold War' and needlessly inflaming tension. The stakes were frighteningly high.

In 1981, Andropov, then head of the KGB, sent a message to his senior officers: 'Never before, starting from the Great Patriotic War and the Cold War years, has it been as acutely apparent as it is now: the imperialists are waging an arms race on an unprecedented scale and are expediting the preparations for war.'[52]

Political warfare was declared. The KGB general in charge was Yuri Andropov, a tall, scholarly looking man with cultured and reserved manners. He was ascetic to the point of fanaticism and his apartment was bare. Despite his stern exterior, he indulged a weakness for American jazz, especially Louis Armstrong. But he remained an uncompromising Cold Warrior. Born in 1914, he was Jewish in origin. When Yuri was five years old his father, a teacher, died and his mother passed away when he was just thirteen. He became a Communist Party organiser, fighting with partisan units behind German lines during the Second World War. As Soviet ambassador in Budapest during the Hungarian revolt in 1956, he demonstrated a capacity for intrigue by helping to lure Hungarian leaders to their death.

'The sad lesson of Hungary', he later admitted, 'was that the truth could not be defended merely with the word and pen but also, if needs be, with the hatchet.'[53]

In 1967 Andropov became head of the KGB but he was also a powerful voice in Soviet foreign policy and led the calls for 'extreme measures' to crush the liberal revolt in Czechoslovakia the following year. He was known for his obsession with conspiracy theories, according to Oleg Kalugin. This found vivid expression in his ardent support for active measures – disinformation, forgery, honey trapping and blackmail. He was fascinated with the creative nature of intelligence and was guided by Lenin's unflinching advocacy of using dirty tricks and falsehoods for political advancement.[54]

Under Andropov, covert active measures were intensified against the USA, which was known as the 'Main Adversary' (*Glavny Protivnik*). The KGB's Service A (forgeries) tasked officers to collect official letterheads and signatures of prominent Americans and other Western leaders, which could be used with scissors and paste to fabricate letters in photocopy form. Some were 'silent forgeries', shown in confidence to Third World leaders to 'alert' them to imaginary imperialist plots. Other documents were leaked to influential newspapers. The most notable was a letter ostensibly written by President Reagan to fuel opposition to Spanish membership of NATO. Dated 23 October 1981, the fabricated letter, leaked to prominent Spanish journalists, urged the King of Spain 'to act... with despatch to remove the forces obstructing Spain's entry into NATO'.

Millions of dollars were poured into KGB coffers to expand active measures and discover political intelligence. One tactic was to place an eavesdropping device inside Congress. KGB officers targeted the House of Representatives Committee on Armed Services which discussed top-secret military issues during closed sessions. According to Oleg Kalugin:

> A bug in the committee room would be an absolute gold mine, and we decided to give it a try. The best way to bug the room would be to send the TASS correspondent to an open hearing. Then, when the hearing was over and reporters and congressmen lingered to talk, the TASS man could plant the bug in a hidden spot and leave. The bug had to be wireless and have a sufficiently strong battery to transmit for an extended period of time.[55]

At the next hearing the TASS correspondent succeeded in attaching the device to the underside of the table. KGB agents eagerly waited with a receiver in a car just a few blocks from the Capitol building. But the bug did not work. It was not a technical fault. The FBI had been tipped off. They disabled the device and waited for the KGB agents to check it. The agents never returned to the scene of that crime and the operation failed but, like repeat offenders, the Soviet spies would revive their covert operations in different guises.

As the Cold War warmed up in the early 1980s, the pressure on KGB officers in Washington DC intensified. The priority was to prevent Reagan from being re-elected and the KGB's three residences were ordered to find incriminating information about the president. All they could discover was evidence of his weak intellectual capabilities and inability to concentrate – hardly a state secret.

The KGB was 'very strategic', a former senior FBI counter-intelligence officer told me. 'They targeted low level political sources and potential assets in foreign agencies who had access to classified documents.' The focus was to recruit agents on the staff of presidential candidates and influential congressmen. This was done by the KGB investigating and profiling congressional candidates. If they demonstrated potential, they would be invited for drinks at the Soviet embassy in Washington DC. However, by the mid-1980s, agent recruitment was more difficult. In previous decades the KGB had exploited the support for Communism to counter Fascism and offered financial inducements. A crude approach was: 'I have money. You have secrets. Let's swap.' But that motivation was no longer enticing.

One of the most effective KGB officers in Washington DC at the time was Yuri Shvets, who recruited a US administration official codenamed SOCRATES. He was advised by Colonel Valentin Aksilenko, his senior officer:

> Psychology is the most potent intelligence weapon today. There was a time when we recruited with ideology but who believes in those ideals any more? Then we switched to money but the standard of living in the West has risen to such an extent that we can no longer afford to pay enough to attract good assets. So only psychology is left. You must look for individuals with certain psychic deviations, primarily adventurers. You can hardly succeed in this task without knowledge of psychology. The James Bond era is over.[56]

Psychological warfare and its approach to intelligence-gathering was – and is – crucial. Many KGB officers during the Cold War had little, if any, experience of living in the West or access to accurate information. Instead, they relied on conspiracy theories about capitalist plotters and Zionist bankers who supposedly operated a secret command centre in the USA, intent on ruling the world. The CIA were the main conspirators – guilty of assassinating JFK, engineering Watergate to oust Nixon and creating an ethnic weapon that would kill blacks and spare whites. While not all KGB officers took these fantasies seriously, their boss, Andropov, certainly had the propensity to believe them.

The most serious conspiracy theory was the KGB's belief that the US was planning a nuclear first-strike attack against the Soviet Union. Codenamed Operation RYAN, a Russian acronym for 'Nuclear Missile Attack', it was launched in May 1981, the largest intelligence operation in Soviet history. Its purpose was to collect intelligence to prove that a full-blown nuclear onslaught was imminent. In fact, RYAN was derived from the paranoid instincts of Andropov and fuelled by the anti-Soviet rhetoric of President Reagan. It was a myth and desperate, pressurised KGB officers resorted to bizarre methods such as monitoring the stocks in British blood banks, the number of animals killed in slaughterhouses and the frequency of meetings between Prime Minister Margaret Thatcher and the Queen.[57] For the KGB, these were sure signs that the UK was preparing for a thermonuclear Armageddon.

Based on fear and Orwellian neurosis, RYAN was a classic case of spies trying to manipulate the facts to prove a pre-conceived theory. And when a leaked US national security council report demonstrated that the West's nuclear arsenal reflected a defensive doctrine, the document was quietly suppressed by the KGB and not shown to the Kremlin.[58]

The politicisation of intelligence-gathering was at its most intense. As former MI6 officer Gordon Barrass recalled:

Few KGB officers serving in the West are likely to have known of the top secret 'psyops' being mounted against the Soviet Union or just how apprehensive the Soviet leadership was becoming. Although the underlying concept of RYAN was sound, some of the information KGB officers overseas were told to look for made them dismiss the whole operation as being ludicrous… However, knowing they would be severely reprimanded if they detected no signs, KGB officers began to make them up, uncertain of what impact, if any, their reports would have on KGB headquarters.[59]

Despite the absence of evidence, Operation RYAN was maintained for most of Reagan's first term in office, as it had the extra benefit of 'informing' KGB officers that the president was a warmonger. It was only abandoned when Andropov died on 9 February 1984.

His successor, Konstantin Chernenko, was a hard-line Cold Warrior but not a conspiracy theorist and he reluctantly realised there was no factual basis for the operation. The legacy of RYAN was how the KGB assessed intelligence. As Christopher Andrew observed: 'The KGB's main weakness in the field of political intelligence was not, as it supposed, in intelligence collection but rather in its ability to interpret what it collected.'[60]

By 1983 the KGB retained the view that they could still have an impact on presidential elections. In previous campaigns, according to former KGB officer Yuri Shvets, several American politicians made an attempt, on the eve of the elections, to establish a communications channel to the Kremlin via the KGB. As a result, the prestige of the residency in Washington DC received such a major boost that Yakushkin, head of the KGB station until 1982, remarked: 'We are in a position to influence the outcome of the US presidential elections, you know.'[61]

On 25 February 1983, nearly two years before the next presidential election, the Centre in Moscow ordered the KGB residencies in the USA to plan active measures to prevent Reagan's re-election. They looked for *Kompromat* ranging from the president's alcoholic father to proving that he was planning to start World War Three. Ambitious and impractical plans were drawn up to sabotage Reagan's campaign by branding him a warmonger, according to a telegram by former KGB officer Vladimir Kirpichenko. The KGB sponsored and facilitated articles attacking Reagan.

During the 1984 campaign, KGB officers throughout NATO countries and around the world were instructed by Moscow to popularise the phrase 'Reagan Means War'. Vladimir Kryuchkov, then head of Soviet foreign intelligence operations and later KGB chief, implored his officers to 'expose' Reagan and the USA, which was intent on 'world domination'.[62] The strategy was to leak stories to the international press that the president was a reckless warmonger. But their influence was overstated and the limitations of their operation were illustrated by the failure of a single residency in a NATO country to popularise the KGB slogan.[63] Despite the KGB's best efforts, Reagan was re-elected by a landslide of votes.

During Reagan's second term in the White House, the KGB's active measures expanded and consumed thousands of officers and hundreds of millions of dollars. 'In the 1980s the KGB implemented a lot more active measures against American politicians than is realised', a former FBI officer told me. 'Their aim was to influence voters by hurting the reputation of the politicians.'

Forgeries and disinformation were the favourite tactic. In 1987 a letter was fabricated to show that William Casey, then director of the CIA, had authorised plans to overthrow Rajiv Gandhi, prime minister of India.

A favourite target was Richard Perle, then assistant secretary of defense and a hostile and articulate critic of the Soviet Union. Known as 'The Prince of Darkness', he was outspoken and an aggressive exponent of the SDI, which the Kremlin regarded as a needlessly provocative programme. And so the KGB forged a letter to Perle which was apparently sent and signed by the president of the Heritage Foundation, a radical conservative think tank.

The letter stated that the Soviet threat was 'a bluff' but one useful to American conservatives and was to be exploited as a trump card in domestic politics. For this political reason, the peace initiative by Mikhail Gorbachev, the new Soviet president, should be declared a 'menace' and vigorously opposed. The Heritage Foundation president apparently stressed the importance of increasing the American military and promoting the SDI.

One day in 1986 this letter was handed to KGB officer Yuri Shvets, who began reading. 'The letter was written in a confidential tone, the way two like-minded people would conduct personal correspondence', recalled Shvets. 'I was somewhat taken aback by the letter's bluntness; not once did he mention US national priorities, concentrating exclusively on the interests of the conservative political community.'

Shvets discussed the letter in the office. 'Who sent it?', he asked a colleague.

'We would also like to find that out', the colleague replied.

Don't be a fool, thought Shvets to himself. The letter literally shouted 'Made in the KGB'.

His KGB colleague added: 'Maybe someone in Moscow will find some use of it. Its basic idea is not bad but the execution is too crude.'

Shvets kept the letter as 'glaring evidence of an active measure stupidly conceived'.[64] When I asked Perle in 2022 about the letter, he confirmed that it was a forgery.

By the 1988 US presidential election campaign, perestroika and glasnost were in full flow. Presidents Reagan and Gorbachev negotiated a nuclear non-proliferation agreement and the end of the Cold War was in sight. It was the inevitable consequence of what the Soviet Union had privately already known for many years: a secret KGB presentation in late 1983 revealed that the US had superior firepower with its land-based strategic missiles.

'It's over, then', said a glum Yuri Andropov, then Soviet premier, who looked like a defendant who has just received a stiff jail sentence. 'We can't do anything at this level of military sophistication. Further military competition with the Americans is pointless unless we are willing to destroy our economy completely. We have to come to terms with the US, even at the price of major concessions… It looks as though we've considerably exaggerated their aggressiveness all along.'

For KGB officers like Yuri Shvets, who attended the presentation: 'It was a historic moment, marking a dramatic revision of the strategic doctrine and foreign policy of the Soviet Union. Gorbachev merely implemented the plans Andropov had drawn up but had not had the time to carry out.[65]

On the surface, one of the casualties of the end of the Cold War was KGB active measures – disinformation, forgery and fake news. In November 1987, Gorbachev was presented with a detailed investigation into the most grotesque KGB active measure of the Cold War: to spread the idea that the deadly AIDS virus was deliberately created by the American government in a biological weapons research centre in Maryland, in order to kill only black and gay people. Codenamed Operation INFEKTION, at first the Soviet premier fiercely denied that the KGB was capable and culpable of such an act. But then he was left alone to read the devastating detailed report. Gorbachev went quiet and shook his head. He apologised and decided to abolish such active measures.

It appeared to be the end of the KGB's involvement in influence operations, forgery, disinformation and interference in American presidential elections. Or so it seemed.

8

ESPIONAGE IN THE UK

Without a maximum of knowledge, you are unable
To put spies successfully in place.
Without humanity and justice you are unable
To send scouts ahead.
Without sure instincts and a penetrating mind you are unable
To judge the authenticity of a report.
Sensitivity! Sensitivity!

Sun Tzu, *The Art of War*

ONE EVENING IN THE EARLY 1960S a secretary who worked for an MP with a special interest in foreign policy attended a smart cocktail party in Mayfair, London. There she met a handsome, articulate diplomat who told her he was based at an East European embassy. Despite the Cold War, it was not unusual for the staff of MPs and ministers to socialise with officials from the Soviet bloc. Both sides knew the rules of the diplomatic game. The woman – who I shall call Miss Montagu – liked the engaging, intelligent diplomat who spoke excellent English. The feeling was mutual and they met again and developed a friendship.

However, the East European – who I shall call Novotny – had an agenda. He was in fact an intelligence officer and while he genuinely liked Miss Montagu, there was a secret mission: she was a secretary at the House of Commons and may have access to political and classified documents. While she found the 'diplomat' attractive, the secretary knew she had to be careful.

During one evening Miss Montagu casually mentioned that her MP had gone abroad, leaving her in charge of his affairs. For the Communist spy it was his golden opportunity. Novotny remarked that such MPs must be well-informed and interested in topical political issues.

'I am also interested in such matters', he remarked. 'Surely you must have a chance to see documents which summarise Western views on current affairs and political developments.'

Miss Montagu was guarded and discreet in her reply: 'It is almost impossible for me to obtain such documents.'

The intelligence officer, whose country was a close and dependent ally of the Soviet Union, was confronted with a dilemma. He was discouraged by Miss Montagu's response but his mission was not lost. After all, he thought, she had used – perhaps deliberately – the word 'almost'. *What is my next move?*, the spy reflected. He was sophisticated enough to realise the offer of cash would not persuade her. She was not that type, he correctly surmised.

After some consideration, Novotny tried a more subtle approach. He asked Miss Montagu for advice on the choice of a ring to send home as a present to his wife. The secretary was not particularly surprised when a few days later she herself received a ring worth about twenty pounds from her new friend. She returned the ring, expressing her polite regret that it was impossible for someone in her position to accept such gifts, especially from a foreign official. Even worse, from someone who represented a hostile nation state.

Despite the flattering attentions of the debonair 'diplomat', Miss Montagu knew she could be dipping her toe into treacherous waters. From the beginning of his approach, she had informed

MI5 and kept them briefed of his polite solicitations. There the friendship ended and they parted courteously as if they were characters in a Somerset Maugham novel. For Novotny, it was the end of a short and hopeful liaison. They never met again. But for one MI5 officer who was familiar with this affair, he was reminded of a phrase used by the Russians for such episodes – 'The scythe has struck a stone', or as we say in English, an irresistible force had met an immovable object.[1]

*

Historically, Great Britain and its political elite has always been a target for the KGB. Throughout the Cold War, the Soviet spies and their subsidiary satellite agencies stationed far more officers in London than other cities. 'Great Britain is still the number two power in the free world', said former Czech intelligence officer Josef Frolik in 1977. 'If you want to compromise them, you have to act.'[2]

The KGB believed that MI6 and the Foreign Office were the unrivalled experts in psychological warfare, deception and slander, even though the Soviet Union was a closed society which made it almost impossible to spread disinformation. They had no hesitation in using any tactic to subvert the political system of what was regarded as the 'decaying, rotting West'.[3]

For the KGB, recruiting an MP was the highest prize because he or she could be used to propagate the Kremlin line openly or covertly via front organisations. And the House of Commons was a relatively easy target because of its openness from a security perspective. If you secured an appointment with an MP or researcher and were afterwards escorted back to the Central Lobby, you could then roam undetected throughout the Palace of Westminster. MI5 was conscious that the KGB was very active in Parliament. In 1971, in rare evidence to a government inquiry on national security, Sir Martin Furnival-Jones, then MI5's director-general, addressed the threat:

One must not suppose that all hostile intelligence service officers are readily recognisable. There was a time indeed when they were readily recognisable. The Russians were because they wore long coats and curiously shaped hats. They do not do so any longer. They have learned that this is counter-productive… I can certainly say that very many members of Parliament are in contact with very many intelligence officers.

The head of MI5 added that Russian spies cultivated MPs not merely to obtain classified information covered by the Official Secrets Act. They were also interested in political intelligence useful to the Soviet Union and even the social lives of the British people.

'No doubt many MPs enter the Commons in the hope of becoming Ministers', added Furnival-Jones. 'If the Russian Intelligence Service can recruit a backbench MP, and he climbs the ladder to a Ministerial position, it is obvious the spy is home and dry… The other information which they are after and show a remarkably voracious appetite for is party political information.'[4]

The KGB decided on two strategies regarding political espionage. Firstly, the black propaganda approach based on forgeries. In the early 1950s they were assisted by the double agent Guy Burgess, who enthusiastically advised agents on how to counterfeit official government documents. He once helped to fake letters supposedly sent by concerned private citizens to MPs with the aim of spreading political chaos.[5] The most notorious smear was in July 1974, when a photocopy of a Swiss Bank Corporation account statement in the name of Edward Short, then leader of the Commons and deputy Labour Party leader, was sent anonymously to journalists. It gave the MP's correct home address and showed a credit balance of £23,000, which would have been deemed illegal. But there was no account number and the police soon established that it was a forgery. While it was never proven, UK intelligence officers believed it was conceived by the KGB.

'I have always suspected that this forged document was a KGB-inspired device to discredit the British government through one of its senior ministers', said the renowned author and security reporter Chapman Pincher, who had the best intelligence contacts at that time.[6]

The KGB's second strategy was to recruit Labour MPs as secret agents of influence. This was partly facilitated through the British Communist Party. Ever since their landslide election victory in 1945, Labour Party leaders were worried about the presence of what they believed were 'cryto-Communists' on their backbenches. On the morning after that election Douglas Hyde, news editor of the Communist *Daily Worker*, received a telephone call and heard a familiar voice.

'The man at the other end announced himself as the new Labour MP for his constituency', recalled Hyde. 'He followed it with a loud guffaw and rang off. I had known him as a Communist Party man for years... By the time the list [of Labour MPs] was complete, we knew that we had at least eight or nine "cryptos" [Communists] in the House of Commons, in addition to our two publicly acknowledged MPs.'[7]

Historians agree that at least twelve Labour MPs were either secret Communists or pro-Soviet in their views and were known at the time as 'The Lost Sheep'.[8]

By the early 1960s the leadership of the Labour opposition was more concerned about Communist and Soviet subversion than the Conservative government. Of course, if a Labour MP expressed pro-Soviet views it did not mean that he or she was a KGB agent or even an asset. But Hugh Gaitskell, the moderate Labour Party leader, and Patrick Gordon Walker, the shadow foreign secretary, were fearful of the damage to their election prospects. And so Gordon Walker wrote to Sir Roger Hollis, then MI5's director-general, and on 5 September 1961 he met his deputy, Graham Mitchell. The shadow foreign secretary brought with him a hand-written letter on Commons notepaper with a list of sixteen Labour MPs who, he believed, 'were in effect members of the CPGB [Communists] pretending to be Labour members or men under Communist Party direction'.[9]

The name at the top of the list was Will Owen, Labour MP for Morpeth, who was also head of a travel firm which specialised in visits to East Germany. Owen later resigned his seat after being charged with giving Czech intelligence agents confidential information which he had learned as a member of Parliament's estimates committee. At his trial in 1970 the MP admitted receiving £2,300 from the Czechs which he had not declared for tax and that he had been a spy since 1954. Despite the security danger, he had demanded free holidays in Czechoslovakia and gifts. Owen also acknowledged he knew that his contact at the Czech embassy was a senior spy. Notwithstanding evidence that he leaked NATO documents, the MP was acquitted on the grounds the information he had leaked was not covered by the Official Secrets Act.

At the meeting with MI5, Gordon Walker asked for information about MPs who were secret Communists and had penetrated the Labour Party. The deputy director-general declined because the request was motivated by party political considerations, not national security.[10]

What was significant about the list of Labour MPs who were suspected Communists and hence potential KGB agents was the absence of certain names. Perhaps the most notorious MP was John Stonehouse, who was recruited by the Czechs in 1962 and continued to be an agent while he was minister for aviation and minister for post and telecommunications in the Labour government, later in the 1960s. MI5 suspected Stonehouse was a spy but did not possess the proof and so he was allowed to be a minister right up until the 1970 election. The truth only emerged in 1974, when Stonehouse faked his own death after securing a false passport in the name of a dead man and 'drowning' off Miami beach while wanted for fraud charges. He later went to jail.

Far less well known were the covert activities on behalf of the KGB carried out by Bob Edwards, the maverick left-wing Labour MP for Wolverhampton. Born in 1905 in Liverpool, his mother was a factory worker and his father worked as a harbour master on the docks. Edwards was a radical young firebrand and led an Independent Labour Party Youth delegation to Moscow in the late 1920s, where he met Stalin and Trotsky. After fighting with the Republicans alongside George Orwell in the Spanish civil war, he worked for trade unions until he was elected as an MP in 1955.

Unlike his fellow KGB agent and trade union leader Jack Jones, Edwards was almost unknown outside Westminster and the ranks of the radical left. But he was on the KGB radar and recruited as an agent of influence in the late 1950s. He remained an enthusiastic exponent of Soviet disinformation measures and conspiracy theories, especially against the CIA, and was occasionally paid. In early 1961 the Labour MP attracted the attention of the CIA and MI5 as the co-author of an eighty-page booklet called *A Study of a Master Spy*, a vituperative attack on the former CIA director Allen Dulles which was in fact written by a KGB officer. The principal allegation was that Dulles had cultivated pro-Nazi business interests just before the Second World War and so had become compromised and illicitly sympathetic to the Nazi cause. 'Hemmed in on all sides by the black slime of Nazi interests, he could not help put a foot in the mire', stated the booklet.[11]

The role of the KGB officer as the ghost-writer of the booklet was not known at the time but the participation of Edwards was suspicious and MI5 launched an investigation. In 1965 MI5 believed they had sufficient evidence that he was a security risk to apply for a warrant to tap the MP's telephone. This was authorised by Frank Soskice, then home secretary, but countermanded by Harold Wilson, mainly because he had told MPs that their phones were not bugged by MI5. The MP therefore remained undiscovered, and later that year became chairman of the Defence and Foreign Affairs Sub-Committee of the Estimates Committee and vice-chairman of the Western European Defence Committee.

'Both would have been of interest to the KGB and there is no doubt Edwards would have passed on all he could get hold of', an MI5 report later concluded. 'We know Edwards' motivation was ideological, although he occasionally accepted money.'[12]

For the next fifteen years the MP's KGB controller was Leonid Zaitsev, head of the foreign intelligence division's directorate T (science and technology) and stationed in London before becoming a major general. They became close friends and the KGB arranged to contact Edwards by radio and dead letter boxes, possibly because they suspected that the MP's phone was tapped.

By the late 1970s Edwards was not as active, although the KGB recognised his contribution in 1980 when he was awarded the Order of the People's Friendship by the Soviet Union. Two years later Oleg Gordievsky discovered the importance of Edwards as an agent while reading intelligence dossiers on active cases in Britain. One was devoted to the West Midlands MP. It was clear that he was a willing KGB informant. When Gordievsky was posted to London he revived old contacts and met Edwards, who remained an unrepentant friend of the KGB and 'was happy to chat about the old days but had very little to reveal about the new ones'.[13]

After losing his Commons seat in 1983, Edwards retired and died on 4 June 1990, aged eighty-five, just before the Soviet Union collapsed. His vision of a Communist utopia remained unfulfilled. He always denied the speculation about his espionage for the Soviets to his fellow Labour MPs and took his KGB secrets to his grave. But the MI5 and Russian intelligence documents proved conclusive and, as Gordievsky reflected, the MP's recruitment was 'lost in the mists of antiquity'.

A close friend of Edwards and a fellow traveller was William Wilson, Labour MP for the neighbouring constituency of Coventry. A solicitor and an army officer, Wilson was also radicalised by the depression and the threat of Fascism of the 1930s. He was motivated by genuine deep-seated socialist ideals. But, as he later acknowledged, he was also a confidential contact of the KGB during the Cold War and a true believer (he once called for full diplomatic relations with Communist Albania and North Korea). Between 1977 and 1983 he was chairman of the British-Soviet Friendship Society, a front for the Soviet Union, whose influence was overstated but valued. In Moscow officials regarded the MP as an influential politician who at crucial junctures reinforced the Kremlin line, although he was not a pro-Soviet advocate in the Commons.[14]

Before he died in 2010, Wilson was asked by Darren Lilleker, the author of *Against the Cold War*, a study of pro-Soviet allegiances in the Labour Party, about his relationship with the KGB. He admitted that through his activities in pro-Soviet friendship societies and his support for the extension of trading links with Eastern Europe, he became a close friend of a 'diplomat' at the Soviet embassy in the early 1970s. And he acknowledged it was not a purely innocent relationship. He was often invited to lunch at the diplomat's expense, during which he discussed the political situation, the Labour Party and 'who in British politics was likely to be favourable to the Soviet Union'. The diplomat turned out to be Anatoly Maisko, the cultural attaché at the Soviet embassy who oversaw the friendship societies. Technically he was not a KGB officer but was defined as a 'co-optee' – a KGB-trained diplomat who operated under a dual brief, according to Oleg Gordievsky, his case officer in London.[15]

Wilson's rationalisation of this relationship was that he did not regard the Soviet Union as a threat to Britain and did not disclose any classified secrets or inside information.

'I was simply extending the hand of friendship', he recalled. 'I didn't tell them anything they didn't already know.'

But he did provide insights into the political scene from within Parliament and information on which MPs would be responsive to Soviet overtures and how to contact them. He also relayed messages and invitations between the diplomat and other contacts. That did not make him an operational spy but it was certainly useful to the Soviet cause.

The value of such an MP was that if a major conflict broke out, the KGB could consult someone who was close to the decision-making process and might provide useful information. 'Wilson's role was as a conduit of understanding', wrote Lilleker. 'He enabled the Soviet leadership to interpret British politics and the imperatives of decision-making from the perspective of someone within the British parliament.'[16]

Wilson was also asked about the brutal invasions of Hungary in 1956 and Czechoslovakia in 1968.

'For him, it was not a question of whether you were a Stalinist or Trotskyist but did you want the Soviet Union to become a truly socialist nation', Lilleker told me. 'In his opinion, defending the Soviet Union and opposing the USA was the way to achieve that.'

When asked about Edwards, his parliamentary fellow traveller was guarded even though it was several years after his death. Both Wilson and Edwards left political archives, but nothing about the Soviet Union, which is not surprising. However, intriguingly, in Wilson's papers there are 'thirty-six files which have been closed for varying periods because they contain particularly sensitive personal information about people who may still be alive'.

Most Labour MPs who were contacted and befriended by Soviet diplomats during the Cold War were aware that these figures were in fact KGB agents. They knew that they were targeted due to their ideologies, but wanted to have a dialogue. As Lilleker remembered:

> What struck me is that they wanted to offer an alternative perspective to the Soviet Union than the black-and-white view that was set during the Cold War. Hence they viewed the relationships with those we might view as [KGB] handlers as mutually beneficial. They were largely naïve, desperate to find evidence that actually existing socialism was possible and that if it was not for US opposition it would flourish... Wilson remained unable to divorce his socialist aspirations for Britain from the success of the Soviet system. To denounce the Soviet model would mean rejecting socialism.

The notion that large numbers of Labour MPs were KGB active secret agents of influence is fanciful. Clearly, some like Edwards were spies and useful to the Soviet cause. But to define an MP who discussed politics with a Russian diplomat as an intelligence agent is misleading and hyperbolic. If an MP spoke to a KGB officer, that does not make him or her an agent – or even an asset or informant. At best, the MP would be a confidential source and provide useful political intelligence and analysis but it would not be classified material. The misunderstanding of that relationship led to false allegations that former Labour Party leader Michael Foot was a KGB agent.

During the Cold War many MPs wanted access to the Soviet perspective and most are adamant they did not disclose secrets and only revealed information that was in the public domain. But that approach was naive and even dangerous. The cultivation of senior British politicians was a high priority for the KGB and officers like Gordievsky needed to prove access and obtain information. The Kremlin certainly believed they had agents inside Parliament and even 10 Downing Street. This perception was exacerbated by some left-wing MPs, who encouraged relations with the Soviet Union. And so even the Labour prime minister, Harold Wilson, was regarded as a potential KGB target.

'I do not for one moment believe, as some in MI5 seemed to believe, that Wilson was a conscious Soviet agent or spy', said Sir John Killick, British ambassador to the Soviet Union between 1971 and 1973. 'But Moscow certainly regarded him as a potential "agent of influence", if not as a "useful idiot".'[17]

The supreme irony is that the Soviet Union preferred dealing with Conservative and right-wing politicians during the Cold War. The KGB and their satellite spy agencies, especially the Czechs, believed Tory MPs could be cultivated, despite the ideological hostility. One successful recruit was Conservative MP and junior minister Ray Mawby, who spied for the Czech security service in return for payment. He even handed over the floor plans of the prime minister's private office in the Commons.

Politically and diplomatically, the Soviets found that negotiating with Conservative ministers was reassuring because there was political certainty. This was in contrast to Labour regimes, who viewed Communism as a perversion of socialism whereas Conservatives were comfortable negotiating with autocracies.

'The Soviet system was very much top down', said Andrew Wood, former British ambassador to Moscow, who was also stationed there twice as a diplomat during the Cold War. 'And so I think many Soviet Communists felt that social democrats were more the main enemy than the Conservatives because at least the Conservatives from their perspective understood and were operating within the parameters of power relationships rather than any nonsense about social justice.'[18]

For the Kremlin and the KGB the ideology and aspirations of Communism and capitalism were starkly opposite and irreconcilable. The Soviet state was founded on a rigid dogma and there was an inherent unyielding conservatism to its society and culture. The liberals were the enemy. And this was vividly illustrated when Sir Curtis Keeble, British ambassador in Moscow at the height of the Cold War, commented on the conservatism of the Kremlin leadership to an archbishop of the Russian Orthodox Church. 'Yes', he replied. 'Conservatism and dogma, the twin pillars of the Orthodox Church and the Soviet state.'[19]

This unlikely relationship can be traced back to at least 1927, when the Conservative foreign secretary Sir Austen Chamberlain remarked that the Soviet government was more willing to shake hands with him than with Labour ministers: 'They regarded Conservatives as their natural enemies but the more moderate Labour leaders they looked upon as traitors.'[20] This remained true after the 1945 election, when Stalin would have far rather dealt with Winston Churchill than the new Labour prime minister, Clement Attlee. And when Khrushchev visited London in April 1956, there were furious rows with the Labour leadership.

After the speaker's lunch, Aneurin Bevan, the left-wing shadow foreign secretary, muttered repeatedly to the British ambassador, Sir William Hayter: 'He's an impossible man.'

The dislike was reciprocated. When Sir William returned to Moscow, an irritated Khrushchev told him: 'Bulganin [Soviet Premier] can vote Labour if he likes but I am going to vote Conservative.'[21]

Inside the KGB there was no party political bias. The aim was to recruit powerful civil servants, MPs and politicians. In 1965 the KGB and their Czech accomplices decided to persuade the new Conservative Party leader, Edward Heath, to become an agent. It was a bizarre plan, even in the world of espionage. Heath was a bachelor and the gossip, unfounded, was that the future prime minister was gay and so could be compromised. And so Czech agents devised a scheme to lure Heath to Prague by inviting him to indulge his passion for organ playing in the city's most prestigious church. Once there, he could be compromised by a handsome young agent and recruited to work for the Czech security service and, de facto, the KGB. Predictably the plan failed when Heath declined the invitation.[22]

The KGB's target was the party in government. In the early 1960s the social network was a priority and so they tasked the charismatic KGB officer Mikhail Lyubimov. Known as 'Smiling Mike'. Lyubimov was a handsome spy who was stationed in London between 1961 and 1965, where he shared a flat at 10 Earls Terrace, just off Kensington High Street. A gifted linguist with a friendly demeanour, he cultivated novelists like Alan Sillitoe and C. P. Snow and was invited to smart parties where he would be introduced half-jokingly as 'the Russian spy'. At one dinner hosted by the historian Lady Antonia Fraser, the KGB officer met Ian Fleming just after the *Dr No* film had been made and a lot of whisky was consumed while they discussed the James Bond movies.

The Conservatives were in power for most of Lyubimov's tenure, but his cover did not remain intact for long. 'I was directed at the Conservative Party and very soon I became well known as a spy in the Conservatives', he recalled. 'I worked very intensively and I was foolish enough at that time to be very active.'[23] He attended the 1962 Conservative Party conference and danced with the activists, and the charming Russian did recruit one agent: a Tory MP's personal secretary. And one woman thought about handing over secret documents but changed her mind. He was predictably less successful when he approached the right-wing columnist Peregrine

Worsthorne, the newly elected MP Peter Walker and Nicholas Scott, then leader of the Young Conservatives.

Unfortunately for 'Smiling Mike', he was expelled from London in 1965 when he was caught trying to recruit a cipher operator. He returned to Moscow and was promoted to colonel before spending his retirement living with his black cat and writing improbable spy novels and plays.

*

By the mid-1960s, MI5's watchers were struggling to contain the elaborate espionage operation being run out of the Soviet embassy in Kensington Palace Gardens. The MI5 surveillance team was coordinated from a control room off Regent's Park, with a huge street map of London on one wall and a constantly crackling radio. But British intelligence simply did not have the numbers to cope with their wily opponents. At least sixty KGB officers operated under cover at the embassy, with dozens more working for military intelligence and two hundred cars at their disposal.

Unknown to the local residents, Russian spies moved into flats and houses on Bassett Road in Notting Hill, Earls Terrace, Kensington and Edith Road, Chelsea. The house at 42 Holland Park had been a well-established residency for KGB officers since at least 1964. It was owned by the Russian state and became notorious in 1983 when the MI5 officer Michael Bettaney dropped an envelope containing security files on three Soviet agents through the letterbox. The inhabitant – KGB station chief Arkady Gouk – assumed that it was a trick and ignored the approach. But the documents were genuine. It was a naive attempt to sell state secrets and the unstable Bettaney was later jailed.

Outside London KGB officers and diplomats used Seacox Heath, a Grade-II listed nineteenth-century castle, as a weekend and holiday retreat. Sitting in the sleepy countryside around Tunbridge Wells, on the border between Kent and East Sussex, the castle is one of eighteen properties in England owned by the Russian state.

The imposing four-storey property, worth millions of pounds, boasts mock-Gothic turrets, chiselled balconies and terraced lawns opening onto its thirty acres of grounds. The estate includes two detached cottages, tennis courts and a football pitch.

The 'dacha' used to be the refuge of the leader of the Hawkhurst gang, Arthur Gray, from which the smugglers led raids across the coast of Dorset. The existing structure, built in a French chateau style in 1871, belonged to the second Viscount Goschen. He gave it to the Soviet Union in 1947 as a gift after Russian sailors saved his son during the Second World War. While the Soviets never mixed with the locals, the Hare and Hound pub was frequented by KGB and security officers, notably Sergei Ivanov, before he was expelled from the UK.[24]

During the Cold War, KGB officers were observed destroying documents. A neighbour was Ruari Chisholm, former MI6 station chief in Moscow. One day his friend John Miller, a foreign correspondent based in the Soviet Union, noticed some late-night activity at the castle.

'From the end of his garden you could sometimes see the KGB burning their shredded secret files on a bonfire', recalled Miller. 'We once sneaked into the back garden and kicked over the ashes for a disappointing reward: the only thing readable was a list of items on a BBC news broadcast.'[25]

As dozens of KGB officers and agents roamed the streets of London, it was difficult for MI5 to monitor their activities. A favourite tactic was the dead letter box – an arrangement whereby a KGB officer would exchange documents, film and photographs with an agent or source at a secret location without meeting. One agent received £8,000 cash in a large hollow artificial brick using elaborate radio communications. By avoiding direct contact, this enabled the spy to avoid being photographed or filmed. During the Cold War a popular venue was the Brompton Oratory, the grandiose Catholic church just behind the Victoria and Albert Museum in South Kensington. A KGB agent filed this report for a collection:

Just to the right of the entrance is an altar. It is a memorial to Englishmen who were killed in the [Second World] war and has a copy of Michelangelo's famous statue 'Pieta' – the dead Jesus Christ in his mother's arms. On the floor below the statue are the words 'Consummatum est'. Just to the left of the altar, as you face it, are two large marble columns which are part of the architecture of the church. Both are very close to the wall. The dead letter box site is behind the column nearest to the wall (the right-hand column) in a tiny little space between the column and the wall.

This part of the church is very poorly lit. It is dark there even in the daytime. The impression gained was that no one stops there... I would suggest leaving a 35 mm film suitably sealed in this place. As a test, I left a film in this spot at 11 a.m. I returned at 6 p.m. and the film was still in place. I took it out and I do not think that anyone had noticed this film during the day. I chose Brompton Oratory because it is in central London and people go in and out all day and no one pays any attention to them. The church is not 'state property' so there are no people keeping a round-the-clock watch on it... I would be inclined to think that there is no safer place in central London.[26]

An alternative place was almost next door, near the smaller Holy Trinity Church on Cottage Place. The actual site for the dead letter box was on the ground, at the base of a large tree facing a statue of Saint Francis of Assisi on a small paved precinct for pedestrians. On one occasion an empty film cassette was left there all day without anyone noticing. Other locations included a signal site on a lamppost in Audley Square in Mayfair. Around the corner in the garden a chalk mark was placed on a bench to indicate that the signal on the lamppost had been read and understood. And in less fashionable areas signal sites were marked in code on a post at the intersection of Gray's Inn Road and Guilford Street and near the Ballot Box pub in Sudbury Hill, north-west London.[27]

*

It was the discovery of a dead letter box in 1967 that led to the largest and most controversial expulsion of KGB officers from London in the history of the Cold War. A Soviet spy called Oleg Drozdov had been filmed by MI5 collecting information left by a British atomic scientist in a London park. It epitomised the scale of KGB espionage operations in the UK, and threatened to overwhelm not just MI5 but the security of the state.

By 1970 there were so many Soviet agents operating in London that MI5 was hopelessly over-extended. Their strategy was to swamp the exhausted MI5 with more intelligence officers than they could hope to keep under surveillance. 'At the time the number of KGB and GRU staff in London threatened to outnumber MI5', said former KGB officer Mikhail Lyubimov, who was stationed in the UK in the mid-1960s.[28] This was confirmed by George Walden, then a senior Foreign Office official on the Soviet desk and later a Conservative minister, in his memoirs.

> Their [KGB] agent-runners in the London Embassy or Trade delegation had begun propositioning very senior aircraftsman or defence industry employees who came their way, regardless of the risk that they might report the approach. When they did, and MI5 told us, we expelled the agent, and then the Russians threw out one of our people in Moscow in retaliation and inserted another KGB man in London, and everything proceeded as before. Since they had about five times as many personnel in London as we had in Moscow, in tit-for-tat reprisals, the British were on a losing ticket.[29]

In the late 1960s the KGB took advantage of the passivity and complacency of the Labour government. The prime minister, Harold Wilson, was unwilling to adopt an antagonistic stance against the Soviet Union and saw the political advantages of diplomatic engagement by carving out a role for himself, notably as a mediator between the Russians and the Americans in Vietnam. And so he was not prepared to allow rampant espionage to interfere with East–West diplomacy.

For many Foreign Office mandarins, this policy was culpable neglect. The KGB were not just outnumbering MI5. Their agents were penetrating – or attempting to penetrate – UK military installations.

'While wanting a facade of good relations with the outside world, the Brezhnev doctrine was based on a real need for Western technology above all', said Sir John Killick, British ambassador to Moscow in the early 1970s. 'A lot of the espionage that went on in Britain was to get technology, no question about it.'[30]

His former Foreign Office colleague, Sir Roderic Lyne, agreed the KGB was intent on any intelligence: 'A certain amount of it was pretty innocuous – trawling public libraries for our scientific and technological knowledge. But clearly a more important task was to get any military information and defence research and to suborn people. They were also seeking to influence the political process – cultivating MPs is a normal part of the diplomatic process but sometimes their cultivation crossed the boundaries of propriety.'[31]

In matters of espionage it is usually the mandarins rather than ministers who prefer a quiet life and do not want to upset diplomatic protocol. In this case the *Yes Minister* syndrome personified in Sir Humphrey was reversed. The Foreign Office pressed reluctant, nervous ministers to act. In late 1970 George Walden was appalled when he read the files.

'Known KGB personnel had been let into Britain under diplomatic cover on the assumption that MI5 would "keep an eye on them" ', he recalled. 'I discovered that it took nine [MI5] men to follow a single Soviet agent. The truth was that we had no serious means of keeping track of them, had little idea of what they were up to and none at all of whether they were doing us serious damage or not.'[32]

For Walden and his colleagues, the Establishment's complacency reflected a wider institutional malaise and an inflated view of itself. He advocated a tough line because 'the Russians knew that we knew that we were swamped with spies and that we did not dare to do anything about it', he said. 'The will to resist their pressures in the field of espionage was rightly seen by the Russians as a gauge of a country's resolution overall and by 1970 the KGB regarded the British as broken-backed.'[33]

Political timidity was the obstacle to a mass expulsion of the Soviet spies. But then the unlikely Foreign Office radicals were blessed with a stroke of good fortune. Oleg Lyalin, a KGB officer working in the Soviet trade delegation, was persuaded to defect by MI5 and become a British agent after they discovered during routine surveillance he was conducting an illicit affair with his secretary. In return, he was promised eventual resettlement for himself and his girlfriend.

Codenamed 'GOLDFINCH', Lyalin was debriefed at a safe house at 24 Collingham Gardens, Earls Court, over several glasses of beer and identified a large number of fellow spies. His cover job had been an importer of clothes, travelling throughout England and buying nothing more security-sensitive than knitwear and woollen socks. But at night and in his spare time the former parachutist and expert marksman devised sabotage operations designed to spread turmoil, for use in time of war. These included maps for Soviet submarine landing sites, plans to use bombs to flood the London tube and even the distribution of poison-gas capsules in the tunnels beneath Whitehall – all on behalf of the KGB. These apocalyptic schemes were regarded as somewhat fantastical but embryonic in character.

The extent of the KGB espionage network revealed by Lyalin shocked the government. But the strategy was to give the Soviets the opportunity to withdraw their agents quietly. While the British never expected this would occur, Sir Alec Douglas-Home, then foreign secretary, took the opportunity of a visit by Andrei Gromyko, the Soviet minister, in late October 1970 to complain about the level of espionage by his embassy staff. He then provided precise numbers. Bizarrely and comically, Gromyko replied 'These figures you give cannot be true because the Soviet Union has no spies' and he asked Sir Alec to put his complaints in writing. On

4 December 1970, Sir Alec sent a letter, mainly to pre-empt any complaints that the government's action was hysterical. It indicated that the Soviets were not expected to stop intelligence-gathering but to scale it back. But he never heard back. This was the ultimate discourtesy to a gentleman of Sir Alec's aristocratic decorum. It was resolved that more radical action was required.

Top-secret meetings were then held in Whitehall with MI5's director-general, Sir Martin Furnival-Jones, and the MI6 chief, Sir John Rennie. On 25 May 1971, the head of MI5 told senior civil servants that in the previous fifteen years the KGB had penetrated the Foreign Office, the Ministry of Defence, the army, the RAF, the Labour Party and the Board of Trade.

'It was difficult to say exactly how much damage was being done', said Furnival-Jones. 'But it was equally difficult to believe that the Russians maintained such a large establishment for no profit. At least thirty to forty Soviet intelligence officers in this country were actually running secret agents in government or industry.'

The MI6 chief, Sir John Rennie, added that the KGB 'attached a high priority to acquiring scientific and technical secrets and to commercial information with military overtones'.

The officials were shocked but also uneasy about the Soviet response to any large-scale expulsions. Sir Burke Trend, the cabinet secretary, asked whether the Russians would increase their illegal operations (KGB agents operating without diplomatic immunity) and create more difficulty. The MI5 director-general replied that this would be difficult as 'illegals' were much more difficult to run and could not themselves actively recruit agents. The Foreign Office permanent secretary agreed that Britain would be 'vulnerable to commercial reprisals and general beastliness, but did not think the Russians would break off diplomatic relations'. MI5 proposed the removal of at least a hundred KGB officers and the cabinet secretary concluded that it would be better to implement the expulsions during the parliamentary recess.[34]

In conditions of strict secrecy, Operation FOOT was put in motion. The strategy was referred to in the Foreign Office as 'the falling ceiling' – designed to make the Soviets watch their step in the future. It was a warning sign as much as a punitive measure. The foreign secretary, Sir Alec Douglas-Home, hoped for a quiet withdrawal of KGB officers and sent a final warning on 4 August 1971. His Soviet counterpart, Gromyko, did not reply, no doubt because the KGB boss was the hardliner Yuri Andropov. Incensed by such diplomatic rudeness, Douglas-Home met the prime minister, Edward Heath, and other ministers on 21 September to make a final decision. The stakes were high but the situation where hundreds of Soviet spies in different guises were roaming the streets of London and infiltrating the government was almost out of control. Heath authorised Operation FOOT to proceed.

Three days later at 3.15 p.m. on 24 September, Ivan Ippolitov the Soviet chargé d'affaires, himself an undercover KGB officer, was summoned to the Foreign Office. He was greeted by Sir Denis Greenhill, the permanent secretary, who read out the charge sheet in a monotonous gravelly voice. Sir Denis told him no further expansion of Soviet diplomats in London would be permitted and any reprisals would lead to more expulsions. He then passed over two lists: one consisted of ninety KGB officers then in the UK and another of fifteen spies who were not at that moment in the UK but held valid re-entry visas. They would not be allowed to return. The Soviet diplomat nervously leafed through the list of expelled KGB officers, which went on for several pages. He did not read beyond the first page. He was asked if there was anything that he did not understand. 'No, no', he replied in a husky voice. 'All is clear. Very drastic measures, Sir Greenhill, very drastic!' After a few standard courtesies, he was shown out. As he was driven back to the Soviet embassy in Kensington Palace Gardens, he saw the billboards for the *London Evening Standard*. The huge headline read – 'KGB OUT'.[35]

When Ippolitov arrived back at the embassy, MI5 watchers were at hand to observe the reaction. Within minutes of his entrance, a man hurtled across the street from the KGB offices on the other side and the phone calls and telegrams to Moscow reached frenetic levels. Meanwhile, George Walden, the diplomat who had done so much to make Operation FOOT a success, went for a celebratory drink at MI5's headquarters in Curzon Street, Mayfair. MI5 spies were usually a repressed, stony-faced crowd, living in intense secrecy and receiving no recognition for their services. But that night they were in high spirits – except there was no alcohol. This was only remedied when an officer opened a vast, imposing safe which was completely full of wine and whisky.[36]

The KGB was furious and Gromyko denounced the 'gross provocation' by Britain. There was some harassment of embassy staff in Moscow, but the Soviet response was relatively muted and fell far short of London's worst fears. The trade repercussions were minimal, and only four embassy staff and a resident businessman in Moscow were expelled. Diplomatic relations were not broken off.

'They [the Russians] gained more from their presence in the open society of London than we did in the closed society of Moscow', recalled Martin Nicholson, a Foreign Office diplomat involved in the expulsions. 'And so for the sake of appearances they [the Soviets] bulked up the numbers of expellees with an assortment of "also-rans".'[37]

Abroad, Operation FOOT was well-received by Britain's allies, who were given the unpublished list of the 105 KGB spies, and in many cases they refused visas to those who had been expelled when they sought new countries for their operations. This compounded the KGB's misery. In Moscow foreign diplomats arrived at the British embassy, flying their flag.

'Nobody was more interested than the Chinese ambassador who wanted to know every detail regarding what we had done to ruin the Russians', said the British ambassador, Sir John Killick. 'He loved it.'[38]

France, hosting a state visit from Leonid Brezhnev at the time, was less enthusiastic. The French security service DST was delighted but their diplomats loftily dismissed the KGB expulsions as 'a traffic accident'.[39]

Despite its success, there had been some overkill in the selection of the expelled personnel. A few of the 105 were genuine diplomats and not spies but the Foreign Office justified it on the sheer scale of the KGB infiltration. One official even quoted Stalin, who said after being asked about the number of innocent people being purged: 'When you chop wood, the splinters fly.' But even Ivan Ippolitov, the Soviet chargé d'affairs who had received the demand for the expulsions, acknowledged they were justified. Many years later he telephoned Sir Julian Bullard, the erudite and intelligent head of the Foreign Office's Eastern Europe and Soviet department. The call was from a public telephone at Heathrow airport, so that nobody could listen in. He told Bullard in confidence the Soviet foreign ministry did not mind the expulsions as much as the British feared. And he admitted the numbers of KGB officers were so huge at the embassy that there was very little space for the genuine diplomats.[40]

However, the Soviet intelligence community were enraged by Operation FOOT. They were especially humiliated that none of their agents, notably their well-connected MPs, had provided any forewarning. 'For all their resources and efficiency', reported Sir John Killick, the British ambassador in Moscow at the time, the KGB leadership were 'out of their minds' with anger that the Kremlin did not retaliate against Britain to the extent they wanted to.[41]

For the KGB, Operation FOOT was a crippling blow to their covert operations in the UK. 'The London [KGB] residency never recovered from the expulsions', said Oleg Gordievsky. 'The KGB found it more difficult to collect high-grade intelligence in London than in almost any other Western capital.'[42] But it was not terminal. Behind the scenes the KGB strengthened their presence by co-opting diplomats and staff at the London embassy. By 1973 nineteen members of the embassy were listed in leaked files as KGB agents and co-optees, notably the deputy ambassador, Ivan Ippolitov.[43]

A major priority remained: commercial and technological intelligence for trade and for military purposes. Dame Stella Rimington, then an MI5 counter-intelligence officer and later head of MI5's anti-subversion branch and then director-general, recalls that 'about 150 Soviet weapons systems depended on technology stolen from the West'.[44] Despite the failing Soviet economy, the Kremlin was still spending vast sums on intelligence operations.

'They [KGB] were offering money or other forms of inducement', recalled Sir Roderic Lyne, a diplomat based in Moscow between 1972 and 1974 and later ambassador.

A very large part of their diplomatic effort and their so-called trade effort in Britain was actually devoted to espionage. We had very large resources deployed in the Security Service [MI5] to counter it and when this came to the crunch, it would land on my desk in the Foreign Office with MI5 – with whom I was in constant touch – saying that they didn't want to grant a visa to Mr X or they wanted to expel Mr Y. And one would have to look at the strength of the case and sometimes the case was not 100 percent convincing.[45]

Despite the setback of Operation FOOT, the KGB was still 'trying to subvert western democracies' during the Cold War, according to Stella Rimington.[46] But the capacity of the KGB residency in London to secure inside intelligence was greatly diminished. Officers resorted to recycling information from open sources and portraying it as coming from confidential contacts. The telegrams sent to Moscow were political analysis based on the party line rather than secrets from within the British government. And implementing active measures was even more challenging. In 1977, Yakov Lukasevics, head of the KGB station in London, was asked by President Andropov whether his residency possessed the means to influence British policy.

'Why yes, we can influence', he replied promptly. 'We have such channels.'

But the former KGB boss was sceptical. 'I do not think you can', he replied. 'I think you are too hasty in answering that question.'[47]

Then two years later, in May 1979, the KGB was confronted by a formidable new political opponent: Margaret Thatcher. Dubbed 'The Iron Lady' by the Kremlin, Thatcher was a staunch Cold Warrior and a resolute, hostile enemy of the Soviet Union.

'The Russians are bent on world dominance and they are rapidly acquiring the means to become the most powerful, imperial nation the world has seen', she declared.

Thatcher was also a strong supporter of the United States, increased military spending and installing more nuclear weapons in Western Europe. Accordingly, the Kremlin wanted to discredit her and portray her as a reckless and dangerous warmonger.

The problem is that the KGB could not recruit an agent inside the Conservative government. And so they resorted to crude active measures and disinformation. A Danish journalist called Arne Herlov Petersen was recruited for the task. He had been a KGB agent of influence since 1973 and used mainly to write newspaper articles favourable to the Kremlin line. A naive, deluded left-wing intellectual, Petersen had been carried away by radical causes and enthusiasm for such improbable anti-capitalist heroes as Kim Il Sung, Pol Pot and Colonel Gaddafi. He used a pseudonym if he ghosted KGB articles, but also wrote under his own name. As the historian Christopher Andrew noted: 'Their literary merit was as slight as their political sophistication.'[48]

Soon after Thatcher entered Downing Street, Petersen was ordered to attack. The first KGB–Petersen production was entitled *Cold Warriors*, which anointed Thatcher as Europe's leading anti-Soviet crusader. While the prime minister would have been delighted by this honour, the KGB was unaccountably proud of the pamphlet. Yet its political analysis was primitive. Thatcher wanted to appeal to 'racist sentiments', promote 'capitalist influence' and wage 'war against the British working class'. The other Cold Warriors were familiar KGB targets – Senator Henry Jackson, Senator Barry Goldwater and the German conservative politician Franz Josef Strauss.

The following year the KGB hired Petersen again to discredit Thatcher. In a pamphlet entitled *True Blues*, the spy made the mistake of attempting satire – always a weak area of KGB active measures – and it carried the feeble subtitle 'The Thatcher That Can't Mend Her Own Roof'. The Danish spy attacked her for 'government incompetence' (which even her harshest critics would not claim), 'personal ties with big business and monopolies interests' (more credible) and for having deliberately 'chosen the war path' (contentious).[49] The pamphlet was published by 'Joe Hill Press', an obvious fake front company as Joe Hill was a well-known American trade union activist immortalised by Joan Baez in her folk song 'I Dreamed I Saw Joe Hill Last Night'.

The choice and deployment of Petersen as an agent of influence reflected the paucity and inept judgement of the KGB in the early 1980s. He made basic mistakes – Thatcher's birthplace, Grantham, was in Lincolnshire not in the suburbs of London. But their publishing joint venture was short-lived as in 1981 Petersen was arrested in Denmark and later charged with collaborating with the KGB. To the dismay of the Danish security service, the 'journalist' was released because the KGB officers had left the country and so could not be summoned to give evidence.[50]

In contrast to the USA, the KGB operation against Thatcher was restrained. During Gordievsky's term at the KGB London residency between 1982 and 1985, he did not witness similar Petersen-style pamphlets or any fabricated documents bearing Thatcher's signature that were comparable with the Reagan forgeries.[51] Instead, the focus appeared to be on political intelligence and analysis rather than active measures. One KGB officer deployed for this task was Maxim Bazhenov, who was stationed in London from 10 September 1980 until he was expelled in 1985, along with twenty-five other spies.

Using his cover as an interpreter and journalist, Lieutenant Colonel Bazhenov (not his real name), spent most of his time attending press conferences and political meetings and interviewing senior politicians, in order to gather intelligence about the Thatcher government. Most events were public, but on one occasion he managed to attend a closed lecture at the London

School of Economics by the commander of NATO naval forces in the North Atlantic – an intelligence coup.[52]

Articulate, intelligent and engaging, Bazhenov prepared for his assignment by reading Graham Greene novels and meeting agents in London. One day in 1982 he arranged such a meeting and there was the usual three hours' driving around to detect any surveillance by MI5. But when he turned on his car radio, the BBC announced that a Soviet military attaché had been expelled from the UK. The KGB officer became concerned, cancelled the meeting and walked around the city for several hours, deciding on his operational strategy. Then Argentina invaded the Falkland Islands and the agenda changed.

The Falklands War was important to the KGB. The Kremlin saw the conflict as an opportunity to portray Thatcher as a warmonger, disrupt UK–US relations and depict the UK and the US as intent on dominating Latin America. The first operation was to fabricate a US department of defense press release, which included provocative – but fake – undiplomatic comments by the secretary of defense, Caspar Weinberger, regarding the Falklands crisis. The forgery stated that US support for the war was conditional on support for a US military base 'from which we will assert our control over the whole of Latin America'.

Copies of this KGB-inspired document were circulated among senior diplomats in Washington DC. Within days a false story was circulated that the Soviet authorities 'had evidence' that the British naval task force was equipped with nuclear weapons. If true, it was extremely damaging to the British but it was classic KGB disinformation. The Soviet state media broadcast the story and some Western journalists were persuaded by KGB agents to publish a version, even though it was untrue.

Back in London KGB officer Bazhenov was using his journalistic cover to assess the political implications of the Falklands War and obtain any inside intelligence. As a Russian, he was able to drink heavily and remember most of what was said and so spent many happy hours in the bars of the House of Commons and in

Westminster pubs. His tactic was to wait in the pub until the accredited defence correspondents of Fleet Street newspapers returned from their closed briefings at the Ministry of Defence and hope that several pints of beer would loosen their tongues. After a few free drinks, the words would invariably flow. Even the most innocent-sounding question could reveal useful insights on the war.

When not hanging around in parliamentary bars, Bazhenov interviewed MPs who might reveal secrets or at least provide a sense of the political zeitgeist of the war. He met Enoch Powell, the controversial Conservative MP, who told Parliament that the conflict would reveal what kind of metal the Iron Lady was actually made of. The KGB officer was surprised to hear that Powell opposed the deployment of American cruise missiles in the UK.

'Based on my knowledge of history, I will always believe that the Soviet Union will never invade Western Europe', said the MP.

The KGB officer also interviewed opponents of the war like Tony Benn, the charismatic leader of Labour's left-wing, and Tam Dalyell, the obsessive campaigner whose Scottish ancestors had served in the tsars' armies and was surprisingly friendly to the Soviet Union.

But Bazhenov's closest relationship was with the veteran Labour MP Denis Healey, former defence secretary and shadow foreign secretary during the Falklands crisis. Despite his party's support for the war, Healey explained to the Soviet 'journalist' that he had served as a major during the Second World War. Unlike most politicians, he had commanded a battalion and witnessed the horrors of war – blood, death and soldiers being maimed for life. And so he preferred to explore diplomatic alternatives.

The intellectual if mischievous Healey made a strong impression on the KGB officer and they kept in touch. The Labour shadow foreign secretary showed him draft articles on the Soviet Union and the spy handed the MP his dissertation on Anglo-Soviet relations. Over long boozy lunches in Soho, they discussed Lenin ('great thinker, weak strategist') and Russian philosophy. An extrovert with a sparkle in his eyes, Healey was suspicious of Bazhenov's true identity.

'Ah, Maxim Bazhenov', he greeted him at their final meeting in a Moscow hotel. 'How is the KGB doing?'

'No worse than usual', he replied. 'I would like to talk to you.'

The interview took place late that night in Healey's hotel room. For his final question, Bazhenov could not resist asking – off-the-record – about Healey's dealings with Soviet diplomats and spies in London while he was the defence secretary between 1964 and 1970. Healey replied:

> You see, Maxim, a good half of Soviet representatives were pure spies and the other half were forced to report to the KGB about their contacts. This is the axiom for us British politicians. The KGB is listened to in the Kremlin. And so by communicating with Russian intelligence, Labour MPs – and sometimes Conservatives – have the opportunity to directly convey our thoughts at a high and influential level. Some of us are afraid of contact with the enemy but I have not been afraid to use this channel and promote my political agenda and goals. And in return you Soviet intelligence officers can learn from us.[53]

The successful outcome of the Falklands War provided a political premium for Thatcher. But the KGB remained unimpressed. As the 1983 election approached, their agents focused on portraying the prime minister as endangering world security by deploying cruise missiles in the UK. Bazhenov met veteran peace activists like Fenner Brockway and secured two interviews with Joan Ruddock, the articulate chairperson of CND, which were monitored by MI5.

'At one time we were able to establish that Ruddock gave an interview to a Soviet journalist who was actually a career KGB officer,' said former MI5 officer Cathy Massiter.[54]

The Kremlin was desperate for Thatcher to lose the forthcoming election. Aggressive active measures were authorised. The KGB compiled a cassette tape of a fake telephone conversation between

Thatcher and President Reagan. The tape surfaced in the press in
the Netherlands. In fact, it was a crudely edited recording of
Thatcher promising to punish Argentina for the loss of HMS
Sheffield during the previous year's Falklands War and Reagan was
heard trying to calm her down. The KGB had spliced together real
recordings of their voices from interviews and speeches and manufactured a conversation which in fact never took place. In early
March 1983, pamphlets and leaflets which were starkly anti-NATO
and anti-Thatcher were distributed to teenage children in British
schools. One booklet, entitled *People Rise Against War*, contained
a photograph of the prime minister with the slogan 'Stop the Mad
Killer', above a graphic of the Union Jack. The material was distributed by the Novosti Press Agency Publishing House, a KGB front
which also circulated official Soviet propaganda.

However, when the campaign was underway the prospects were
bleak for the Kremlin. On 16 May 1983, three weeks before the
poll, Viktor Popov, the Soviet ambassador in London, summoned
a meeting of diplomats and KGB officers to discuss the election.
While they searched for evidence of Labour Party progress in the
polls, the consensus was that the Conservatives would win handsomely. There was nothing they could do to influence the result.
But the Kremlin disagreed. A week later the embassy in London
received the text of a Soviet letter about nuclear disarmament,
which Moscow believed could enhance Labour's prospects. On 23
May, the KGB residency in London received a telegram announcing
that 'an important document' containing 'themes' should be introduced into Labour campaign speeches. This was a highly ambitious
task and not made easier by the fact it took four days to decipher
the telegram, which was written in a curious mixture of English
and Russian. As the KGB did not have agents inside the Labour
campaign headquarters, the residency regarded the demand as
hopelessly impractical and took no action. Two weeks later
Thatcher won a landslide election victory.[55]

After the 1983 election, KGB officers in London focused on the
deluded and distorted analysis by the Kremlin that the Reagan

and Thatcher administrations were planning for nuclear war.[56] But when Operation RYAN was disbanded after President Andropov's death in 1984, it signalled the final days of active measures aimed specifically at Thatcher and Western leaders. His successors, Chernenko and Gorbachev, were both critical of the quality and value of the KGB reporting from London.

Yet the end of the Cold War was partly due to two successful KGB intelligence operations in the USA. When Gorbachev became president in March 1985, he realised that while Thatcher and Reagan's confrontational rhetoric was dangerous and provocative, they were not on the verge of launching thermonuclear war. This was mainly due to intelligence and documents sold to the KGB by Aldrich Ames, who worked on Soviet operations at the CIA, and Robert Hanssen, an FBI officer who had access to secret US assessments on Gorbachev and the prospect of a nuclear conflict. The material strengthened Gorbachev's conviction that there were no offensive NATO plans and Operation RYAN was a fantasy based on conspiracy thinking rather than reality.[57] The Cold War drew to a close not with a bang, but a whimper. None of the protagonists believed a new Cold War using the same intelligence methods would return twenty-five years later.

9

THE NEW COLD WAR

Secret operations are essential in war; upon them the army relies
to make its every move. An army without secret agents is exactly
like a man without eyes or ears.

Sun Tzu

War is the continuation of politics by other means
General Carl von Clausewitz

Thank God there is the FSB. All power is from God and so is theirs
Father Alexander, Church of the Holy Wisdom,
August 2001

IN THE FINAL HUMILIATING MONTHS OF the Cold War, even the
KGB faced public criticism for its repressive role at home and
its controversial operations abroad. Its First Chief (Foreign
Intelligence) Directorate (FCD) was publicly ridiculed even by
some KGB officers. The FCD was accused of having 'profaned the
essence of intelligence work', one officer told *Izvestia*. 'We served
mainly (Communist) Party interests. To please our bosses, we
passed on doctored and slanted information, in accordance with

the slogan "Pin everything on the Americans, and everything will be OK". That's not intelligence. It's self-deception."[1]

The dramatic decline in its status was highlighted when the Nobel Prize-winning dissident, Andrei Sakharov, an uncompromising opponent of the KGB, was acknowledged by Gorbachev as 'the commanding personality' at the 1989 Congress of People's Deputies in Moscow. This was a man once described by Yuri Andropov, former head of the KGB, as 'Public Enemy Number One'.[2]

Bizarrely, the usually hard-line KGB chief Vladimir Kryuchkov reacted by launching a public relations campaign. Like a politician who cannot accept that his or her policies are unpopular or unworkable, he blamed the perception rather than the substance. 'The KGB should have an image not only in our country but worldwide which is consistent with the noble goals I believe we are pursuing in our work', he said.[3] A media office was opened and Kryuchkov called for more East–West intelligence collaboration against terrorism and drug trafficking.

The Soviet secret state also resorted to desperate measures to revive its reputation. The male-dominated KGB even made an unintentionally comic attempt to use female glamour to improve its image. In January 1990 it announced, amid a blitz of Russian press and TV coverage, the appointment of Katya Mayorova as 'Miss KGB', the world's first holder of a security service beauty title. Ms Mayorova wore a bullet-proof vest 'with an exquisite softness like a Pierre Cardin model', according to *Pravda*, and she also had the ability to deliver a well-aimed, lethal karate kick to her enemy's head! During press interviews, Miss KGB's knowledge of espionage tradecraft was limited to giggling and smiling silently through all her answers. And when she was asked to pose for a photograph, she sidled up to a bust of Felix Dzerzhinsky, the revered head of the Cheka secret police, and positively cooed. Given that Dzerzhinsky had ordered mass torture and executions, this was perhaps not the image that the KGB spin doctors wanted to convey for the 'New KGB'.[4]

By the summer of 1991 such desperate and risible measures to revive the KGB's reputation were not working and Ms Mayorova had disappeared. As the very existence of the Soviet Union was under threat, Kryuchkov resorted to familiar conspiracy theories to explain the crisis, unable to admit that the Communist economic model was not sustainable. He blamed the CIA for their war against the Soviet state and a Western plot, 'akin to economic sabotage', to 'deliver impure and sometimes infected grain as well as products with an above level of radioactivity'.[5] But Kryuchkov was a conspirator as well as a conspiracy theorist. In August 1991, while Gorbachev was on holiday in Crimea, the KGB chief was the chief organiser of an attempted coup. And at the heart of his manifesto was the complaint that Gorbachev had been too tolerant of ideological subversion (free speech) which undermined the one-party state. 'Malicious mockery of all the institutions of state is being implanted', he said. 'The country has in effect become ungovernable.'[6]

The coup failed and the state agency most under attack was the KGB. Kryuchkov was arrested for treason and the old KGB guard was purged. The symbolic collapse was the toppling of the huge statue of the founder of Soviet intelligence, Dzerzhinsky, outside the Lubyanka, the KGB's headquarters. Crowds cheered as Lenin's brutal spymaster was toppled from his pedestal and unceremoniously taken away on a lorry.

Soon after Boris Yeltsin became president, the old Soviet intelligence apparatus was disbanded. 'The KGB must be liquidated', said his chief of staff, Sergei Stepashin. The KGB had been an integral part of the Soviet system and its abrupt disintegration left behind a vast bureaucracy. Prior to 1991, the agency employed an estimated 480,000 people, of whom 260,000 were agents. When the Communist regime fell, nearly half of the KGB's staff were dismissed and its budget was slashed. On 30 August 1991, less than three weeks after the attempted coup, a major reform to depoliticise the KGB was announced. The purely political police directorates were abolished, some of its functions were redistributed and the remains of the KGB were merged into a new agency: the FSB.

In 2022 the FSB has, to a considerable extent, become the KGB incarnate. There are some key differences. Instead of upholding the Communist or any other ideology, the FSB seeks to preserve the president's personal power. It implements targeted repression against individual political opponents, not against mass movements. And, unlike the KGB, it can intervene in the economy, offering fresh opportunities for corruption.

Yet the FSB inherited the KGB's infrastructure, archives and many of its agents. While several KGB officers left Russia and offered their services to Western intelligence and the private sector, just as many moved to the new agency. Attempts to reorganise the KGB were in fact superficial and cosmetic. Consequently, the FSB has preserved much of the KGB's mindset, operational tradecraft and hostility to the West.

'Communist ideology has gone but the methods and psychology of its secret police have remained', said Alexei Kondaurov, an MP at the time.

The FSB leadership publicly broke with the past, but over time FSB officers, including Putin, head of the agency before becoming president, increasingly identified with their predecessors. The new generation of intelligence officers regarded the FSB as a true descendant of the blood-soaked Cheka. In fact, monuments to its founder, Felix Dzerzhinsky, were erected in the offices of its regional departments.[7] And Vasily Stavitsky, head of FSB public relations from 1999 until 2001, even published a poem which became an FSB official hymn:

Always at the front
Always at one's post
Don't touch Russia –
A Chekist is always vigilant

Officially, the KGB had been disbanded and the billionaire oligarchs wielded immense political power over President Yeltsin in the 1990s. But in reality and operationally, especially abroad, the KGB was revived in a different guise and recovered its old espionage powers. This was apparent during a visit to Moscow in December 1991 by Stella Rimington, then MI5's deputy director-general.

'I wanted to establish what scope there was for a reduction in the espionage attack by the KGB on this country [UK]', recalled Rimington. 'It seemed to me not unreasonable to expect that if the Cold War was over, there should be less aggressive spying.'

During her stay Rimington was invited to meet Yevgeny Primakov, then head of Russia's foreign intelligence directorate and later foreign minister. One evening the deputy head of MI5 was driven in the ambassador's Rolls-Royce to an address in a leafy Moscow suburb, which she took to be an old-style KGB safe house. She recounted 'we had somehow slipped into a James Bond film and that reality had become confused with fiction'. During a brief and cool discussion, Rimington told Primakov there was much scope for collaboration, especially on terrorism and organised crime. But if there was to be sincere cooperation, she added, the level of Russian espionage in the UK should be reduced. Her proposal was greeted with scorn and dismissed. It was a ridiculous idea, he replied. Espionage would continue to be necessary for the defence of Russia and their security service would engage at whatever level they chose.

Two years later, in late 1993, an FSB officer commented: 'There are friendly states but not friendly intelligence services.' This was 'a sentiment which characterised the nature of our "co-operation" with the Russians for years to come', Rimington added, who was by then MI5's director-general.[8]

During the Yeltsin years the old certainties were gone. The reassuring Soviet state had vanished and the Russian people faced economic uncertainty and poverty as they adapted to the new and chaotic post-Communist life, dominated by corruption and commercially motivated murder and kidnapping. Meanwhile, avaricious oligarchs siphoned off the wealth of the nation, when valuable state assets were sold off cheaply. This sense of uncertainty and the frailty of the Russian character was identified by the American diplomat George Kennan in his famous essay 'The Sources of Soviet Conduct', written at the dawn of the Cold War in 1947:

> The present generation of Russians have never known spontaneity of collective action. If consequently anything were ever to occur to disrupt the unity and efficacy of the [Communist] Party as a political instrument, Soviet Russia might be changed overnight from one of the strongest to one of the weakest and most pitiable of national societies.[9]

The collapse of the Soviet Union confirmed Kennan's prophecy. The new Russia did not have a clear ideology or purpose apart from a vague patriotic devotion to the nation as a 'great power' and hostility to foreign enemies. For most of the 1990s Russia endured economic peril while the oligarchs exported billions of dollars abroad via offshore companies and trusts and allowed production to stagnate. It was the rising price of oil, gas and other commodities from March 1999 onwards, coupled with increased production, that rescued the country from bankruptcy and enabled Russia's economic recovery. And so when Putin became acting president in late 1999, he was in a strong position and consolidated his power by appointing former KGB officers into the most powerful government positions. Known as the '*Siloviki*' (power guys), several KGB veterans were executives in Gazprom, Russia's biggest company, and Gazprombank. The overwhelming majority of Russia's elite had ties to the security services. Putin was creating a neo-KGB state.[10]

The KGB was back in the guise of the FSB and eventually Cold War hostilities were restored. Putin does not trust anyone and thinks the internet was a 'CIA project' to spy on the world. 'He doesn't believe anyone at their word or believe any spoken or printed word', said former KGB officer Sergey Zhirnov. 'He believes only in secret information.'[11] In effect, Putin has governed Russia by reviving Cold War espionage. This has made it difficult to assess the world accurately. During the Cold War the KGB were so addicted to espionage that they only trusted information if it was obtained by illicit means. This was also a failing of the British.

'Sometimes the assessments at the London end [the Foreign Office] were over-influenced by secret information', recalled Sir Reginald Hibbert, a Russian-speaking former diplomat and aide to former foreign secretary Ernest Bevin. 'People tend to believe that if it is secret, then it must be true which, of course, very often is not the case. In fact, no better an example of what happens to you if a foreign policy is based entirely on secrets is that of the Soviet Union. Over-reliance on the KGB ensured that the Soviet foreign policy was largely unsuccessful.'[12]

The influence of intelligence on Russian foreign policy during the Putin years has been crucial. The legacy of the Cold War is that the KGB were highly effective in gathering secret intelligence but fell short in assessing its value and relevance.

'One of the things to understand about the KGB that made it different from American intelligence', said former CIA director Robert Gates, 'is that it really had no analytical capability. You had all these spies out there reporting information and there was no one analysing it for accuracy or for whether it was real or not.'[13]

An extra obstacle the Soviets faced in assessing the West based on KGB intelligence was the pressure to 'force an excellent supply of [KGB] information from the multifaceted West into the over-simplified framework of hostility and conspiracy theory', according to Sir Percy Cradock, chairman of the UK Joint Intelligence Committee between 1985 and 1992.[14]

*

'There was no change after the Cold War. The KGB just changed the name of the agency', former CIA officer John Sipher told me over lunch in Maryland, USA, in March 2022. 'They may have lost political influence but operationally they were the same', added Sipher, who was stationed in Moscow between 1992 and 1995 and now runs a film company that makes spy movies. The tradecraft was the same. Most – if not all – CIA officers in Moscow were under surveillance twenty-four hours a days, usually by car.

'Thousands of FSB officers were assigned to monitor the movements of officials and diplomats of what they called "unfriendly nations" by car, foot and electronic surveillance', said former CIA officer Steven Hall, who was stationed in Moscow between 2010 and 2012.

'The FSB were always trying to catch our agents doing something for which they could be blackmailed', added Sipher. 'We called it "dolphin surveillance" – sometimes under the water, occasionally over the water.'

The Russian paranoia about the Americans was unrelenting. In response, the CIA noticed that most FSB officers were white, male and heterosexual. It was no secret that most Russian intelligence officers were racist, misogynistic and homophobic. And so the CIA increasingly deployed black, female and gay agents on the streets of Moscow. This was highly effective because the FSB could not believe such people could be spies. 'I think the new FSB officers were less interested in collecting intelligence, and more operational and interested in destabilising the West', reflected Sipher.

The KGB was now called the FSB but *Kompromat* was still a top priority. And Putin did not hesitate to use it as a political weapon, primarily against his critics, often in conjunction with cyberwarfare. The FSB did not even pretend it was for national security reasons. Instead it was wielded as a crude political weapon to smear and destabilise Putin's political opponents. Sex tapes and videos with images of critics, activists and comedians consorting with prostitutes and sniffing lines of cocaine were leaked regularly. The most notable was in 2016 when a tape was distributed of Mikhail Kasyanov, former prime minister and a Putin challenger, in bed with a female activist while trash talking his own colleagues.

The release of the video immediately derailed Kasyanov's campaign and his coalition bombed in the subsequent parliamentary elections.

Kompromat was a coherent and carefully managed part of Russia's foreign policy. After a honeymoon, the resumption of Cold War hostilities between Russia and the West made such tactics even more important. On 6 July 2009, seven months after Barack Obama was sworn in as president, a four minute eighteen second video appeared on an obscure Russian website called informacia.ru, which showed a portly 37-year-old British diplomat called James Hudson, deputy consul general in Yekaterinburg, having sex with two prostitutes while drinking champagne. The 'story' was followed up by *Komsomolskaya Pravda* and the tabloid website life.ru. Two days later the *Sun* in London published extracts from the video and a prominent article headlined 'Our Man in Russia pulls out after spy films his Urals sex'. Hudson, an experienced diplomat who had served in the Balkans, Hungary and Albania, promptly resigned.

It was a classic honey trap. Even the headline on the video – 'Adventures of Mr Hudson in Russia' – was reminiscent of the Cold War. Further investigation revealed that the website informacia.ru was used by hackers and had ties to the FSB and Russian intelligence.[15]

A month later the same website published a video of a similar ilk. This time the victim was the American diplomat Brendan Kyle Hatcher, based at the US embassy in Moscow. The video contained surveillance footage of Hatcher making phone calls to an escort agency in order to meet a prostitute. It then cut to a scene where a couple were together in a hotel bedroom in the dark. The clear implication was that Hatcher was having sex with a prostitute.

The video was then posted on informacia.ru and KP.ru and reprinted in *Komsomolskaya* – the same media outlet as the Hudson entrapment. But the difference in this case was that the video was a fake. The surveillance footage of Hatcher making the phone call was real but it had been taken several years previously when he was visiting Moscow as a private citizen. The clip of a couple having sex was not the diplomat, but the FSB had manufactured and spliced together genuine and fake footage to make it look like Hatcher. 'This was a fake hit job', said the then US ambassador to Moscow, John Beyrle. 'Clearly the video we saw was a montage of different clips, some of which are clearly fabricated. I have full confidence in him and he is going to continue work here at the embassy.'[16]

Hatcher was targeted by the FSB because he worked in the US embassy's political section and responsible for liaising and working with human rights organisations, NGOs and religious groups. In the mindset of the FSB, these were CIA front groups and so he needed to be removed, or at least discredited.

The Cold War was back and the Russians, unlike the West, adopted a long-term strategy. Videos, photographs and documents – real and fake – were carefully filed away.

'Russia is willing to play a long game, put large resources into things that may not bear fruit for many years to come', said former FBI counter-intelligence officer Clint Watts. 'The accumulation of these operations over a long period will result in a major political impact. And they know that.'[17]

This was a powerful weapon for the FSB – giving it a key advantage over the short attention span of the Americans. But then the internet and social media arrived. And that changed the operational rules of the game. The old methods were supplanted. Instead of typewriters, letter-writing campaigns, telex and fax machines, shortwave radios and rotary printing presses, now there were websites, social media accounts, hackers, troll factories, retweets and view counts. In the old Cold War, a disinformation operation could reach 100,000 people via a newspaper, but now millions could be messaged instantly.

The essence of the internet – its speed, anonymity, openness, ubiquity, immediacy in combinations and, above all, its love of controversy – makes it ideal for Russian influence operations. 'Its decentralised nature allows hidden actors to reach large audiences quickly', argues the BBC security correspondent Gordon Corera. 'Its algorithms can be gamed by those who understand it. Its frictionless anonymity was perfect for the type of identity transfer that spies used to engage in but were finding harder to do in the world of biometrics and databases. The new online world was perfect for a Putin judo slam.'[18]

During the second Obama administration (2012–16), relations with Putin turned icy, almost freezing. Russia saw the political advantage of the hacking and dumping of large volumes of data and traffic on social media influence campaigns. It set up an organisation called the Internet Research Agency (IRA), which employed 400 Russians to post pro-Kremlin propaganda online under false identities, including on Twitter, in order to create the illusion of a massive army of supporters. Based in St Petersburg, their job was to create social media identities that made it look as if they were Americans. It was very intense work. 'Two 12-hour days in a row, followed by two days off', recalled former employee Lyudmila Savchuk. 'Over those two shifts I had to meet a quota of five political posts, 10 non-political posts and 150–200 comments on other workers' posts.'[19]

These 'specialists', as they were described by the IRA, were the online version of the old KGB disinformation specialists, forgers and fantasists. But the difference is that sometimes the KGB artisans and operatives were subject to scrutiny and occasionally detected. Now the internet provided anonymity and so the specialists could implement dirty tricks without recourse. As the old joke goes, on the internet no one knows you are a dog and no one knows you are a Russian either. Disinformation was now distributed faster to vast numbers of people and with far less chance of being caught. 'Plant, incubate and propagate has been replaced by tweet, retweet and repeat', argued Steve Abrams in his essay 'Beyond Propaganda – Soviet Active Measures in Putin's Russia'.[20]

The amount of craftsmanship and work required from the new disinformation specialists was also lower than in the previous Cold War.

'Digital storage made it possible to breach targets remotely and extract vast amounts of compromising material', argues Professor Thomas Rid.

> The internet facilitated the acquisition and publishing of unprecedented volumes of raw data at a distance and anonymously. Automation helped to create and amplify fake personas and content, to destroy data and to disrupt. Speed meant that operational adaptation and adjustments could take place not over years, months and weeks but in days, hours and even minutes. Activist culture meant existing leak platforms outperformed purpose-created ones. And the darker, more depraved corners of the internet offered teeming petri dishes of vicious, divisive ideas and guaranteed a permanent supply of fresh conspiracy theories.[21]

The new Kremlin took full advantage of this new political hybrid warfare. In 2015 the IRA specifically targeted the United States, the old enemy. The specialists were divided into day-shift and night-shift teams linked to US time zones. The aim was not to inform and educate but to divide and influence. And the troll factory workers were given extensive and precise guidance on how to implement the operation. 'Our goal was not to turn the Americans towards Russia', said one worker. 'Our task was to set Americans against their own government – to provoke unrest and discontent.'[22]

Suddenly, young men and women – often using attractive pictures and pretending to be American – started posting about US politics, especially critical comments about the Obama administration. All social media was part of the campaign and the trolls used virtual private networks (VPNs) to hide the fact that they were really in Russia – the digital version of a fake postal mailing address. If their account was closed down by Facebook for being suspicious, they would email administrators back and cite free speech and the US constitution.

In the run-up to the 2016 presidential election, these fake profiles multiplied and the information war was declared. The growing polarisation of American politics – as exemplified by Donald Trump vs Hilary Clinton – offered fertile ground and the Russians exploited the divisions in American society. Fake social media pages on the sensitive issues of race and immigration were created and then automated accounts – known as bots – amplified the provocative messages from these accounts. On the surface the US media reported these were the views of real American voters. In fact, they had been fabricated by the Russian keyboard warriors.

By the time of the election campaign, policies were posted online and events were organised as if they were real Democratic initiatives. More than 100,000 real Americans were contacted through fake US personal online accounts. They had no idea they were communicating with Russian intelligence agents because, of course, they did not speak to them. It was all online.[23] The IRA were also active. They created social media accounts and robots purely to send out hundreds of thousands of comments and messages on Twitter and Facebook, which highlighted disinformation and suppressed accurate data. And when a voter posted a positive comment about Clinton, then the bots drowned this posting by an overwhelming tidal wave of negative disinformation. The pro-Clinton comment was not deleted but swamped by a vast tsunami of links, hostile comments and fake emails – all automated and none of them real or authentic.

In parallel, the GRU implemented a 'hack and leak' operation against Clinton's campaign. On 19 March 2016, eight months before the vote, Clinton's campaign chairman John Podesta clicked on an email link that looked like a security notification from Google telling him to change his password. As a result, the GRU hackers secured access to 60,000 emails. It was a targeted reconnaissance mission. Known as 'Fancy Bear' and 'Cozy Bear', these hacker groups then sent 'spear phishing' emails to 300 Democratic officials and Clinton activists. Using malware to explore the Democratic National Committee's (DNC) computer networks, they harvested thousands of emails and attachments and then deleted computer logs and files to obscure evidence of their covert activities. Despite the carefully planned operation, the emails empowered crazy conspiracy theories, including the presidential candidate running a child sex pornographic ring from the basement of a pizza parlour. This fantasy was based on the fact that John Podesta had once exchanged emails with the owner of the restaurant.

By the following month the Russian spies had broken into the DNC's virtual office. It was like an online version of Watergate. But this time it was foreign intelligence agents hacking into emails and taking screen shots, not right-wing security operatives breaking into the DNC's office late at night, looking for documents.

'We did attribution back to the Russian government', said Shawn Henry, a former executive assistant director of the FBI and chief security officer of CrowdStrike. 'We believed it was the Russian government involved in an espionage campaign – essentially collecting intelligence against candidates for the US Presidency.'[24]

The hack was an old-style active measure – or influence operation – to damage Clinton's prospects of winning the presidency. The thousands of hacked emails were saved and carefully leaked in stages during the three months before the election. Some were released strategically to distract the public from media events that were either beneficial to the Clinton campaign or harmful to Trump. Others were published on Russian websites, transferred to Wikileaks via intermediaries and sent to the mainstream media. Codenamed 'Project Lakhta' by the Kremlin, an investigation by Robert Mueller, former FBI director, discovered substantial evidence of Russian online interference in the 2016 election, which he described as 'sweeping and systematic' and which 'violated US criminal law'.

While the evidence of Russian intelligence online active measures against Hilary Clinton is overwhelming, it is not clear to what extent – if at all – they secured Trump's election victory.

'Measuring the actual impact of trolling and online influence campaigns is probably impossible', said Kate Starbird, one of the world's leading researchers of online disinformation campaigns. 'But the difficulty of measuring impact does not mean that there is no meaningful impact.'

Statistics can be misleading. A year after the 2016 election, a *New York Times* headline declared 'Russian Influence Reached 126 Million Through Facebook Alone'. On the face of it, that is a huge section of the electorate. But as Professor Thomas Rid argues in his definitive book *Active Measures*:

> In reality the pre-election reach of the Internet Research Agency was far less, for two reasons: only about 37 percent of Facebook's number of 'impressions' were from before 9 November 2016 [the rest were after]. And impressions are not engagements, only what a user may have scrolled past, perhaps absentmindedly... Online metrics, in short, created a powerful illusion, an appealing mirage.'

In a fair-minded assessment, Rid argues the irony is that the metrics created an opportunity for disinformation about disinformation by exaggerating its impact.[25]

For the FSB and the GRU, their mission was accomplished. Hostility to Hilary Clinton, who had been secretary of state during Obama's administration, superseded any enthusiasm for Donald Trump. Indeed, the Russian elite regarded Trump as a figure of ridicule and were shocked by his political rise and success. One veteran former Russian military intelligence officer told me he had assumed – wrongly – that US presidential candidates were vetted in advance. 'The KGB were aware of Trump's notorious business practices in the late 1980s', he told me. 'In 1990 Trump wanted to meet President Gorbachev. We regarded him with suspicion and a joke because of all the bankruptcies. We did not take him seriously and so I personally signed the document which prevented Trump from meeting Gorbachev.'

Measuring the impact of whether the activities of Russian intelligence agencies finally succeeded in their favoured candidate being elected as US president in 2016 is almost impossible. They tried to back their preferred candidate in 1960 (Stevenson) and in 1968 (Humphrey) and actively conspired against Goldwater in 1964, Reagan in 1980 and 1984 and Clinton in 2016. But the lesson of the 2016 election is that Putin authorised the intense active measures, hacking and disinformation as part of a much more profound political strategy than electing a failed businessman and reality TV show host. His agenda was not to engineer a specific outcome in the election but to cause disunity and disruption for their own sake.

Indeed, Putin's real purpose was – and is – to weaken and destabilise the USA, sow discord between NATO and EU allies, undermine transatlantic security ties (thus strengthening Russia's position in Europe), disrupt the US economy, especially on energy policy, and create chaos in the West. This agenda is much more important than an individual candidate or a useful idiot in the White House. If Putin can achieve this aim, then he believes Russia will be revived as a great power and the Soviet Union will be restored.

'There was never the aim to influence anyone', said Vladimir Yakunin, a confidant of Putin, who was delighted by Trump's election but in the context of a defeat for the Western liberal world order. 'There was the aim to raise Russia from its knees.'[26]

*

Espionage and active measures are not just an integral part of foreign policy but they also feature in actual military wars. This emphasis on disinformation in conflict zones was highlighted by General Sir Nick Carter, Britain's chief of defence staff, in his annual lecture in 2019. He warned that 'the idea of political warfare has returned'. Missiles, ammunition and tanks still matter, he reassured his military audience, but authoritarian rivals like Russia increasingly try to undermine the West using disinformation, cyber-attacks, assassinations and agents of influence. The West has underrated or misunderstood this threat at its peril. The Americans, as the influential diplomat George Kennan pointed out at the outset of the Cold War, viewed war 'as a sort of sporting contest outside of all political context' while the Russians grasped 'the perpetual rhythm of struggle, in and out of war'.[27] For Russia and Putin, war is the continuation of politics by other means, as Clausewitz remarked in the nineteenth century.

In the new Cold War, technology has enhanced the impact and effectiveness of disinformation so that its incarnations are more sinister, insidious and pernicious. Waves of trolls and bots promoting pro-Putin and Kremlin hashtags during the Ukraine invasion have been unleashed with a speed and magnitude that was impossible before the internet and have influenced popular opinion on a scale never before possible.[28] In the twenty-first century, as David Omand, the former director of the UK eavesdropping agency GCHQ, wrote: 'subversion and sedition are now digital'. But their underlying purpose, as tools of disinformation, remains the same.[29]

During the invasion of Ukraine in 2014, a new doctrine, named after General Valery Gerasimov, chief of Russia's general staff, was devised which integrated cyber-attacks, disinformation and covert diplomacy as part of the military campaign. This emphasis on deception, secrecy and manipulation was inspired by *The Art of War* by Sun Tzu (although this would never be admitted by the Kremlin). Indeed, the advocacy of non-military tactics during war by the foreign secretary, Lord Palmerston, in 1849 was once quoted by a KGB officer during the Cold War: 'Opinions, if they are founded in truth and justice, will in the end prevail against the bayonets of infantry, the fire of artillery and the charges of cavalry.'[30]

Using devastating new technology, the importance of information warfare has been an integral part of Russia's intelligence blitzkrieg and foreign policy. Influence operations have now been weaponised by Putin's regime not just to convince the population of the righteousness of a war but to sustain their support during the conflict. This is what happened in Ukraine in 2022 and enabled the war to continue despite the military setbacks. Russian intelligence agencies have been influenced by and are adopting the techniques from the KGB manual during the Cold War – only the technology has changed. The parallels are striking.

By 2018 the increased focus on and resources for the Russian intelligence agencies had become ironically transparent. An estimated 33% of the Federal budget was spent on security. Much of this money was spent on buying and maintaining new equipment but some went on personnel. Under Putin, Russia had become a colossal security state. The FSB employed 387,000 people, with another 13,000 people in the SVR (foreign intelligence) and an estimated 380,000 in the GRU. In stark contrast, the UK had just 16,868 people devoted to intelligence across all of its seven agencies, mostly in GCHQ.[31]

A new generation of Russian intelligence officers was taking over. They were colder and harder and more interested in money but also more conscious of the humiliations of the past, like their president. In *Russians Among Us* by Gordon Corera, there is a revealing account of a conversation between a former KGB operative and a serving FSB officer:

> One American recalls witnessing the tension at the end of a long vodka-drinking session after a liaison meeting. An older Russian officer reminisced wistfully about the good old days of the Cold War, when the two spy services went head-to-head. But a young FSB officer reacted angrily. The older officer's generation was the one that lost the Cold War, he said bitterly. His generation was determined to restore Russian pride and would take the fight to the enemy.[32]

This hard-line historic mindset manifested itself in the Russian invasion of Crimea and the Donbas region in early 2014 and the rest of Ukraine in 2022. The conflicts can be traced back to a speech by Putin in February 2007 at a Munich security conference, when he criticised what he called the United States' monopolistic dominance in global relations. Using Cold War language, he claimed the USA has adopted an 'almost uncontained hyper use of force in international relations' and wanted a world 'in which there is one master, one sovereign'. As a result 'no one feels safe'.

The speech raised the stakes. Almost immediately the FSB recruited senior members of the Ukrainian special forces and some from the security service of Ukraine, known as the SBU. Over the next seven years about 50% of the security forces were enlisted by FSB operatives, mainly at pro-Russian events at their embassy in Kiev and sometimes by using *Kompromat* techniques. The FSB spent an estimated $200 million per year in bribing and persuading Ukrainians to become Russian agents of influence or informants, according to the Ukrainian lawyer and author Yuri Shulipa. He said that these funds are derived from the state and Russian oligarchs but are ultimately controlled by the Kremlin.[33]

The FSB's overt purpose was to persuade Ukraine to integrate more fully into Moscow's regional economic and military structures, such as the customs union. But their secret agenda was to undermine, divide and weaken Ukraine and its security services, according to Valentyn Nalyvaichenko, head of the SBU between 2006 and 2010. His investigation resulted in five FSB officers being arrested for espionage. The SBU discovered digital voice recorders, a video camera inside a fountain pen, a tiny container for storing digital data inside a keychain and a memo with instructions for undercover FSB operations.

After Nalyvaichenko left the SBU in 2010, the new president of Ukraine, Viktor Yanukovych, conspired with the FSB and the Kremlin, especially in the weeks before the invasion of Crimea in February 2014.

'Before the invasion, the FSB inserted their own agents into the Crimea government, its parliament and its law enforcement offices', Nalyvaichenko told me. 'It was not difficult for the FSB to do so because Yanukovych, the prime minister Azarov and the head of the FSB were pro-Putin and pro-Russia. And unfortunately there was no SBU which had become a branch of the FSB.'

In November 2013, Yanukovych was ousted as president but refused to leave office. This resulted in violent clashes and Ukraine was on the brink of civil war. Meanwhile, behind the scenes a group of forty-three FSB and GRU generals and officers and Vladislav Surkov, deputy chief of staff to Putin, twice secretly visited Yanukovych in Kiev.

'According to our investigation, Surkov and FSB officers were actively engaged in activities against the Ukrainian people and protesters', said Nalyvaichenko. 'The FSB and Surkov were plotting with Yanukovych to allow Ukraine to be under the political and military control of Moscow. As far as I was concerned, the FSB officers were financing and supporting terrorism and involved in the execution of protesters.'

It was during this tense and dangerous period that Yanukovych and the SBU allowed a group of twenty high-ranking FSB officers to stay at a secret counter-terrorist facility near Kiev, where they were given access to the internal data and computer software of the ministry of interior. The FSB officers – heavily armed – copied everything and stayed for several days before they flew back to Moscow on 20 February 2014.

On returning to the Kremlin, the FSB was in possession of a treasure trove of top-secret, classified documents and discs. Using this stolen data, the 18th centre of the FSB set up a system for hacking MPs in the Ukrainian parliament, civil servants and military officers.

'This unit operates as a special institution inside the FSB where almost 1,500 people work around the clock', Nalyvaichenko told me. 'They operate through the social media networks through robotic messaging systems, and deliberately send out messages and texts to make people panic over several days. When your mobile phone is under attack by this robotic calling system, you cannot make a call to anyone or text a message for several hours.'

For the Ukrainian citizens of Crimea, it was much worse. From the day of the invasion – 20 February 2014 – the FSB used the stolen database for disrupting their lives. The data was used to place all people at train and bus stations under surveillance. This enabled the FSB to arrest all military and police officers and their families. Hundreds of people were detained by the FSB.

However, the popular protests against the pro-Putin regime and the deadly clashes in Independence Square were overwhelming and on 22 February 2014 the Ukrainian parliament voted to remove Yanukovych from office. A warrant for his arrest was issued, which accused him of 'mass killing of citizens' and high treason. Documents found in the presidential palace revealed that Yanukovych had siphoned off hundreds of millions of pounds from state budgets and hidden them in offshore companies and foreign bank accounts. He then moved to Moscow where he is under the Kremlin's protection and supervision.

Two days later Nalyvaichenko was restored to his position as head of the SBU. On returning to his office, he found files which disclosed how between 2012 and 2014 the FSB had registered and funded several satellite, digital and technology companies in the United States as a cover for their covert activities. 'We found that the FSB inserted the relatives of an FSB general into these US companies as shareholders and beneficiaries', the former head of the SBU told me. 'We went to the American government and delivered our information and evidence. They investigated our claims and then closed down these companies.'

A year later, in June 2015, Nalyvaichenko resigned as head of the SBU after President Poroshenko was elected. But he has remained a senior and influential member of the Ukrainian parliament, especially on security matters. He told me that the FSB have been using every possible cyber-attack at their disposal, both before and after the invasion of Ukraine in 2022. Based partly on the data stolen in February 2014, the FSB cyber-attacked Ukraine government websites, television channels, radio stations, banks and corporations.

'The FSB is very active on social media, telegram channels and public online forums and using these platforms to send out disinformation, fake news and trying to create panic among our people', he said. 'They are also using social media to find intelligence about the Ukrainian armed forces and their personnel.'

The hostile use of social media by the FSB during the 2022 war is an extension of the active measures and influence operations used by the KGB during the Cold War. Nalyvaichenko agrees. During his first stint as head of the SBU in 2008, he authorised the declassification of the KGB archives in Ukraine, which revealed horrific crimes against humanity by the Soviet Union just after the 1917 revolution and in the 1930s during the mass famine. Buried in the files his colleagues found evidence of how Russian intelligence agencies falsified reports and fabricated witness statements against the Ukrainian liberation movements. The documents accused the Ukrainian insurgents of crimes which they demonstrably never committed. These 'stories' and 'cases' were then sent to newspapers in the UK and Western Europe via their agents of influence.

As the declassified dossiers also included evidence of false claims of the murder of Jews in Ukraine, Nalyvaichenko flew to Tel Aviv and delivered copies of the files to his counterpart in Mossad and Israel's minister of public security. What these files and the FSB cyber-attacks and recruitment of agents in 2014 and 2022 demonstrated to Nalyvaichenko is that the disinformation, forgery and active measures deployed by the KGB during the Cold War have not vanished into the mists of time. These covert operations are very much in use in Putin's war in 2022. The ghosts and shadows of the KGB continue to haunt the West and their role in implementing Russia's secret agenda remains as insidious and influential as ever.

The old KGB techniques of subversion, surveillance, sexual blackmail, influence, deception, forgery and political intrigue are in 2022 deployed in the service of new military ambitions in Ukraine. But the work of Russia's intelligence agencies, operating as a clandestine branch of government, shines a light not just on the country's foreign policy. The nature of these KGB and FSB covert operations also reveals the way in which Russia, especially its political elite, regards itself and its role in the world. Throughout the Cold War the KGB was the custodian of the Marxist faith, answerable only to the Communist Party and retaining the deluded belief that the Soviet Union was an invincible global power. In 2023 its successor, the FSB, operates like a private army for Vladimir Putin, as a means for preserving and expanding that power and influence, but it is characterised by brutality, deception and repression. The legacy of the KGB lives on.

Appendix: List of KGB Forgeries

In *1984*, Winston Smith invents a war hero called Comrade Ogilvy while 'rectifying' historical documents at the Ministry of Truth. His job is to falsify the past in accordance with the Party's latest version of reality and provide written examples of 'doublethink'. Comrade Ogilvy, who did not exist in the present, now existed in the past. A few lines of print and a couple of fake photographs brought him into life. 'And when once the act of forgery was forgotten, he would exist just as authentically, and upon the same evidence, as Charlemagne or Julius Caesar', wrote George Orwell.

George Orwell, *1984*, Secker and Warburg,
London, 1949

Afghanistan: Embassy Telegram

In 1980, a falsified embassy telegram appeared in Islamabad, Pakistan, suggesting links between the late President Amin of Afghanistan and the CIA. The KGB aimed to discredit the CIA as well as Amin himself, whom Soviet security forces had unsuccessfully poisoned and finally shot in 1979.

Africa: 'Aviation Personnel International' Letter

In 1982, a fabricated letter from a US aviation personnel company to a South African general, A. M. Muller, discussed US assistance for helicopter pilot recruitment and hinted at US involvement in the failed 1981 coup attempt in the Seychelles Islands. The forgery insinuated covert US–South African military collaboration as well as US-sponsored interference in African governments.

Africa: British Cabinet Paper

A highly successful forgery of a UK Cabinet paper contained 'imperialist' designs on Africa, including opposition to the All-African Trade Union Federation. Russian diplomats and pro-Soviet media circulated this document in African countries to drive a wedge between NATO powers and the developing African nations.

Africa: US Government Document

In 1980 a President Carter administration document was circulated which suggested there was anxiety in the USA about connections between black Americans and Africans. Although the president's press secretary denounced it as a forgery, the document was published several times over the next few years, notably in Nigeria and the Upper Volta. The fake KGB memo sought to undermine US diplomatic relations with African states.

Chernobyl: US Information Agency Letter

In 1986, a forged US information agency (USIA) letter to a US senator suggested influencing European newspapers to exaggerate the mortality rate of the Chernobyl disaster. Leaking this letter would portray the USA as deceptive and meddlesome, making false claims in the European press. However, the Soviet forgers had used a USIA letter containing a unique marking as their template, allowing US authorities to trace the forgery.

'Destabilization Guide': US Army Manual

In March 1975, the Turkish newspaper, *Baris*, mentioned a US Army manual covering techniques to destabilise countries where US diplomats and troops were stationed. The KGB also sent the bogus army manual directly to the president of the Philippines, which led to its exposure.

Egypt: CIA Report

In 1979, a Cairo-based magazine claimed that a CIA report had branded Islamic groups detrimental to US goals in the Middle East and recommended ways of suppressing, dividing and eliminating these organisations. This CIA report was one of a series of Soviet forgeries designed to undermine US-Egyptian relations.

Egypt: US Ambassador's Letter

In 1979, the Syrian newspaper *Al-Ba'th* published the contents of a faked letter from the US ambassador to Egypt, which included plans to repudiate and remove President Sadat as he was disinclined to serve US interests. The KGB hoped to discredit the USA in the Middle East.

Egypt: US Embassy Dispatch

In 1977, the Egyptian embassy in Belgrade received a dispatch which purported to originate from the US embassy in Tehran, suggesting that the USA had agreed to Iranian and Saudi plans to overthrow President Sadat.

Egypt: US Official's Speech

In 1976, a speech, allegedly by a member of the US administration, insulted Egyptians and urged 'a total change of the government and the governmental system in Egypt'.

Egypt: US State Department

A fabricated US state department document, delivered anonymously to the Egyptian embassy in Rome in 1977, contained insults to President Sadat, other Egyptians and Arab leaders, including King Khalid of Saudi Arabia.

Europe: US Department of Commerce

Ahead of a 1982 summit, a fabricated US economic policy document, which twisted US trade policy to cause friction with European partners, was distributed in Brussels. US officials confirmed that it was a forgery to destabilise US–European relations and the story was never published.

European Gas: US Department of Commerce Memo

In 1982, a fake department of commerce memorandum relayed the recommendations of an imaginary 'Special Presidential Working Group on Strategic Economic Policy' to cancel USSR–West European gas pipeline arrangements. The memo was sent to officials and journalists to cause friction between the USA and Western Europe.

Falklands: US Government Press Release

A US government press release reported false, provocative comments concerning the Falklands crisis attributed to secretary of defence Caspar Weinberger, such as how supporting the UK would lead to a US military base exerting control over South America. The forgery sought to undermine US relations with South American nations as well as with the UK, as it contained allusions to influencing British politics.

Ghana: US Embassy Report

Disrupting diplomatic relations between the US and African states was a priority for the KGB. In 1983 an alleged US embassy report was leaked to the Ghana government in which Ambassador Thomas Smith urged his CIA officers to 'prove themselves' by overthrowing President Rawlings of Ghana. The document caused a media uproar and the Ghana government accused the US of planning a coup. Although Ghana later accepted the 'diplomatic' report was a forgery, US–Ghana diplomatic relations were severely damaged for some time.

Greece: US Diplomat's Letter

In 1982, a forged letter and intelligence study purportedly from a US deputy secretary of state to the US ambassador to Greece outlined plans for a possible military coup, depending on the outcome of the then-upcoming Greek elections. The intent was to sabotage US–Greek relations.

'Holocaust Papers': US Department of Defense

US military planning documents nicknamed the 'Holocaust documents' were doctored to show supposed US nuclear targets in Western Europe. Although denounced as fake following initial publication in the Norwegian magazine *Orientering* in 1967, this forgery resurfaced over twenty times in various countries in the years that followed.

Indian Elections: British High Commissioner Telegram

Ahead of the 1967 Indian elections, a forged telegram from the UK high commissioner, John Freeman, to the Foreign Office was sent to journalists. The telegram suggested improper US funding of right-wing Indian politicians in order to boost left-wing candidates.

Italy: NATO Memo

A fabrication of a military handbook suggested that NATO exercises had been responsible for two civil aviation accidents in Italy in 1980 and 1982. The forgery supported rumours and fears of NATO responsibility previously printed in the left-wing Italian press.

Italy: NATO Press Release

Soviet intelligence faked a NATO recommendation to move its 'quick reaction' military division to Italy to combat the political unrest there. The fabrication implied that NATO might interfere with Italy's domestic politics. The Soviets hoped to spread fears among NATO members that they may lose a degree of sovereignty.

Italy: Trade Union Letter

In 1983 the KGB falsified a letter from America's largest trade union, the AFL-CIO, to Luigi Scricciolo – an Italian trade union activist who had been investigated for his dealings with an extreme Marxist–Leninist group and had admitted spying for the Communist Bulgarian regime. The letter hinted that Scricciolo was secretly channelling CIA funds via the AFL-CIO to a Polish trade union. The KGB forgery surfaced in a Sicilian newspaper and was designed to discredit the AFL-CIO and

Scricciolo while suggesting the CIA was covertly supporting Polish trade unions.

Latin America: Reagan Memorandum

In 1983, the KGB faked a memo from President Reagan to the CIA and secretaries of state and defense calling for an 'Inter-American Permanent Peace Force' to be created to protect US interests in Latin America. The document, designed to make the USA seem overbearingly imperialistic, was sent to officials in a Latin American country.

Lebanon: US Department of Defense Document

A falsified 1982 department of defense document suggested that the USA and Israel had plans to collaborate on an invasion of Lebanon. Soviet intelligence circulated the document amongst Arab countries and communities living in Europe in order to discredit the USA.

NATO First-Strike Strategy: US Secretary of State

In 1979, a letter from NATO Supreme Allied Commander Alexander Haig to Secretary-General Joseph Luns discussed a nuclear first-strike strategy and urged 'sensitive' action to 'jolt the fainthearted in Europe'. However, the forgery was easily detected because Haig always used the more familiar 'Dear Joe' rather than 'Dear Joseph'.

Nigeria Assassination: Lagos Embassy

A bogus 1983 document purporting to be from the US embassy in Lagos alleged that the US ambassador, Thomas Pickering, had approved plans to assassinate the major opposition candidate in the Nigerian presidential elections. Two major Nigerian newspapers were fooled and printed the allegations.

Papal Assassination: Rome Embassy Cables

In 1983, two forged cables supposedly from the US embassy in Rome suggested a conspiracy between the USA, pro-US Italian politicians and Italian intelligence to blame the attempted assassination of Pope John Paul II on the Soviets. Only one, left-wing, media outlet published the story, while others quickly denounced the cables as fake.

Peru: US Diplomatic Message

In 1983, a faked diplomatic telegram leaked in Lima, Peru, purported to show US intentions to sell nuclear cruise missiles to Chile. The goal was to stir up tensions between Peru and Chile as well as between Peru and the USA. However, Peruvian newspapers later denounced the story as a product of Soviet forgery.

Poland: US National Security Council Memorandum

Zbigniew Brzezinski, the Polish-born US national security adviser to President Carter, was the target of the KGB throughout the Cold War (see Chapter 7 for details). A prominent Spanish newspaper published a fabricated US national security council memo in which Brzezinski told President Carter to destabilise Poland as it was 'the weakest link in the chain of Soviet domination of Eastern Europe'. The document was outed as a forgery by the US state department but resulted in tension between the US and Poland.

South Africa: Northrop Corporation Letters

In 1982, faked letters from US defence company Northrop Corporation invited South African General Muller to observe Tiger Shark aircraft flight tests as a potential customer. This forgery hoped to show that a US company, with the permission of the US government, sought to violate the arms sale embargo to South Africa.

South Africa: US Defense Mapping Agency

Soviet intelligence forged a US Defense Mapping Agency letter, replete with spelling and grammar irregularities, which offered South African General Dutton access to US satellite images of Angola, Mozambique and Zambia. The forgery implied US–South African military cooperation but it was not convincing, not least because General Dutton had long since retired.

Spain: NATO Information Service

In October 1981, Soviet forgers sent journalists a series of letters with information packets that falsely listed Spain as a NATO member. These letters appeared to treat Spain's democratic institutions, which were still debating NATO membership, with disregard and contempt; however, journalists spotted the forgeries.

Spain: Reagan Letter

In 1981, the KGB, posing as US President Reagan, wrote a letter to Spain's king, Juan Carlos, urging him to suppress certain left-wing groups and join NATO. However, they sent the letter not to the king but to Spanish newspapers, who largely ignored it.

Sweden: US Officials

Following the 1981 discovery of a Soviet submarine in Swedish territorial waters off Karlskrona, the KGB forged messages from supposed US government officials offering journalists details of a secret US agreement to use the Karlskrona base for intelligence. The aim was to alleviate the Soviets' embarrassment at the discovery of its 'whisky-class' submarine by providing a pretext for its presence. The affair became known as the 'Whisky on the Rocks' incident.

UK: Reagan–Thatcher Tape

In May 1983, two weeks before the UK General Election, the KGB compiled a cassette tape of a fake telephone conversation between Prime Minister Margaret Thatcher and President Ronald Reagan. The tape surfaced in the press in the Netherlands. In fact, it was a crudely edited recording of Thatcher promising to punish Argentina for the loss of HMS *Sheffield* during the previous year's Falklands War and Reagan was heard trying to calm her down. The KGB had spliced together real recordings of their voices from interviews and speeches and manufactured a conversation which in fact never took place.

US Foreign Policy: National Security Council Memorandum

In 1986, the KGB falsified a US national security council (NSC) memo detailing global US foreign policy strategy for 1985–8. The document highlighted US plans for a first-strike nuclear capability and included ideas offensive to various foreign governments. This forgery reinforced recurring KGB narratives concerning their 'main adversary, the USA'.

Bibliography

Albas, Yevgenia. *The State within a State – The KGB and its Hold on Russia, Past, Present and Future*, Farrar, Straus, Giroux, New York, 1994

Aldrich, Richard. *Espionage, Security and Intelligence in Britain, 1945–1970*, Manchester University Press, Manchester, 1998

Aldrich, Richard and Cormac, Rory. *The Black Door – Spies, Secret Intelligence and British Prime Ministers*, William Collins, London, 2016

Andrew, Christopher. *Defence of the Realm: the Authorized History of MI5*, Allen Lane, London, 2009

Andrew, Christopher and Gordievsky, Oleg. *KGB – The Inside Story*, HarperCollins, London, 1990

Andrew, Christopher and Gordievsky, Oleg. *Instructions from the Centre*, Hodder and Stoughton, London, 1991

Andrew, Christopher and Green, Julius. *Stars and Spies – Intelligence Operations and the Entertainment Business*, Bodley Head, London, 2021

Andrew, Christopher and Mitrokhin, Vasili. *The Sword and the Shield – The Mitrokhin Archive and the Secret History of the KGB*, Allen Lane, London, 1999

Bagley, Tennent. *Spymaster – Startling Cold War Revelations of a Soviet KGB Chief*, Skyhorse Publishing, New York, 2013

Barrass, Gordon. *The Great Cold War*, Stanford University Press, Stanford, California, 2011

Barron, John. *KGB – The Secret Work of Soviet Secret Agents*, Bantam Books, New York, 1974

Bazhenov, Maxim. *My Teacher – Philby: a History of the Confrontation Between British and Domestic Security Services* (Мой учитель Филби. История противостояния британских и отечественных спецслужб), Eksmo (Эксмо), Moscow, 2020

Bedell-Smith, Walter. *My Three Years in Moscow*, J. B. Lippincott, Philadelphia & New York, 1950

Belton, Catherine. *Putin's People – How the KGB Took Back Russia and Then Took on the West*, William Collins, London, 2020

Beschloss, Michael. *The Crisis Years*, Edward Burlingame Books, New York, 1991

Bower, Tom. *The Perfect English Spy – The Unknown Man in Charge during the most Tumultuous, Scandal-Ridden Era in Espionage History*, William Heinemann, London, 1995

Bullard, Margaret. *Endangered Species – Diplomacy from the Passenger Seat*, privately printed, 2021

Caute, David. *Red List: MI5 and British Intellectuals in the Twentieth Century*, Verso, London, 2022

Corera, Gordon. *The Art of Betrayal – Life and Death in the British Secret Service*, Weidenfeld and Nicolson, London, 2011

Corera, Gordon. *Russians Among Us – Sleeper Cells and the Hunt for Putin's Agents*, William Collins, London, 2020

Courtney, Commander Anthony. *Sailor in a Russian Frame*, Johnson Publications, London, 1968

Davenport-Hines, Richard. *Enemies Within – Communists, The Cambridge Spies and the Making of Modern Britain*, William Collins, London, 2018

Deriabin, Peter and Gibney, Frank. *The Secret World – The Terrifying Report of a High Officer of Soviet Intelligence*, Arthur Barker, London, 1959

Dobrynin, Anatoly. *In Confidence*, University of Washington Press, Seattle, USA, 1995

Dorril, Stephen. *MI6: Inside the Covert World of Her Majesty's Secret Intelligence Service*, Simon & Schuster, New York, 2000

Dzhirkvelov, Ilya. *Secret Servant – My Life with the KGB and the Soviet Elite*, Harper and Row, New York, 1987

Haslam, Jonathan. *Russia's Cold War – From the October Revolution to the Fall of the Wall*, Yale University Press, 2011

Hayter, Sir William. *A Double Life*, Hamish Hamilton, London, 1974

Herbert of Munster, George. *Political Sketches of the State of Europe from 1814–1867*, Edmonston & Douglas, Edinburgh, 1868

Kalugin, Oleg. *Spymaster: My 32 Years In Intelligence and Espionage Against the West*, Basic Books, London, 2009

Kaufman, Robert. *Henry M. Jackson – A Life in Politics*, University of Washington Press, Seattle, USA, 2000

Kaznacheev, Alexander. *Inside a Soviet Embassy*, Robert Hale, London, 1963

Kevorkov, Vyacheslav. *Victor Louis – The Man Behind the Legend* (Виктор Луи: Человек с Легендой), Seven days (Семь Дней), Moscow, 2010

Khrekov, Anton. *King of Spy Games – Victor Louis, Special Agent of the Kremlin* (Король шпионских войн. Виктор Луи – специальный агент Кремля), Phoenix (Феникс), Rostov, 2010

Khrushchev, Nikita. *Memoirs of Nikita Khrushchev: Volume 3, Statesman, 1953–1964*, The Pennsylvania State University Press, University Park, 2007

Knightley, Philip. *The Second Oldest Profession*, Pan Books, London, 1987

Lilleker, Darren G. *Against the Cold War – The History and Political Traditions of pro-Sovietism in the British Labour Party, 1945–1989*, Tauris Academic Studies, London, 2004

Lownie, Andrew. *Stalin's Englishman: The Lives of Guy Burgess*, Hodder and Stoughton, London, 2015

Lucas, Edward. *Deception – Spies, Lies and How Russia Dupes the West*, Bloomsbury, London, 2012

Lucas, Edward. *The New Cold War: How the Kremlin Menaces Both Russia and the West*, Bloomsbury, London, 2012

Macintyre, Ben. *The Spy and the Traitor*, Penguin, London, 2019

Macqueen, Adam. *Private Eye – The First 50 Years*, Private Eye Productions, London, 2011

Mallaby, Christopher. *Living the Cold War – Memoirs of a British Diplomat*, Amberley Publishing, Stroud, 2019

McKeever, Porter. *Adlai Stevenson: His Life and Legacy*, Morrow, New York, 1989

Miller, John. *All Them Cornfields and Ballet in the Evening*, Hodgson Press, Kingston-upon-Thames, 2010

Miner, Steven Merritt. *Stalin's Holy War: Religion, Nationalism, and Alliance Politics, 1941–1945*, University of North Carolina Press, Chapel Hill, 2003

Murphy, David, Kondrashev, Sergei and Bailey, George. *Battleground Berlin – CIA vs KGB in the Cold War*, Yale University Press, New Haven, 1999

Nicholson, Martin. *Activities Incompatible*, Privately printed, 2013

O'Brien, Helen. *Regina Nopii – Cabaretul Eva*, edited by Silvia Colfescu, Vremea MC IMEX Publishing House, Bucharest, Romania, 1996

Omand, David. *How Spies Think: Ten Lessons in Intelligence*, Penguin Random House, New York, 2020

Pegues, Jeff. *Kompromat – How Russia Undermined American Democracy*, Prometheus Books, New York, 2018

Pincher, Chapman. *Inside Story – A Documentary of the Pursuit of Power*, Sedgwick and Jackson, London, 1978

Putin, Vladimir. *First person: an astonishingly frank self-portrait by Russia's president Vladimir Putin*, Public Affairs, New York, 2000

Rid, Thomas. *Active Measures – The Secret History of Disinformation and Political Warfare*, Profile Books, London, 2020

Rimington, Stella. *Open Secret – The Autobiography of the Former Director-General of MI5*, Hutchinson, London, 2001

Romerstein, Herbert and Levchenko, Stanislav. *The KGB Against the Main Enemy – How the Soviet Intelligence Service Operates Against the United States*, Lexington Books, Lexington, 1989

Rositzke, Harry. *The KGB – The Eyes of Russia, The Secret Operations of the World's Best Intelligence Organisation*, Doubleday, New York, 1981

Shultz, Richard and Godson, Roy. *Dezinformatsia – Active Measures in Soviet Strategy*, Pergamon-Brassey's International Defense Publishers, Washington DC, 1984

Shvets, Yuri. *Washington Station – My Life as a KGB Spy in America*, Simon & Schuster, New York, 1994

Sixsmith, Martin. *The War of Nerves – Inside the Cold War Mind*, Profile Books, London, 2021

Soldatov, Andrei and Borogan, Irina. *The New Nobility – The Restoration of Russia's Security State and the Enduring Legacy of the KGB*, Public Affairs, New York, 2010

Walden, George. *Lucky George – Memoirs of an Anti-Politician*, Allen Lane, London, 1999

Weinstein, Allen and Vassiliev, Alexander. *The Haunted Wood – Soviet Espionage in the Stalin Era*, The Modern Library, New York, 2000

West, Nigel. *Historical Dictionary of Sexspionage*, Scarecrow Press, Maryland USA, 2009

West, Nigel and Tsarev, Oleg. *The Crown Jewels*, HarperCollins, London, 1998

White, Duncan. *Cold Warriors – Writers Who Waged the Literary Cold War*, Little Brown, London, 2019

Wolf, Markus with Anne McElvoy. *Man Without A Face – The Memoirs of a Spymaster*, Jonathan Cape, London, 1997

Wright, Peter. *Spycatcher – The Candid Autobiography of a Senior Intelligence Officer*, Penguin, London, 1987

Zubok, Vladislav. *War on the Rocks*, University of North Carolina Press, Chapel Hill, 2007

Zubok, Vladislav and Pleshakov, Constantine. *Inside the Kremlin's Cold War – From Stalin to Khrushchev*, Harvard University Press, Cambridge, Massachusetts, 1996

Acknowledgements

A MEASURE OF THE FEAR THE RUSSIAN intelligence agencies generate is that many of the people I spoke to during my research for this book were anxious to remain anonymous. Some preferred only for their first names to be used.

However, I am delighted I can acknowledge George Nixon, my brilliant researcher, who did a fantastic and tireless job in tracking down obscure documents from archives, compiling profiles of individuals and tracing sources. His Russian language skills were also useful. And his contribution to compiling the Notes and References and the Appendix was indispensable. I cannot thank him enough. I am also most grateful to Thibault Krause for his incisive and diligent research as well as facilitating access to an important archive. And I would like to thank Joshua for his highly professional research contributions.

In Ukraine, I was privileged to interview and receive the cooperation of Valentyn Nalyvaichenko, head of the Security Service between 2006 and 2010 and 2014 and 2015, and now an MP. His first-hand insights into the role of the FSB, the successor of the KGB, before and during the invasion by Russia in 2022 were invaluable. I was also fortunate to be advised by David regarding this section of the book.

For expert analysis, I am indebted to Edward Lucas, author of *Deception* and *The New Cold War*, and Dr Andrew Foxall, former director of Russia and Eurasia Studies at the Henry Jackson Society.

For the chapter on the Eve Club, the precise recollections of Brian Boyce, the renowned former detective chief superintendent of the Metropolitan Police, provided a fascinating inside track. I am also grateful to Clive Entwistle, the award-winning TV producer and crime journalist, for sharing his memorabilia and memories of the club's remarkable owner, Helen O'Brien.

While this is the first book focusing on KGB's covert operations in the political arena, I would like to pay tribute to other historians who have written about Russia's most ruthless intelligence agency. I drew on excellent books by Dr Christopher Andrew (*KGB* and *The Mitrokhin Archive*), *Enemies Within* by Richard Davenport-Hines and *KGB* by John Barron. I was also impressed by books on the Cold War by Martin Sixsmith (*War of Nerves*), Gordon Corera (*Art of Betrayal* and *Russians Among Us*) and Gordon Barrass (*Against the Cold War*)

I also appreciate the contributions of the following:

Richard J Aldrich, Catherine Belton, Gill Bennett, Tom Bower, Michael J Bracey, Sir Bryan Cartledge, Rory Cormac, Stephen Dorril, Henry Elwell, Kate Fall, William Ferroggiaro, John Fox, Anna-Maria Galojan, Adrian Gatton, Nicholas Gilby, Janet Gunn, Steven Hall, Paul Halloran, Don Jensen, Robert Kaufman, Darren Lilleker, Nicholas Louis, Tom Mangold, Ella Marsh, Ileana O'Brien, Richard Perle, Giorgina Ramazzotti, John Sipher, Ralph Ward-Jackson, Charles Webb, Michael Weiss, Andrew Wood.

I do not speak Russian and so I would like to thank Jasmine Wastnidge, David Clarke and Jurga Zilinskiene at the superb Guildhawk company for their high quality translation of Russian documents.

This book is partly based on historical documents and so I am grateful to the staff at the UK National Archives, London School of Economics, Essex University and the Bodleian Libraries at University of Oxford.

My agent Charlie Viney gave me wise counsel and always believed in this project and so I hope I have repaid his faith. Tony Hirst did an excellent job in copy-editing the text. I am also grateful to Alex Christofi for commissioning this book. The team at Oneworld Publications improved my manuscript immeasurably with astute, intelligent and diligent editing.

Finally, this book was written in an idyllic and picturesque area of Sweden with the love, intelligent support and care of my girl-friend Lisa. I could not have written it without her.

Mark Hollingsworth
London

Notes

CHAPTER 1: THE COVERT ART OF WAR

1. Thomas Rid, *Active Measures – The Secret History of Disinformation and Political Warfare*, Profile Books, London, 2020, pp. 329–31.
2. Julia Ioffe, 'How State-Sponsored Blackmail Works in Russia – The Art of Kompromat', *The Atlantic*, 11 January 2007.
3. Rid, pp. 329–31.
4. Ioffe, 11 January 2007.
5. Ibid.
6. Vladimir Putin, *First person: An Astonishingly Frank Self-Portrait by Russia's President Vladimir Putin*, Public Affairs of Perseus Books Group, New York, 2000, p. 22.
7. Sun Tzu, *The Art of War*, Pax Liborium, 2009.
8. Oleg Kalugin, *Spymaster: My 32 Years in Intelligence and Espionage Against the West*, Basic Books, London, 2009, pp. 335–6.
9. Chris Bowlby, 'Vladimir Putin's formative German years', BBC News, 27 March 2015.
10. Putin, p. 69.
11. Ibid.
12. *The Economist*, 'The Making of a Neo-KGB State', 25 August 2007, p. 28.
13. Catherine Belton, *Putin's People – How the KGB Took Back Russia and Then Took on the West*, William Collins, London, 2020, p. 36.
14. Bowlby, 27 March 2015.
15. Putin, p. 79.

16. *The Economist*, 25 August 2007, and *Der Spiegel*, 'Kremlin Riddled with Former KGB Agents', 14 December 2006.

17. *Der Spiegel*, 14 December 2006.

18. Alena Ledeneva, quoted in Adam Davidson, 'A Theory of Trump Kompromat', *The New Yorker*, 19 July 2018.

19. Steve Abrams, 'Beyond Propaganda: Soviet Active Measures in Putin's Russia', *Connections QJ*, 1, 2016, pp. 5–31, esp. p. 8.

20. Edward Lucas, *Deception – Spies, Lies and How Russia Dupes the West*, Bloomsbury, London, 2012, p. 7.

21. Toomas Hendrik Ilves, 'Digital Society, Cybersecurity, and Anti-Disinformation', an interview with *Ukraine World* on Digital Security, 18 June 2018.

22. Andrei Soldatov and Irina Borogan, *The New Nobility – The Restoration of Russia's Security State and the Enduring Legacy of the KGB*, Public Affairs, New York, 2010, p. ix.

23. Sun Tzu, *The Art of War*, quoted by Richard H. Shultz and Roy Godson, *Dezinformatsia – Active Measures in Soviet Strategy*, Pergamon-Brassey's International Defense Publishers, Washington DC, 1984, p. 13.

24. Ibid.

25. Joseph Conrad, quoted by Sir William Hayter, *A Double Life*, Hamish Hamilton, London, 1974, p. 131.

26. Peter Wright, *Spycatcher – The Candid Autobiography of a Senior Intelligence Officer*, Penguin, London, 1987, p. 34.

27. Richard Davenport-Hines, *Enemies Within – Communists, The Cambridge Spies and the Making of Modern Britain*, William Collins, London, 2018, p. 4; and Christopher Andrew and Oleg Gordievsky, *KGB – The Inside Story*, HarperCollins, London, 1990, p. 17.

28. Vladimir Putin, 'Interview with Lionel Barber', *Financial Times*, 27 June 2019.

29. Davenport-Hines, p. 4; and Andrew and Gordievsky, pp. 18–20.

30. George Herbert of Munster, *Political sketches of the State of Europe from 1814–1867*, Edmonston & Douglas, Edinburgh, 1868, p. 19.

31. John Barron, *KGB – The Secret Work of Soviet Secret Agents*, Bantam Books, New York, 1974, p. 88.

32. Ibid.

33. Kalugin, p. 297.

34. Barron, p. 402.

35. Barron, p. 88.

36. Davenport-Hines, p. 12.

37. Barron, p. 458.

38. Ibid.

39. Vladimir Putin, 'Vladimir Putin's annual news conference', Presidential Administration of the Russian Federation, 20 December 2018; and Vladimir Putin, 'Gala evening dedicated to the Day of the Security Service Worker' (Торжественный вечер, посвящённый Дню работника органов безопасности), Presidential Administration of the Russian Federation, 20 December 2014.

40. Tennent Bagley, *Spymaster – Startling Cold War Revelations of a Soviet KGB Chief*, Skyhorse Publishing, New York, 2013, p. 171; and Davenport-Hines, pp. 13–14.

41. Miranda Carter, *Anthony Blunt – His Lives*, Macmillan, London, 2001, p. 154.

42. Richard Aldrich and Rory Cormac, *The Black Door – Spies, Secret Intelligence and British Prime Ministers*, William Collins, London, 2016, pp. 155–6.

43. Gill Bennett, 'Counter-Disinformation and the Tools of the Intelligence Trade: an Historical Perspective', a lecture at the University of Cambridge Intelligence Seminar on 14 February 2020.

44. Davenport-Hines, p. 1.

45. George Orwell, 'You and the Atom Bomb', *The Tribune*, 19 October 1945.

46. Davenport-Hines, p. 32.

47. Stephen Dorril, *MI6: Inside the Covert World of Her Majesty's Secret Intelligence Service*, Simon & Schuster, New York, 2000, p. 743.

48. Vladimir Putin, speech at a meeting of the Russian Popular Front's (ONF) interregional forum, 25 January 2016.

49. Quoted by 'Radio Moscow', English language broadcast, 28 June 1962.

50. Private papers of Sir Patrick Reilly, Oxford.

51. Kalugin, p. 5.

52. Edward Lucas, *Deception – Spies, Lies and How Russia Dupes the West*, Bloomsbury, London, 2012, pp. 12–13; Martin Sixsmith, *The War of Nerves – Inside the Cold War Mind*, Profile Books, London, 2021, p. 351.

53. Ilya Dzhirkvelov, *Secret Servant – My Life with the KGB and the Soviet Elite*, Harper and Row, New York, 1987, p. 124.

54. Sixsmith, p. 366.

55. Ibid.

CHAPTER 2: AGENTS OF INFLUENCE

1. Gordon Corera, *The Art of Betrayal – Life and Death in the British Secret Service*, Weidenfeld and Nicolson, London, 2011, p. 13.

2. Ibid., pp. 13–16.

3. Ibid., p. 15.

4. Peter Foges, godson of Hans-Peter Smolka, 'My Spy – the Story of H.P. Smolka, Soviet spy and inspiration for *The Third Man*', *Lapham's Quarterly*, London, 14 January 2016.

5. Richard Davenport-Hines, *Enemies Within*, William Collins, London, 2018, pp. 493–4.

6. Ibid., p. 240.

7. Peter Foges.

8. Duncan White, *Cold Warriors – Writers Who Waged the Literary Cold War*, Little Brown, London, 2019, p. 198.

9. The National Archives, KV 2/4169, MI5 report by Brooman-White, 12 September 1942.

10. Christopher Andrew and Oleg Gordievsky, *KGB: The Inside Story*, Hodder & Stoughton, London, 1990, p. 325, and Davenport-Hines, p. 241.

11. Andrew and Gordievsky, *The Inside Story*, pp. 325–6, and Davenport-Hines, p. 241.

12. Corera, p. 19.

13. The National Archives, KV 2/4168, Letter from Rex Leeper of the Foreign Office, 1 September 1939.

14. Peter Foges.

15. Davenport-Hines, p. 277.

16. Tom Bower, *The Perfect English Spy – The Unknown Man in Charge During the Most Tumultuous, Scandal-Ridden Era in Espionage History*, William Heinemann, London, 1995, p. 56.

17. Steven Merritt Miner, *Stalin's Holy War: Religion, Nationalism, and Alliance Politics, 1941–1945*, University of North Carolina Press, Chapel Hill, 2003, pp. 246–7.

18. Davenport-Hines, p. 278.

19. Andrew and Gordievsky, *The Inside Story*, p. 325, and Peter Foges.

20. David Caute, *Red List: MI5 and British Intellectuals in the Twentieth Century*, Verso, London, 2022, pp. 120–4.

21. The National Archives, INF 1/676, quoted in J. G. Hicks, 'Was the Left's Thunder Stolen? Soviet Short Films on British Wartime Screens',

Global Studies Institute, 2017, p. 12; and The National Archives, INF 1/677.

22. Andrew and Gordievsky, *The Inside Story*, p. 328.

23. Caute, pp. 120–4.

24. Andrew and Gordievsky, p. 328.

25. Duncan White, p. 226.

26. Andrew and Gordievsky, *The Inside Story*, p. 327.

27. The National Archives, KV 2/4169, MI5 memorandum 173A, 12 September 1942.

28. Christopher Andrew and Vasili Mitrokhin, *The Sword and the Shield – The Mitrokhin Archive and the Secret History of the KGB*, Allen Lane, London, 1999, p. 158, and Davenport-Hines, p. 312.

29. Davenport-Hines, p. 313.

30. Nigel West and Oleg Tsarev, *The Crown Jewels*, HarperCollins, London, 1998, p. 158.

31. West and Tsarev, p. 158.

32. Davenport-Hines, p. 494.

33. Andrew and Gordievsky, *The Inside Story*, p. 325.

34. Miner, pp. 277–8.

35. Harold Caccia, ONS 3341/1, Foreign Office memorandum by Harold Caccia, 28 April 1964.

36. John Barron, 'KGB: The Secret Work of Soviet Agents', *Reader's Digest* Press, New York, 1974, p. 37.

37. Christopher Andrew and Oleg Gordievsky, *Instructions from the Centre*, Hodder and Stoughton, UK, 1991, p. 56–7.

38. Richard Shultz and Roy Godson, *Dezinformatsia: active measures in Soviet Strategy*, Pergamon Press, Oxford, 1984, p. 176.

39. Ibid., pp. 178–9.

40. Andrew and Mitrokhin, pp. 605–6.

41. Ibid., p. 607.

42. Ibid., p. 608.

43. Ibid., p. 614.

44. Ibid., p. 614.

45. Vyacheslav Kevorkov, *Victor Louis – The Man Behind the Legend* (*Виктор Луи: Человек с Легендой*), Seven days (Семь Дней), Moscow, 2010.

46. Barron, p. 240.

47. Ibid., p. 243.

48. Ibid., p. 243.

49. Peter Deriabin and Frank Gibney, *The Secret World – The Terrifying Report of a High Officer of Soviet Intelligence*, Arthur Barker, London, 1959, pp. 353–4.

50. Kevorkov.

51. The National Archives, FCO 168/6087, Disinformation, 1 January 1981, pp. 14–15.

52. Sir Brian Barder in 'The Role of H. M. Embassy in Moscow', held 8 March 1999 (Institute of Contemporary British History, 2002, https://www.kcl.ac.uk/sspp/assets/icbh-witness/moscow.pdf), p. 26.

53. Kevorkov.

54. Ibid.

55. Tom Bower, *Maxwell – The Final Verdict*, HarperCollins, London, 1995, p. 159.

56. Ibid., p. 161.

57. Ibid., p. 161.

58. Ibid., p. 161.

59. Catherine Belton, *Putin's People: How the KGB Took Back Russia Then Took on the West*, William Collins, London, 2020, pp. 53–4.

60. The National Archives, FCO 168/6087, Lionel Shearer, Interview with Jennifer Louis, 'The Mystery Woman of Moscow'.

61. Anton Khrekov, *King of Spy Games – Victor Louis, Special Agent of the Kremlin* (Король шпионских войн. Виктор Луи – специальный агент Кремля), Phoenix (Феникс), Rostov, 2010.

62. Sir Curtis Keeble, 'British Diplomatic Oral History Programme', 2001, p. 113.

CHAPTER 3: FAKE NEWS

1. Sun Tzu, *The Art of War*, Pax Liborium, 2009.

2. *The New York Times*, 'Operation InfeKtion: How Russia Perfected the Art of War | NYT Opinion', 12 November 2018.

3. Ibid.

4. Martin Sixsmith, *The War of Nerves: Inside the Cold War Mind*, Wellcome Collection, London, 2021, pp. 332–3.

5. CIA, 'Soviet Covert Action and Propaganda', a study presented to the Oversight Subcommittee of the Permanent Select Committee on Intelligence, House of Representatives, USA, 6 February 1980.

6. *The New York Times.*

7. Ibid.

8. David Murphy, Sergei Kondrashev and George Bailey, *Battleground Berlin - CIA vs KGB in the Cold War*, Yale University Press, New Haven, 1999, p. 447.

9. Sixsmith, p. 335.

10. Rodric Braithwaite, a letter to the *Irish Times*, quoted in Margaret Bullard, *Endangered Species - Diplomacy from the Passenger Seat*, privately printed, Oxford, 2021, p. 56.

11. Sixsmith, p. 336.

12. Tennent Bagley, *Spymaster: Startling Cold War Revelations of a Soviet KGB Chief*, Skyhorse Publishing, New York, 2013, pp. 166–8.

13. Bagley, p. 185.

14. The National Archives, FCO 168/4602, 'The Role of the Russian Intelligence Service in Subversion', p. 1.

15. Allen Dulles, speaking on a televised round-table on 29 March 1964, quoted in CIA, 'The Soviet and Communist Bloc Defamation Campaign', September 1965, pp. 8–10.

16. *Pravda*, November 1964.

17. Sixsmith, p. 334.

18. Christopher Andrew and Oleg Gordievsky, *Instructions from the Centre*, Hodder and Stoughton, UK, 1991, p. 51.

19. Oleg Kalugin, *Spymaster: My Thirty-Two Years in Intelligence and Espionage Against the West*, Basic Books, New York, 2009, p. 54.

20. Lawrence Britt (Ladislav Bittman), speaking before the Subcommittee to Investigate the Administration of the Internal Security Act and Other Internal Security Laws of the Committee on the Judiciary United State Senate, 5 May 1971.

21. *The New York Times*, 'Operation InfeKtion: How Russia Perfected the Art of War | NYT Opinion', 12 November 2018.

22. The National Archives, FCO 168/6087, 'Disinformation', p. 5.

23. Kalugin, p. 54.

24. Ibid.

25. Bagley, p. 175.

26. Ilya Dzhirkvelov, *Secret Servant - My Life with the KGB and the Soviet Elite*, Harper and Row, New York, 1987, p. 290.

27. Ibid.

28. Pete Earley, *Comrade J: The Untold Secrets of Russia's Master Spy in America after the Cold War*, Penguin, New York, 2008. Quoted by Thomas Rid in *Active Measures – The Secret History of Disinformation and Political Warfare*, Profile Books, London, 2020, p. 291.

29. Catherine Belton, *Putin's People: How the KGB Took Back Russia Then Took on the West*, William Collins, London, 2020 p. 480.

30. Norman Reddaway, reviewing Richard Shultz and Roy Godson, *Dezinformatsia: Active Measures in Soviet Strategy*, Pergamon Press, Oxford, 1984 in *International Affairs*, 60, 4, Autumn 1984, pp. 706–7.

31. Evidence supplied to the Subcommittee on European Affairs of the Committee on Foreign Relations United States Senate, 12–13 September 1985, pp. 16–17.

32. Alexander Kaznacheev, *Inside a Soviet Embassy*, Robert Hale, London, 1963, pp. 172–3.

33. 'Soviet Active Measures' (documentary), US National Archives And Records Administration, 1984, Arc Identifier 54826 / Local Identifier 306.9798.

34. Evidence supplied to the Subcommittee on European Affairs of the Committee on Foreign Relations United States Senate, 12–13 September 1985, p. 81.

35. Herbert Romerstein and Stanislav Levchenko, *The KGB Against the Main Enemy – How the Soviet Intelligence Service Operates Against the United States*, Lexington Books, Lexington, USA, 1989, p. 314.

36. Richard Helms, speaking before the Subcommittee to Investigate the Administration of the Internal Security Act and Other Internal Security Laws of the Committee on the Judiciary United State Senate, 2 June 1961, p. 14.

37. Ibid.

38. Bagley, p. 182.

39. Shultz and Godson, p. 150.

40. Lawrence Britt (Ladislav Bittman), speaking before the Subcommittee to Investigate the Administration of the Internal Security Act and Other Internal Security Laws of the Committee on the Judiciary United State Senate, 5 May 1971.

41. Romerstein and Levchenko, p. 272.

42. Rid, p. 266.

43. Ibid.

44. Ibid.

45. Ibid.

46. Sixsmith, pp. 344–5.

47. Ibid.

48. Ibid.

49. Yuval Noah Harari, 'Nationalism vs. globalism: the new political divide' on TED Dialogues, February 2017.

50. Belton, p. 480.

51. Rid, p. 12.

52. Yevgenia Albas, *The State within a State – The KGB and its Hold on Russia, Past, Present and Future*, Farrar, Straus, Giroux, New York, 1994, p. 175.

CHAPTER 4: SEDUCTION AND SURVEILLANCE

1. Sir Curtis Keeble, 'British Diplomatic Oral History Programme', 2001, p. 81.

2. Dennis Amy, 'British Diplomatic Oral History Programme', 1998, p. 7.

3. Martin Nicholson, *Activities Incompatible – Memoirs of a Kremlinologist and a Family Man, 1963–1971*, privately printed, 2013, p. 67.

4. David Easter, 'Soviet Bloc and Western Bugging of Opponents' Diplomatic Premises During the Early Cold War', *Intelligence and National Security*, 31, 2016, p. 29.

5. Ibid., p. 30.

6. Sir Curtis Keeble, 'British Diplomatic Oral History Programme', 2001, p. 82.

7. Christopher Mallaby, *Living the Cold War – Memoirs of a British Diplomat*, Amberley Publishing, Stroud, 2019, p. 110.

8. Sir Patrick Reilly, private papers, MS. Eng c.6922, folio 58, quoted in Easter, p. 34.

9. The National Archives, PREM 11/2992, Record of a Conversation between the Prime Minister and Mr Khrushchev at the Soviet Embassy on 16 May 1960, quoted in Easter, p. 47.

10. Dennis Amy, 'British Diplomatic Oral History Programme', 1998, p. 12.

11. Sir Rodric Braithwaite, 'British Diplomatic Oral History Programme', 1998, p. 8.

12. Sir Bryan Cartledge, 'British Diplomatic Oral History Programme', 2007, p. 16.

13. Easter, p. 42.

14. Ibid., p. 35.

15. Ibid., p. 35.

16. Sir Curtis Keeble, 'British Diplomatic Oral History Programme', 2001, p. 111.

17. Dobrynin, p. 358.

18. Ibid.

19. Sir John Killick, 'British Diplomatic Oral History Programme', 2002, p. 28.

20. Easter, pp. 40–1.

21. Robert Gillette, 'Sophisticated New Devices : KGB Eavesdropping Pervasive, Persistent', *Los Angeles Times*, 13 April 1987.

22. Interview with Marshall Brement, Frontline Diplomacy: The Foreign Affairs Oral History Collection of the Association for Diplomatic Studies and Training (FAOHC), The Library of Congress, quoted in Easter, p. 31.

23. Harry Rositzke, *The KGB – The Eyes of Russia, The Secret Operations of the World's Best Intelligence Organization*, Doubleday, New York, 1981, p. 88.

24. Sir Curtis Keeble, 'British Diplomatic Oral History Programme', 2001, pp. 109–10.

25. Ibid.

26. Markus Wolf with Anne McElvoy, *Man Without a Face – The Memoirs of a Spymaster*, Jonathan Cape, London, 1997, p. 124.

27. Timeline World History Documentaries, *The Spy Who Loved Me: When East German Spies Broke Hearts In The Cold War*, TV documentary.

28. Markus Wolf, p. 71.

29. Oleg Kalugin, *Spymaster: My Thirty-Two Years in Intelligence and Espionage Against the West*, Basic Books, New York, 2009, pp. 257–8

30. John Barron, *KGB: The Secret Work of Soviet Agents*, Reader's Digest Association, New York, 1974, pp. 160–1.

31. Nigel West, *Historical Dictionary of Sexspionage*, Scarecrow Press, Maryland, USA, 2009, p. xxvii.

32. Barron, p. 164.

33. Gordon Corera, *Russians Among Us – Sleeper Cells and the Hunt for Putin's Agents*, William Collins, London, 2020, p. 146.

34. West, p. 32.

35. Former assistant FBI director William Sullivan in testimony before the US Senate Church Committee, 1 November 1975, quoted in West, preface.

36. Gordon Corera, *The Art of Betrayal*, Weidenfeld & Nicolson, London, 2011, p. 231.

37. Oleg Kalugin, quoted in West, preface.

38. Walter Bedell-Smith, *My Three Years in Moscow*, J. B. Lippincott, Philadelphia & New York, 1950, p. 186.

39. Barron, p. 17.

40. Nicholson, p. 73.

41. John Miller, *All Them Cornfields and Ballet in the Evening*, Hodgson Press, Kingston-upon-Thames, 2010, pp. 260–1.

42. Simon Freeman and Barrie Penrose, 'My KGB Chambermaid by British Envoy', *Sunday Times*, 22 February 1981.

43. Ibid.

44. Christopher Andrew and Vasili Mitrokhin, *The Sword and the Shield – The Mitrokhin Archive and the Secret History of the KGB*, Allen Lane, London, 1999, pp. 531–2.

45. The National Archives, FCO 158/206, Top Secret: Cadogan Committee – Cadogan Report, box 9.

46. Corera, p. 229.

47. Richard Aldrich and Rory Cormac, *The Black Door – Spies, Secret Intelligence and British Prime Ministers*, William Collins, London, 2016, p. 211; and Christopher Andrew, *Defence of the Realm: the Authorized History of MI5*, Allen Lane, London, 2009, p. 493.

48. Eric Alterman, 'A Newsmaker in Every Sense of the Word', *The New York Times*, 19 April 2012.

49. Edwin Yoder Jr., 'Joe Alsop resisted Soviet blackmail in the 1950s', *The News & Observer*, 18 January 2017.

50. Andrew and Mitrokhin, pp. 529–31.

51. Ibid.

52. Philip Knightley, *The Second Oldest Profession*, Pan Books, London, 1987, pp. 385–7.

53. Ibid.

54. Dennis Amy, 'British Diplomatic Oral History Programme', 1998, p. 7.

55. Wolf, p. 150.

56. Barron, pp. 188–90.

CHAPTER 5: ANATOMY OF A SMEAR

1. Commander Anthony Courtney, *Sailor in a Russian Frame*, Johnson Publications, London, 1968, p. 130.
2. Ibid., p. 13.
3. Gordon Corera, *The Art of Betrayal*, Weidenfeld & Nicolson, London, 2011, p. 52.
4. Courtney, p. 45.
5. Ibid., p. 41.
6. Ibid., pp. 53–5.
7. MI5 documents obtained by the author.
8. Courtney, pp. 62–4.
9. Ibid.
10. Ilya Dzhirkvelov, *Secret Servant – My Life with the KGB and the Soviet Elite*, Harper and Row, New York, 1987, p. 174.
11. MI5 documents obtained by the author.
12. Commander Anthony Courtney, House of Commons, Hansard, Vassall Case (Tribunal's Report), Volume 677: debated on Tuesday 7 May 1963, col. 339–40.
13. Harold Gurden, House of Commons, Hansard, Espionage – Volume 837: debated on Friday 26 May 1972, col. 1839, quoting Harold Macmillan on 14 November 1962; and Courtney, pp. 72–3.
14. MI5 documents obtained by the author.
15. MI5 documents obtained by the author.
16. The National Archives, FO 371/189001, Brimelow to A. A. Russell (Consular Dept), 26 March 1966; PREM 13/483, T. Bridges (FO) to M. Reid (No.10), 18 June 1965; and conversation between Cdr. A. Courtney, MP, and Wilson, 29 June 1965, quoted by Geraint Hughes, 'Giving the Russians a Bloody Nose', 17 August 2007, *Cold War History*, pp. 6, 2, 229–49, 232.
17. Corera, p. 204.
18. Stephen Dorril and Robin Ramsay, *Smear – Wilson and the Secret State*, Fourth Estate, London, 1991, p. 347.
19. MI5 documents obtained by the author.
20. Christopher Andrew, *Defence of the Realm: the Authorized History of MI5*, Allen Lane, London, 2009, p. 522.
21. Courtney, p. 142.
22. Ibid., p. 149.
23. Ibid., p. 151.

24. Adam Macqueen, *Private Eye – The First 50 Years*, Private Eye Productions, London, 2011, p. 234.

25. Naim Attallah, *Singular Encounters*, Quartet Books, London, 1990, p. 346.

26. Courtney, p. 154.

27. Corera, p. 227.

28. MI5 documents obtained by the author.

CHAPTER 6: ALL ABOUT EVE

1. *Daily Telegraph*, Obituary, 20 September 2005.

2. Helen O'Brien, *Regina Noptii – Cabaretul Eva* (loosely translated as 'Queen of Clubs'), edited by Silvia Colfescu, published by Vremea MC IMEX Publishing House, Bucharest, Romania, 1996. Never published in the UK.

3. Henry Porter, *Illustrated London News*, May 1988.

4. Veronica Horwell, Obituary, *Guardian*, 29 September 2005.

5. Terry Kirby, 'Soho in the Sixties', *Independent*, 22 September 2005.

6. Porter.

7. Helen O'Brien, memoir.

8. Ibid.

9. Lawrence Britt (Ladislav Bittman), speaking before the Subcommittee to Investigate the Administration of the Internal Security Act and Other Internal Security Laws of the Committee on the Judiciary United States Senate, 5 May 1971.

10. Jake Ryan and Abul Taher, 'Key aide to Prime Minister Harold Wilson "spied for Czechoslovakia and passed on details of phone calls with President Lyndon Johnson"', *Mail on Sunday*, 11 November 2019.

11. Kirby.

12. Helen O'Brien, memoir.

13. Ibid.

14. Horwell.

15. Kirby.

CHAPTER 7: OPERATION WHITE HOUSE

1. Yuri Shvets, *Washington Station – My Life as a KGB Spy in America*, Simon and Schuster, New York, 1994, pp. 158–9.

2. Allen Weinstein and Alexander Vassiliev, *The Haunted Wood - Soviet Espionage in the Stalin Era*, The Modern Library, New York, 2000, pp. 140–50.

3. Ibid.

4. Ibid.

5. Ibid.

6. Ibid.

7. Ibid.

8. Ibid.

9. Vladislav Zubok, *War on the Rocks*, University of North Carolina Press, Chapel Hill, 2007, p. 47.

10. Weinstein and Vassiliev, p. 285.

11. Ibid.

12. Ibid.

13. Michael Beschloss, *The Crisis Years*, Edward Burlingame Books, New York, 1991, p. 32.

14. Ibid.

15. Bruce Dearstyne, 'The Russians Tried Once Before to Meddle in a U.S. Presidential Election', History News Network, Columbian College of Arts and Sciences, 29 December 2016; and Porter McKeever, *Adlai Stevenson: His Life and Legacy*, Morrow, New York, 1989, pp. 428–30.

16. Ibid.

17. Ibid.

18. Ibid.

19. Beschloss, p. 33.

20. Vladislav Zubok and Constantine Pleshakov, *Inside the Kremlin's Cold War - From Stalin to Khrushchev*, Harvard University Press, Cambridge, Massachusetts, USA, 1996, p. 238. Also, see Christopher Andrew and Vasili Mitrokhin, *The Mitrokhin Archive - The KGB in Europe and the West*, Allen Lane, London, 1999, p. 236.

21. Nikita Khrushchev, *Memoirs of Nikita Khrushchev: Volume 3, Statesman,1953–1964*, The Pennsylvania State University Press, University Park, 2007, pp. 295–6.

22. Interview with Oleg Troyanovsky (translation) hosted on The National Security Archive on the The George Washington University website.

23. David Gardner, 'JFK files contain explosive new claims Russia "had information" that Vice President Lyndon Johnson was behind assassination', *Evening Standard*, 27 October 2017.

NOTES

24. Lawrence Britt (Ladislav Bittman), speaking before the Subcommittee to Investigate the Administration of the Internal Security Act and Other Internal Security Laws of the Committee on the Judiciary United State Senate, 5 May 1971.

25. Ibid.

26. Herbert Romerstein and Stanislav Levchenko, *The KGB Against the Main Enemy*, Lexington Books, Lexington, USA, 1989, p. 273.

27. Anatoly Dobrynin, *In Confidence*, University of Washington Press, Seattle, USA, 1995, pp. 52–3.

28. Ibid.

29. Mike Feinsilber, 'Soviets Tried to Turn 1968 Election Against Nixon, Envoy Says', *AP News*, 15 September 1995.

30. Oleg Kalugin, *Spymaster: My 32 Years In Intelligence and Espionage Against the West*, Basic Books, New York, 2009, p. 124.

31. Dobrynin, p. 266.

32. Christopher Andrew and Oleg Gordievsky, *KGB – The Inside Story*, HarperCollins, London, 1990, p. 538.

33. Ibid.

34. Andrew and Mitrokhin, pp. 311–12.

35. Robert Kaufman, *Henry M. Jackson – A Life in Politics*, University of Washington Press, Seattle, USA, 2000, p. 99.

36. Dobrynin, p. 269. Also see Gordon Barrass, *The Great Cold War*, Stanford, California, 2009, pp. 186–7.

37. Andrew and Mitrokhin, p. 312.

38. Ibid.

39. Author's documents.

40. Andrew and Mitrokhin, p. 313.

41. Kaufman, p. 234.

42. Dobrynin, p. 338.

43. Andrew and Mitrokhin, p. 313.

44. Ibid., p. 379.

45. Dobrynin, p. 375.

46. Andrew and Mitrokhin, p. 314.

47. Ibid.

48. Rowland Evans and Robert Novak, 'Brzezinski – Kremlin Target', 'Inside Report' publications, 22 October 1978.

49. S. Vishnevsky, 'Kontseptsiya Konfrontatsii' (The Concept of Confrontation), *Pravda*, 24 July 1978.

50. Andrew and Mitrokhin, p. 315.

51. Dobrynin, p. 459.

52. Jonathan Haslam, *Russia's Cold War – From the October Revolution to the Fall of the Wall*, Yale University Press, New Haven, 2011, pp. 210–11.

53. Kalugin, pp. 294–5. Also see John Barron, *KGB*, Bantam Press, London, 1974, p. 97.

54. Kalugin, p. 101.

55. Kalugin, p. 101.

56. Shvets, p. 23.

57. Andrew and Gordievsky, p. 2.

58. Shvets, pp. 124–5.

59. Barrass, p. 291.

60. Andrew and Mitrokhin, p. 720.

61. Shvets, p. 159.

62. Andrew and Gordievsky, p. 140.

63. Ibid., p. 590.

64. Shvets, p. 140.

65. Ibid., p. 129.

CHAPTER 8: ESPIONAGE IN THE UK

1. Anonymous author, *Their Trade is Treachery*, Beautiful Books, London, 2010, pp. 25–6. This book was first published in 1964 by HMSO but with restricted distribution and circulation.

2. Josef Frolik, Interview with *This Week*, Thames Television, ITV, 7 July 1977.

3. Martin Sixsmith, *The War of Nerves – Inside the Cold War Mind*, Profile Books, London, 2021, p. 343.

4. Martin Furnival-Jones giving evidence to the Franks Committee, Franks Report, Appendix, 1972, p. 16.

5. Tennent Bagley, *Spymaster – Startling Cold War Revelations of a Soviet KGB Chief*, Skyhorse Publishing, New York, 2013, p. 181.

6. Chapman Pincher, *Inside Story – A Documentary of the Pursuit of Power*, Sedgwick and Jackson, London, 1978, p. 189.

7. Christopher Andrew, *The Defence of the Realm – The Authorised History of MI5*, Penguin Books, London, 2009, p. 411.

8. Ibid., p. 411.

9. Ibid., p. 412.

10. Ibid., p. 413.

11. Allen Dulles, speaking on a televised round-table on 29 March 1964, quoted in CIA, *The Soviet and Communist Bloc Defamation Campaign*, September 1965, pp. 8–10.

12. Andrew, p. 527.

13. Ben Macintyre, *The Spy and the Traitor*, Penguin, London, 2019, quoted by David Sanderson, 'Veteran MP Bob Edwards was honoured by the Soviet Union', *The Times*, 15 September 2018.

14. Darren G. Lilleker, *Against the Cold War – The History and Political Traditions of pro-Sovietism in the British Labour Party, 1945–1989*, Tauris Academic Studies, London, 2004, p. 197.

15. Ibid., p. 197.

16. Ibid., p. 198.

17. Sir John Killick, 'British Diplomatic Oral History Programme', 2002, p. 22.

18. Sir Andrew Wood, 'British Diplomatic Oral History Programme', 2003, p. 16.

19. Sir Curtis Keeble, 'British Diplomatic Oral History Programme', 2001, p. 83.

20. Richard Aldrich and Rory Cormac, *The Black Door – Spies, Secret Intelligence and British Prime Ministers*, William Collins, London, 2016, see Introduction, pp. 1–7.

21. Sir William Hayter, *A Double Life – The Memoirs of Sir William Hayter*, Hamish Hamilton, London, 1974, p. 139.

22. Andrew and Gordievsky, p. 522.

23. Gordon Corera, *The Art of Betrayal*, Weidenfeld and Nicolson, London, 2011, p. 223.

24. Davies, Hugh, 'Time, Comrades, Please', *Daily Telegraph*, 7 April 1983.

25. John Miller, *All Them Cornfields and Ballet in the Evening*, Hodgson Press, Kingston-upon-Thames, 2010, p. 162.

26. Christopher Andrew and Oleg Gordievsky, *Instructions from the Centre*, Hodder and Stoughton, UK, 1991, p. 102.

27. Ibid.

28. Mikhail Lyubimov, 'Time to be gentlemen again', *Sunday Telegraph*, 12 May 1996.

29. George Walden, *Lucky George – Memoirs of an Anti-Politician*, Allen Lane, London, 1999, p. 144.

30. Killick, p. 25.

31. Sir Roderic Lyne, 'British Diplomatic Oral History Programme', 2006, p. 20.

32. Walden, p. 143.

33. Ibid., p. 144.

34. Richard Aldrich, *Espionage, Security and Intelligence in Britain, 1945–1970*, Manchester University Press, Manchester, 1998, p. 160.

35. Martin Nicholson, 'Activities Incompatible', privately printed, 2013, pp. 168–71.

36. Walden, p. 148.

37. Nicholson, p. 172.

38. Killick, p. 25.

39. Nicholson, p. 175.

40. Margaret Bullard, *Endangered Species – Diplomacy from the Passenger Seat*, privately printed, 2021, p. 111.

41. Richard Davenport-Hines, *Enemies Within*, William Collins, London, 2011, p. 511.

42. Christopher Andrew and Oleg Gordievsky, *KGB – The Inside Story*, HarperCollins, London, 1990, p. 436.

43. Martin Sixsmith, p. 577.

44. Stella Rimington, *Open Secret – The Autobiography of the former Director-General of MI5*, Hutchinson, London, 2001, p. 140.

45. Lyne, p. 21.

46. Rimington, p. 140.

47. Andrew and Gordievsky, *Instructions from the Centre*, pp. 189–90.

48. Andrew and Gordievsky, *KGB – The Inside Story*, p. 591.

49. Ibid., p. 591.

50. Ibid., p. 592.

51. Ibid., p. 592.

52. Maxim Bazhenov, *My Teacher – Philby: a History of the Confrontation Between British and Domestic Security Services* (Мой учитель Филби. История противостояния британских и отечественных спецслужб),

Eksmo (Эксмо), Moscow, 2020, not available in English, referenced from a private translation.

53. Ibid.

54. Nick Davies, *Observer*, 24 February 1985. Cathy Massiter said: 'Joan Ruddock did not know that the Soviet journalist was a KGB officer but it provided the grounds for MI5 recording her as a contact of a hostile intelligence service which was ridiculous'. On that pretext MI5 opened a file on the CND chairperson. Also see 'MI5's Official Secrets', 20/20 Vision Productions, Channel 4, 8 March 1985.

55. Andrew and Gordievsky, *KGB – The Inside Story*, p. 592.

56. Ibid., p. 592.

57. Barrass, p. 395.

CHAPTER 9: THE NEW COLD WAR

1. *Izvestia*, quoted in Christopher Andrew and Oleg Gordievsky, *Instructions from the Centre*, Hodder and Stoughton, UK, 1991, p. 128.

2. Christopher Andrew and Julius Green, *Stars and Spies – Intelligence Operations and the Entertainment Business*, Bodley Head, London, 2021, p. 343.

3. Andrew and Gordievsky, p. 301.

4. Andrew and Green, p. 344.

5. Andrew and Gordievsky, p. 302.

6. Andrew and Green, p. 344.

7. The Dossier Center, 'Lubyanka federation: How the FSB determines the politics and economics of Russia', Atlantic Council, 5 October 2020, pp. 6–8.

8. Stella Rimington, *Open Secret – The Autobiography of the former Director-General of MI5*, Hutchinson, London, 2001, p. 238.

9. George Kennan, 'The Sources of Soviet Conduct', *Foreign Affairs*, 1947, p. 26.

10. Steve Abrams, 'Beyond Propaganda: Soviet Active Measures in Putin's Russia', *Connections* QJ 15, 1 (2016), pp. 5–31, esp. p. 17.

11. Sergey Zhirnov, Interview with *Euromaidan Press*, 24 November 2018.

12. Sir Reginald Hibbert, 'Role of HM Embassy in Moscow', ICBH Witness Seminar, Institute of British Contemporary History, 2002.

13. Gordon Barrass, *The Great Cold War*, Stanford University Press, Stanford, California, 2011, p. 384.

14. Ibid., p. 384.

15. Andrei Soldatov and Irina Borogan, *The New Nobility*, Public Affairs, New York, 2010, p. 236.

16. John Beyrle quoted by Matthew Cole and Brian Ross, 'U.S. Protests Russian "Sex Tape" Used to Smear American Diplomat', ABC News, 23 September 2009.

17. Clint Watts interviewed by *The New York Times*, 'Operation InfeKtion: How Russia Perfected the Art of War | NYT Opinion', 2018.

18. Gordon Corera, *Russians Among Us*, William Collins, London, 2020, p. 358.

19. Adrian Chen, 'The Agency', *The New York Times*, 2 June 2015.

20. Abrams, p. 20.

21. Thomas Rid, *Active Measures*, Profile Books, London, 2020, p. 434.

22. Corera, p. 358.

23. Ibid., p. 364.

24. Ibid., p. 365.

25. Ibid., p. 432.

26. Catherine Belton, *Putin's People*, William Collins, London, 2020, p. 480.

27. George Kennan, 'The Inauguration of Organized Political Warfare', US State Department hosted on the Wilson Center Digital Archive, 30 April 1948.

28. Corera, pp. 179–80.

29. David Omand, *How Spies Think: Ten Lessons in Intelligence*, Penguin Random House, New York, 2020, p. 180.

30. Viscount Palmerston, House of Commons, Hansard, Russian Invasion Of Hungary, Volume 107: debated on Saturday 21 July 1849, col. 813.

31. Dr Andrew Foxall, *Putin Sees All and Hears All: How Russia's Intelligence Agencies Menace the UK*, Henry Jackson Society, London, 2018, pp. 7–9.

32. Corera, pp. 179–80.

33. Yuri Shulipa, interviewed by Victoria Kirillova, 'Enemy agents of the Kremlin: how the FSB undermines Ukraine' (Вражеская агентура Кремля: как ФСБ подрывает Украину), *Cyprus Daily News*, 24 December 2021.

Index

active measures 5–6, 7, 55, 56; *see also* disinformation; forgery; honey trapping
Adenauer, Konrad 99
Afghanistan 263
Africa 62–3, 65, 76, 264
Agayants, Gen Ivan 58, 59, 67
Agee, Philip 78
agents of influence 6, 8, 37–40, 67, 70–1
  and British politics 213, 215
  see also Louis, Victor; Maxwell, Robert; Pathé, Pierre-Charles
AIDS virus 208
Aksilenko, Col Valentin 203
All-African Trade Union Federation 76, 264
Allen, Richard 191
Alliluyeva, Svetlana: *Twenty Letters to a Friend* 45
Alsop, Joseph 113–14
Ames, Aldrich 239
Amin, Hafizullah 263
Amy, Dennis 88, 91
Anderson, Jack 195
Andrew, Christopher 192, 205
  The Mitrokhin Archive 42
Andropov, Yuri 46, 48, 50, 115, 205, 207–8
  and Britain 229, 232
  and death 239
  and Sakharov 241
  and USA 197, 200–2, 204
Angleton, James Jesus 64
Anglo-Russian Business Consultants Ltd 126–7, 129
anti-Communists 58, 59, 73, 128, 159, 175
  and Nixon 185, 189, 190
anti-NATO campaigns 66

anti-Semitism 27, 65–6, 74, 199–200
anti-Soviet sentiment 23, 28, 57, 59, 192–3, 197–8
Arab nationalism 75
ARCOS (All-Russian Co-operative Society) 13–14
aristocracy 147, 149, 150, 152–3, 168–9
Armstrong, Robert 169, 170
Artha-shastra 9
Artuzov, Artur 58
Asia 62–4
assassinations 8, 11
Astor, David 26
Astor, William, Lord 26
Attlee, Clement 220
Austria, *see* Vienna
autocracy 10

Baldwin, Stanley 14
Barder, Sir Brian 47
Barrass, Gordon 204–5
Barron, John: *KGB* 106
Bayer, Gerhard 99
Bazhenov, Maxim 234–7
BBC 30–1, 36
Bedell-Smith, Gen Walter 105, 106
Belton, Catherine: *Putin's People* 5
Benckendorff, Count Alexander von 11
Benn, Tony 236
Berlin 56, 60, 66
Berlin Wall 6
Berry, Frank 77
Bettaney, Michael 222
Bevan, Aneurin 57, 220
Bevin, Ernest 246

301